THE LOST HOURS

THE LOST HOURS

A THRILLER

LYNN TAVERNIER

NEW YORK

Books should be disposed of and recycled according to local requirements. All paper materials used are FSC compliant.

This is a work of fiction. All of the names, characters, organizations, places, and events portrayed in this novel are either products of the author's imagination or are used fictitiously. Any resemblance to real or actual events, locales, or persons, living or dead, is entirely coincidental.

Published in the United States by Crooked Lane Books, an imprint of The Quick Brown Fox & Company LLC.

Crooked Lane Books and its logo are trademarks of The Quick Brown Fox & Company LLC.

Library of Congress Catalog-in-Publication data available upon request.

ISBN (hardcover): 979-8-89242-219-2
ISBN (paperback): 979-8-89242-287-1
ISBN (ebook): 979-8-89242-220-8

Cover design by Heather VenHuizen

Printed in the United States.

www.crookedlanebooks.com

Crooked Lane Books
34 West 27th St., 10th Floor
New York, NY 10001

First Edition: September 2025

The authorized representative in the EU for product safety and compliance is eucomply OÜPärnu mnt 139b-14, 11317 Tallinn, Estonia, hello@eucompliancepartner.com, +33757690241

10 9 8 7 6 5 4 3 2 1

For Don,
Without whom this book
could not have been possible.

The belief in the supernatural source of evil is not necessary; men alone are quite capable of every wickedness.

Joseph Conrad

CHAPTER

1

I WOKE IN DARKNESS to the sound of the dull scrape of a low-hanging branch against the wood shingle exterior and what felt like soft wings grazing my nose. I could just make out the faint outline of tiny black ears canted in anticipation.

"I'm awake, dude," I whispered.

No need for a clock, we had a routine; it was four in the morning. I scratched beneath his chin and as Tom lay his head on my shoulder and purred, my mind drifted to the day ahead. By five I'd be making the slow uphill run to Beavertail, then perch atop the headland to witness the first bursts of gold shrugging off the darkness and giving way to a dusty blue sky. Those moments felt like a ceremonial initiation, a new start. A perfect beginning to my vacation week. A whisper of crisp salt air wafted in through the open window and I sighed, thinking how much I needed this.

My cell phone rang, breaking my train of thought. The number was blocked; never a good sign. I tapped the decline icon. To my dismay, Mr. or Mrs. Persistent hung up and redialed. The phone droned impatiently, and my resolve not to answer skittered into the ether.

"Detective Stuart."

"Stuart, O'Sullivan here. Sorry to call so early. Unusual situation."

That godforsaken word.

"No problem, sir."

"I understand you're on vacation, but this is nearby and won't take more than a few hours of your time."

My participation wasn't optional.

"Tragic accident. Young gal. There was a big to-do—a party before her wedding. The family is prominent. The Philbricks. Do you know them?"

Christ. Hope Philbrick. So this was it. O'Sullivan thought I might be friendlier, more emissary and less cop. While Hope was at least five years my junior, our lives had been socially intertwined: our families, members of the same private clubs. We hadn't been friends, but there had been that one time.

"No. Well, socially."

"Right. We've agreed to keep it quiet, off the scanner and out of the news. Fell from a steep rock ledge. Multiple eyewitnesses. You'll need to take statements and get her to Newport. We're sidestepping protocol as a favor to the family. Emergency services will transport the body. She'll arrive DOA at Newport Memorial. Are we clear?"

"We are. What about DelCarmen?"

"You won't need a partner on this. If it makes you feel better, he can file the report for you. And Stuart? It might be best if you didn't ask too many questions. And keep to the script. Understood?"

There it was. O'Sullivan's big stick. Six months earlier, I'd received my first letter of reprimand. Despite the severity of my indiscretion, the outcome had been a win for the department. Still, he dangled my job like a hard-fought fish dancing at the end of a tattered line. But O'Sullivan hadn't said to keep it by the book. The directive was to do what I was told. The line went dead before I could reply. I dialed DelCarmen.

"All good?" he asked. As usual, he sounded as if he'd been awake for hours.

"I've been called out to an accidental death. In Jamestown." I repeated my conversation with O'Sullivan.

He whistled. We silently considered the oddity of the call, and how it was out of our jurisdiction.

"The dead girl's father's a big muckety-muck, right?"

"He is."

"It's probably nothing. But if you want company, I can be there in twenty-five."

"I'm good. If it feels off, you'll be my first call."

"Don't be a hero," DC said, then hung up.

I dressed, then rooted around for my car keys, patting my jacket pockets, upending my purse, then groaned remembering the walk home from the Gannie, my go-to watering hole, and the hours before when I dropped my car at the garage for service. I was spending the week at the carriage house at my mother's Jamestown property and if I needed to go off island, I'd take one of hers.

My footsteps echoed across the cobbled courtyard of the six-bay garage that stored my mother's fleet. Rusted metal tracks screeched as I lifted the door, sending a mouse scampering across the stone; a gray owl had it in its talons before I could blink. The realization that the skillful predator had been watching, waiting for its moment long before I arrived, did little to ease my pang of guilt.

I shook my head in a feeble attempt to cast off the disturbing image, then turned and scanned my options. When my eyes found the hulking remains of my late father's 1979 Pontiac Parisienne station wagon, fond memories unfurled like footage from an old movie reel. With seating for about seventy-five, its exterior had been a creamy white with brown panels, its interior, an indestructible greenish-brown Naugahyde. At present, it was a mottled shade of dirt and corrosion with the still pristine Naugahyde.

I opened the door to the Parisienne, slid behind the wheel, and turned the key; the V8 engine coughed then emitted a throaty growl like some prehistoric beast warning me to stay back or suffer the consequences. The wagon had ushered me safely through more near-disastrous journeys of my teenage years than I cared to remember. *I'd take my chances*, I thought, as I reversed out of the garage and shifted into drive.

CHAPTER

2

I WOUND ALONG THE southernmost part of the island toward the public park that included the Beavertail Lighthouse and a two-room museum that housed its centuries-long history. Beavertail embodied contradiction. Its center was a serene grassy expanse, offering miles of unrestricted ocean views, and held aloft by a precipitous rocky perimeter where unrelenting waves pummeled the stone, dragging anything in its wake into the Atlantic.

One seventy-five Beavertail Road, or the Crow's Nest, was easy to miss with an entrance set back from the road. No lights, no fanfare; old money didn't advertise. Modest stone pillars flanked the dirt driveway. Twenty feet farther, a steel security gate blocked my path. I cranked open the window; a tinny voice asked me to state my name and my business.

"Detective Andrea Stuart, Providence Police." I held out my badge toward the voice and, no doubt, a surveillance camera. The gate slid away, and I eased the land yacht forward.

It was a quarter of a mile up a gentle sloping rise before I saw the lights of the house. As I turned into the car park, the grand old Victorian materialized, illuminated from below by subtle landscape lighting, its facade kissed by the gaze of the waning full moon.

The Crow's Nest had been a nineteenth-century sea captain's estate and, accordingly, sat at the island's highest elevation, providing a clear view from the widow's walk of a ship's return from sea. In ruin when the Philbricks bought it, painstaking reconstruction had reclaimed its stately beauty. The red cedar shingle exterior had weathered to a hue of burnished smoke and was trimmed in a rich hunter green. Multiple stone chimneys jutted above the gabled roofline.

I climbed the mahogany stairs to the half-moon covered porch spanning the length of the house. Ceiling fans circled lazily overhead; Chopin tinkled from invisible speakers. A uniformed officer stationed at the front door welcomed me as if I were a guest at the party. I flashed my badge and his smile faded.

"Log?" I asked.

His pudgy cheeks bloomed bright pink. "No log," he said, averting his eyes. "I was told it wasn't necessary."

Preston Philbrick had well-placed friends, one of whom had, no doubt, leaned on the department for privacy. Not unusual for a man with his financial wherewithal.

Stepping into the foyer, I took in my surroundings. In the study to my right, leather-bound books filled floor-to-ceiling mahogany shelves. On the walls hung a history of privilege: antique hunting rifles, photos of a handsome chestnut Arabian midjump, and aerial views of a boat with masthead sloop rigging under sail.

A woman with stiff blond hair sat in a wingback blankly staring into the dying embers of a fire. I hadn't seen her in some time. The once beautiful socialite Penelope Philbrick looked old, small, and broken.

A resplendent living room dominated the center of the house. Glass-paneled doors receded into pocket openings, creating a seamless transition between the interior wood floor and the exterior bluestone patio. Beyond, a swimming pool held hundreds of water lanterns shimmering like jewels on its glass-like surface and teetering precipitously at its vanishing edge.

The officer at my side cleared his throat. I turned and read his nametag. "Okay, Fisher, bring me up to speed."

"As you probably know, the deceased, Miss Philbrick, fell from the observatory near the stairs leading to the dock."

I feigned interest in specifics I'd already received.

"No witnesses," he added.

Officer Fisher had my complete attention.

"No witnesses?" I repeated.

Fisher nodded.

"Who found her?"

He flipped through his notebook. "Miss Philbrick's fiancé. Edward Field."

"When was that?"

"We received the call a little before three AM."

"Was she still alive?"

He shrugged. "They called for the rescue, right?"

"Right," I said, then crossed the living room and stepped through to the patio.

I followed a grassy pathway matted by recent foot traffic and bordered by yellow and white wildflowers that glowed in the darkness, their heady scent mixing with the brisk salt air. The path opened to a sizable clearing fronting the edge of the cliff. Grasses, scruffy shrubs, and spicy-scented beach roses rambled at will. Smoke coiled from the chimney of a fieldstone fireplace tucked behind a stand of birch trees off to my right.

Straight ahead was the observatory platform spanning roughly twenty-five feet, yet I saw neither the view, nor a barrier preventing stargazers from tumbling over its edge until the moon slunk from behind its shroud and the sea appeared, moody and majestic, along with the lines of sleek steel cabling that glinted like thinly wrought blades in its light. As I descended the stairs built into the cliff, a mournful wailing mingled with the crashing surf. Two flights below, a female EMT pleaded with a disheveled-looking man.

"Come on now, Eddie. We need to get you to the house." She spoke to him like he was a child and she was his babysitter.

"Andrea Stuart," I said as I approached.

"Sherry Gladstone," said the EMT. "This is Miss Philbrick's fiancé, Eddie."

His eyes were bloodshot, his pupils dilated, and despite the September chill, his skin glistened with sweat. Eddie listed to the left. Sherry swung a formidable arm around his shoulder, then lumbered with her ward up the stairs.

"That's right, Eddie. Okay, one more. You're doing fine." Her voice faded as they receded upward into darkness.

When I turned back, a portable field light flashed on. Fifty feet below, the body of Hope Philbrick lay swaddled in semitranslucent layers of vibrant persimmon-colored chiffon that radiated in stark contrast with the impenetrable blackness of wet stone and the sea swelling at her tiny island grave. With her left arm cradled beneath her head, her body a semicircle, and a slight flush in her cheeks, I imagined an energetic girl overcome by exhaustion, dropping to the ground and falling into a deep, untroubled sleep. From my vantage point, Hope Philbrick could have been the muse for Frederic Leighton's *Flaming June*. The uncanny likeness of the tableau below me to the work of art I'd considered that terrible morning eight years earlier rattled my soul.

Three more techs waited at the dock. I introduced myself and they stepped aside. My romantic bird's-eye musing had been a visual sleight of hand. Hope Philbrick's arm was not cradling her head but splayed behind her back at an unnatural angle; her legs were not curled as if in sleep but gruesomely twisted beneath her body. Dark patches of blood stained her dress, coated her shattered skull, and seeped along the coils of her flaxen hair. Hope's right eye, cloudy and lifeless, was half open, blindly staring into the inky darkness of the bay. Sea spray had dampened the bodice of her dress, exposing her right breast, the nipple protruding through the chiffon in a manner that looked obscene. *Flaming June* rocketed through me like the thunderous crack of a lightning bolt. I'd seen countless bodies and some even more grotesque, yet never had I felt compelled to remove my jacket, to cover them, to shield them from the eyes of those at my side. I desperately wanted to take Hope in my arms, whisper words of comfort, and gently rouse her from what certainly was a terrible misunderstanding.

I looked up; the observatory was directly above. Instead of turning right toward the stairs, she must have toppled over the railing, plunging roughly fifty feet onto the rocks below. From above, it appeared to be a straight drop and an accidental fall seemed feasible. From below, I realized the upward projection of the field light had obscured the jut of stone at the cliff's base, and from this perspective, a fall seemed questionable. In my mind's eye I saw her arms cartwheeling helplessly, felt the terrified realization of her rapidly approaching fate, and heard her earsplitting scream slice the night sky.

CHAPTER

3

I ADDRESSED THE FIELD supervisor. "Has anyone touched the body?"

His gaze shifted toward the landing above. "Miss Philbrick's fiancé was all over her."

"Help Gladstone get him to the house and please tell Officer Fisher I'll be up in a few minutes. Everyone should stick around. I'll need to talk to the family."

The field supervisor signaled to a member of his team. Without hesitation, the young man hiked up the steps, taking them two at a time.

I looked from the observatory to the hideously disfigured body on the rocks, wondering if this was what it seemed to be. Could she have drunkenly stumbled in the dark, lost her footing, and fallen to her death? I'd witnessed my fair share of the inexplicable resulting from too much alcohol to rule it out. Besides, who would want Hope Philbrick dead, anyway? She'd been known as down-to-earth, sweet. Then again, I'd gone off to boarding school then college sixteen years earlier—home only for holidays and summers—and hadn't lived full-time in Jamestown since. I heard DelCarmen's voice saying things change, people change. While it was possible, I didn't believe it was absolute. Then I thought about her fiancé. The Philbrick fortune was rumored to be massive. It was a moot point—the wedding wouldn't happen now.

Taking one last comprehensive look at the scene in front of me—the long deep-water dock, the sailboat, dinghies, all tied up tight—I considered the nonexistent promised eyewitnesses. Had O'Sullivan lied to me, or had he been given faulty information? He deserved the benefit of the doubt. But O'Sullivan hadn't minced words when he said I had a reputation for being difficult, a word that could mean a multitude of things, but in my world it meant only one thing: difficult cops didn't last long on the force. If this went badly, I'd be the one left holding the bag.

As I stood debating the pros and cons of disobeying his orders, a sobering gust of wind kicked up off the water, sending an unsettling chill up my spine and breathing the last gasp of life into Hope Philbrick's party dress. The skirt floated up, then tenderly draped her wrecked body as the air seeped away.

I'd worked my first cases with John Riordan, the medical examiner in South County. He'd given me his cell phone number and said to call if I ever needed anything. This would qualify. Like a cat who has caught the scent of its prey, the prickle of a decision skittered across my nerve endings.

"Change in plans," I announced to the waiting medical team. "I'm sending her to South County. I'll call ahead." They looked at me and shrugged. I switched on my phone's camera and shot the body and the scene to the extent possible, noting significant hypostasis on the underside of her right arm. The pooled blood meant she hadn't been moved, and the scene hadn't been staged. Within two hours after death, rigor mortis begins in the face, then advances to the larger muscles. I pulled on a glove and touched her shoulder. It was rigid. I checked the time. Five thirty. She'd been dead approximately three hours; at last, something that felt accurate.

"Do you have anything to wrap her extremities? And protective gear?" I asked. The field supervisor nodded. "Suit up and wrap her with minimal contact. Give me a half hour with the family and I'll follow you to South County Hospital."

Setting off up the stairs, the sound of the surf grew less urgent as I climbed, the hum of crickets signaling solid ground. I went to the observatory platform and to the section of railing from which she'd likely fallen and checked the area for scuffing, clothing fragments, any sign of a struggle or to indicate something other than an accident.

Nothing.

I continued down the path feeling like I'd been blindfolded then pushed into a minefield. O'Sullivan's warning to "keep to the script," echoed in my head. My mind raced for another solution, but nothing better surfaced. Appeasing O'Sullivan would be tricky if I took her to South County, but my reasoning didn't need to be accurate, just plausible. O'Sullivan had said they wanted to keep this out of the news. Maybe I'd tell him the press regularly worked the staff at Newport Memorial and Hope's death would make tomorrow's front page if I brought her there. That was a thing of the past, but it just might work. I took a deep breath and dialed. He answered on the second ring.

"Dr. Riordan, sorry to wake you," I said, trying to sound upbeat. "It's Andie Stuart. You said to call if I ever needed anything. I'd like to take you up on your offer."

"Oh, baby." His voice had an early morning rasp.

I rolled my eyes. "I've got a high profile dead girl. It's an accidental death, but something feels off. She's slated for Newport, but I thought South County would be more discreet."

"I see," he said, his tone less than enthusiastic. "Slightly unorthodox."

"Department brass are calling the shots, sidestepping protocol."

"And you're sidestepping the sidestepping. The less I know the better," John said. "You realize it's Saturday?"

"Actually, it's Sunday."

"Even worse."

"I don't expect her to be pushed to the front of the line. A slot in next week's regular schedule is fine. I just need a change of venue. All I'm asking is that you call them, let them know to expect us so I don't have an issue when I show up. It'd be a huge favor."

"Well, this favor might require a little quid pro quo—"

I should have known better.

"My mistake for thinking you meant what you said. I'll figure it out," I said, and hung up.

My angst ratcheted up another notch and my insides twisted as I walked toward the house. The image of Hope Philbrick and her momentary likeness to *Flaming June* unnerved me, opening a floodgate and trotting out unwelcome memories that I couldn't shake even after all these years. That morning, one clumsy foot dutifully followed the other and somehow I found myself standing at the office door of the college's nurse practitioner. Kay Mathews surveyed my bruised cheek and split lip and sat me in a chair. She took my trembling hands in both of hers.

"What happened?" she asked, searching my face.

I wracked my brain; nothing apart from muffled noises and blurred images surfaced. I wasn't sure what had happened, so I said, "You need to help me get into rehab."

Kay frowned, worried eyes again going to my bruises. "What makes you think that?"

"I have a problem. Rehab is the only solution," I said, feeling more businesslike.

"It's all going to be okay, but you've got to tell me what happened."

I sobbed quietly, desperate for her words to be true. My gaze wandered to the mesmerizing print that hung across from where I sat. *Flaming June* dozed peacefully in all her gauzy saffron splendor. My eyes fell upon the oleander bouquet on the ledge above where June lay and I wondered if June had drunk the juice from the delicate red blooms and was not sleeping at all but languishing in the merciful sleep of death. That death might have been kinder to me spun in circles.

My cell phone rang, disrupting my thoughts. I'd expected it to be DelCarmen, but when I checked caller ID, the incoming number was blocked. Shit. O'Sullivan. I stuffed the phone into my jacket pocket. It rang again. I twisted my neck to the right then left; it crunched like brittle twigs underfoot. Dull pain drummed behind my eyes. Retrieving the phone, I stabbed at the quivering green symbol on the screen.

"Detective Stuart," I said.

"I'm calling from my landline," said John. "Please don't hang up. I'm sorry. It's late—early. I was trying to be cute. It came out badly."

"Don't sweat it."

"I meant what I said. I called South County. They're expecting you. I'm up and getting dressed."

"That's unnecessary," I said, but was suffused with relief.

"Too late. I'll meet you in an hour."

Dread ballooned in my chest, but the swelling crescendo of my inherent need to be certain, to do what was right, snuffed out the sound of O'Sullivan's directive. I wasn't going to do what I was told; I was going to do my job. Thinking of the irony—that doing either might result in the same—demotion or worse, dismissal, made me want to laugh or cry or both. The image of Hope Philbrick's dead body flickered across my mind's eye.

I straightened up and thought: *let them try.*

CHAPTER 4

THEY WERE WAITING in the great room. Preston Philbrick paced its length, his head bowed, his hands clasped behind his back. Penelope Philbrick sat on the edge of the sofa looking shell-shocked. A tall, heavyset young man stood beside her. Hope's fiancé, Eddie, was nowhere to be seen.

"Andrea Stuart," I said, introducing myself as I approached Preston Philbrick.

He paused and eyed me carefully. He was taller than I remembered, an imposing figure standing at least six two or three, his hair various shades of gray swept back from his angular, tanned face. After an uncomfortably long minute, a hint of recognition materialized and he accepted my outstretched hand. "Oh yes, of course, Andrea. It's been some time."

I took his hand and offered my condolences, then reached for Penelope's, conveying the same. Tears tumbled along her cheeks.

I scanned the room. "Is Hope's fiancé here?"

"This is Jeffrey, Edward's brother. He's just driven down from Cambridge," Preston said, as if this answered my question. I looked more closely at Jeffrey, who wore jeans and a hoodie emblazoned with the Harvard seal.

"Will he be joining us?"

"Edward was horribly distraught. We called our family physician. He's given him a sedative to help him rest."

As if on cue, a door off to the left opened, and out stepped a man in his late seventies carrying a well-worn black leather medical bag. The doctor turned to meet our collective gaze. With a full head of shaggy white hair almost obscuring his eyes, he conjured the image of an old sheepdog. Preston joined him and ushered him toward the entryway. The front door opened and closed and the doctor was gone without introduction.

"Edward's asleep in the guest room," Preston said as he rejoined the group.

A housekeeper with a worried face set a tray of four steaming mugs of coffee on the cocktail table. Her eyes, red and swollen, met mine; a lift of her chin indicated I should help myself. I retrieved a pad and pen from the pocket of my jacket and cleared my throat.

"Just a brief formality."

No one spoke.

"The party was a prenuptial for Hope and Eddie, uh, Edward?"

"Yes," said Preston. "For the most part, friends of the couple. We thought it'd be nice since some acquaintances wouldn't be invited to the wedding. Roughly a hundred and fifty guests, but the actual number who attended is anyone's guess."

I scribbled on my notepad. "To the best of your ability, please tell me who else was in attendance, in terms of staff?"

"It was catered, so chefs, servers, bartenders, and, of course, the band," he said.

"And as you understand it, what happened?"

"Quite simply, Hope had too much to drink."

"She wasn't much of a drinker," Penelope said. "She'd been nervous about the new caterer. I'm not sure she'd even eaten."

"Edward brought Hope to Penelope's herb garden," Preston said, "hoping she'd settle down. They quarreled, and he left her there."

"Did he say what time it was?"

Penelope shook her head. "He didn't."

"Did they quarrel often?"

Husband and wife exchanged a look.

"Of course not," Penelope said. "It upset Edward to no end. He blames himself for leaving her."

"And then what happened?"

"We don't know," said Preston.

"I need to understand where everyone was." I turned toward Penelope.

"I wasn't feeling well," she explained. "I went upstairs and took a bath, then went to sleep."

"Did you note the time?"

"I'd say it was about eleven."

"And you, Mr. Philbrick?"

"I was mingling with guests. Someone needed to be available to give instructions to the caterer."

"And your housekeeper?"

"Rosa?" he asked.

"Yes," I said, hoping we spoke of the same person.

The housekeeper, a carafe of coffee in her hand, froze. Penelope and Preston spoke at the same time. I held up a hand.

"Rosa, can you tell me—"

A flash of terror spread across Rosa's face.

"Rosa's English is minimal," Preston interrupted. "When I came up at the end of the evening, I passed her on the stairs. She was heading to the kitchen to finish up."

"What time was that?"

"If I had to guess, it was twelve thirty or thereabouts."

Rosa retreated toward the kitchen. I made a note to speak with her; we could work around her English and my flimsy Spanish.

"Did either of you notice anything unusual at any point during the evening? Uninvited guests? Anyone getting out of hand?"

Preston answered for both. "No, not at all."

"How did you learn about your daughter?"

"Rosa . . . She woke me, said there'd been an accident," Preston said. He dabbed his eyes with a white linen handkerchief.

"Edward found her?"

"Yes," said Preston.

Penelope dropped her head into her hands and sobbed. Jeffrey patted her back.

"I'll need to speak with Edward," I said, handing Preston my card. "Please call me as soon as he's available to talk." I closed my notebook, signaling the end of my intrusion on their grief.

"I'll see you out," he said.

Rosa appeared at the table and gathered the coffee mugs. "Gracias. El café . . . delicioso," I said, exhausting my high school Spanish repertoire.

Rosa met my gaze. Preston stepped forward.

"Please understand that our staff have been with us for a long time. They are like family and are grieving as well."

I followed him through the front door and onto the porch. The ceiling fans had stopped turning and the music no longer played.

"What happens now?" he asked.

"Emergency Services will transport her to South County Hospital."

"South County? I was told Newport."

I delivered the lie. "Yes, but if we take her to Newport, you won't avoid the media. South County will be more discreet. From there, they'll transport her to the supplementary morgue annexed to the hospital."

He took a calming breath. "Yes, yes. You're quite right. South County will be fine."

"The medical examiner is meeting me. Strictly routine. He'll release her as soon as he can. Is there a particular funeral home?"

Preston's shoulders slumped. "Yes, of course, Belmont Hughes in Newport. Forgive me. It's been a long night."

As I retreated toward my car, the moon cast a thin ribbon of shadow, mimicking my strides like the ghost of a companion. I prayed the next few hours would prove my instincts wrong. But doubt and questions populated then multiplied in my mind like a tangle of quick-growing vines. And I, like Alice in pursuit of the white rabbit, felt powerless to resist curiosity's gravitational pull into the vortex and, I feared, down the inevitable rabbit hole.

CHAPTER

5

Dr. John Riordan stood in the autopsy suite decked out in scrubs, booties, and a clear surgical mask pushed atop his scrub cap.

"This is above and beyond," I said as I approached the autopsy table.

"I have paperwork to catch up on. I figured I'd meet you and kill the proverbial two birds and still eke out some semblance of a Sunday."

John was tall, an all-American athletic type in his midthirties. His hands seemed better suited for basketball or football, or for a woman's hips, than for dissection.

"A fortunate confluence of events."

John nodded. "But more important, I'm here because I'm a man of my word. I would very much appreciate a do-over."

His apology sounded practiced; not a hint of playfulness in his eyes. I'd been on the fence, but leaning toward him being a player. Now I was unsure. The word "goofball" popped into my head.

"Do-over granted."

John pressed his hands together as if in prayer.

I held up an index finger. "One condition," I said. "That you do me the same. I was on edge. I overreacted."

"All forgotten," he said, and pulled his protective face shield in place.

With great care, John unfolded the sheet, exposing the body of Hope Philbrick on the table between us. Autopsies rarely bothered me, but she was someone I'd known. The patchwork of deep plum mottling covering her skin, and the glint of sharp tools beneath stark florescent lighting, made me queasy.

I watched in silence as John completed the first steps: the body photographed, material scraped from beneath the fingernails, anything foreign found on the surface of the body, all collected, noted, then packaged for storage or testing.

He switched on the voice recorder and began the visual external examination. This amounted to a general description of all identifying features and concluded with a diatribe of medical terminology that detailed the contusions, lacerations, and broken bones resulting from the fall from a fifty-foot ledge. I'd seen Hope from afar—in town, at social events—throughout the years. My mind veered back to the only time we'd ever met. She might have been ten, and I'd been fifteen or sixteen. Our exchange had seemed inconsequential, but now it seemed relevant; I remembered that after, I'd felt like a wise big sister. My hands suddenly felt clammy.

"Was she dead before going over?" I asked.

John frowned, but indulged me. "Let me show you a few things that suggest that wasn't the case." He gestured to her neck. "I started my exam by checking for signs of asphyxiation. There's no bruising in the soft tissue between the larynx and the esophagus, consistent with any kind of strangulation. There are, however, signs of cyanosis." He gestured to her head and neck and said, "The skin is visibly blue. And look here." He pointed to the skin around her eyelids and lips. "This is petechial hemorrhaging, tiny red dots indicative of ruptured blood vessels. I'm guessing severed vertebrae of the upper spine contributed to both, but I won't know conclusively until I do the internal. Without getting too technical, there are always exceptions. Cyanosis and petechiae rarely develop if the victim doesn't struggle. We can be fooled if we aren't thorough."

He picked up one of her hands. "There are no defensive wounds here or on the arms where you'd likely find them, no stab wounds on the body. I collected traces of skin from beneath the fingernail of the index and middle fingers on her left hand. But testing will be a challenge since the sample is negligible. The tips of the fingers had been, albeit superficially, submerged in water—traces of salt support that. Otherwise, all the lacerations suggest ante mortem blunt force trauma."

I replayed what I'd once done for Hope; a lump formed in my throat.

John met my gaze. "My opinion may change, but at present, I believe she was very much alive when she struck the rock formation."

Given the absence of protocol and the compromised scene, this had the whiff of what cops whisper about after a long shift and too many drinks—those fabled quashed inquiries. I'd stepped up once before on Hope's behalf and knew I needed to again. Hope Philbrick would receive the due diligence she deserved, consequences be damned.

CHAPTER

6

FOR REASONS UNKNOWN to the civilized world, criminals don't work a nine-to-five. Sleep is therefore patchy for the cops who pursue them. Most get used to catch-as-catch-can. But without regular sleep, I can't think. And since thinking is essential to getting the job done and preventing my ass and the rest from being blown to bits, I needed a nap.

Wrapped in a white terry-cloth bathrobe, my black sleep mask pushed atop my head, I fished through a basket of assorted bath salts kept next to the tub. A packet with a flowery mauve Victorian motif caught my eye. I plucked it from the mix and read the label: Batherapy. Sounded promising. Pushing the power button on the Jacuzzi, the jets whirred to life and tiny eddies swirled in the tub, dissolving the violet-colored crystals into the steaming water; a nauseating, flowery scent mixed with the steam and filled the bathroom.

Why do I believe anything I read?

I flipped on the exhaust fan, lit a dozen vanilla-scented candles to rid the bathroom of the Eau de Aunt Mabel smell, turned off the lights, and headed into the kitchen. I put the kettle on the stove, set a cup with two bags of chamomile tea, opened the meat chiller and retrieved a whole roasted turkey breast, carving three generous slices, which I ate without fork, knife, or condiments while I waited for the water to boil.

Mug of tea deposited on the bath tray and L-tryptophan in the form of turkey headed for digestion, I drew the shades, turned on the Bose, and slipped into the steaming bath. The candlelight twinkled in the half-darkness. Luciano Pavarotti's tender yet powerful voice mingled with the gurgling water. The opening chords of "Ave Maria" felt like a fine cashmere wrap, blanketing my soul with its prayer, easing the images of death from my mind. I closed my eyes. The music drifted up, caressing the timbered gable peaks, the odd, churchy cut-glass windows then wafted over me, my taut jaw and shoulders softening in the water's warmth. Twenty minutes later, perfectly groggy, I dried off and climbed into bed, pulling the down comforter over my body, the sleep mask over my eyes, and the pillow over my head.

After what felt like two minutes had passed, I rolled over and reached for my phone. Two hours almost to the minute. A missed call from John. I tapped the redial icon.

"Hello, Dr. Riordan. What do you have for me?"

"Preliminary lab results. She died from her injuries resulting from the fall. Time of death between midnight and two AM."

"Superb."

"Except she wasn't drunk."

I frowned. "What do you mean, 'she wasn't drunk'?"

"Blood alcohol level was .002 percent."

I thought this over. A blood alcohol level at that number was negligible—the equivalent of one glass of wine or beer consumed within an hour. "Could the sample have been compromised?"

"Doubtful."

I knew the answer but asked anyway. "Any reason to rerun the test?"

John cleared his throat. "Tests for blood alcohol levels are straightforward. We're waiting for the full toxicology report. With any luck we'll find evidence of a drug in her system that mimicked intoxication and supports the accidental death theory."

"When will we hear more?"

"Sometime tomorrow. Tuesday at the latest for the preliminary screenings for drugs and therapeutics. The official report may take some time."

I threw back the covers, rolled out of bed, and headed into the closet. When I flipped on the light switch, the row of five Styrofoam heads crowned with wigs on the top shelf made me jump. Alabaster white with eyes of the blind and the reproachful lips of the dead, they glared menacingly. Given the sheer size of her home, I couldn't understand why my mother's creepy seventies wigs needed to live here or exist at all. I collected myself, then tucked the phone under my ear and struggled into a pair of jeans.

"Any looky-loos poking around?" I asked.

"Not a one."

"Can you hang on a sec?" I enabled the phone's speaker and set it on the dresser while I hooked my bra together, then pulled a T-shirt over my head. "Family requesting her release?"

"Not as far as I know."

"You are the best."

"Tell everyone you know."

"It's not a long list."

"Whatever you can do."

I smiled, then felt uneasy. Except for DelCarmen, colleagues got under my skin and I, them—a dependable symbiotic relationship. This impromptu smiling business was odd. "Please call my cell as soon as you hear something. I'm headed back to the house. Most likely I'll have some follow-up work for you, which is going to suspend my much-needed vacation."

"And which vacation was that? It looked like you were on the job this morning."

"The vacation that was supposed to start yesterday."

"I see. I suppose if I was any kind of gentleman, I'd make it up to you."

"Oh . . . uh . . . that's kind of you to offer, but you've done enough. No need to make anything up to me."

Before he could insist further, I ended the call, grabbed a blazer then headed downstairs and out the door. I needed to talk to Eddie Field.

CHAPTER 7

Everyone has dirty laundry. An endless supply feverishly breeding in baskets behind closed closet doors that easily outpaced the long-suffering washing machine. Likewise, troublesome blemishes don't discriminate. Rich, middle, and poor wrangle alike: scrubbing, soaking, magic solvents, more scrubbing and soaking, and the stain becomes barely discernible. Yet we never completely rid ourselves of its existence. Lady Macbeth knew about spots; she knew the terrible truth of how they came to be.

Edmond Locard, the "Father of Forensics," claimed that every contact leaves a trace. Despite harboring a fondness for many things French, especially Champagne and Chanel No. 5, romantic prejudice hadn't swayed me. The French guy was correct. His essential premise was simple: wherever we sit, stand, walk—wherever we are—we leave something behind. That unique something can be connected to us—a hair, fibers from our clothing, from the carpeting in our car or home, dirt, spittle—minute traces of our DNA. The list is long. The evidence is there. One simply needs to be thoughtful, diligent, and it will be found.

As I drove to the Crow's Nest, I mulled this over. The problem with the Locard premise as it applied to Hope Philbrick was that the area where any evidence could have been found had been trampled by a hundred and fifty party guests, domestic help, the catering crew, and a ten-piece band. To make matters worse, no one had been logged in and accounted for. Even if the stars were in some sort of cosmic alignment and we had an ample supply of magic fairy dust and could put something together, there wasn't a chance in hell we'd ever make it stick. I considered what John had said about finding a drug in Hope's system that mimicked intoxication, how that might explain what had happened and put an end to this story. It would simplify everything; the Philbricks could bury their daughter, and we could get out of their way.

This led to my dirty laundry theory: the Philbricks hadn't lied; instead, they'd omitted details in order to keep Hope's indiscretions under wraps. It wasn't uncommon for a family to circle the wagons in an attempt to preserve the reputation of their deceased family member. My thoughts shifted to that day at our small neighborhood beach. Propped on my elbows at the end of the pier, lazily watching gulls circle in the heat of the afternoon sun, high-pitched banter prompted a glance over my shoulder. A gaggle of girls, maybe ten or eleven years old, dropped towels and kicked off flip-flops. I'd never met Hope, but recognized her; smaller than the others, she hung back as the rest plummeted cannonball style over the end of the pier. The drop was fifteen feet, but another twenty through the shimmering green to the sandy bottom made it daunting. "Just jump already," they'd called up to her. As they continued to taunt, the jabs turned cruel; Hope fought back tears.

I got to my feet, sidled up next to her, then pitched forward, my hands on my knees so we were shoulder to shoulder. We stood a good five feet from the end of the pier, both pretending we could see over the edge. "Not for me," I said, shaking my head. She eyed me hopefully. "But I'll race you to the float from the beach." With a whoop of delight, she'd taken off at a run. By the time I reached its ladder, she stood atop the platform, hands on her hips and a smile of triumph on her face. And I wondered if John had been right, that she'd been under the influence of a drug and whatever she'd been on, had been powerful enough to eliminate her fear, to prompt her to do things she'd never consider. An ache of memory confirmed it was more than possible.

Through the glass-paneled kitchen door I watched as Rosa, the housekeeper, removed a plate of untouched eggs from in front of Eddie Field, who sat alone at the kitchen's center island. When I knocked, Rosa dropped the plate in the sink, wiped her hands on her apron, and hurried to the door. She smiled and held it open for me.

"Good morning, Rosa," I said, then turned and greeted Eddie.

He was muscular; his bulky shoulders and chest stretched the limits of his glacier-white Fruit of the Loom, and his eyes, still bloodshot, had a wild look about them. Eddie appeared to be coming down from some rough stuff. I wondered if it was the sedative from the doctor, the booze, or both. He showed no sign of recognition when I handed him my card and offered condolences. Pen in hand, I took the stool directly across from him. "Do you prefer Edward or Eddie?"

He shrugged. "Either works."

Eddie seemed friendlier.

"Well, Eddie, again, I'm sorry to intrude, but it's procedure after an accident with a death resulting that we need to file a corroborating report. Are you okay with answering a few questions?"

"I'm not sure what I can add to what you already know," he said. "Hope was drunk. She was going to her boat. She fell. It was a horrible accident."

I decided to play along.

"Can you tell me what she was drinking?"

"White wine."

"Any idea how much?"

He shook his head. "There were servers handing out drinks, taking empties. It wasn't like I was pouring her a glass from one bottle and could keep track." It exasperated him that I didn't appear to understand the protocol of catered affairs.

"And?" I prompted.

"And it became . . . uncomfortable. She did things. Things she normally wouldn't."

"Like what?"

"Like dancing with other guys."

"You were among friends."

"The bartender wasn't a friend."

"Given her alcohol consumption, her behavior might make sense."

"Maybe," he said, meeting my eye, and using none of the typical tells for deception.

I considered telling Eddie about Hope's blood alcohol level, but decided to see how big of a hole he'd dig and if that would result in an admission that he and Hope had used drugs the night of the party and resolve this whole thing. "Were you concerned when you noticed she was drinking more than usual?"

"I guess that's the point. I hadn't noticed. One minute she was fine and the next . . ." He shook his head.

"I see. At what time did she become visibly intoxicated?"

"After nine, maybe closer to ten. I wasn't checking the time."

"And how about you? How much had you had to drink?"

"Early in the evening, I was careful not to overdo it. But later on, not so much."

"I understand you argued. Can you tell me about that?"

He picked at his lower lip. "Like I said, I saw Hope dancing. She was a little too friendly. It pissed me off. I pulled her off the dance floor so we could talk."

He'd sidestepped the question. I'd circle back.

"Did Hope take drugs?"

"Absolutely not."

I told him that the toxicology report would verify what was in her system and repeated my question. His swift, unfaltering denial felt genuine. It stuck in my craw.

"What happened next?"

He stared off, presumably reliving images from the previous night. "I grabbed a bottle of water and led her to the herb garden. We sat on one of the benches."

"Is that where you argued?"

He cocked his head. "It wasn't an argument. I asked her what the hell had gotten into her and she laughed at me, told me to lighten up."

"Did it get physical? Pushing, scratching—anything?"

"I held her hand, encouraged her to drink some water. Five or ten minutes later she became annoyed, chucked the bottle of water into the corner of the garden, and told me to leave her alone." He hesitated. "So, I did. That was the last time I saw her before—"

I finished the sentence. "Before finding her on the rocks?"

Tears soaked his cheeks.

"What time was it when you left her?"

"No idea."

"Where did you go?"

"I wandered around."

"Can you be more specific?"

"Around. I don't know," he snapped.

"Did you see anyone? Talk to anyone?"

A small shake of his head.

"Okay, then what?"

"After a while, I went back to the party."

I repeated my question about the time.

"Maybe about eleven," he said. "Then the guys dragged me to the poolside bar. Insisted we drink shots. That's when I sort of overdid it."

"I'm going to need a list of your friends and their numbers." I pushed a pen and paper in front of him. He jotted down three names and phone numbers. "When did it occur to you to look for her?"

"It was getting late. The caterers were packing up. Me and the guys went into the kitchen, rooted around for leftovers. I realized I hadn't seen her for a few hours."

"Where did you check first?"

"The house. Her room, the guest room."

Rosa cleared her throat as if she had something to say. Eddie shot her a look. She turned and busied herself with the dishes. I made a note to question her with DelCarmen; it'd be easier in her native language.

"What happened next?"

"My buddies and I spread out, walked the grounds, called her name. Then I went to the boat." With a sharp intake of breath, he said, "I saw her when I went back up." Eddie dropped his head into his hands; his shoulders shook as he sobbed. "I had nothing to do with it, just a fucking accident."

"Were you aware that Hope was afraid of heights?" It was a guess, but an educated one.

Eddie lifted his head from his hands and glared.

"She'd been up and down those stairs her whole life."

"It wasn't the stairs she fell from, Eddie. It was the observatory. And yes, I think a fear of heights would impact the circumstance of her death. I think she'd be hard pressed to go near the edge."

Eddie wiped his face with the back of his wrist. "You can think what you want," he said. Then, as if to say our conversation was over, he thumped his palms on the countertop, stood, tipping his stool on its side, then strode from the room. I blinked, taking in Eddie's erratic behavior. All the mixed signals, initially truthful then some of what he said, deliberately thin. He had to know Hope hadn't been drinking, but his insistence that she didn't use drugs rang true. It didn't mean Eddie was lying nor did it make him guilty of anything, but my intuition was sounding an alarm.

Rosa stared in disbelief, her lower lip wobbled. We reached the overturned stool at the same time. "Let me help," I said, resetting the stool.

Training discouraged emotional involvement, yet in that moment, something inside severed as I recognized Rosa's unacknowledged loss for a girl she had, no doubt, loved. I placed my hand on her shoulder. She lifted her weary eyes to meet mine; silent tears dripped from her chin.

"I'm sorry," I said. "For Hope." She nodded, lifting the hem of her apron to her cheeks. After a few moments, I asked, "Can you show me the herb garden?" Her face clouded over in confusion. "Los herbas . . . herbos," I said, taking a hatchet to her language.

Rosa untied the apron from her waist and pushed open the kitchen door, a flick of her head indicating that I should follow. We had walked a short distance to the side of the house when she stopped. Rosa's eyes scanned the windows of the upper floors. I followed her gaze in time to see the curtains of a third-floor window swing back into place. Emitting a small moan, she spun and hurried away.

"Rosa! Wait! What's the matter?"

She turned and pointed beyond where I stood. "Alli. There." Seconds later, the kitchen door slammed shut. I looked up. The curtains were still. Another interesting moment. *Rosa's edginess wasn't subtle*, I thought, as I walked on alone.

Wrapped in a tall hedge of mature privet, the herb garden was secluded. Neat rows and semicircular pathways of pea gravel created a visual mini-maze. In its center, two benches faced each other; gazing balls and statuary sat amid rows of plantings. I closed my eyes. The sound of music, revelry in the distance; Hope and Eddie in the dark, seated on a bench, the thump of the water bottle landing on pea stone. I ran through plausible scenarios. She'd been flirting with other men; it had angered Eddie. She told him to leave her alone. Did that mean she rebuffed Eddie's advances, or had she asked him to leave? Did Eddie walk off? That part of his story seemed unlikely. Perhaps Hope left Eddie, and he followed her to the observatory. If they then fought, it would explain the skin beneath her fingernails. Somehow she fell. An accident? Murder? My mind returned to the elusive motive. Did rage overtake reason? History is littered with examples.

The walk to the observatory took less than a minute. I stepped to the right of the high-top table, bent over the railing, and looked down. Sturdy and wide, the top rail caught me below the breastbone; it was roughly four feet high. I recalculated the distance to where she landed on the rocks—four or five feet from the cliff wall. I'd hoped to see something different in the light of day, but my eyes hadn't played tricks and the darkness hadn't skewed the perspective: it wasn't even close to a straight drop.

CHAPTER

8

WHAT LEVEL OF cosmic manipulation does it take to turn something tragic into something of value?

I'd been home for a week-long stay with my parents at the end of August, nearing the end of my third year on patrol. A week after I returned to Boston, my dad suffered a devastating heart attack. I wasn't ready to return to Rhode Island, but six months after his unexpected death, Mother wasn't coping and I knew it was time.

I applied for a transfer and was accepted to the Providence Police. Out of the box, it was difficult not to notice Julian DelCarmen. He and his partner were almost mythical highfliers; their collective solve rate was off the charts. When the two breezed, shoulder to shoulder, through the detective division, eyes lifted, necks craned, and a hush fell over the room as if some hypnotic pheromone wafted in their wake.

Six months after I passed the promotional exam to the rank of detective, DelCarmen's partner of eight years was killed during a routine detail. Until that time, I'd floated, hadn't been assigned, but within a month, DelCarmen and I were partnered. At first I thought the pairing was so that DelCarmen, the senior detective, could evaluate my viability, but then it occurred to me that no one had been beating down the door to fill the vacancy. DelCarmen was beyond brief with colleagues who interpreted him as dismissive, but I couldn't imagine he was shunned because of his communication style. It made perfect sense—to me, anyway—that his priorities didn't include meaningless chitchat, his linguistic prowess reserved for witnesses and higher-ups. I concluded that my selection as partner had been driven by ego, that DelCarmen hadn't wanted a partner; he only wanted a warm, compliant body to fill the empty seat next to him.

If my parents had been confused about my reasons for joining the force, my colleagues were even more so. In their world, educated, wealthy women didn't dump their privileged lives to become a cop. There was a reason, and they wanted to know what it was. A partnership with DelCarmen seemed to be the answer to my sticky situation. It'd be a relief to sit in companionable silence during the endless hours of a surveillance detail, unconcerned about dodging the typical probing personal questions I had no intention of answering. If nodding my head and retrofitting DelCarmen's utterances with subjects, pronouns, or even verbs was the price of admission, it was a pittance to pay for the seat next to the best of the best. And that's how the past two years had gone. Although he seemed to know private details I hadn't shared, we asked no personal questions, and other than the occasional lighthearted barb, discussions were strictly business. I didn't know if he had a partner or children or even a pet. Once I saw a duffel bag in the trunk of his car that contained a slew of baseball bats and guessed he played in some adult rec league, but that was the extent of what I knew.

But, of course, I'd been dead wrong about most everything I assumed about Julian DelCarmen, including the reason he chose me.

* * *

At eleven on Sunday morning, DelCarmen answered on the first ring.

"How'd it go?" he asked.

"We've got some work."

"Vacation?"

"The good news is I didn't buy airline tickets. Got a pen?"

I heard the click of his Parker Jotter retractable. Of course, he had a pen.

"His name is Edward Field, middle initial *b* like 'bravo.' We should look at ex-girlfriends, his finances, family, bad habits, the gamut. But

I'm most interested in drugs. I googled the engagement announcement; he's a relatively new veterinarian."

"Right."

"We need to know if for any reason he'd want to murder his fiancée—a very wholesome, all-American type with boatloads of money."

"Your dead girl from the island?"

"Yeah. Are they talking about that downtown?"

"Not."

"Not what? Did you mean they 'are not'?"

"Correct. Someone steal your ride?"

"It's in the shop. Don't they have lives?"

"Ah, interesting question." I imagined his hazel eyes narrowing, his thumb and index finger caressing his bottom lip as if considering a complex puzzle.

"When will they find someone else to harass?"

"When you stop taking the bait."

Without further conversation, DelCarmen ended the call. It didn't matter how he did it. He had a vast reservoir of motives I had yet to understand, that spun and whirred and produced results. He would have what I needed within twenty-four hours.

CHAPTER

9

My phone rang before I could pocket it. "What can I do for you now?" I asked with feigned exasperation.

"That's a loaded question, Miss Stuart."

"Very funny, Dr. Riordan." I cringed. God had invented caller ID to avoid moments like these. "I thought you were DelCarmen."

"Sorry to disappoint."

"Not at all. I've been anxiously awaiting your call. For professional reasons, naturally."

"Naturally."

"What do you have for me?"

"A preliminary report. It'll be finished in a few hours. Thought I'd detour through Jamestown later this afternoon and hand-deliver it. Besides, my Sunday is already shot to hell, not to mention your vacation. Perhaps we could meet so we can discuss any questions you might have? For a drink. My treat."

Dread flapped like a frantic caged bird. "As in a date?"

"Absolutely not. We couldn't go on a date."

It felt like someone had stuck out their foot, and blindly, I'd stumbled over it. I scrambled for a brilliant, witty comeback, but my brain was busy trying to right itself. Instead, I said, "Ah, right. Best not to mix business with pleasure."

"It's not that, but if things didn't work out, a woman licensed to carry a gun scares the crap out of me."

I chuckled.

"Consider it a peace offering. Shall we say Leo's at five?"

"A peace offering," I repeated like some half-wit, then mumbled something that might have sounded like "sure."

"See you then," he said, and hung up. I stared at my phone, a large question mark formed on my face.

Sunday was turning out to be an interesting day. Mother had invited my brother, Peter, and me for lunch—she'd even mentioned she felt like cooking—which was odd. While there'd been extensive warming and serving, she hadn't technically cooked since Dad passed. At about the same time, she'd been diagnosed with macular degeneration. She hadn't appeared visually impaired—she drove, watched television, read intricate sheet music when she played the piano—and was mum on the subject of her troubled vision unless she cited it as the reason to bow out on a social event. Concerned or perhaps hoodwinked, Peter had offered to hire a driver. Who did he think she was, Mother had scoffed, Miss Daisy? And I wondered if compromised vision was more socially acceptable to her than sadness.

I rambled along the quarter mile from the guest cottage to the main house. Mother and Peter were in the kitchen sipping cold white wine and nibbling on something that looked as if it had been prepared elsewhere.

"This looks yummy," I said, kissing Mother on the forehead and appraising the feast spread across the kitchen's butcher-block center island. I breathed in the faint smell of jasmine and vanilla, and it occurred to me I couldn't remember when she had last worn perfume.

"So, what's up?" I asked, slipping onto a stool.

"Isn't it possible that a mother wants to enjoy the company of her children with no ulterior motives?"

"Anything is possible," I agreed.

Her eyelids shimmered, her lipstick, freshly applied. There was an agenda.

"First things first," she said. "At the end of the month, the Historic Preservation Society is holding its annual fundraiser. Silver Oak Equity is hosting at Marble House. I can't go, so I'm asking you both to attend—to represent the family."

This was an event she and my father never missed. It had been four years. Peter and I hoped that this year she'd attend.

"Do we both have to go?" I asked.

"Peter is between girlfriends, so to speak. And you are . . . Well, either of you would need an escort, so going together simplifies things."

I turned to Peter, made an *L* with my thumb and index finger and held it to my forehead. He mouthed the word "sorry," shrugged his okay then pulled the wine from the chiller, poured a glass, and nudged it in my direction. Mother's olive-green silk blouse matched her eyes. She wore a long strand of pearls and pearl earrings—her event jewelry. I took a long swig of the wine and leaned left, taking in her heels and tailored cream-colored trousers.

"Looking quite snazzy. Are you going out?" I glanced at Peter, who pretended to brush crumbs from his tie. A tie? An ominous feeling surfaced.

"Goodness, no." She waved dismissively. Her cheeks flushed pink.

"This is nice," I said, as I loaded up a delicate bone china plate and scoured the possibilities. I looked at Peter, who refused to meet my eye and remained suspiciously mute.

"It's great to have you here for the week," she began. "It'd be even better if you came more often and took some time from your job."

She said the word as if it was a newfound untreatable disease. Everyone in the family had jobs. In her defense, my abrupt change in career path had been a shock. I'd been accepted to the prestigious doctoral program in American Studies at Harvard. While taking summer school classes to complete my undergraduate degree, I deferred my acceptance and, without a word to anyone, took the civil service exam then enrolled in the Boston Police Academy. That fall I hadn't pretended to attend Harvard; my family had simply assumed.

"It's great to be here, and I come when I can," I said.

"Well, your brother and I," she said, gesturing, "are concerned that you're too focused on this . . . this career. When exactly was the last time you had a date?" she asked. "With anyone, I mean."

After training, I took a job with the Boston police as a patrol officer. It gave me a reason to get up in the morning. The world I'd been born into scooted aside as if creating room for one more on the couch. A sense of purpose filled the empty space while I hovered somewhere in between. Yet Mother still hadn't understood that my occupation and my retreat from an active social calendar resulted from one event. That the former hadn't caused the latter.

"I'm fine. Dating is fine," I lied.

I looked from Mother to Peter, but couldn't read either of them. Was there such a thing as a dating intervention?

"I'm not a lesbian," I said.

"Thank heavens." She looked skyward, laying a hand across her chest. "You know how much I adore your Uncle Jerome and his . . ."

"Partner," I supplied.

"Yes, partner. But you're my daughter. I wouldn't know what to do or say."

"I have no doubt that you'd figure it out." I couldn't repress a smile.

"Now that we've straightened that out," she said, "when did you last have a date with a man? Other than a friend."

I cleared my throat. "Let's see. Michael Lang, you remember him. He asked me out, oh, about three weeks ago for dinner."

"I do remember him," Mother said, brightening. "Where did you have dinner?"

"Something came up. I had to take a raincheck."

Her shoulders slumped. "Let me rephrase. When did you last have a date and didn't cancel at the last minute?"

I twisted my neck left, then right. It crunched like peanut brittle.

"I'm having a drink later—with a doctor." I cocked my head and opened my eyes wide.

She looked hopefully at Peter, who had the look of a gazelle trapped between two lionesses. "A doctor." She sampled the word, savoring its possibility.

"Anyone I know?" asked Peter.

"He speaks," I said, and Peter winced.

"His name is John Riordan."

"Not sure I've heard of him. What kind of medicine does he practice?"

"He's a forensic pathologist, the medical examiner in South County."

"That's . . . nice, Andie," Peter said. Mother made a face.

"Both of you need to relax. Just no one special yet."

"How could there be?" she said, shaking her head and seeming to wonder how I could overlook the obvious.

"Mother, enough, okay? You've been telling me this sort of thing my entire life." I drained my wine and held out my glass for a refill.

"It's different now," she said. "It used to be that god-awful habit of saying what you think the minute it floated into your head. That was immaturity. Now it's . . . it's . . . You scare them," she blurted out.

Peter nodded enthusiastically, and I flipped him the bird.

"Scare them? What on earth are you talking about?"

"Just look at you!" She eyed me like I'd sprouted antlers. "Perhaps 'scare' is the wrong word. You intimidate them," she said, satisfied with her new assessment.

"That's me, intimidating. Let's see: educated, in shape, and not to mention the M-O-N-E-Y."

"It's not that," Mother said, exasperated. "It's your approach."

"My approach?"

"Exactly," agreed Peter. "What about that thing a few months back? With Howard."

"How can you even bring him up? I'm not looking to meet men in bars."

"It's a well-respected golf club, not a pool hall—they call it the 'Gathering Room,' for Christ's sake. Howard had been trying to show you the correct setup for a chip. Next thing I know, you've got him on the floor in a headlock."

"You don't know," I said, my voice shrill, quavering. "His hands were all over me. Besides, are you not the self-proclaimed authority on all things love related, who has informed me more than once that men like bitchy women?"

"That wasn't bitchy. That was thuggish." Peter sighed, frustrated.

He had a point. "Fine," I said, and drank the last of my wine. "I'll work on it." I fluttered my eyelashes and made a production of checking the time. "Would you look at this? And we were having so much fun. Let's do this again soon."

I blew dramatic kisses, gathered my jacket, and gave them my prom queen wave at the door. Glancing back, their look of desperation frightened me. An image of Mother threatening with a gas can while Peter readied a Zippo flashed across my mind's eye. I traipsed back into the kitchen.

There had been one opportunity for me to explain and for her to understand how it had all begun, but our chance had come and gone, and I'd been unable to forgive her for how it had played out. But as the years passed, I realized that my stubborn inability to let it go had scattered the fuel then lit the fire that burned the bridge between us. Now I didn't know how to reach across and take the olive branch she held. My wounded inner child refused to grow up.

"The important point is that I'm okay. The job is good for me. It grounds me. And because I'm passionate about my job, it doesn't mean dating is out of the question. It means the right person hasn't come along yet." I continued with rhetoric that would placate, wouldn't wound. Mother listened, scrutinized for tells in the same manner I assessed a suspect. When I promised I'd try, I meant it.

Her lips curled at the corners, she raised the eyes we shared to meet mine and finally, almost imperceptibly, she nodded. Peter flashed an appraising smile. I'd won the battle, yet I knew the war was far from over. Mother would have one foot in the grave and still muster the energy to wag a disapproving finger at me.

CHAPTER

10

JOHN RIORDAN LEANED on the stone wall that fronted Leo's, a quaint bistro on Jamestown's main drag. As I made my way up Narragansett Avenue, I watched John scan the handful of pedestrians who strolled past. The sun shone from behind, setting his angular facial structure in relief. His shock of blond hair flashed brilliantly in the fading light. I was a block away when he saw me and grinned.

This was not a date.

Conceived and constructed around a European beech that stood sixty feet tall, its spread almost as wide, Leo's was the embodiment of an elegant treehouse. The tree's massive trunk hurtled upward through its center; tiny white lights draped its limbs. Beneath the canopy of leaf and bough, candles sparkled on tables dressed in white linen. Strains of a live jazz trio wafted onto the street. John wore jeans, a white button-down, and a well-worn dusty-blue corduroy blazer; a manila file folder, tucked under one arm. He was more athletic than his scrubs revealed. Despite his intimidating stature, he exuded gentleness and warmth. For the first time in a very long time, I wasn't planning my exit strategy before we even said hello.

"Thanks for coming," he said.

"Thanks for that report." I gestured to the file folder.

"There's no room at the bar. Hope it's okay that I got a table."

I looked over; the bar was three deep. "That's fine," I said, lying.

We trailed the host along a flagstone path covered by a rustic wooden pergola. Stone pots placed at the supporting beams contained flowering vines that wound their way up and through overhead slats. More glittery white lights strung here and there lit our way. We arrived at a table for two dotted with votive candles and a vase with a small bouquet of salmon-colored tea roses in full bloom. John helped me into my chair. I breathed in the delicate aroma of rose and smiled.

"Well," I said. "It's been quite a day."

"I can imagine," John said, settling into the chair across from me.

I laughed and shook my head. "I'm not sure you can."

"Try me."

It had been a long time since anyone had said they wanted to hear about my day and meant it. I envied the intimacy my parents had enjoyed. I knew that whatever you went through during the day, no matter how mundane or trying, once shared with the right person, it could be left behind. That right person had been my mother or father as a child; as an adult, he should be called "soul mate." But I didn't know. It was, for me, entirely theoretical.

"It's the job," I said, surprising myself. "Some days are a blur. Don't get me wrong, I love it. But I'm getting that nagging feeling that life is passing me by."

"We all wrestle with that. At some point, we think we've arrived at that intangible place called 'success.' One day you wake up and realize that your job takes up the lion's share of your time and all the going out and fun stuff you thought you'd be doing isn't happening."

"Definitely not happening," I agreed. Then I heard myself ask, "So, not enough time for your girlfriend?"

John hit his forehead and made a theatrical popping sound. I imagined the lightbulb flashing above his head. "I knew there was something I keep forgetting to do." He pulled a pen and notebook from the breast pocket of his jacket. "If I don't write everything down, it never gets done," he said, wetting his index finger, turning the page to a blank sheet, furrowing his brow. "Get girlfriend," he mouthed as he wrote, his eyes darting from me to his notepad.

"Very funny. I assumed, you know, a guy like you." I shrugged. "Thought you'd have one."

"Oh, there are women," John said. "One after the next. Problem is they're nonresponsive."

"As in stiff?" I laughed.

He pointed a finger at me. "Exactly! I'm getting a complex." A waiter appeared. "Andie, have you tried their pear martini?"

This was the problem with not sitting at the bar: I couldn't watch the bartender make my drink.

"Andie?" John prompted, disrupting my thoughts.

"Ah, no, I haven't," I said.

"How's that possible?" John asked. "It's Leo's signature drink. Ice cold. The perfect hint of ginger and lemon. You haven't lived until you've had one." He arched an eyebrow.

"Sounds delicious," I said, feeling the rumble of anxiety like a distant train approaching the station.

Ten minutes later the waiter delivered two martini glasses, tawny yellow and filled to the brim, small fragments of ice shimmering along the surface, a skewered slice of pear draped across the top.

"Do you need a few minutes?" the waiter asked.

"We weren't planning on food, but I'm starved. Andie, how about we split a few appetizers?"

"My resuscitation skills are weak. We should order something."

"Great." John scanned the menu, then ordered enough food to feed a small village. "Let's start with that. Okay?" he asked, shrugging boyishly.

I lifted my martini. "Here's to something new," I said, considering my options: spill or trust.

John raised his glass. "I like that. To something new."

I watched John sip, then listened as he extolled the bartender's skillful preparation. I tamped back my irrational objections, lifted the glass to my lips and allowed a mouthful of the pear martini to slide down my throat. As promised, it was wonderful.

The waiter brought a tomato and fresh mozzarella salad and an extra plate. John served, then dug in. "I know this is a business meeting, but I can't think on an empty stomach." He picked up the pepper grinder and gestured. I nodded. "What can I tell you?" he asked, finally.

"What was Hope Philbrick on?"

"Don't know yet."

"Will you test for ketamine? Her fiancé is a vet."

"We test for an entire spectrum of that class of drug, ketamine included."

"I know the drill for the turnaround time."

"It may not help, but I've requested the lab expedite the tox screen. Fair warning, when I get the full toxicology report, it might change what I currently think about this."

"I'll take your first impressions with a grain of salt."

"Murder seems the least likely. An accident more likely, but I can't rule out suicide."

"Interesting," I said. "I believe she had a fear of heights. If she was going to kill herself, it seems unlikely she'd choose to do it this way."

"Unlikely, yes. But if she'd been on drugs that contributed to irrational thoughts and the lack of inhibition, there you go."

"So, if something happened to set her off, it could have been the perfect storm."

"Exactly. Again, I'm on the fence. Deaths due to falls are tricky. The pathology will tell you one thing, but not everything."

"Meaning?"

"Meaning that the injuries she sustained suggest there was one massive impact to the head, indicative of a dive. However, without the rest of the picture, we can't be conclusive about the manner of death. You know: murder, suicide, or accident."

"Is the impact what killed her?"

"She suffered massive head injuries that would have been sufficient to kill her. However, she severed the vertebrae that contain the nerves that control the diaphragm. More than likely, she asphyxiated shortly after impact. One or the other. Happened within minutes, or less."

"So, it's not a possibility she was dead before she went over?"

He shook his head. "It might have looked as if she'd sustained injuries not related to the fall, but the bruising was most definitely postmortem."

Within a few minutes of clearing our plates, our waiter delivered crab cakes with a serpentine of horseradish sauce at the edge of the plate. While we noshed, I processed what John had said. I knew that if the victim remains alive for even a short time after the injury, the blood continues to flow through the tissues, showing up as a bruise on different parts of the body. Prime example: a blow to the scalp most often reveals itself as a black eye.

"Could she have been pushed?"

"It's possible, if she was in position. You know." He raised his arms overhead, mimicking a dive. "But the more likely scenario is that she dove, either by mistake or on purpose."

The waiter reappeared with an eggplant dish. John scanned the proffered wine list and without fluster or indecision, ordered a lovely bottle of white Bordeaux, reminding me of an unfussy version of my father, who understood the subtleties of pairing wine with food.

"We've got nothing so far to suggest that she was suicidal."

"Andie, she was getting married. Puts people over the edge all the time." A wry look spread across his face. I rolled my eyes. "You seem unconvinced. Is there something else?"

"The whole thing doesn't fit in the nice box I have for it in my brain. If it's an accident, I need to be certain."

"Look, Andie, you probably know better than anyone. Sometimes we don't get all the answers because they're lost or never there to begin with. Sometimes you only get half the answer and it sends you in the wrong direction."

It was an important point, one I tended to forget. The waiter stopped at the table. John looked apologetically at me and said, "If there's a speck of food in my fridge, it's got an acute case of green acne."

"Harsh," I said, shaking my head. "Be my guest, but I'm done."

He ordered a plate of rigatoni Bolognese and devoured it as we chatted happily about nothing. We both enjoyed golf. John claimed a basic proficiency in the sport was a requirement for his medical degree, and I claimed to have potential. John practiced his one-liners and shared amusing stories of growing up with four brothers. The whole thing felt easy.

"How about you? Are the bars littered with the men whose hearts you've crushed?"

"That would ordinarily be the case, but dating isn't on the agenda these days."

"That's too bad. How come?"

"It might ruin my chances."

"For what?"

"For getting into the nunnery, of course."

"The nunnery. I see." He feigned seriousness. "So, you're Catholic?"

My parents raised me as an Episcopalian, but I no longer found solace in my religion. My senior year at college made me question and doubt everything.

"I'm currently a practicing doubter—waiting for a sign."

"Anything promising?"

"The certainty of the existence of hell," I said without hesitation.

"That's pretty definitive." I could see the cogs in John's head shift into gear. "What do you get if you're an insomniac, an agnostic, and dyslexic?"

I shrugged.

"Someone who stays up all night wondering if there really is a dog."

John slapped his knee and howled and it made me smile. We sipped the wine slower and slower. When the waiter removed the empty bottle and, piece by piece, everything else from the table, we got the not-so-subtle hint and meandered to the hostess station.

"Thank you, Dr. Riordan, this has been a relaxing end to a hectic day." I held up the manila file folder. "And thanks for your attention to my case." I turned to go.

"Just a minute, young lady." John gently twisted me to face him. "Where are you parked?"

"I'm fine." I waved dismissively. "I'm just down at the pier. This is Jamestown. If a pigeon gets out of line, I have my Glock in my purse."

John placed his hands on his knees and stooped so we were eye to eye. "If I don't walk you to your car, the pack of wolves who raised me will hunt me down and skin me alive. Perhaps you can find it in your heart to help me out?"

There it was. The easiness.

I smiled and said, "But, Grandmother, what big teeth you have."

John straightened, the space between us less than a foot. He extended a large, smooth hand. A tide of panic I struggled to conceal washed over me. It seemed so simple, yet I felt paralyzed, my insides cresting the terrifying pinnacle of a roller-coaster track.

"I haven't bitten anyone since I was three," he said, softly.

My shoulders relaxed, the breath I held seeped between my lips, and a hint of a smile formed on my lips. He reached out tentatively, slowly laced warm fingers through my own, then gave my hand a gentle squeeze. We walked in companionable silence to my car. He gave the land yacht a once-over.

"Is this what you drive?"

"You like?"

He stood back considering me, then took both of my hands in his. "I enjoyed not having a date with you, Miss Andrea Stuart."

I took a deep breath. "It was very nice not having a date with you, too, Dr. John Riordan."

"What are the chances you'd consider not going out with me again?"

"Chances are good."

I wished my words were truthful, but knew they were not.

CHAPTER

11

THE GUEST COTTAGE was the former carriage house to my parents' estate. When we were children, our parents had given strict orders to keep out. Mother said it was unsafe; Dad said it was where the ghosts lived. Neither swayed our resolve to pry open rotting boards and see what all the intrigue was about.

Shortly after Dad passed away, Mother hired a team of contractors to install a proper kitchen, two full bathrooms, re-shingle the exterior, and to replace the old wooden doors that once accommodated nineteenth-century carriages with floor-to-ceiling windows.

Prized possessions of Peter's and my childhood artwork carefully preserved in frames better suited for masterpieces, hung alongside nautical-themed oils and watercolors. A pictorial history of my family's life by the sea filled the gaps on the walls. Mother's beachcombing excursions loaded the cottage with the typical bowls of emerald-green and sky-blue beach glass, delicate pearl white shells. Remnants of salty nets and driftwood collected on shelves, tables, and the mantel. All the weather-beaten and lost or discarded possessions that washed up on the shore, now unified by their misfit status, had been given new purpose; as if still a part of the gentle ebb and flow of the sea, they lulled, reassured and soothed. Unknowingly, Mother had created a haven for my adrift and battered soul.

Giving up my apartment on the West End of Providence and moving home wasn't an option, but soon something needed to give. Mother was notorious for calling in the middle of the night with some calamity that required immediate attention. Showing up in the morning was crisis provoking. While I was in Boston, Peter shouldered the responsibility. When I moved home, we took turns. The late-night drive to Jamestown soon got old. Within six months of my return to Rhode Island, I was dusting the furniture and putting fresh linens on the bed in the cottage for whenever I needed to stay.

I lit a fire under the supervision of Tom Collins the Second, my recently rescued pound kitty. The first Tom Collins was my grandmother's all-black cat named for her favorite adult beverage. When Grandpa died, Tom became Grandma's cocktail-hour companion. I'm sure that Tom wasn't a gin-swilling feline, but his company was easily bought with fresh salmon or tuna. There was a resemblance and as the years drifted past, I began to doubt there'd be other opportunities to pass on family names.

I settled on the couch in front of the fire with John's report. Haunting, large-format colored close-ups showed Hope Philbrick's body in dehumanizing sections. For cops, self-deception was essential to self-preservation. I'd endeavored to hit delete on the mental file of the undignified images of her dead body and pictured her as she'd been in life, clinging to random sightings of Hope over the years and the photos throughout her parents' home in which she'd been smiling, vibrant and very much alive. Yet before my eyes was the disturbing reality of a life stamped out in its prime.

I turned to the last page. Final Pathological Diagnosis: inconclusive and awaiting toxicology report. Opinion: none stated. Great. I flipped back to the beginning. The report outlined the usual: clothing, identifying features, external examination, internal examination, and so forth.

The body is that of a well-developed, well-nourished Caucasian female, age twenty-five. The body measures sixty-two inches in length and . . .

I scanned the external examination; not much of her body had been unscathed.

Massive blunt force trauma to the head resulting from the velocity of a one hundred and seventeen-pound body from a height of approximately fifty feet and initial direct impact on a rock formation . . . inner table and outer table of the skull and diploes are shattered, radiating fractures spread outward from the sight . . . the spinal cord is severed at the third, fourth, and fifth cervical vertebrae (C3, C4, C5) . . . asphyxiation resulting.

It was horrifying in black-and-white print. There was little need for the photos. I flipped forward.

Genitalia are those of a normally developed woman. Minor laceration of posterior fourchette. Minor abrasions noted on the labia minora. A small amount of dried and semifluid blood is present on the anterior aspect of the vagina . . . a minimal amount of thin watery red fluid is present . . . tearing is noted . . . incision into the underlying subcutaneous anal tissue discloses significant contusion involving the superficial muscular layer.

Why the hell hadn't John mentioned this?

The toenails are neatly trimmed and clean.

My throat was dry and my hands, clammy. I closed the file, reached for my cell phone, and dialed John.

"What's up?" he asked.

"Is there a chance she was raped?"

There was a considerable silence before he answered. "When a woman is raped, she fights. We see similar injuries from case to case. I saw nothing to suggest this."

"But if she'd been high on some sort of drug, wouldn't she have been less likely to resist?"

"That's the correct assumption. Keep in mind, however, that the genital injury described in the report is much disputed and open to interpretation. The favored term is 'vigorous consenting intercourse.' Both share similar patterns except for defensive wounds."

"Was there semen?"

"There wasn't. Or to be clear, none discernible with the naked eye."

"What does that tell you?" I asked.

"Whoever she had sex with used a condom. The encounter was energetic or rough and produced normal secretions and abrasions and, while it's hard to be definitive, it likely occurred in the hours before her death. If you like, I'll revisit my notes and the photos."

"That'd be great," I said.

"And if need be, I can send the fluid samples to the lab for analysis."

"I'll let you know. Perhaps we can talk tomorrow."

"Sounds great," he said. "Leo's was fun—"

An old fear simmered, grabbed the wheel, and swerved to head off the dangerous turn in the conversation. I heard myself interrupting, saying something about my mother beeping in and that I'd call him. An hour later, I turned off the lights and sat gazing at the fire, considering the details of the autopsy. I dozed, falling into one of those intermediate states when I had the distinct feeling of being watched. My eyes fluttered open; lumps of orange embers pulsed in the grate as the antique clock on the mantel chimed twelve times. It was midnight and twenty-four hours since Hope Philbrick's death.

CHAPTER

12

THE NEW DIGS of the Providence Police Department at 425 Bradley Street were a vision of glass and steel. The modern angular structure was out of place in Providence's downtown of mostly red brick or stone Neo-Georgian–styled buildings. Perched between a bend of the city's three merging highways and the up-and-coming West End of Providence, the offices had lots of natural light and so-called views—even if it was of the passing traffic.

The detective division overlooked the staff parking. Despite my better judgment, I swung the Parisienne into the lot and waited at the booth to be cleared, then pulled into a space toward the back. At eight o'clock on Monday morning, the detective division was in full swing. A barrage of feigned compliments, whistling, and cheering greeted me.

"Holy shit, Stuart. Sweet ride."

"Stuart, retro is a good look for you."

I waved and nodded like a politician greeting her adoring constituents. This wasn't the first, nor would it be the last time my presence created some adverse stir. I was from another world of blue and try as I did to fit in, I wasn't one of them and never would be and worse, no one wanted me to forget it.

DelCarmen sat in front of his computer in the cubicle we shared. Steam wafted from a cup of coffee on my desk; it smelled freshly brewed. A jolt of affection morphed into suspicion. I dropped my bag, sat down, and shrugged off my blazer.

DelCarmen lifted his chin. "Rethinking vacation?"

"As a matter of fact, I'm on the beach in Bermuda sipping a boat drink," I said.

He whistled. "Someone run over your dog?"

DelCarmen held up his hands in response to my scowl. I looked over my shoulder. "Captain in?"

"Out for the day."

"Perfect."

"Anything beyond first impressions and blood alcohol?"

I gave DelCarmen a rundown of my discussion with John and Eddie Field, and about the text I'd sent to a friend at the Jamestown PD hoping for local knowledge. "What about you?"

DelCarmen swiveled in his desk chair, pulled out his notepad, clicked his Parker Jotter, and flipped backward through the pages. "Preston Philbrick, CEO of his own private equity firm, no financial details available. Main office in Boston, satellite in Jamestown. Lots and lots of family money. Gives prolific amounts of cash and time to several worthy groups, most notably, Newport Memorial. He's on their board of trustees and sponsors that big corporate blood drive they have at the hospital to benefit the blood bank every year. Want the full list of his philanthropic affiliations?"

I shook my head.

"Had a fender bender three years ago. Rear-ended a car at a stop sign, turned around and drove home."

"A hit and run?"

"Days later, when they finally tracked him down, he said he hadn't known he hit anyone. The locals suspected he'd had a couple of drinks and wanted to avoid a Breathalyzer." DelCarmen flipped forward in his pad. "The Philbricks maintain homes in Jamestown and in Boston. She's here full-time, he's back and forth. The Mrs. is a quiet lady. No fancy clubs or hobbies—"

"Odd," I said, thinking about a photo in the study of Penelope Philbrick in the center of a group of men, all wearing the same shorts and T-shirts and standing on the dock in front of a twelve-meter sailboat. "Something makes me think her family had been involved with the New York Yacht Club racing circuit."

"Not on their, or any boards, for that matter. Not within the last ten years, anyway," DelCarmen said and continued, "she had a sister, her twin. In private care since she was a child. Died four years ago."

He met my eye, and I shrugged.

DC scribbled on his notepad. "The fiancé, Edward Field, East Side kid. No social media. His father was a big-time exec with GE, retired a few years back. Rumored to have a long battle with alcohol. His mother left town when Eddie was sixteen and according to the neighbor, Eddie stepped up."

"That says something," I said.

"Went to Boston College on a football scholarship, then Tufts Cummings School of Veterinary Medicine. He's worked at the Veterinary Wellness Center in Warren for the past two years."

"Right. The vet."

"Just. He appears to have been in some sort of limbo. The typical path is an eight-year stint—undergrad and grad school—but it took him roughly ten years and he didn't specialize."

I did some quick math and realized that our time as students in Boston had overlapped for three of them. "Maybe he's not a scholar."

"You asked about drugs. It's not much, but he interned at the Bay Clinic in Sharon where he met the deceased when he cared for her schnauzer three years ago. Anyway, they reported stolen ketamine. Field quit his job right before anyone started poking around. The person I spoke with said that his departure was abrupt and frankly, suspicious."

"Ketamine, interesting."

"No priors—not even a parking ticket. He's got two brothers. Jeffrey, a choirboy. Senior at Harvard."

I recalled the waspy sort hovering over Penelope. "Go Crimson," I said, waving an imaginary pennant.

"Then there's Jacob," he said, like a white-gloved waiter removing the silver cloche from an iced bowl of caviar. "No rap sheet, but a boatload of speeding tickets. Funnily enough, he sells for Altman Auto Dealership in Newport."

"Maybe Bentley and Ferrari owners don't believe speed limits apply to them," I said.

"Drives a vintage Ferrari. The word is that he does well."

"I can feel a 'but' coming."

DC offered a rare smile. "Jacob plays high-stakes poker. Deep into Carmine Figueroa. The guess is two hundred large—and he isn't making the juice."

"A man in need of some cash."

DC nodded. "Want the rest?"

"You have the floor," I said, with a dramatic sweep of my arm.

"A Mr. Edward Bradford Field was married on July third of this year to a Miss Hope Elizabeth Philbrick. Justice of the peace, Martha's Vineyard, Massachusetts."

"Huh. Interesting." Letting this sink in, I twisted a strand of hair around my index finger until it pinched. "Well, this changes things. We have a motive. Let's get Daddy Philbrick on the horn and see if he has time for us. We need to know if there's a prenup in place."

DelCarmen made the call, and fifteen minutes later we were en route to Jamestown.

CHAPTER

13

We were shown into the second-floor study. Shadow overwhelmed daylight, saturating the room with grief. Sheer draperies swelled in the cool breeze trundling in through a pair of open patio doors.

Preston Philbrick stood before a wrought-iron demilune balustrade, gazing skyward. Rosa Rodriguez cleared her throat. He turned and muttered his apologies as he approached, then gestured for us to sit.

Presentation panels with fabric swatches and paint chip cards pinned to them covered the desk. In opposite corners of the room, easels held larger boards with illustrations of what appeared to be the reception area of a commercial building. Each offered a different color scheme for paint and furnishings.

"We are refreshing our office space and I need to make decisions," he said, gathering the design panels and setting them on the credenza behind his desk. "Last week it was a priority, today it's . . . it's pointless and on hold."

"Understandable," I said.

Preston settled into his chair, then turned his attention to me. "How can I be of help, Ms. Stuart?"

"As Detective DelCarmen mentioned on the phone, we have some questions about Edward Field. We hoped you could clarify a few things."

"Yes, please," he said, gesturing for me to begin.

"Were you aware that Hope and Edward were married on July third?" I said.

Preston gave a weary sigh. "I was," he said. "It wasn't something I had any control over."

"Was there a prenuptial agreement?"

"Not at the time. However, Hope came to me after it was done. I agreed to keep the marriage from her mother. Penelope would have been very hurt. I didn't want that. Our attorney drafted a postnuptial agreement to be signed to protect her interests . . ." His hand fluttered as if he was trying to summon the right words. A pretense, of course, since old-monied families didn't discuss their wealth.

"When was that signed?" I asked.

"It was supposed to be signed today."

"Since they were legally married, Edward would be entitled to her money, would he not?"

"Most of it is safe in trust, but he stands to gain a sizable amount."

"How sizable?" I asked.

"Enough for Edward to move forward in comfort."

His words conveyed no resentment and, oddly, no emotion of any kind.

"Did she have a reason to harm herself?" DelCarmen asked.

Preston closed his eyes and gave a decisive shake of his head.

"Perhaps you could tell us about Hope," said DC, his voice soft. "What was she like as a child?"

Preston considered the question before answering. "My firm's headquarters is in Boston. For many years I spent the early part of the week there and then Jamestown for the weekend. And, of course, the nature of my work dictates that I spend roughly six months of the year in Europe. It meant I was away during much of her critical growing-up years." He swiped at a tear that rolled down his cheek, then collected himself and continued. "For the most part, Hope never gave us any trouble. Of course, children will be children, try things, become influenced by their peers. Parents don't always have complete control over them."

"When you say she was influenced by her peers," DC prodded, "were you concerned about drugs?"

"What parent isn't?" Preston said.

"Did she use recreational drugs, Mr. Philbrick?" I asked.

He paused for an uncomfortably long minute, then shook his head. I continued.

"Was she taking any prescription medication that could have had an adverse reaction when mixed with alcohol?"

"That I cannot tell you." He raised his eyes to meet mine.

"We can check with Mrs. Philbrick while we're waiting for the toxicology report," I said.

"I'd rather you didn't. Penelope is devastated, and the sedatives she's taking make her confused. It'd be more reliable if you checked with our doctor."

I flipped backward through my notepad. "Dr. Maxwell?" I asked.

"Yes, that's right. He has all our medical records."

"What do you know about Jacob Field?" DelCarmen asked, switching gears.

"Let me put it this way." Preston leaned back in his leather desk chair and rocked while he surveyed the ceiling. "Jacob loves his expensive cars, a different girl on his arm every night, Bellevue Avenue parties, and like the rest of the crowd he runs with, can't keep away from the wager. I wasn't privy to the details, but the last I heard, he was asking Edward and Hope for money to pay off his gambling debt. It was disturbing. Edward seems to be forever cleaning up after his very troubled brother."

"Was Eddie going to help him?" I asked.

"I made it quite clear to Edward and to Hope and to Hope's mother that I would not let the likes of Jacob Field adversely affect the Philbrick name. Oddly enough, Hope agreed with me. She forbid Edward to help his brother, not with her money, anyway." Preston swiveled in contemplation, then sighed. "But Edward has been the mother and father to both of his brothers since . . . since their mother abandoned her family and his father lost his way. An admirable effort on Edward's part. Jeffrey is soon graduating from Harvard," he added, with an approving nod.

"Was Jacob invited to the party?"

"Absolutely not."

"Is there a chance he was there?"

"That's an interesting question." Preston studied me. "He didn't come through the gate, but it's possible. Some guests arrived by boat, and he owns some sort of a speedboat, docks it in Newport. I didn't see him, but that doesn't mean he wasn't there."

"The people he owes money to will hurt him if he doesn't pay," I said.

"We make our own beds, Ms. Stuart," Preston said as he checked the caller ID on the cell phone vibrating on his desk. He excused himself and answered it. When Preston hung up, he looked at us apologetically. "I'm sorry," he said. "I must attend to this. If there's anything else, please let me know and I will make time."

"Thank you, Mr. Philbrick. We'll need a complete list of guests, personnel, the catering company, the band—anyone on the property Saturday night," I said.

"Yes. Of course."

We stood and DelCarmen handed him his card. "I'll have my personal secretary forward it to you. I presume email is acceptable?" Mr. Philbrick said.

"It is. Thank you," DC said.

As we made our way toward the kitchen door, my phone chirped. It was a text from Steve O'Donnell, my friend on the Jamestown force. His message said there were a few random things, but nothing germane.

I texted back: *Whatever you can tell me would be great. Give us an excuse to catch up. Meet for a beer at the Gannie?*

A beer at the Gannie, for sure. The only thing I can think of is the terrible tale of the Edmund Fitzgerald.

Huh?

Mrs. Philbrick's sailboat sank.

Looking forward to hearing all about it.

"My friend at Jamestown PD says there's nothing relevant," I said. "Want my thoughts?"

"Shoot."

"Eddie's the guy with a row of dinner plates spinning on tall flimsy sticks. He hurries from one to the next—his brothers, his father, his job, her parents, even Hope—keeping the peace, preventing missteps; each needs something different. The plates twirl and twirl, yet there's always one that can't find its rhythm. He's the perpetual pain in Eddie's side; wobbling, forever threatening. Eddie is desperate not to let him careen out of control, and crash and burn."

"I take it we need to speak with Mr. Crash and Burn."

"We do."

CHAPTER 14

SUGAR MAPLES LINED the half-mile drive. In another month, they'd put on a spectacular fiery-red display. Riders atop graceful stallions trained in the riding arena off to the right and a dozen or so horses grazed in a field just beyond it.

The drive curved left and led to a semicircular car park fronting a massive stone structure that resembled an English country manor. You'd never dream it housed a dealership, even for uber-luxury vehicles. Before DelCarmen could shift into park, the equivalent of a valet hurried toward the car. DC rolled down the window, waved his badge, and pulled into a space reserved for a future Bentley owner.

The reception was evocative of the concierge desk at a boutique hotel. The woman who greeted us was striking, with an aristocratic aquiline nose, generous flecks of amber and gold in her large brown eyes, and her hair pulled into a lustrous, long ponytail. As if we'd been expected, she said Mr. Field was finishing a call and would be with us in a few minutes.

While we waited, I glanced behind a three-quarter wall that concealed a vast showroom. Sunlight gushed through its great glass walls, dazzling the high-polished chrome of the handful of new model and vintage Bentleys and Ferraris displayed.

Jacob Field strode toward us like a man who had the world by the shorthairs. He was tall, perfectly coiffed, his hand-cut navy silk suit slack on his lanky frame. He greeted us as if we were long-lost friends and whisked us off to a conference room. We sat at an antique burled walnut table in hand-tufted caramel leather chairs with a gold nail trimmed finish. A series of original etchings that depicted the evolution of the Ferrari and Bentley designs blanketed the walls.

We declined the proffered beverages from his assistant, who materialized out of thin air. "Nice spot," I said.

Jacob smiled. "It's the former estate of the late Senator Hughes. He had it designed after a visit to the English countryside. It was a struggle to get the zoning approved, but ownership went the extra mile, convinced this would be an ideal setting for what we do."

Bull's-eye, I thought, admiring the lovely, well-oiled charade.

"We know you're busy," said DC, "but we need to ask you a few routine questions."

"About Hope?" Jacob asked. "So tragic." A faint bluish haze smudged his deep-set eyes.

I nodded. "What time did you arrive at the party on Saturday?" I asked, as if I had confirmation that he'd been there.

Jacob cleared his throat and adjusted his tie but didn't hesitate. "Early. A little after six. We had other commitments, but of course, we wanted to stop by."

"You weren't on the guest list," I said, matter of fact.

"Does a brother need a formal invitation?" he asked with a laugh.

"You arrived by boat?"

"Yes," Jacob said. "My X35 MasterCraft."

"An X35," I said, pretending to be impressed.

Jacob beamed. It was a hell of a boat with a hell of a price tag. I was guessing somewhere close to a hundred thousand. And, of course, the docking fees in Newport weren't modest.

"And the name of your companion?" DC asked.

"Ah," Jacob said, his smile brightening. "I was with the lovely Mariana. Mariana Bucci."

"We'll need Miss Bucci's information," DC said.

Jacob pulled out his phone and scrolled through his contact list. He jotted down her phone number and email address and handed them to DC.

"Had you known Eddie and Hope were already married?" I asked.

He fiddled some more with his tie, then said, "Of course, I knew. We're brothers."

"We understand that Carmine Figueroa is looking for repayment on a debt," I said, while DC sat back and observed.

Jacob frowned as he considered my statement, then his smile returned. "Well, that's not entirely accurate. He's giving me some time to rearrange my finances. And we, you know, worked out a mutually agreeable payment plan."

I said, "Sort of unusual. A bookie offering a payment plan once you've lapsed."

"My case is different," said Jacob. "Sales. Some months it's tricky. Some months it's a windfall." He gestured as if at any moment thousand-dollar bills would cartwheel from the ceiling. "He knows I'm good for it."

"Did you ask Eddie for money?" I asked.

"Is that what he said?"

"He's your brother and married to a very wealthy woman," I said, dodging his dodge.

"I might have mentioned it to him," said Jacob, patting the pockets of his suit jacket, his eyes eventually finding the cell phone on the table.

"Did he turn you down?" I asked.

He pursed his lips. "Hope wasn't in favor."

"Did Eddie say he'd lend you the money? Perhaps quietly?"

"Like I said, I had an arrangement and didn't need his help."

"But you asked him?" I persisted.

"Yes, I asked him. It would have been simpler, and less expensive, but I worked it out."

I moved on. "Does Eddie do drugs?"

Jacob's eyes sparkled. "Eddie loves the uptown perks that come with the Philbrick son-in-law gig—the yacht, the clothes—but he's got a bit of 'downtown bad boy' in him."

He'd skirted the question, so I asked again.

"I shouldn't say," Jacob said, feigning reticence. "Recreational, perhaps," he added as if I'd badgered him into telling me.

"Like what?" I asked.

He made nonsensical spluttering noises as if I had questioned his virtue. "I wouldn't know exactly, but vets have access to drugs."

"Are you referring to ketamine?" I asked, playing along.

"You didn't hear it from me." Jacob put an index finger to his lips.

"What about Hope? Did she dabble?"

"I'm not very good at the couple thing, but it seems to me that the same sort of people are drawn to each other."

"Was there some reason or need for the first ceremony?"

Jacob shrugged, his knobby shoulders flimsily propping up his suit jacket. "Eddie was over the moon about it. He said it was their own little secret thing."

"And what about their relationship, any recent rifts that come to mind? Nerves? Regrets?"

He shook his head. "Happy as clams, those two."

"What time did you leave the party on Saturday?" I asked.

"We arrived at Swing at about eight. Bruno was on the door."

DC and I exchanged glances. He nodded.

We stood, and I said, "Thank you for your time, Mr. Field. We'll be in touch to set a time for you to come in and give us your formal statement."

He walked us to the door, his unflappable demeanor unchanged.

"Thoughts?" asked DC, as we got into the car.

"He had no qualms offering up big brother. Even if he wasn't physically there and his hands are technically clean, it doesn't mean the needed cash isn't driving this bus," I said.

"That's about the size of it," DC agreed. "Jamestown's on the way back to the city. Let's see what Eddie has to say."

We stopped by Swing and picked up the surveillance tapes from Saturday night. DC drove, and I contemplated the age-old question of the virtues of blood and water, and wondered if Eddie Field's familial bond held sway over his marriage vow.

CHAPTER

15

We stood at the observatory watching Eddie Field as he prepared the boat for sail. For a large man with a bulky build, he moved with the ease of a dancer as he methodically furled and secured lines, checked the rigging, and stowed loose objects.

DelCarmen lifted his chin in Eddie's direction. "Ten words or less."

"All over the map. He's sad, angry."

DelCarmen nodded and started down the stairs. I fell in step behind him. At the midway point, he stopped and looked up at the observatory. "Where'd she land?"

A downward glance conjured the image of Hope Philbrick's splayed body, twisted in bloodstained gossamer tangerine. I pointed toward the inky cluster of stone laden with tentacles of seaweed that jutted above the lumbering swell. DelCarmen looked from the landing to the rocks, then paced off its length and made mental calculations for the rest of the distance out from the cliff.

"Athletic?" he asked.

"From everything I've been told. If I'm not mistaken, she sailed competitively. I don't know what that means in terms of athleticism, but it's something."

We continued to the end of the dock and waited for Eddie to reappear on deck. Empty boxes littered the wharf and two, full of provisions, sat in the aft cockpit. We stood port side listening to the sound of cabinet doors systematically opened, then slammed shut. Eddie was cursing to himself.

"Permission to come aboard?" I called.

Eddie appeared at the threshold and squinted, plummy half-moons cut beneath his eyes. His face darkened as he looked between us. He nodded toward the cockpit, and returned below. We took this as an invitation and climbed aboard, then planted ourselves on the bench seats.

Five minutes later, Eddie stood before us, a defeated look on his face. "Sorry," he said sheepishly. "Trying to find something I just had my hands on."

"Eddie, this is my partner, Detective DelCarmen. We need to ask you some questions about Hope."

Eddie reached across and shook DelCarmen's hand, then sat in the bench seat across from us. This was a different Eddie, a gentler sort. "Please," said Eddie. "I'm getting ready to head out, but no real rush."

"I can see that," I said, eyeing the boxes more closely. It didn't look like it was going to be a short trip. "Where you headed?"

"Block Island. My friend's parents' summer home. He's there for the week. I'll be back in a day or two," he added.

"Lots of stuff," I said.

"I'm going to be staying on the boat for a while, here." Eddie gestured to the cove.

"We need some help with a few things for clarification," I said. "Why the wedding before the wedding?"

Eddie stared out over the water. "Hope wasn't anything like her parents," he said finally. "She didn't need the great white parade—that's what she called it. That was for them; the private ceremony was for us."

"It wasn't so secret, though. Your brother knew. Had to have been others. So why not wait?"

"Like I said, it was for us."

"Did you realize you'd be heir to her estate upon her death?" I asked.

"I agreed to sign a prenuptial agreement," said Eddie.

"But that didn't happen, and now you're entitled to, as her father put it, a sizable amount of money."

"It wasn't about the money. I have a job."

"You've recently become a vet, but spent a long time as a technician. Any reason?" asked DelCarmen.

Eddie ignored the question. "Like I said, I don't care about money. I wanted to be with Hope. With the private ceremony, we wanted to consummate our relationship."

The direction of the conversation shifted before I'd intended, but I went with it. I'd circle back.

"Consummate as in, have sex for the first time?"

"Hope was a virgin until our marriage. She wanted me to be her first and her last."

I lowered my voice. "Did you have sex with Hope the night she died?"

"Not that it's any of your business but, no, we didn't," he answered evenly. I almost believed him.

"Well," I continued, watching him, "then you wouldn't have been her last."

"What the fuck do you mean by that?" Eddie asked.

The other Eddie was back.

"Hope engaged in some rough sex the night she died. Do you want to rethink your last answer? There was an awful lot of partying going on that night. Maybe you've forgotten some details?"

"I didn't forget any of the details. We didn't have sex," Eddie said.

I looked at DC and nodded. It was his turn.

"Let's get back to your former job, the one at the Bay Clinic in Sharon," DC said. "You were a technician at a prestigious veterinary clinic, then you up and quit. What happened?"

"I didn't like the job." Eddie looked away and raked a hand through his hair.

DC clicked his retractable and flipped through his notes. "I spoke with Marcia Rathbun this morning. She confirmed that until the last few months, you were working out well and they'd planned to offer you a full-time position. But then there was a problem with missing drugs—ketamine. They suspected someone who had access stole it."

"Lots of people had access," Eddie said.

DC continued, "You quit the same week they reported the theft to the police. She said the timing was suspicious."

"She can say whatever she wants. I quit because I didn't like it."

"Were you and Hope using ketamine on Saturday?" DelCarmen asked.

"No," Eddie said.

DelCarmen locked eyes with Eddie and spoke slowly. "You know ketamine, kit kat, special k, whatever it is you call it, is a fun party drug, but if you do a little too much or mix it with booze, it can be a real bitch on your memory."

Eddie stood up and got in DelCarmen's face. "Get the fuck off my boat."

"Sit down, Eddie," I said, "and listen carefully. You've got some real problems here. It'd be in your best interest to work with us."

Amazingly enough, Eddie sat.

"You know what I think?" I continued. "I think you're buried under a mountain of responsibility. Picking up the slack when your mother left, caring for your brothers, your father. In the beginning, it's a few things every now and again. Before you know it, you're pinned under the burden of what everyone else needs."

Eddie wiped the tears from his face with the back of his hand and said nothing.

DelCarmen picked up where I left off. "Now you've got this great girl, but you can't always be yourself. You aren't exactly what her parents consider suitable as a prospective husband. And you want to be Eddie, not Edward. I mean, who the hell is Edward, anyway?"

The weight of Eddie's stress was palpable. It was easy to imagine how it could become overwhelming and slip out of control.

"Maybe that scene was working for you on some level," DC continued. "But it was becoming increasingly difficult to be who everyone needed you to be. Hope, her parents, Jacob, your dad, all sucking the life out of you. And maybe it's not how you wanted to handle it, but you know, it was an accident. The drugs, a little rough sex, one thing led to another, you panicked."

Eddie raised his head from his hands and looked from me to DelCarmen. "You need to leave," he said.

"One more time," I said, "were you and Hope using special k the night she died?"

"For the last fucking time, she didn't use drugs. She was drunk."

"No, Eddie," I said. "In fact, Hope's blood alcohol level was negligible."

"That's not possible," he said.

His shock felt genuine.

"We can work with the truth. Accidents happen all the time," I said. "You had sex in the garden, followed her to the observatory, and then what happened?"

"I can't tell you. I . . . I don't know. I left her in the garden."

"We had a very interesting conversation with your brother Jacob," DelCarmen said.

"Jacob's a liar. He's the one you should ask about drugs. He'll say and do anything to support his habit."

"We don't care about the missing ketamine; it's a two-year-old closed case. Our sole concern is what happened to Hope," I said.

Eddie appeared to be weighing his options. "When I was working at the Bay Clinic, Jacob got the job at Altman. He came to me, said he had an issue with drugs, ketamine specifically. It's popular with his crowd, but almost impossible to kick without professional help. I begged him to go to rehab. He said he'd lose his job; he needed to slowly wean himself off. He promised me."

His gaze swiveled between us, pleading for understanding.

"So, I stole the drugs. Gave him small amounts. I kept stealing and kept hoping. But like all things Jacob, he'd just been playing me, using me to support his drug habit. Then a colleague said management was looking into missing ketamine. I panicked. Quit."

"Was Jacob threatening you?" I asked.

"Not in a way that made me nervous, but he's always been a wild card. He had information that could bury me, ruin my career before it even started."

"What happened when he showed up at the party?" I asked.

"Hope was furious."

"Did he ask you for money?"

Eddie nodded. "Two hundred and seventy-five thousand. I told him he was on his own."

"Not even a little help?"

"Not one fucking dime."

"And then?"

"Hope lost it. Told him to leave. She wasn't polite about it. And he just pretended the words hadn't been said. Looked at his watch, said it was time for him to get going. He slapped me on the back, wished us well, went to find his date."

"Would he have hurt Hope?" DC asked.

Eddie considered the question. "Even as little kids, if you stood in his way, didn't move fast enough, he'd push you aside or to the ground, take what he wanted. It could have been someone else's favorite toy or the toothpaste, it didn't matter. He didn't think twice about it, didn't think it was wrong. So, I don't know."

"Those guys he's screwing with show up with baseball bats when their clients don't come up with the cash. You know that, don't you?"

Eddie bristled.

"Jacob told us you were going to bail him out of trouble," DelCarmen continued, trying to push Eddie a bit more.

"I told Jacob he'd better run and hide, that I couldn't help him." Eddie buried his face in his hands. When he looked up, tears streamed down his cheeks. "I didn't give her drugs, and I didn't kill her for money. We had our whole lives . . . Don't you understand? We wanted a family. We had plans. There was nothing . . ."

We could no longer make sense of Eddie's words, yet understood his grief-stricken attempt to describe what he had with Hope, what was to be, and now, without warning, what he'd lost.

DelCarmen flicked his eyes in my direction and we stood. "Listen, Eddie," I said. "I know your world is upside down. A lot of confusion—"

"You know nothing about my world." His voice was a hoarse growl.

He was right, of course. "Let us help you," I said. "We *can* help you."

DelCarmen leaned in and with great gentleness said, "If you want our help, and clearly you need it, call. Work with us. The alternative will not serve you well."

Eddie stared off as if remembering. "We made love early Saturday morning. It was tender, gentle," he said.

When I asked if they'd used a condom, he shook his head. Then summoning what felt akin to sincerity or maybe desperation, he looked from me to DelCarmen.

"I would have never hurt her," he said. "I'll give you whatever you want."

"Good," said DelCarmen. "That's very good."

CHAPTER

16

I DIALED JOHN TO ask if the results were in for drugs in Hope's system, specifically ketamine. He was one step ahead.

"No ketamine, but close. She tested positive for Rohypnol."

"Rohypnol?"

As the name clicked, my heartbeat accelerated. It was eight years and a lifetime ago when I first learned what Rohypnol was, the power it possessed. John was speaking, but the series of sounds that reached my ears were unrecognizable as words. His voice faded and my thoughts tumbled backward to that late afternoon.

I woke beneath a mound of blankets, a damp towel draped across my forehead. The sound of Kay's hushed voice as she sent a student on his way helped me remember I'd come to the college's medical office. Drawing a gritty tongue across cracked lips, the taste of bile prompted images and sensations like a flurry of leaves in a windstorm: the cold metal of the bowl thrust beneath my chin, shaky legs unwilling to support me, warm, strong hands and the sound of springs groaning beneath my weight. I scanned my memory for the events of the hours before. Nothing beyond an ache of dread materialized.

When the office door closed, I dragged myself off the cot and into the armchair. The college's nurse practitioner, Kay, filled a cup with ice chips and a spoon and placed it in my shaky hands. She opened a warm can of ginger ale and set it on the table next to me. When I'd gained some sort of composure, she asked, "Better?"

I sipped the ginger ale, crunched a few chips of ice, and nodded.

"You asked for my help. To get you into a rehab program. Do you remember that?"

I shrugged.

"I can help you, but I need to know what happened."

The kindness in Kay's puddle-blue eyes stretched across, reached into my fragile, spent mind, and held me, promising to shoulder the crushing burden of my shame, my fear, for as long as I would need. I recounted how Kari Lindstrom and I had walked to Joe's in the Back Bay, and planned to take a rideshare back to campus. We took a table, ordered a beer, and looked at the menu. I favored whatever citrusy craft beer was on tap; Kari ordered the same. The beer arrived in chilled glasses.

"And then what?" Kay asked.

"We ordered one of those thin crust pizzas and two more beers."

"Tell me about the second round of beer."

"It was just . . . beer . . ." The back of my head throbbed as I searched my memory. An image appeared of the two sweaty pint glasses on the table, the look of dismay on Kari's face. "When the beer finally arrived, the glasses weren't, you know, filled. No head on them."

"They'd been poured then not delivered right away."

"Well, yeah, it was busy."

Twenty minutes later, we flagged down the server and asked about the pizza. She said it wouldn't be much longer. "And by the way, that last round was on your secret admirer."

We turned, scrutinized the bar, but the trajectory of downlighting from the bar's gantry offered a mass of headless suit jackets, the glint of gold buttons.

"Which suit?" Kari asked.

"The one wearing one of those expensive Swiss watches," said the server.

Kari laughed. "I bet they're all wearing those."

"His played a pretty melody. Chimes on the hour or something like that. Classical. Piano. You know the one." She snapped her fingers as if that might jar her memory. "French. Dun dun." Her voice cracked as she sung the second note at a range much higher than the first.

I recalled the murmuring, then the hush as it settled over Carnegie Hall, my mother squeezing my hand in anticipation of the piece of music she'd practiced incessantly. When I was a child, she called it the Moon Song. At eighteen, and with years of French under my belt, she used its correct title and, as we waited for the soloist to take his seat at the piano, she whispered that this third movement was meant to be a reprieve before the dramatic finale, that it conveyed the sense of a sad, but beautiful dreamlike calm, then finally, delivered clarity. As she spoke, I imagined the moon slipping from behind a cloud to reveal a magnificent star-filled sky.

"*Clair de Lune*?" I asked.

"Hot damn!" She pointed at me. "Now that we've got that straight, let me check on that pizza," she said, and hurried off.

We clinked glasses and drank and soon, neither of us cared about the pizza. Kari said something about the bathroom. I watched her lurch into the crowd as if through the lens of a camera on a painfully slow shutter speed. Snap. Blur. Snap. Focus. Blades of light from the dim table lamp made me blink, shield my eyes. I squinted, scanned the room, but she was gone.

"And then I thought I should check on Kari."

I stood. So hot. *God, where's the bathroom?* Bodies leaned in from the shadows, funhouse large, then receded, funhouse small. The floor shifted beneath my feet. I shuffled left amid muffled voices, a burst of laughter; watched my hand reach for the back of a nearby chair. Light bounced from a chunky gold pinkie ring on a hand that had taken hold of my forearm. The suit's other arm slipped around my shoulder, righting me. As he walked me toward the door, the last thing I remembered before tumbling into a slow, swirling eddy that dimmed and quieted until my mind was as black as a starless sky and as silent as the ocean floor, was the tinkling of the pretty piece of music I thought of as my mother's Moon Song.

"That's all I can remember," I said.

She sat there nodding, putting it together.

"I'm going to tell you something and you need to listen, to hear me." Kay inched closer and squeezed my hand. "This was not your fault, and you must promise me that you won't blame yourself."

"What the hell are you talking about, Kay? Of course, it's my fault."

"Andrea, you don't have a drinking problem. You were drugged. Your beer sat on the bar unattended. Someone slipped something into the beer. Typically, it's Rohypnol. Have you ever heard of that? Sometimes they call it other names."

I sat there, paralyzed. Kay's words slowed, lumbered in my direction, but my brain refused to assemble them into intelligible sentences. I let them drift past.

"Andie?" Kay's voice echoed softer.

"Did I lose you?" John said.

I steadied my breathing. "Yeah, John. I'm here. Bad cell area."

"I said she tested positive for Rohypnol. I'm assuming it was a bootleg."

"Why do you think that?"

"Because Rohypnol never received FDA approval. The side effects were too severe. It's approved for distribution throughout Europe, Mexico, and who knows where."

In my attempt to bury what had happened to me, I knew the drug's name, but had refused to research it, hadn't known any of this.

"What was it used for medically?" I asked.

"It was developed to treat insomnia, sleeping disorders. But it's widely used to facilitate sexual assault. For that purpose, it's bootlegged. They call it many things, like roofies . . ."

I glanced at DC, who drove one-handed, a finger in his right ear, earpiece in the left, talking on his phone. John continued, albeit louder, as if nothing was wrong.

"It has a way of showing up in girls' drinks, popular among the university set. The research shows it's mostly about the attacker and their insecurities—fear of rejection—and their warped sense of justification. The women are always hot for them, if you know what I mean. They walk, they talk, are agreeable to all advances, and for the most part, never remember a thing."

I fought down the bile that licked at the back of my throat.

"Thanks, John. Is there anything else?"

"Worst-case scenario is death resulting. We find that with the fake pharmaceutical varieties. They lace their pills with some nasty household cleaner and it's kaput."

"You got lucky. The next one might not be so fortunate," Kay whispered in my ear.

"Is there a way to distinguish between the bootleg and the script?" I asked.

"It depends what they lace it with," he said. "When the full toxicology comes back we'll see, but it'll be tricky to be conclusive. I hate to simplify things, but sometimes people take drugs or are given drugs mistakenly. Lots of people have old drugs in their medicine cabinets for years. It might be something they pick up when they're traveling because they can't sleep. No malicious intent, just your garden variety stupidity."

The contents of my medicine cabinet came to mind. Drugs prescribed, tried and unhelpful, still in residence. John's words made sense, but unease shook me. Rohypnol wasn't just a drug. It was a drug used with specific intent.

"I hear you. If there's anything further, let me know," I said, and ended the call.

"DC, we need to visit with her doctor. Hope tested positive for Rohypnol."

"Address?"

I flipped through my notepad. "Eighty-seven Walcott."

DC made a neat illegal U-turn while I called ahead to make sure the doctor was home.

Dr. William Maxwell's office was adjacent to his home on Walcott Avenue overlooking Jamestown Harbor, the Newport Bridge, and on most days, Newport itself. The white-shingled Victorian with its matching eyebrow dormers and pretty scrolled gable trim sat up high and well off the road. A thick privet hedge wrapped the terraced yard and lent privacy to the porch that spanned the front and side of the house. A small wooden sign that read W. Maxwell, M.D., General

Practitioner swayed in the breeze. The man I'd seen at the Crow's Nest on Sunday morning waited for us at the side entrance, an elderly golden retriever obediently at his side. Dr. Maxwell had caterpillar-style brows that framed his blue eyes; his cheeks and nose were streaked red with broken capillaries. He swatted away the badges we held out for his review.

"I've got my guard dog," he said, chuckling. "Andie, is it?" he asked, looking at DelCarmen.

"Detective Andrea Stuart and this is my partner, Detective Julian DelCarmen," I said.

Dr. Maxwell screwed up his face.

"Andie and DC," I said, taking his outstretched hand.

"Ah, yes, better. Well, come in, please. This is Lady," he said. Then, in a whispered aside, "More of a fraidy-cat than a guard dog." He patted the golden retriever on her head, then led us into the office. Metal file cabinets lined two of the four walls. Well-thumbed books with scraps of torn paper marking passages of interest filled floor-to-ceiling shelves. More books were stacked on the floor and the desk, and loomed precariously on chairs when shelf space was no longer available. Dr. Maxwell surveyed the room like he was just then wondering where it all had come from. "Oh goodness," he said, shaking his head. "This won't do. Follow me."

Dr. Maxwell mumbled to himself as he negotiated past cardboard boxes that cluttered the hall. We trailed behind him through a door that led into an examining room and another that led into the main house, and finally into a lovely sitting room carefully furnished with two rolled-arm upholstered chairs and a well-worn brown leather recliner. A bank of windows delivered the soothing cadence of the bay.

"Will you join me for cocktail hour? It is," Dr. Maxwell made a grand gesture of pulling back the cuff of his shirt sleeve and looking at his watch, "five o-seven," he said with a little skip in his voice, humming as he ambled off. He returned several minutes later with a battered wooden tray that held three double old-fashioned glasses, a bottle of Dewar's scotch, ice, and an assortment of mixers.

"Ladies first. What's your pleasure?"

"Thank you, Dr. Maxwell," I said, a smile spreading across my face.

"Please, my friends call me Max."

"I'd love some of that club soda, Max, hold the scotch." I leaned toward him and lowered my voice. "I'm afraid I overdid it last night."

His eyes twinkled as he inclined his head and mimicked my tone. "Take my advice, I have lots of experience with this sort of thing. A little of this," he lifted the bottle, "and you'll be as right as rain." He turned to DelCarmen.

DC smiled and said, "Technically, I'm still on the clock."

"If you reconsider, no one's going to be the wiser." Max gestured he was zipping his mouth and throwing away the key, then hummed as he poured what appeared to be two generous fingers of scotch for himself.

"So, what can I help you with?" he asked, landing heavily on the recliner.

"Hope was your patient and you're close to the family. This can't be easy for you," I said.

His already watery eyes pooled with tears. Max reached into his breast pocket and retrieved a wrinkled cotton handkerchief, removed his glasses, and wiped his eyes. "She was a special young lady. I delivered her, you know," he said, his voice cracking.

I patted his arm, then retrieved my notepad. "We are trying to piece together the details of how Hope died and have some background questions. Could you tell us if she was taking any prescription medications?"

"She was on birth control, nothing else."

"When did you prescribe that?" I asked.

"Back in June. She was a funny one." He smiled.

"How so?"

"I presume you know about Martha's Vineyard by now."

"We do."

"If you want to know about Hope, this was typical. She was a lot like her mother, strong willed, though not half as reckless." He took a long sip on his drink. "That's another story, but all connected, I suppose. Hope came to tell me that she intended to marry, that she was ready for birth control. She told me about the ceremony on the Vineyard and the plans her mother had for a large wedding. I gave her what she needed and wished her well."

"Did she say why they decided to elope before the planned wedding?" I asked.

"Hope and Eddie had wanted something small. Her mother balked, so they agreed to the big celebration and arranged their own thing, without her mother's knowledge. Everyone would be happy."

DelCarmen and I shared a glance.

"Did you treat her for any other ailments or illnesses?" DelCarmen asked.

"Hope has always been a very healthy young lady. Nothing other than the usual, all very much routine."

"Did Hope suffer from a fear of heights?" I asked.

"Funny you should ask. She actually suffered from visual height intolerance, a lesser form of the phobia. All that means is that she didn't much care for heights with an unobstructed edge." He chuckled. "She had no trouble driving over the Newport Bridge, but hated being in the passenger seat."

I considered the observatory with its nearly invisible steel-cabled railing, then of the thick wooden slats on the stairs to the wharf that made the descent feel enclosed, secure.

"What about insomnia? Did she ever mention she had any problems sleeping?" I asked.

"What? Insomnia?" he repeated, fiddling with his hearing aid. "Ah no," he said, finally.

"Hope had a drug called Rohypnol in her system," I said.

"Rohypnol?" Max shifted in his chair and cleared his throat. "That isn't something I can prescribe."

I knew the answer, but asked anyway.

"Because?"

"Because the FDA didn't approve it."

"Where do you think she might have gotten it?"

Dr. Maxwell inspected his glass and jiggled his ice. "Like I said." Those three words resonated like the clunk of a bad penny. "I can't prescribe it."

His response prompted me to ask again. "I understand you can't prescribe it, but do you have any idea where she would have gotten it?"

"I do not," he said, meeting my gaze.

"Did anyone else in the family suffer from insomnia?"

"Not that I can recall."

The tells continued. Using words typically contracted and the convenient, fence-straddling ability of recall.

"Well, that's not entirely true, Penny—that's what I call her—had trouble, but it wasn't what I considered insomnia. And I guess it's not true that Hope had always been healthy. She had a rough start."

"How so?" I wondered if I could glean anything from his excursion around my question.

"Hope was a preemie. Twenty-eight weeks. Spent two months on a ventilator. And with low blood volume, of course, she needed blood. Penny needed blood. Even I gave because we were in short supply of their type."

"Mr. Philbrick wasn't here for the birth?"

Max coughed. "General practitioners did it all back then."

"You mentioned Mrs. Philbrick had trouble sleeping," I said.

"When Hope finally came home, she fed often, slept irregularly, and like many young mothers, Penny became sleep deprived. I'm sure, like everything else, it passed. Heard nothing more about it."

DC uncrossed his legs and recrossed them, right over left. This was the equivalent of the queen shifting her handbag from one arm to the other as a signal to her ladies-in-waiting to interrupt a conversation, her plea to be rescued. DC's signal meant I should move on.

"How did Penelope and Preston take to Eddie?" I asked.

"How shall I say this?" Max chose his words carefully. "Penny was determined not to do the same thing to her daughter that had been done to her."

"What do you mean by that?"

"Penny's parents were old school, old money. It was important to them that she marry well."

"They didn't approve of Preston?" I asked.

Max laughed. "They loved Preston. It was the suitor before Preston they disapproved of."

"Can you tell us about that?"

"Quite simply, Penny met a young man, they fell in love, and he proposed. The young man in question was considered unsuitable for Barty and Lois Harrington's daughter. He didn't have the right pedigree."

"Hmm," I said.

"Don't judge them too harshly," he said, as if he could read my mind. "It wasn't unusual back then, and especially with that crowd."

"And?" I prompted.

"And then Preston stepped up. He'd been smitten with Penelope from the time they were children. In the early years when their families spent just the summer months in Jamestown, they'd been neighbors. But he was twelve years older, so she hadn't given him a thought. Preston is an only child and isn't much for the word no. Pulled out all the stops—boatloads of flowers—flew her to Paris to see her favorite opera, and to meet his mother. Eventually she came around."

"His mother?" I asked.

"Well, yes. His mother is French. His parents divorced when Preston was a teen. She moved back to Paris, and Preston split his time between households. Not an easy feat, but they made it work."

The queen shifted her handbag, and I changed the line of questioning.

"Was their relationship good? Mrs. Philbrick and Hope?"

Max shrugged. "Penny is a tough woman. At times outright bullheaded. She adored her daughter, but that's not to say they didn't have their moments. And Hope was allowed to make decisions for her life that had been denied to Penny. I expect this caused some acrimony, but I don't know."

"I understand Mrs. Philbrick had a twin," I said.

"Oh, yes." The subject brought a spark to his face. "They were mono-mono twins. Are you familiar with the term?"

DC and I shook our heads.

"Quite interesting, medically. Not only do they come from the same egg, but in utero, they share both a placenta and an amniotic sac. Very rare. Unfortunately, this causes many issues with development and survival. And with the Harrington twins, Penny thrived but Bea had been born without the ability to communicate or care for herself. The unfortunate part of the story is that Penny didn't know about her sister until she was a grown woman."

"Until she was a grown woman?" I repeated.

Max nodded. "They didn't think Bea would live. Not the right thing, of course, keeping it from Penny, but back in those days, that's what they did. It was typical of prominent families to shutter mentally disabled children from public view. You'll no doubt recall the Kennedy child."

"I'm sure it was a shock when Mrs. Philbrick learned she had a sister," DC said.

Either the scotch was having the desired effect, or Max didn't get many visitors.

"Indeed, it was. But then it was almost like a saving grace, a new start for Penny. They couldn't communicate in the normal sense, but somehow, they did. They were good, happy years."

"And then Bea died?" I asked.

"Hmm? Ah, yes," said Max, looking over the side of his recliner as if he'd dropped something. "About four years ago. It was an odd, sad turn. No one knows what happened," he said, still feigning distraction.

Trying to discern the subtext, a feint, or an omission, was suddenly exhausting. I no longer had the strength to Miss Marple my way around Marcus Welby. Unbeknownst to my conscious mind, a decision had been made.

"Did Hope have questions about her sex life?" I asked, releasing the clasp of the gold bracelet on my left wrist and cupping it in my right hand.

Max abandoned his search, looked up, and smiled. "With Eddie? Oh, goodness no." Max's cheeks reddened as he waved away the suggestion. "We didn't discuss that."

DelCarmen asked, "Do you know if Hope took recreational drugs?"

"I don't know, of course, but I doubt it. She said she was looking forward to being a wife and a mother. It was the same conversation I'd had with Preston all those years ago. Both were only children, both wanted big families."

Max examined his drink, swirled the ice in his glass then gleaned the last drops of scotch from it. He stood abruptly and shuffled the glasses on the tray like those long-doomed deck chairs. Lady nuzzled her head into his hand and Max was visibly relieved.

"It must be five forty-five," he announced. "We walk like clockwork three times a day at the forty-fives—nine, one, and five. She doesn't need this to remind me." Max pulled back the cuff of his sleeve and tapped his watch, then patted the dog's head.

I slipped my bracelet into the crevice between the cushion and armrest.

"We'll leave you to it," I said, standing.

Max led us through to the side door. We thanked him for his time.

I turned, eyed the file cabinets, certain Max's history had been selective. He was the reluctant keeper of Philbrick family secrets: secrets that piqued my interest.

CHAPTER

17

"NOT THE CAN of corn I expected," I said as DC pulled away from the curb.

"In Providence, we call a soft target a ground ball."

"All the hesitation, diversion, memory qualifiers—it was textbook. The question is, why?"

"Everyone lies, Stuart."

"Dr. Maxwell didn't lie. He committed the sin of omission. Doddered when it suited him and was to the point otherwise. He knows something," I said, directing DelCarmen straight through the intersection.

"Perhaps he does," said DelCarmen. "Might suspect something but doesn't know it to be true. Maybe he thinks it could harm and not help."

"He didn't seem to have any filter when it came to family history."

"But none of it was privileged or damaging. We need more information and maybe another shot at him. Formally."

I nodded. "Did you buy the legitimacy of the private ceremony?"

DelCarmen considered the question. "The doc did. But that's a tough one."

"You never mentioned a best friend or a maid of honor."

"Hope's college roommate. Didn't attend the party," DC said, exiting onto the bridge.

"We should talk to her. If there was pressure to get married sooner than planned, it'd be something they'd have discussed."

"We'll call her in the morning."

"The twin who lived," I said, changing the subject. "Couldn't have been easy for Mrs. Philbrick."

"Depends on who you are," said DC.

DelCarmen eased into the high-speed lane and accelerated to eighty-five miles per hour. Gray streaks of vehicles and landscape ticked past.

"What do you think?" I asked. "Hope had a healthy dose of Rohypnol in her system. Where'd she get it?"

"The simple explanation is that someone, likely Eddie, gave her the drug. Probably both took it, thought it would settle their nerves. She was tiny, he's a big guy. Same dose would devastate her. A little alcohol, and bam."

"Eddie denied giving her anything. Felt genuine."

"If I were Eddie, I'd lie, too. You said he was out of it Sunday morning."

"He said he'd been drinking shots."

"Might explain it," said DC, "but might not. Here's what I think. They have a quicky. He uses a condom, so he doesn't get anything on her dress He's strung out, and the sex is rough. It sets her off. She goes toward the observatory, and he follows. They argue and she goes over."

I wondered why he'd have a condom given that Hope was taking birth control pills, then recalled the countless wallets we'd inventoried—a condom was as common as a driver's license. "How does she go over?"

"She's telling him to leave her alone—don't forget—she's strung out, too. She climbs up on one of those high-top tables or that railing. He reaches for her. Maybe she dives thinking she'll make the water, but it's low tide, dark, and she can't tell."

DelCarmen pulled up behind an SUV doing sixty-five in the high-speed lane, muttered something about there being a special place in hell. He blasted a brief yelp on the emergency vehicle siren and the SUV jerked to its right into the travel lane.

I rolled my eyes. "Maybe, but we should explore the possibility that he did what he said he did, that he left her in the herb garden and doesn't know what happened."

"If there was someone other than Eddie, she'd have had defensive wounds. What did the ME say about that?"

"The term he used was 'vigorous consenting intercourse.'"

"It started out as consensual and got rough."

"But if she was high, maybe it wasn't consensual. The drug is what disturbs me. If it came from Eddie, where'd he get it?"

"We'll put out some feelers. In the end, the source won't make a damn bit of difference."

"I beg to differ. The drug is most commonly associated with drug-facilitated sexual assault. We need to be certain we aren't overlooking someone other than Eddie who may have come along after."

"Beg all you want, but don't let the lack of critical evidence make you overthink this."

I felt the sharp sting of his arrow.

"And by the same token, don't let it make you oversimplify things."

The phone rang. Caller ID said it was the South County Hospital. Perfect timing to diffuse the moment.

"Detective Stuart," I said.

"Am I catching you at a bad time?" asked John.

"DelCarmen and I are headed back to Providence. What's up?"

"It's about your case. You busy later?"

It sounded reasonable. "I could make some time."

"Can you meet me at the Gannie in an hour or so?"

It was six. I calculated time necessary to freshen up and so forth. "How about seven thirty?"

"See you then." John ended the call before I could rethink my decision.

* * *

We swung into the Bradley complex a few minutes later while I was still stewing about DC's reluctance to consider an alternate scenario—my alternate scenario. The third-floor detective division was quiet.

Captain O'Sullivan paced in his office, a phone pressed to his ear. He waved me in as I went by and motioned for me to sit. DC didn't give me a backward glance as he continued toward our cubicle. O'Sullivan strode back and forth, loosening his tie. A line of sweat darkened his dress shirt along the length of his spine. He mumbled an unhappy string of acknowledgments into his handset. The squawk and screech that filtered from the phone sounded like a hysterical blue jay. The captain stopped, looked at the handset, then slammed it onto its cradle when he realized the jay had hung up.

"Stuart, I've got good news for you. You can get started on that vacation of yours. Thanks for your fine work with the accidental in Jamestown. Appreciate you handling it." He nodded, forced a smile, then looked back at the pile of paperwork he'd begun sifting through.

I leapt to my feet, put my hands on my hips and the unfortunate "What the fuck?" look on my face. "I haven't filed my report yet. And the medical examiner hasn't made any final determinations. With all due respect, sir, what are you talking about?"

O'Sullivan raised both eyebrows and tilted his head. He continued with a calmness that sent a shiver down my spine. "I've reviewed the preliminary. It's going to be ruled an accidental death. DelCarmen can file the final report. And stay away from the beat. Word has it that you could stand some downtime." He met my eye and added, "And any more trouble won't be good for your career."

O'Sullivan's reference to my first major infraction filled the office like a poisonous gas. He busied himself with his paperwork. I didn't move.

"Work with me, Stuart. Running interference for you is a full-time job. One more than I signed up for. Understood?"

O'Sullivan's eyes said: this conversation is over.

"Understood," I said, yet screams of "No!" filled my head. Pretending to straighten my jacket, I eased my hands from my hips and reconfigured my face into a smile. "I'm appreciative about getting some time off, but there are unanswered questions. I can't dump it on DelCarmen. In another day or two, I'll have it all wrapped up." I held up my three middle fingers and said, "Scout's honor."

"There's nothing to suggest anything else. If I've missed something, by all means." He swept his arm, pretending to invite further discussion.

"You've got to admit the way it went down raises some questions."

"That was all about privacy and negative publicity."

Miss Congeniality flitted away. "Was it? I was told there were eyewitnesses. I'm assuming you were told the same. Somewhere along the line, someone was lied to, and as a result, the scene was not secured, potential evidence compromised. The implications of the blatant misinformation raise a big red flag with me."

O'Sullivan's face reddened, sweat glistened on his forehead, and the veins pulsed at his temples. I thought he might be having a stroke or doing some odd deep-breathing exercise. Either way, he hadn't liked what I had to say, but it struck a chord.

"Is that all you have?" he asked.

"The preliminary tox screen showed Rohypnol in her system."

"Kids use that like they used to use Quaaludes."

"It's an old drug, originally manufactured to treat insomnia, the side effects so dangerous the FDA wouldn't approve it. There are more easily accessible party drugs out there. It's troubling."

"Any other physical evidence?"

Had he not heard me?

"The Rohypnol finding is significant. There is something we're not seeing."

"I disagree. So I'll ask one more time, what else do you have?"

And DelCarmen had also disagreed. It shook my confidence. He had ten and O'Sullivan, at least twenty years more experience. Even so, they didn't know what I knew about Rohypnol. I'd been its victim. I drew myself up to my full height.

"It appears she engaged in either very rough consensual or nonconsensual sex in the hours before her death."

"What did the fiancé say?"

"He said they had sex in the morning but not that night. Denies it was rough."

"Do you think he was lying?"

I shrugged.

"Did the ME have an opinion?"

"Not on his radar. I'm following up."

"Motive?"

"The fiancé was actually her husband. The couple married this past July in a private ceremony, no prenup. He stands to inherit a pile of cash—cash he needs. His brother is up to his ears in gambling debt. We think it's motive enough and need to verify one way or the other."

"Already hitched, huh? Were the parents aware?"

"The father was, after the fact. At the deceased's request, he kept it quiet. She didn't want to upset her mother. Ironically, the prenuptial agreement was supposed to be signed today."

O'Sullivan rubbed the back of his neck.

"Captain, we might all reach the conclusion that this was a tragic accident, but we need to be certain. Hope Philbrick deserves our due diligence. Let me do the job I was asked to do."

O'Sullivan sighed heavily. "Look, Stuart, you've ruffled some feathers and I'm up to my ass in alligators. And frankly, you have a piss poor case for anything—"

"On the first day I made detective, you told me to finish what I start. You said that detectives working a homicide are the voices of those who can no longer—"

"I tell everyone the same bloody thing!" he snapped.

Captain O'Sullivan examined the ceiling, shaking his head, involved in some sort of debate with his internal tribunal. I waited a beat and said, "I may have nothing except a girl high on drugs who dove from a cliff, but I need to be sure."

He took a deep breath, looked me in the eye, and nodded. "I will defer to your judgment. But—"

"Thank you, sir."

"Don't thank me yet." O'Sullivan raised his five-finger stop sign. "Here's what I'm willing to do. DelCarmen can take it from here. Detective Long is available to assist. If you want answers, let DC and Long do it quietly. I'll give them to the end of the week before I shut it down. DC has four days to bring me something solid. Otherwise, we have an accident. I'll update the major and we'll do what we can to hold everyone off."

"But—"

"But nothing! You clearly do not fully appreciate the level of pressure I'm dealing with to get this thing closed and keep it out of the news." He pointed at me and narrowed his eyes. "You stay away from this, or I will personally see to it that you're back in uniform and walking the West End on the graveyard shift. Have I made myself perfectly clear?"

"Perfectly, sir."

Four or five sarcastic responses sprung to mind, but I thought better of it. I nodded and left without another word. Retreating from the room, I slammed into DelCarmen.

"Whoa, lady, you in a hurry for that date?"

"Hardly, and for your information," I advanced toward him and stabbed at his chest with my index finger, "it is not a date."

DelCarmen retreated, holding up his hands. Why did I feel the need to deny I had a date? It could have been a date. And what did it matter if it was? I stared at the ground then looked him in the eye. "You get to wrap it up. I'm officially back on vacation. Long will be assisting."

"Fair enough," he said.

I wanted to repeat my concerns about the Rohypnol, but I'd already been shot down twice. "I'm being pushed aside," I said, feeling red splotches flare on my cheeks.

"That's not what this is." A tender smile spread across his face. "He's trying not to mess with your vacation. Thinks he's doing you a favor."

I had insisted I continue with the case, but it hadn't mattered. "You have the go-ahead to subpoena Eddie's phone and bank records."

DC nodded. "I have the list from Philbrick's personal secretary. I'll get Long here first thing to start working on it. We'll contact the bestie."

I held up a finger. "Ask the admin to compile the sexual assault cases for the last ten years in and around Newport and South County. Leave them on my desk."

"Why?" he asked, an edge to his voice.

"Rohypnol is widely used in drug-facilitated sexual assault. We don't know where the drug came from. It's highly unlikely we'll find anything, but no harm for me to see if there might be a connection."

He leveled me with a stare, as if in disbelief. I folded my arms, met his eye, and let the silence speak.

Finally, I said, "I'll use my spare time the way I want."

After an uncomfortable minute, he nodded, turned, and hurried off. I left the building thinking my attitude about everything would be much improved by a beer, or possibly two.

CHAPTER

18

HEADING SOUTH TO Jamestown, I thought about DelCarmen. His prickly side had never been leveled at me; then again, I'd never been lead on a case before, even though it'd only been for a mere twenty-four hours. Our partnership might never survive his ego if he couldn't handle what would inevitably happen again.

My thoughts moved on to Steve O'Donnell and his sister, Kate, who'd been my best friend since kindergarten. Kate went west for college and never looked back. Steve stayed in Jamestown and joined the tiny local force.

I knew too well how tragedy can reshuffle the deck and deal a future you'd never considered. Kate had been six and Steve fourteen when their mother died. Her final errand before heading home that Friday afternoon was a quick stop at McCord's: they were out of milk again. Steve in the passenger seat and Kate, strapped safely in the back, were spared when a blue Ford pickup failed to stop or even slow as it approached the four-way intersection at Narragansett Avenue and North Main Road, barely a hundred yards from the McCord's parking lot. Without so much as the squeal of brakes to warn her, the Ford plowed into the driver's side door, leaving their mother with no time to do anything except scream.

It had been the loss of his mother that nudged Steve toward his future employment. Their father had been overwhelmed with the prospect of raising two children on his own, and Steve picked up the slack. At first it was small things: walking Kate home from school and helping with homework. When puberty hit and Kate and I developed breasts bigger than the pimples on our faces and clogged the phone lines with calls to each other about boys, Steve made us his mission. He was going to prevent any missteps by two goofy teenage girls if it was the last thing he did. I was included in the surveillance simply because Kate and I were inseparable.

I dialed Steve's cell phone and smiled when I heard his familiar voice.

"Is this Steve O'Donnell, the real inspiration for the saying 'Big Brother is watching you'?"

"In the flesh. Andie, it's so nice to hear from you."

"The kids and wife are well?"

"Let's see, my kids are eating me out of house and home, and my wife knows no bounds with the credit cards. Life couldn't be better," he said, laughing. "How about you? No significant other yet?"

"No one special."

"It's all I hear about from my Aunt Louise. You know she's in that garden club with your mother. According to my aunt, your mother is some storyteller."

"If she tells your aunt I've run off with a handsome Greek shipping tycoon that'll make Onassis seem like a pauper, it's a lie."

"Yeah, I think I heard about him."

We both laughed. "I need some cheering up. I thought I knew about the sinking of the *Edmund Fitzgerald*, but now I'm certain I don't."

"It's what one of the guys at the station called it, and, like these things do, it stuck. Not so amusing, however, so if you'd prefer a more lighthearted tale, I've got plenty of mailbox mishaps, stories of wandering lawn ornaments, and the cringe-worthy hoisted up flagpoles."

"Well, curiosity has, you know . . ."

"I do know," he said. "A while back—maybe eighteen or nineteen years ago—Mrs. Philbrick takes Hope, who's maybe five years old, out for a sail on her boat, this seventies Bristol 40. Gorgeous old masthead sloop."

"I saw photos of it on the wall in her study. Wasn't sure whose boat it was."

"Her dad sailed, but she trained, crewed her parents twelve meter, raced. So, it's late in the day and she sails out of the cove and into the bay, twenty minutes later she's taking on water. Happens so fast and with her daughter, she'd barely enough time to drop the dinghy and get the kid and herself into it. So the sailboat goes under and she gets the dingy going, but not ten minutes later, it runs out of gas."

"Oh, no."

"You got that right. She's got no radio, no emergency flares and no oars, just a dead outboard and a rope."

"Don't all dinghies have oars?"

"That's standard, but that wasn't the case. They'd just had the cushioned seating replaced and, the thought was, that the oars and the other safety equipment hadn't been reinstalled."

"A pretty big oversight."

"It was. So, the kid's in the dinghy and she ties the rope around her waist, jumps in, and starts to swim. It's early June, the water's cold, but she's smart and finds the current, but she's in like sixty-degree water for almost two hours and the light is fading. By some miracle she's spotted and they tow her and Hope in."

"Did they ever raise the boat?"

"Yeah, weeks later. I can't remember, either a hose or the bilge drain plug had been missing. She claimed the boat had been tampered with. Hard to prove since it had been bouncing around at the bottom of the sea and either could have been dislodged."

"What about the gas in the dinghy?"

"Hadn't checked it, but said she hadn't needed to, it'd been full and unused."

"Anything come of it?"

"After they towed her in, they sent her to the hospital to get checked out. Physically she was fine, but I heard she'd been transferred to Bingham for a few days, if you get my drift."

I did get his drift. Bingham was a psychiatric hospital.

"The guys that handled it chocked it up to her having issues that contributed to negligence and not maintaining the boat. Long and short of it, they say she never sailed again."

"For what it's worth, if I had to do what she did, they'd need to send me to Bingham, too."

"Funny that her daughter became a pretty accomplished sailor."

"Kids are pretty resilient."

"They are. Sorry I can't help with what you're working on."

"If nothing else, your story adds a bit of perspective. Good to know who I'm dealing with."

I thanked Steve, and we agreed to catch a beer when schedules allowed and ended the call as I pulled up in front of the Gannie.

CHAPTER

19

LIKE SCHOOL UNIFORMS for teenage girls, the Narragansett Café was the great equalizer. Age, lineage, and account balances held no sway; once inside, patrons played on the same field. Bikers shot pool with hedge fund brokers, gray-haired hippies swilled alongside hipsters, and every now and again the occasional dog would wander in and curl up in a corner to nap in the island's warm, familiar cocoon. While the Gannie meant something subtly different to everyone, its considerable voice delivered a universal message: no matter what, we all belonged.

The bar was moderately crowded. The crack of a break shot followed by simultaneous moans and whoops emerged from a pool match at the far end of the room. Out of the corner of my eye, a set of flailing arms caught my attention. The arms were attached to a handsome man in jeans and a faded blue button-down with an irresistible mane of sandy hair that fell softly about his face. His smile widened and my composure deserted me. I became acutely aware of every movement of my too-long arms, clunky legs, and clown-shoe size feet as I approached the empty barstool next to him.

"Saved you a seat," John said, moving out the stool.

"Thanks." I sat and peeled off my blazer.

"Can I get you something to—"

Before he could get the words out, Lady Di, who declared the bar a non-constitutional monarchy and she, its self-appointed matriarch, delivered a Peroni on draft.

"A VIP," said John.

"A regular," I corrected, then gestured for him to start.

"It's kind of funny. I got a phone call from my boss, who had a few questions about the Philbrick autopsy. Then he basically asked me to push it through, suggesting that the death was accidental."

I nodded and sipped my beer.

"Andie, I don't get calls like that, and no one has ever dictated my findings to me unless they're standing beside me at the table discussing the autopsy at hand."

The thought was disturbing. "What do you plan to do?"

"Wrap it up. It looks like I will determine her death was accidental unless you come up with something that suggests otherwise."

"Well, I have concerns, a slew of unanswered questions, and a potential suspect with a motive, but I won't be looking into any of it since Captain O'Sullivan has just pulled me from the case. DelCarmen and Long are taking it from here. I'm back on vacation."

"Is Long that super short guy with the buzz cut?"

"One and the same. They call him Shorty."

"Clever," John said. "But it's a good thing, right?"

"Which part? The vacation part or the jerking me around part?"

"The vacation part. Why do you think you're being jerked around?"

I shrugged. "It's pretty obvious that the department is getting heat to shut it down."

"From whom?"

"Most likely from the family. This guy has connections and accordingly has asked for help keeping it under wraps. Who knows? It could go all the way to the governor's office."

"Is that unusual?"

"Welcome to Rhode Island, the Pay to Play State." I laughed. It was the Rhode Island political way of life: hefty campaign donations ensuring plum political appointments, new or revised legislation that benefited Mr. Donor's business, or even better, Mr. Politician himself. The old boys' club at its finest.

"And all along I thought our motto was The Ocean State."

"Ah, but we have both a motto and a nickname. The Ocean State is our official nickname. The Pay to Play State is my unofficial nickname for the state."

"So, what's our motto?" John asked.

"Our official motto is 'Hope,' inspired by the biblical phrase, 'Hope we have as an anchor to our soul.'"

It was a lovely thought. That hope could keep our soul safe, tethered and afloat, preventing passage into a troubling sea. I toyed with my cocktail napkin.

"When a guy with a lot of influence like Philbrick is involved, this sort of top-down hushing up could be nothing. Maybe he doesn't want his family's privacy to be compromised. Or the media to get involved, which could open the door to dig up unrelated nasty truths and display them above the fold in black-and-white print." I finished by tearing the napkin in two.

"I suppose you can't blame them for wanting privacy, and I guess that might explain the phone call, but it alters nothing on my end. The cause of death was straightforward, but motive is what will change my determination of manner of death from unknown to accident, suicide, or to homicide. And motive is your responsibility. I'll wait until your department has completed their due diligence."

"If you can hold off until the end of the week or longer, that'd be great. Can you dance around it for that long?"

"A cha-cha, or a waltz?" John did hokey-pokey hands.

I made a face.

"As long as you need," he assured me.

"DelCarmen believes she took the Rohypnol, or her fiancé gave it to her to help her calm down and she had an adverse reaction with alcohol. All that's possible, but some pieces of the puzzle are still nagging me."

"Which ones?"

I thought *Rohypnol.* Instead, I said, "The scope of her physical injuries—the sexually related ones. You mentioned her sexual encounter took place in the hours before her death, can you be more definitive?"

"If this was one of those cop shows on television . . ." he mused. "Certainly within twenty-four hours of my examination, but more likely within eight to ten."

I nodded, thinking it wasn't in my nature to back away until all the pieces slotted into place, nothing shoehorned for convenience or niggling at me in the middle of the night.

As if reading my thoughts, John said, "Maybe a little time off is what you need." He held my gaze and raised his glass. "To you and your vacation."

We clinked glasses, and I drained the last of my beer. John waved, coughed, and said, "Excuse me" a few times, trying to get the attention of Di, who was having an in-depth conversation with a man at the other end of the bar. Before I could stop him, John did the unthinkable and whistled. There was a collective gasp and a few dozen heads whipped around in alarm.

Di turned and slowly approached; she cocked her head and pointed to her ear. "Was that a whistle?" she asked.

I swung my arm in front of him and whispered, "These stools are ours at the pleasure of The Lady."

John spluttered the appropriate amount of fear and apology.

Di put both hands on the bar, leaned in, narrowed her eyes, and asked, "Bus station?"

"That's about right," I said. Then, in a quiet aside to John, "I'll explain later."

Di opened her hand in my direction, indicating my patronage held weight at her bar. She addressed John: "You get your first and last pass." Then to me, "Are you ready for one more, hon?" I nodded and Di set off to get the beer.

"I take it only one beer is coming," said John.

"If I had to guess," I said. "We can share."

We chatted while I watched Di attempt to draw beer from the tap system that hiccuped and filled several pint glasses with jets of foam.

Di strutted the length of the bar. "Tap system . . ." She dragged a finger across her neck. "It's kaput. We got plenty in the bottle."

"We'll take two Peronis," John said.

"Honey," Di said, shaking her head. "Newport's across the bridge. Domestic only in the bottle. How about a couple of Buds?"

John frowned then scanned the row of bottles on the shelf above Di's head. "Oh, how about Blue Moon?"

Di flinched as if she'd been kicked, then opened a palm in my direction. "She doesn't do fruity," Di said.

The patrons to our left and our right looked between me, John, and Di, likely hoping for fireworks. I cleared my throat. "As luck would have it, I have some Peroni at the house," I said, surprising everyone, especially myself.

"Really?" John asked.

"Really," I replied.

"I'll take the check," John announced. Our audience applauded; my cheeks flushed.

"You can meet Tom," I whispered.

"Who's Tom?" he whispered back.

"The man of the house."

"Can't wait," he said, dropping a stupid amount of cash on the bar. "Shall we?"

CHAPTER 20

JOHN GAZED AROUND the living room. "Very nice," he said. "I'm not sure what I was expecting, but it wasn't this."

"It's my mother's guest cottage, but it's comfortable and it works whenever I need it."

I sent John toward the kitchen. "Beer is in the fridge. I'll be the Girl Scout and light a fire."

"Yes, ma'am," said John, saluting. "What was that about the bus station?" he called over his shoulder.

"Di thinks all the lost souls wait to be collected at the bus station."

"Wow, that bad, huh? And the Blue Moon, geez. It was as if I'd farted in church."

I smiled. "You're fine." I wedged newspaper between the logs in the grate and set fire to it, then lit the candles on the mantel.

"Would you have collected me? At the bus station?"

An image of John leapt into my head. He sat on a bench beside a row of mammoth-sized buses, a backpack between his feet, content, self-assured, waiting for the right person to arrive, for the rest of his story to begin.

"I would have."

John carried two Peronis and an opener to the couch. Just as he was about to sit, I noticed the lump under the blanket and stopped him. "As promised, the king of the castle." I lifted the blinking black fur ball from under the blanket. "This is Mr. Tom Collins the Second. Tom, say hello to Dr. Riordan."

"You named your cat after a cocktail?"

"I named him after my grandmother's cat. She named her cat after a cocktail."

"That explains everything."

Tom wiggled from my grasp and landed with a graceful thump. He didn't so much as give us a backward glance as he strutted off into the kitchen, his tail high in the air.

"You have made a fine first impression."

"I never fail to electrify the felines of the world," he said with a wry smile.

John set the beers on the cocktail table and held out his hand. "May I have this dance, Miss Stuart?"

I inclined my head, my heartbeat ratcheted up a notch. "To what?"

"Shh. Listen."

"I don't hear anything," I whispered, feeling the heat as it colored my earlobes.

"Every home has its own song, its own rhythm."

Entwining warm fingers between my own, he gently pulled me to my feet. We stood inches apart. A sweet smile that asked for trust formed on his face. The sound of the wind whistling through the limbs of the ancient beech trees that shrouded the cottage seeped through the walls. The wood crackled and spit in the grate and a myriad of echoes and thuds unique to a turn-of-the-century cottage filled the silence, feeling newly comforting. Shadow and light from the fire and the candles flickered along the walls, the ceiling.

John took my right hand in his left and folded our arms between us. We swayed in front of the fire. Time slowed; everything beyond where we stood faded away. Delicate sensations became oddly heightened: the brush of his cheek along my ear, his heart beating against my breast, the warmth of his hand in mine, a whisper of his breath on my neck. Eventually, and most naturally, the song came to an end. John stepped back and raised my hand to his chin. When I didn't pull away, he brushed his lips across the back of my hand, sending a twinge through my body that can only be described as electric.

He smiled. "Peroni?"

"Thank you." I felt a sense of relief that felt like warmth.

He opened the beer and proposed a toast. "To Tom."

"To Tom," I concurred.

"To intervening for me with Lady Di." He clinked his beer bottle with mine.

"That was a close one."

"And for rescuing me at the bus station."

"Ah, but we didn't say anything about rescuing. That's a different conversation altogether."

"Because?"

I sighed. "Because I don't believe it's possible to rescue another person. A hand up, sure. Guidance, absolutely. Knowing someone else believes in you, powerful. But in our darkest moments, we need to save ourselves."

"Very deep."

I shrugged. "Besides, that pack of wolves did an admirable job."

"It looks green, doesn't it?"

I thought about his question. "The grass on your side of the fence?"

He nodded. "Suffice it to say that my grass hasn't always been so lush."

"A man with a checkered past. Now we're talking."

We sat in easy silence listening to the hiss and pop of the wood as it burned in the grate. The concept of coincidence, and that I had never believed in it, clawed at me.

"You know what bothers me?" I asked, before I could stop myself.

"Is this a working type of what bothers you?"

"It is."

"Then I object."

"You object? You're a doctor."

"What's your point?"

"I'll bite. On what grounds?"

He pulled back the cuff of his sleeve and glanced at his watch. "On the grounds of . . . of after-hours thinking."

"After-hours thinking?"

"Apparently you haven't heard about the new law requiring that all after-hours thought and discourse be nonwork related."

"Correct, Mr. Orwell, I hadn't heard of that," I said and made a face.

"Have you ever noticed," John said, "that you don't just turn your head, instead you turn your entire body? This is a guess, but is your neck always so stiff?"

"And sadly, perpetually sore."

John held up his hands. "They're magic. Just your neck and upper back."

My expression read skepticism. "Really?"

"A man of my word."

Another hopeful smile appeared and I nodded.

"Now, turn around. That's right. A little closer. Lean back." I closed my eyes and John put the heel of his palm into my shoulders and slowly kneaded, one side then the other, then he applied pressure to the base of my skull. "This may mess up your hair," he said.

"I'm drooling; the messy hair will complete my unhinged look."

John chuckled. "Now, take a deep breath. That's right. One more." He used his index and middle finger in strong circular motions. "I'm going to work your pressure points for ten-second intervals. This may be initially uncomfortable, but it'll give you some relief. Okay?"

I mumbled my assent. "Hey, you're not half-bad at this. And you know, if the ME thing doesn't work out . . ."

"I'll keep that in mind." A few minutes later, he said, "Okay, I've reconsidered. I want to know what bothers you."

My cheeks flushed. "Well, it wasn't important. I just . . ."

"Important or not."

"I lied when I said I could buy into the coincidence of it all. It's starting to feel less and less like one. In fact, I don't believe in coincidences."

"At all?"

I shook my head.

"Feel better now?"

I nodded and smiled. A few minutes later, I closed my eyes. The tension in my neck eased. The last thing I remembered before falling asleep was John, his legs stretched along the edge of the couch, his socked feet wiggling, and the sound of the wood crackling in the grate.

CHAPTER

21

IN THE DREAM, I watch from the shadows as the door swings open and a thump of bass fills the night air. A couple spill into the hazy ribbon of light. At first glance, I don't recognize her. But when I see the alabaster neck and the crimson beret, there is no doubt. As always, his face is shadowy, obscure. She swivels her head in my direction and her luminous gaze vaults across the darkness. Her eyes find mine, hold them; she nods as if we've agreed to something.

My lens rotates 180 degrees at dizzying speed. As if through her eyes, I see myself nod in grim acceptance. The lens jerks and swivels like a tilt-a-whirl, my breath catches as I complete the circle. Time stops, then the scene resumes as if we'd never made eye contact.

She turns, stumbles, giggles. I see the glint of a pinkie ring as he steadies her and leads her by the hand along the wet sidewalk; the opening notes of *Clair de Lune* tinkle from his watch chime and fade in their wake. She follows with childlike anticipation; her instinct for apprehension is temporarily unavailable. I want to call out, warn her. Panic grips my throat and squeezes.

The couple and my opportunity vanish. Shame eviscerates me. The low guttural whimpering I hear is the agony of a wounded animal; the bitter taste of salt on my tongue suggests it is my own. And yet I know how the story ends; I know I have already failed her.

* * *

I thrashed into consciousness, kicking upward beyond the familiar narrative as if breaking free from a tangle of razor-sharp grass binding my legs at the bottom of a murky pond. When I breached darkness into daylight, weight and warmth and a snippet of crimson disappeared from beside me like a clump of dust sucked into a vacuum. My heart pounded as the dream receded like a wave toddling into the arms of the sea. The confusing moments between sleep and wakefulness ebbed; I shivered as I scanned the empty room, then thoughts of Elizabeth overwhelmed me like a rogue wave.

I fumbled into shorts and running shoes and headed for the door. The sharp click of its latch prompted the memory of a voice heard before I'd been fully awake, urging me to trust my instinct.

I ran along the four miles of winding, uphill roads that led to the lighthouse at Beavertail, thinking about the dream, my dream. Always a variation of the same scenario, always with exacting cinematic clarity; this time, however, it felt different, as if Elizabeth had reached across time, had spoken, had asked. And I'd agreed, but to what I didn't know.

My fixation on the drug had, no doubt, prompted the dream—it had been more than a year since the last. And while I didn't have opinions about the afterlife or messages from the dead, this—whatever this was—wasn't going to be ignored.

Twenty minutes into my run, I settled into a comfortable pace, my mind disengaged from the actions of my arms and legs. Each step, the rhythmic clicking of a metronome. This simple act of finding my stride was my saving grace.

* * *

That September of my senior year at college, my future felt secure. Everything I'd worked for was coming to fruition. One ordinary night out with a classmate for pizza, a drug slipped into my beer, and my world turned on a dime.

By late October, nothing was the same. Shattered and lost, crippled with relentless panic attacks that choked my airway, I drank just enough to keep my mind from racing, my hands from shaking, and to scrape through the day. But it wasn't the solution; unexcused absences and incomplete work piled up. My imagined world read like a Stephen King novel, and when I disconnected the plug from the phone jack, it shrank, and I became a frenzied bird in a tiny cage. I needed something to grab on to, something to break my fall. Graduation jitters, my professors said. I told my parents the same. The decision to take a leave of absence for the rest of the semester to rethink my next steps seemed in keeping with my character: conscientious, thoughtful to a fault.

It was all an enormous lie.

I packed up and headed home on the last day of Elizabeth's life, but I hadn't known that then, wouldn't learn of it for months. The universe delivered what I could handle and when I could handle it.

After the endless, white-knuckled drive, I lugged my two suitcases up three flights of stairs, shut my bedroom door, leaned against it, and closed my eyes, breathing in the familiar scent of lemon oil. This room. Every familiar crevice that I thought I'd outgrown, that I'd so casually abandoned, welcomed me like a wise grandmother one could never disappoint. Old friends and adventures cocooned in worn bindings waited patiently on floor-to-ceiling shelves. The dependable *tick, tick, tick* of the clock on the bedside table hummed a soothing lullaby.

I dropped into the overstuffed reading chair, set my feet on its ottoman, and pulled a wool throw over me, relishing its warmth. The view from the window had been unchanged for a hundred years. The sun was low in the western sky, but my mind's eye supplied an image of the neighboring farm's cattle grazing in the pasture, and in the distance, sailboats gliding across the bay. An hour later I thrust open the French doors to the balcony, and a thick blanket of sea air and the whispers of a million crickets drifted in. And that night, finally, I found sleep.

While I thought I'd broken the spell, daybreak offered no peace. Trapped in sleep, dread crept upward, thick, black, and cold, winding in and around, drumming electric against my ribs. Disturbing images played before my eyes; angst tightened its grip. I woke to the sound of Mother at her piano playing *Clair de Lune*. What had once been the soundtrack of my happy childhood brought fresh tears to my eyes, and dread simmering at the base of my stomach.

I pulled on sweats and sneakers, and headed out for a walk. My mind raced. I picked up speed. The need to focus distracted me from the endless search for answers that never came, the missing pieces that hung in the air just out of reach that I struggled to remember and to forget at the same time. Amid the steady rhythm of my footsteps, I found a quiet place. That same weekend I begged my mother to play anything else while I was home. She scanned my grief-stricken face, caressed my sunken cheek, then, without question, nodded.

* * *

As I ran this morning, adrenaline settled my jangly nerves. Arriving at Beavertail lifted me further. I spent an hour climbing the sheer embankments, finding foothold after foothold and pulling myself up a challenging route I hadn't dared try before. Reaching the pinnacle of the headland felt like an impossible win, as if I'd gone the distance with the great Ali.

I lay atop the bluff with the morning sun on my face, mesmerized by the thunderous sounds of the churning sea and saltwater spray. The setting infused me with a strength I felt nowhere else, as if a loose plug had been jammed back into its socket, the mainspring newly coiled on my self-confidence.

My mind turned to Dr. Maxwell. I'd missed something, but not something that had been said; it was something sidestepped. But the case was no longer mine, I had to let it go, let DC handle it. The echo of that voice telling me to trust my instinct chimed like a bell, igniting an internal switch, a need that endorphins wouldn't mollify. I wouldn't walk away. I'd finish my inquiries one way or another until I was satisfied we had the right answer.

I popped in my earbuds and set off, the wind at my back, my sights steady. Turning up the volume on a live recording, I let the drumbeat set my pace and became lost between the layers of brass, guitars, vocals, and harmonica, no longer conscious of the road or my feet as they struck pavement. The crowd, in tandem with the music, lifted me a fraction higher, the saxophone breathing new life into my weary limbs, my aching soul. And when I asked for more, my body delivered; soon I was hauling ass as if my life depended on it and sprinting for home.

In the kitchen, Tom wound between my legs. As I spooned his salmon supreme or whatever the hell it was into his bowl, I saw the note tucked beneath a half-full beer bottle on the kitchen island.

It read: *Your snoring is very cute. Just kidding. Didn't want to wake you. Thanks for a great evening. John.*

I puttered: folded and tucked away the stack of blankets John had draped over me, deposited the beer bottles into the recycling bin, then headed upstairs to fill the tub. I emptied half the bag of Epsom salts into steaming water, narrowed the blinds, then lowered myself in and soaked.

An hour later, as I sat in the kitchen sipping peppermint tea, my cell phone shimmied on the countertop. It was John. Waiting in vain for the telltale chirp, it rang again.

"You up, sleepyhead?"

"Good morning to you, too."

"Big kid that I am, I'm envious of your vacation." He paused and when I said nothing, he continued, "So, I cleared my afternoon. Was wondering if you'd join me for a round of golf?"

"What if you get a case?" I asked stupidly.

"And on the eighth day," John said in a booming, theatrical voice, "God created refrigeration."

"So, that's what happened on the eighth day. Sounds like a possibility. Where and what time?"

"How about two thirty?"

"Where did you have in mind?"

"I'm a member at The Country Club."

"*The* Country Club. Very swanky," I teased. "Can I call you back? I need to check my datebook."

"Just let me know."

I hung up and dialed my mother—a first of sorts. Not since the tenth grade had I sought her advice where the opposite sex was concerned.

"I don't know, Mom. Mixing business and, you know, I think he likes me. It might not be a good idea to encourage him. I mean . . . he's a colleague." I sounded no different from when I'd been in tenth grade.

"I'm not following, dear." The sound of an emery board grated rhythmically in the background. "Is there something else on your agenda today that conflicts? Something else you'd rather do?"

I drew a big fat zero. "Uh, no."

"It's a round of golf, nothing more. Don't read too much into it. You might enjoy yourself. If it's a bore, you can bow out after nine. You said you'd try."

"I did, Mom. Thanks. I'll call him."

I dialed John. "Golf sounds nice," I said, my insides in knots. "I have a few things I need to take care of this morning. How about three? Maybe we can hit a few balls before heading off?"

"Perfect. Meet me at the bag drop," John said.

"See you then," I said, a new feeling, one of pride, bubbling up inside.

CHAPTER

22

AT FIVE MINUTES to ten, I called Dr. Maxwell and left a message about my lost bracelet, telling him I'd be stopping over. At ten AM, fifteen minutes after the walk scheduled for the morning forty-fives, I rang his doorbell.

I thought about O'Sullivan's warning and my first reprimand. Without remorse, I'd risked my job and jail time for the good of the case and the victims when I overlooked that tiny thing I was supposed to uphold called the law. That morning, as I asked my opening question, I unwrapped a sports bar. The crinkle of the wrapper prompted the man sitting across from me to ask me to repeat the question. If he couldn't hear me, could the tape hear him? An hour later, I suspected he was on the cusp of asking for an attorney, yet on the verge of a confession. Around and around swirled the knowledge that despite his grandfatherly cardigan and wire-rimmed glasses, he was a merciless predator; he had to be stopped. As he asked for counsel in his soft whisper of a voice, I crumpled the plastic wrapper of my sports bar. The tape recorded a strident crackling sound mixed with muffled words and then my voice said that'd be fine, "that" being unclear, but first we should discuss what he and I both knew. Over the next few hours, he described how he'd dedicated the last thirty years of his life to counseling and educating the boys who'd attended the afterschool program he ran for at-risk preteens. These boys needed a father figure to help them "understand" their budding sexuality. He'd done the unthinkable as he groomed and manipulated them to satisfy his own whims. In the months following his confession, dozens of victims came forward. Despite how I'd done it, the significance of the outcome for those boys felt powerful. It'd been a huge win for the department, still my fellow officer in the interview had had a quiet word with O'Sullivan. And since then, O'Sullivan had scrutinized my every move.

After I'd analyzed it to within an inch of its life, I admitted to myself that the decision had been a mistake. Even so, I'd do it again and again and again under similar circumstances. This hardly felt like a similar circumstance, but the disquiet that sprung from the knowledge that Rohypnol had been in Hope's system made me open the door.

"Dr. Maxwell?" I said, anticipating silence. "You left the door unlocked. Hello, it's Detective Stuart, from yesterday." I retrieved my gold bracelet, retreated to the office, pulled on latex gloves, and assessed the file cabinets lining the walls. The *P*'s were at the bottom of the second cabinet. And voilà, three fat files.

I selected Hope's, which was half the size of her parents'. Last date of examination, Wednesday, June 21, 2018 . . . prescribed birth control . . . notes of their discussion as Max had described. All presented in a meticulous printing style that betrayed the clichés of the medical profession and slanted in a way that said *lefty*. Nothing appeared out of the ordinary. No mention of insomnia. Skimming through the file—through Hope's brief time on earth—it was clear she had much to look forward to, the world and all its benefits at her disposal.

Penelope Philbrick's file was thick; several folders encompassed her medical history. I skipped forward to Hope's birth. As Max had described, he'd delivered Hope by cesarean section twelve weeks before the due date. There were brief notes as if from a discussion: *Baby not sleeping more than two hours at night . . . longer periods during the day.* Further along: *Medication for jetlag? Fluni?* Two years after Hope's birth, Dr. Maxwell diagnosed a second pregnancy. There were similar notes: *Penelope eight weeks along . . . distressed. Complications?* The pregnancy was terminated three weeks later. A scrawl in the margin noted that Preston was in Europe, but Penelope would have her housekeeper to take care of her.

It was ten twenty. I photographed the pages of Penelope's file I didn't have time to read. Time was at a premium and I needed to choose: either review Preston Philbrick's or Penelope's deceased twin, Bea Harrington's, file. I opted for Bea Harrington's. It contained years of routine monthly evaluation forms. Boxes similarly checked month after month. No illnesses, no hospitalizations. Nothing noted in the margins. I returned all as I'd found it.

It was ten forty when I retraced my steps to the entry, deposited the prepared note on the hall table, and pulled the door tight behind me.

CHAPTER

23

DelCarmen picked up on the first ring. "How's vacation?" he asked.

"Not as much fun as it is in the movies," I said. "The Philbricks need to be told in person about the Rohypnol finding. I'd like to volunteer."

"Because?"

"Because the Philbricks should hear it from someone they know."

"The face-to-face is what's critical. Long and I can handle it."

"I'm right here," I said.

I heard what sounded like unhappy banging in the background. "If you must," DelCarmen said finally.

"And listen, has admin compiled those sexual assault reports?"

"Waste of time," he said.

"I've got plenty to waste," I said.

DelCarmen grumbled something that sounded like "I'll check," then hung up.

I dialed the Philbricks. To my surprise, Mrs. Philbrick answered. She told me to come when it suited me, but if I needed to speak with her husband, he wouldn't be home until closer to noon.

It was almost eleven thirty when I knocked at the kitchen door. Nothing but an echo. I tried the handle, but it was locked. I trotted around to the front entrance and rang the doorbell. A delicate melody of chimes announced my arrival. Minutes passed and finally, heels tapped along the wood floor. The faint shadow of a woman darkened the frosted glass panels; moments passed during which I imagined that the advantages and disadvantages of opening it were being weighed.

The door swung open, and Penelope Philbrick gazed at me with tired eyes, her lips pressed into a thin smile, a thick headband encircling her hairline. "Rosa mustn't be well. She didn't come to work today. I have a terrible habit of ignoring the doorbell," she murmured in apology.

She turned, and I followed her into the great room. Penelope gestured for me to sit in an armchair, then dropped noiselessly into its companion. At forty-nine years old, the deep creases on Penelope Philbrick's pale, fragile skin and the mere wisps of her eyebrows were striking in the stark light of day. Trying not to gawp, my gaze leapt around the room, finally landing on the spines of the three cumbersome tomes on the subject of mythology on the coffee table. Atop the books sat a twelve- or fourteen-inch bronze sculpture of a horse.

"Joseph Campbell was a master storyteller," I said. "One of my mother's favorites." I pointed to the books.

"Oh," she said, vaguely.

I looked more closely at the sculpture of the horse, an Arabian, its breed unmistakable by its high-held tail. I made another attempt to fill the silence. "Is that one of Josie Meyer's pieces?" I asked, gesturing.

She met my eye and nodded. "That was my Cricket. I commissioned the sculpture after he died."

"Ah, a jumper," I said.

"A fine jumper, but in his heart, he was a dancer, a showman. Everyone gave me the credit, but I simply held the reins while he danced. I used to think that if the orchestrated movement of his limbs was sound, they'd emit a symphony."

The confident glint in his eyes, the long, arrogant neck, and the position of his powerful body made it appear as if he might leap from the table. "Josie captured his spirit."

"He'd been my birthday present the year I turned eighteen. My best friend." Then she seemed to be elsewhere, away with her thoughts, as she pressed a tissue to her eyes and collected herself.

"I'm sorry for intruding," I said. "This can't be easy."

Penelope held up a hand and shook off the apology. I stared at the long, jagged scratch on her right forearm. She followed my gaze and pulled her sleeves to her wrists.

Unplanned, I asked the question I already had an answer to regarding her whereabouts on the night Hope died. "Before we begin, I'm sure we discussed this, but couldn't find it in my notes. Can you remind me where you were on Saturday from eleven forward?"

Penelope hesitated. "I was in my room," she said, then stopped. "Then . . . I . . . took a bath and went to bed."

"Can anyone confirm that?"

"Rosa."

It was the same answer she'd given that Sunday morning. I nodded, then continued. "Are you fond of Eddie, Mrs. Philbrick?"

She narrowed her eyes. "Fond or not, my opinion didn't matter. Hope's happiness was what mattered. Would he have been my choice as a partner for my daughter? The answer is no. But a parent needs to trust that they've given their child the wisdom to know that their choices are right for them."

It wasn't much, but it had been honest.

"What brings you here today, Miss Stuart?"

"I've received preliminary results from the toxicology reports and wanted to discuss them with you and your husband."

"He should be here any minute," she said, fishing through the pockets of her cardigan and muttering to herself when she came up empty. I retrieved tissues from the box on the table to my left and handed them to her. She dried her eyes then said, "Please, tell me what the report says, about Hope."

"Are you sure?"

She nodded.

"The toxicology report indicates that Hope had a large dose of a drug called Rohypnol in her system. Are you familiar with that drug?"

She shook her head, her eyes shimmered. "I can't say that I am."

"It was never approved by the FDA, but it's prescribed in Europe and Mexico to treat insomnia, and is sometimes produced and distributed illegally, as a fake narcotic. Often used as a recreational drug. Those fake versions can be dangerous."

Penelope fanned herself as if having a hot flash.

"Rohypnol, fake or not, combined with alcohol—even the smallest amount—doubles or triples the effect."

She drilled me with her luminous sapphire eyes.

"My daughter did not take drugs."

"I didn't mean to suggest she did, Mrs. Philbrick. Quite the contrary. I'm wondering if Hope could have taken this by accident. Or perhaps someone, maybe Eddie, might have given it to her?" I waited a beat. "Thinking it was something that could ease her jitters the night of her prenuptial."

The tears flowed over her swollen cheekbones. The front door swung open and slammed shut. "Penelope," called Preston, his footsteps echoing on the wood floor as he made his way to the great room.

"Well, Ms. Stuart." He approached, stood beside his wife, and placed a hand on her shoulder. "This is a surprise. I expect there is a reason for your visit?"

"The results of the toxicology report. Thought it best if you heard it from someone you knew."

"Yes, of course." He sat next to his wife. Her hands curled in tight fists, but relented when he laced his fingers between hers.

"A drug called Rohypnol was found in Hope's system."

Preston cocked his head. "What on earth is that?"

"It's an old drug—seventies, early eighties—prescribed to treat insomnia. But because the side effects were severe, the FDA never approved it. It's available by prescription in Europe, but it's often produced and distributed illegally."

"Do you mean bootlegged?"

I nodded. "Do any of Hope's friends give you cause for concern?"

Preston Philbrick considered the question and shook his head.

"Could Eddie have given it to her? Maybe to calm her down."

"She had been understandably nervous," he said.

"It would be prudent if we searched her room and her boat. If we find something, we'll be able to put this to bed with no further intrusion. If you have no objection, that is?"

"None whatsoever. Edward will be returning from Block Island in a day or two. I will let him know to expect you."

We searched all five bedrooms and their en suite bathrooms. An eclectic mix of antique and modern furniture was artfully arranged; someone had a thing for highboys. I removed the medicine vials found in the vanities of three of the five bathrooms. Preston took something for high blood pressure. An over-the-counter sleep aid and a prescription to combat anxiety for Mrs. Philbrick. I left a week's worth of each and bagged the rest.

Hope's room hadn't been tidied: clothes were strewn over the desk chair, the bed, the closet floor; makeup was in disarray on the bathroom vanity. I found birth control pills in the bedside table, unopened fish oil gummies in the medicine cabinet. A corner of her laptop protruded from beneath the bedclothes. Before I could ask, Preston gestured that I should take it.

We walked into the foyer. "We appreciate your thoroughness and attention to your work." He lowered his voice and with a look of deep concern, said, "However, I'm worried for my wife's well-being. She isn't sleeping, and lack of sleep and the medication she's taking is making her confused. I must ask that if you have more questions, to please call me."

I walked to the car, replaying my conversation with Penelope. She'd been highly emotional; no doubt I'd upset her. But she hadn't seemed doped or confused. I thought about her reaction to the Rohypnol finding. The look of angst on her face. Had I crossed every last t regarding Penelope Philbrick? Confirming that she'd been in her room at eleven o'clock on the night of Hope's death remained an open item. It was time to speak with Rosa Rodriguez.

CHAPTER

24

COMMUNICATIONS INFORMED ME that there were roughly a hundred cars registered statewide to people with the last name Rodriguez, yet none to a Rosa Rodriguez, nor was there a driver's license issued in that name. A search for her green card on the ICE database and with local utility companies turned up the same. Her legal first name was not Rosa. We'd find her, but it would take time.

While I conducted fruitless social media searches in the driveway of the Crow's Nest, two men—one, tall and skinny, his companion, short and squat, a variety of gardening tools balanced over their shoulders—ambled toward an outbuilding of sorts. A more creative idea presented itself. I closed the phone, pulled up beside them, and cranked open my window. They were having a lively discussion in Spanish.

"Hola," I said, making a mental note to pick up *Spanish for Dummies*.

"Hola," said Short and Squat, with no trace of an accent.

Oh, thank God.

"Do either of you know Rosa Rodriguez?"

Short and Squat translated, then said, "Ramon says she works at the house."

"Does he know her home address?" I flashed my badge. "She didn't come to work today. I'd like to speak with her."

Short and Squat repeated my question. Tall Man shook his head.

"Ramon doesn't know, and neither do I," said Short and Squat, "but Rosa rides to work with her cousin Felipe."

Ramon added something in rapid-fire Spanish that I didn't understand.

"Ramon says they come up from the Hill with a few other guys." He inclined his head toward a silver compact that was parked at the far end of the garage. It had a significant dent in the driver's side door.

"Is he around?" I asked.

The two jabbered on longer than I expected it would take to ask and answer the question. Ramon shrugged and made gestures indicating Felipe might be at the far end of the earth.

"He's done today at twelve thirty. Why don't you wait around? You can catch him before he leaves."

I checked my watch. I had ten minutes.

"Thank you," I said, shifting into drive. I continued down the service road and noted the plate and make of the car. Once on the main road, I backed into an adjacent driveway. Already in a social media sort of mood, I typed "Penelope Harrington equestrian" into the phone's search engine. Dozens of old articles materialized from *Country Life* and *Equestrian* detailing her and Cricket's success in dressage and show jumping. Then I saw the reason for her tears: a newspaper article about the electrical fire, twelve years earlier, that engulfed the barn at her family's horse farm in Little Compton, and was to blame for the death of the four horses, including Cricket, trapped inside. A portable heater had been left running in the tack room. They didn't name Penelope, but the article hadn't needed to: she'd been the sole rider in the family, and the person who managed the stable had been out of state. Penelope's look of angst became clear: she'd been to blame.

My phone buzzed; a missed call from DelCarmen. I tapped redial.

"What happened at the Philbrick house?"

"Neither had heard of Rohypnol. He gave me free rein to search his bathroom vanities. Clean as a whistle. Out of an abundance of caution, I have their meds and Hope's laptop."

"What'd they say about where they were from eleven forward?"

"No change to their original statements. Mrs. Philbrick said she took a bath, went to bed. Rosa could provide her alibi. Mr. Philbrick was mingling and in constant contact with the catering coordinator."

"I have the caterer's contact info. What else?"

"I want to speak with Rosa Rodriguez. Preston Philbrick responded for her during my initial interview. And she was skittish. I want to hear it from her."

"Didn't you just come from the house?"

"A no show for work."

"We'll handle it."

"I'm playing golf later this afternoon. I have plenty of time."

"Once again, I'm capable of interviewing a witness."

"And I'd like to be there when you do. I need to follow through on this one, no questions asked."

"What's her address?" he asked.

"I'll pick you up."

Backing down wasn't an option.

"Is that a yes?" I asked.

"This is the wrong fucking hill to die on. In fact, it's not even a fucking mound."

"So be it."

"And a fucking mistake to poke O'Sullivan's hive."

"He's not going to know."

"You don't get it, do you?"

The silence stretched between us like an exposed nerve.

"You understand the risks and potential consequences?"

Before I could answer, the silver Corolla turned out of the entrance to the Crow's Nest, kicking up sand as it fishtailed onto the paved road. I gave it a minute, then followed.

"Her legal name isn't Rosa, so no address yet, but I'm tailing her cousin, Felipe. She travels to work with him. I think I'm headed up to the Hill."

"Pull him over and get an address."

Instead, I rattled off the license plate number and asked him to run it.

"Because?"

"No emergency vehicle lighting and my ability to communicate with anyone named Felipe is sketchy. Run the plate. I'll pick you up."

Twenty minutes later, I turned off the highway and followed the Corolla onto Atwells Avenue. As I approached Bradford Street, I flashed my lights at DelCarmen, who was leaning against a utility pole. I stopped, and he hopped in. He was always quiet, yet this felt different; he bristled with anger. I didn't care.

We wound through the narrow side streets of Federal Hill, passing endless rows of decrepit tenement houses. Laundry strung on lines zigzagged between them; their exterior pastel paint was dull and peeling. It was trash day. The streets were lined with dented metal garbage cans, many on their sides rolling back and forth from occasional gusts of wind; loose trash was scattered in the street. Men in their late teens and early twenties stood like shadows in doorways, watching.

The Corolla pulled over and stopped. Two men wearing stained T-shirts and cargo pants got out. One waited on the sidewalk digging his hands into his pockets, while the other spoke with the driver through the front passenger side window.

DelCarmen checked behind us. "Pull up next to him."

I pulled abreast of the Corolla, blocking traffic. We stepped from the car and within seconds, DelCarmen had Felipe Rodriguez pinned against the driver's side door, his badge in Felipe's face.

"Don't fuck with me and you'll be fine. Claro?"

I cringed at his tough-guy routine. His anger should have been directed at me, not at our witness. "Tell him I need to talk to his cousin," I said.

"She didn't show this morning," said Felipe. Of course, his English was near perfect.

"Address?" I asked.

"Carter Street Apartments."

"Did you call her?"

"She didn't answer."

"Does she do this often?"

"Maybe once."

"What time do you pick her up?"

"Six thirty."

"Call her," DC said.

Felipe pulled a phone from his pants pocket and dialed. "Straight to voice mail."

Without protest, Felipe climbed into the back seat of the wagon. I handed DelCarmen the keys. He slipped behind the wheel and drove the few blocks to Rosa's building, then dropped me out front.

Doors slammed and outbursts from sitcom laugh tracks filtered beneath doors and through thin walls as I climbed the stairs. The door to apartment 3E was ajar, its flimsy casing splintered. Latin music played from within. I drew my gun, unlocked the safety, nudged open the door with my right elbow, and slid inside.

The radiators hissed and clanked, spewing steam into the dark parlor. Figurines and framed pictures of Mary and the baby Jesus presided over a flock of bulky, old-fashioned furniture. Potted plants hung in clusters from macramé twines, creating an indoor jungle of exotic vegetation. Traditional Spanish music streamed from an antique console radio atop an ornate sideboard in the dining room. It looked as if a cat had tried to claw its way onto the dining table, pulling the tablecloth and anything on top to the floor. Potting soil and pottery shards coated a lipstick tube, wallet, hairbrush, and a set of keys that had tipped from a black handbag. A variegated spider plant dislodged from its pot lay dying on the wood floor. I pulled on gloves and picked up the wallet; it contained crisp hundred-dollar bills.

In the kitchen, a sweaty container of cream and an unused mug sat on the counter. The glass coffee pot was full and cold to the touch. Photos of dark-haired girls in simple white dresses with matching veils, eyes downcast, their hands wound with rosary beads and clasped in prayer, blanketed the wall.

From the doorway of a bedroom, I noted open dresser drawers and a half-packed cloth satchel on the bed, a stack of neatly folded clothing beside it. A second bedroom, doubling as a sitting room, was dark and untouched; the bathroom, tidy. Retracing my steps into the kitchen, I retrieved a flashlight from my trouser pocket.

The door to the basement stairwell was open. I stopped on each step as I descended and listened, but heard nothing except the water that trickled circuitously through the building's plumbing. At the bottom, I pressed my body flat to the wall and felt for the light switch. It was in the "on" position; yet, when I toggled it, the basement remained dark. The beam from the flashlight stretched along the low ceiling: a light bulb, smashed and jagged in its socket, hung from a lone electrical wire. I directed the flashlight to my right along stone foundation walls encrusted with black mold, then to the left over a group of coin-operated washing machines and dryers. Moving toward a glimmer of daylight, I passed ancient snowman furnaces wrapped like mummies with asbestos insulation, hot water heaters, rusted and leaking, abandoned machinery and tools, broken bikes, and discarded toys. Cobwebs brushed my face and caught in my hair.

I stepped around a mountain of overstuffed black garbage bags, and there, as if trying to swim away, lay Rosa, her head resting on her left ear, her right hand with its bloody knuckles reaching forward; she had died mid-crawl. A thick smear of blood the width of her body trailed approximately four feet behind where she lay. There was no guessing how Rosa had died; a bloody flashlight lay on the ground beside her.

I pulled on gloves and felt her jaw, noting its rigidity, then slipped two fingers under her elbow, lifting it without resistance. Rigor wasn't complete. I checked my watch; it was ten minutes past one. It took approximately twelve hours for a body to become fully rigid, which suggested that she was killed somewhere between five and eight this morning. Following the killer's path up the back cellar stairs and out to the parking lot, I dialed DC.

"Can I cut this guy loose?"

"You better hang on to him. His cousin is dead."

When I emerged from behind the building, DC leaned against the bumper of the wagon, and Felipe sat in the back seat with his head in his hands. DC joined me on the sidewalk.

"How?" he asked.

"In the basement. Flashlight to the head. A big one. She was running, she'd packed, a wad of cash in her wallet. Is this a coincidence, or are the two deaths connected?"

"Coincidence."

"Flashlight, DC? Strange choice for a weapon. We can't rule out that this might be connected to Hope Philbrick's death."

"We're not going to. You asked, and I answered. Experience tells me one event has nothing to do with the other. Time of death?"

"Maybe between five to eight this morning. Hard to say; it's at least ten degrees colder in the basement."

DelCarmen asked no further questions, offered no rejoinder; instead, he looked at his watch. "What time's golf?"

"Golf? I can't go golfing."

"You don't have to go golfing, but you can't stay here."

He was right. I'd gotten my one wish from the genie's bottle. It was my turn to give one back, let him save face, but ego is a delicate dance. I bickered and held my ground until finally, I took a deep breath and nodded. DelCarmen beamed in triumph, and in that moment I thought I might know what it felt like to be one half of an old married couple.

"Shorty's on his way," he said, helping Felipe out of the back seat. "We'll take it from here." He tapped on his phone's keypad, then put his hand over the mouthpiece and said, "I'll call you with regular updates." He waved me away with the back of his hand, put the phone to his ear, and said, "No, we don't need an ambulance. Send the men from the morgue. Yeah, that, too. No. Now. I'll secure the scene."

I was smiling as I climbed into the Parisienne and drove off.

CHAPTER 25

MY PHONE RANG as I pulled up to the cottage. Caller ID said it was central station. I hit decline and waited for the chime that indicated a voice mail. O'Sullivan barked about me being off the case and floated the term "insubordination," which was a mistake to ignore. What the hell, did he have a tracking device on my wagon?

As usual, DC had been right: it was time to back off and let the hoopla die down, even if for a few hours. Putting the Philbrick cursor in my brain on hold, I hustled upstairs for a quick shower, slipped into a golf skirt, then pulled a white T-shirt over my head. When I opened the tailgate of the wagon to stow my clubs, I saw Dad's old set of Wilsons, right where they'd always been and, I decided, where they'd stay.

I revved up the Parisienne and pointed the Beast in the direction of The Country Club, a haven for a dying breed of old-moneyed WASPS who had successfully defended their private snooty club from the new wealth that yipped at their heels. The new-moneyed yippers were content to play at the other clubs, for now.

I checked my phone. Two more missed calls: one that was "private," which was never good, and one from DelCarmen. I hit redial.

"Criminals in custody?"

"It's been an hour."

"You're slipping."

DC ignored my razor-sharp humor. "Crime scene guys are here, Hadley and Bonner are canvassing the neighbors, and Shorty's trying to get in touch with her two grown daughters. Look, Stuart, I know you think this is something, but this isn't an unusual event down here. Besides, Shorty got a hit with someone on the catering staff," he said, with an uncharacteristic skip in his voice.

"Wow, who?"

"Frank Moran was one of six bartenders at the Philbrick party. He has a significant sheet, the most interesting, marital rape that was never prosecuted, but an abundance of every flavor of assault charges. He might be a fit."

"Interesting," I said. "What did you say his name was?"

"Frankie 'The Man' Moran. Also known as 'Federal Hill' Frankie. Sound familiar?"

"Was he a boxer?"

"He's retired. Had a promising career, but some sort of injury ended it. Booze, pills, young women, in and out of trouble over the years. Back in the day, he worked as a heavy for a few bookies."

"Debt collection?" I asked.

"Exactly. He's reinvented himself as a celebrity bartender in Newport."

DC explained that a little over a year ago Moran was picked out of a lineup for aggravated assault and rape. That night he'd been working in the city at a part-time job he's since quit—the same bar where the victim and her friends had been. They flagged him on a surveillance camera near where she was attacked. He said he'd left work and was going home, but his statement couldn't be verified since he'd neglected to clock out. It looked like he'd followed her.

"The victim ID'd him. About a month before trial, she dropped the charges, said he wasn't the guy."

"Just like that?"

"Just like that. Shorty and I will bring him in as a person of interest."

"Seems like a stretch."

"It gets better. Shorty spoke with the catering supervisor, who said Moran left his bar about ten o'clock and never came back. And we have a waiter who saw Moran and the deceased walking away from the party about the same time."

"Wait, are you making this up?"

An audible sigh followed. I imagined DelCarmen massaging his temples.

"You understand my skepticism, right?" I said. "It sounds like someone dialed up casting and asked for the perfect suspect for a crime, and then poof, here's this guy with a rap sheet, means, opportunity, and what, no alibi? Sounds too good to be true, don't you think?"

"Sometimes you get lucky, or this guy was sloppy or stupid or both. Listen, we've verified. Didn't you tell me that Eddie Field mentioned something about a bartender?"

Eddie *had* said Hope had been dancing with a bartender.

"Mea culpa. Must be one and the same. Tell me about the victim."

I heard the rustle of paper. "Denise Ryan. Twenty at the time. A college student."

"Witnesses? Cameras?"

"Neither. She was dragged to an adjacent alley, beaten and raped. Reportedly blacked out, woke up, then drove herself home. Didn't leave her apartment for three days."

"Is that when she reported it?"

"Yeah."

"Where is she?"

"Lives and works in Newport. From the Midwest." He flipped through pages. "Indiana. Came here for school."

"Got an address? I'm passing through Newport."

"Go golfing. Shorty and I will talk to the girl."

I sighed. Silence had become my new superpower.

"Fine, talk to the girl, then go golfing."

"As God is my witness."

DC took a deep breath. "She's the day manager at Fuel on lower Thames. She's there today until five."

I dialed John. "I'm going to be late, a half hour at most. I've got to make a stop in town. Work related," I added.

John made schoolyard chicken noises. "You scared, Stuart? I can see it coming. At three thirty, you'll call with another lame excuse."

"Start practicing, Riordan. You're going to need it."

CHAPTER 26

THE CROWD AT Fuel was light for a Tuesday afternoon. A wiry twentysomething with slicked-back blond hair and heavy eyeliner sauntered over to the counter. The tag on his shirt said his name was Jared. I ordered a small regular. Jared frowned.

"We have a lofty or perhaps a towering?" he said, as if speaking to a six-year-old. He held up two cups and waggled them at me.

For fuck's sake, I thought. I met his eye. Jared glared—hadn't been kidding—still waggling his cups.

"I'll take the highfalutin'," I said.

He bristled.

"That small one, thank you." I leaned forward and tapped on the cup to ensure we were both speaking the same ridiculous cup-size language.

"And what kind of coffee can I fill this with?" Jared asked with an impatient smile and a flutter of his eyelashes. He pointed to the extensive list of coffee options on the wall behind him.

"Just . . . uh . . . you know . . ." I scanned the list. "Uh, something . . ."

"Do you prefer a bold blend? Maybe something smooth?" he said, drawing out the words "bold" and "smooth."

I had a sudden urge to hop over the counter, hit him upside the head, and tell him to mind his goddamned manners. Drumming my fingers on the glass case, I gave him the once-over, glanced at my watch, and thought better of it. "Yeah, smooth. Smooth is perfect. Hey, is Denise busy?" I asked, looking around.

"One lofty Sierra Madre," Jared announced. "That'll be four ninety-five. I'll see if she's available," he said, disappearing through the back.

I took my ridiculously expensive cup of coffee to the far corner and waited. Jared returned with a petite dirty blond in tow and pointed at me. The blond made her way to the counter and said, "I'm Denise. Can I help you?"

"My name is Andrea Stuart. I'm a detective with the Providence Police. Can we talk in private?" I asked quietly. Denise eyed my short pink skirt and arched an eyebrow. I retrieved the badge from my hip pocket. She stiffened, then nodded for me to follow. I trailed her through the back of the store and out to the service entrance. Denise pulled a pack of Winstons from the breast pocket of her shirt. Her hands shook as she fumbled with her lighter. She drew hard on her cigarette, then leaned against the wall and stared.

"Did they get him?" she asked after a long minute.

"I don't know," I said, my heart breaking for her.

She narrowed her eyes. "So, what are you doing here?"

I knew how difficult it was to be directly reminded of rape. It opened old wounds and brought you back to terrifyingly dark places. "We're bringing in the guy you identified as your attacker on something unrelated. I need to ask why you dropped the charges."

"Because he wasn't the guy," she said, sending clouds of smoke into the air.

"They had a good case," I said.

"It was all circumstantial, no DNA, no nothing except my testimony."

Denise had waited three days to report the attack. In the meantime, she'd showered a hundred times and thrown away her clothes. I knew why. I knew how dirty she felt.

"He was at the right place at the right time. He had a history," I said.

"He was at the wrong place at the wrong time. And so was I. Look, you don't know," she said, angrily stubbing out her cigarette and lighting a second.

"Yes, yes, I do know," I said evenly.

Our eyes met. She scrutinized my face until the realization crystalized, then she nodded. "Did they ever get the guy?" she asked softly.

"They didn't," I said. *And they never will*, I thought. In my mind's eye, I retreated through the heavy glass doors of the police station affiliated with the college. Kay, the college's nurse practitioner, had explained that this person was likely a predator, other women would be at risk; I'd promised to file a police report. Yet during the two-hour wait to speak with a detective on duty, my nerve deserted me. I'd convinced myself that my hazy memory and the few facts I had would help no one. I left without filing a report.

"It's like I'm waist deep, walking upstream, trying to put one foot in front of the other. There are days when I can barely keep myself upright," she said.

While my lack of memory softened the blow, four months after my assault, I learned about Elizabeth's death and, like Denise, the iron-fisted grip of guilt and blame clung to me like a second skin made of lead.

"Absolving yourself from responsibility is difficult. It's hard to accept there was nothing you could have done to change what happened."

Denise understood the words, but agreeing with them was another hurdle. "I'm sorry," she said, "for what you went through."

"And for you," I said, recalling my deepest and darkest regret.

I hadn't slept in days, had somehow formalized my leave of absence, had packed God knows what. All I could think about was getting in the car and going home. Elizabeth Samms held the exterior door to the dorm as I trundled down the hall, a suitcase in each hand. She wore her signature blood-red beret with unflinching confidence.

"Looks like you're moving out," she said with a smile that faded to concern as she scanned my gaunt face.

"Just the weekend," I lied, regretting that I hadn't bothered with makeup to conceal the deep shadows beneath my eyes. "Warm weather stuff I'm not going to need," I said, gesturing to one of the suitcases. "You look nice," I said, changing the subject.

"Got to kick it up a notch when you go to Joe's. Don't really want to, but they'll kill me if I pull a no-show. Again," she added, rolling her eyes and stepping past me.

I froze. Then called out. "Elizabeth," I said.

She turned.

I managed three words. "You take care."

With a piteous, quizzical look, she offered a tentative wave of her hand. I watched her walk along the sloping curlicue path until she turned the corner and disappeared toward Back Bay.

Joe's was the same bar I'd been at. Her friends had lost track of her—thought she got bored, returned to campus. Someone thought they saw her entering her dormitory with a man, but all the person could say was that he didn't look like a student. Elizabeth was found dead in her dorm room the next day—she'd choked on her own vomit. The autopsy revealed Rohypnol, a potential sexual assault. Without witnesses or a DNA match, the case quickly became cold. Had I reported my assault, a notice would have been sent to students, the bar's ownership notified; safety measures taken. I will never stop wishing for another chance to relive that moment in the doorway. While I no longer took responsibility for what happened to me, I took all the responsibility for what happened to Elizabeth.

We stood in silence. Denise dragged on her cigarette. "It was the voice," she said finally. "I'll never forget it. I was in court when he entered his plea. When I heard him speak, I wasn't sure he was the one."

"Is that what the second lineup was all about?"

"Yeah, the lawyer's idea. He called it a 'voice parade,' made them read something. That time, I knew it wasn't him," she said, crushing her cigarette into small pieces with the toe of her boot. She looked up, her eyes rimmed red. "My life was wrecked, over. I wasn't going to destroy his."

I imagined her coming to in the alley, shivering, confused. The fully formed memory of the hours before jolting her into a terrified frenzy.

"Your life isn't over," I assured her.

A herculean well of strength surfaces and drives her home. She doesn't remember any of the forty minutes it takes. She bolts the door and draws the shades. In the shower, she scrubs until her skin is raw and the water runs cold.

When she said nothing, I said, "Your life is worth fighting for, Denise. And make no bones about it, it is a fight. The good news is that I know you can do it."

Days pass in a blur of panic; nothing she does makes her feel clean. Unable to leave the apartment unless she runs out of cigarettes or alcohol. Too ashamed to tell her family, her friends.

I asked the question I knew the answer to. Sadly, it was the same answer I'd have given. "Have you had any counseling?"

She shook her head.

"Don't you think it's time?" I asked, digging a business card from my hip pocket. Shame seeped like venom through my veins as I advised her to do what I'd never been able to. "Call my cell phone number and leave your contact information. There's a group. I'll set you up with them. They're wonderful—"

"I can't." She wrapped her arms around herself, looking at the ground. "I've never talked about it," she said, her voice a childlike staccato.

The bruises are long gone. Time does what they say it will and as the years slip past, the active mind begins to wriggle free. Yet, cruelly, the body remembers, delivering a wave of crushing panic the same time, year after year, almost to the day, lasting for weeks, months. Mechanics for managing are employed, and for the time being the anxiety is crammed back into its box.

"It's the only way forward," I said, as much to myself as to her.

The hypocrisy of my words delivered an intense wave of fatigue that leached into my bones. Tears covered her cheeks, her breath ragged heaves. My heart splintered, and the words sprung unbidden from my lips.

"How about we go together?"

Denise wiped her cheeks with the back of her sleeve, looked at the card in my outstretched hand, then looked away.

"Okay, here's the deal," I said, standing taller. "If you don't call me, I may have to come back here and beat up on snooty Jared." I swung my head toward the shop. "And escort you personally. It's entirely up to you. Fair warning, I tend to make a scene. So, what's it going to be?"

Her gaze shifted to the card, then she looked me in the eye. "I'd like that," she said.

"The part where I beat up Jared, or where we go together?"

"It'd be great if we could go together," she said, the corners of her mouth forming a crooked smile.

"It gets better," I said. "Your life is out there in some sort of holding pattern, just as it was the minute you stepped out of it." I looked up and pointed, tracing the lines of an imaginary airplane circling above. "It's right there, waiting for you to grab hold and take it back."

"I'll call," she said, taking my business card and stuffing it into the front pocket of her jeans.

* * *

I wound through the narrow streets of Newport and dialed DC. "Date over?" he asked.

"Your guy, Frankie, didn't rape her," I said.

"Are you sure?"

"No question. Your boxer might be our missing link in what appears to be a tragedy of errors. But, as someone smarter than me so rightly advised, we shouldn't put all our eggs in one bastard."

"I'll let you know when we find him."

"Leave that case file on my desk, will you?"

"The rape victim?"

"Yeah. I'm going to look into it when I get back from vacation."

I disconnected the call before he could ask why.

CHAPTER

27

I PULLED OVER AND fished through my bag for my emergency Xanax. I lay my head against the steering wheel and closed my eyes. Fifteen minutes later, I felt its magic. My heartbeat steadied and the nagging thoughts, like the tiny filaments of a dandelion released with a soft breath, drifted, as if on a rolling breeze. But there was something else, something new that materialized from the haze: the strength of the promise I'd made to Denise and to myself buoyed me. I put the car in gear and drove on.

Crisscrossing Newport, I made my way along the ten miles of the iconic southern tip of Aquidneck Island, of which Newport is a part. Locals took hairpin turns at breakneck speeds while tourists crawled along, rubbernecking to get a glimpse of a turret, a veranda, or a gated private drive belonging to the magnificent history that dots Newport's coast.

I turned into The Country Club. The setting was unassuming, the acceptable dress code was shabby chic, the car of choice, The Old Rust Bucket; the Parisienne was right at home.

John chatted with a young man at the bag drop who looked to be no older than fourteen. I pulled up and rolled down my window.

John smiled. "May we take your clubs, miss?"

I pointed to the rear of the car. John opened the tailgate and lifted my golf bag. "Holy cow. What on earth is in this thing?" John rummaged through the bag. "Uh oh, I think you're missing something."

"Impossible," I said.

"I don't see your third putter."

"Very funny." I stepped from the car. John eyed my legs and smiled.

He handed the young man a tip. "Luke, please park Miss Stuart's car."

"Yes, sir, Dr. Riordan. Will you be riding or walking today?"

"Riding, Luke. Thanks."

"Is he old enough to drive?" I whispered as Luke slid behind the wheel and fumbled with the manual seat adjustment.

"He is today," John said, as we strolled to the putting green.

John wore khaki shorts and a pale blue Polo shirt. I watched him putt. Without a visor or a hat, his hair seemed to impede his vision, yet one ball after the next found its way into the hole. John caught me staring. "What?" he asked.

"I'm developing my strategy for our match."

"I see."

"Here's the deal. I get two strokes a hole and six mulligans a side. And if I lose a ball, I don't have to take a stroke. It doesn't count as a lost ball."

"Why would it?" John feigned seriousness.

"My point exactly."

"Well, strokes should be based on handicap—"

"Handicap?" I said with mock incredulity.

"Right. How dare I suggest you have a handicap. Never mind. One stroke a hole and three mulligans a side," John countered.

"And your definition of a mulligan is?"

"A strict do-over. From the tee only. If you hate your shot for any reason, you can take another without penalty."

"Deal." I offered my hand.

We shook, and he leaned close and whispered, "I've been hustled, but, okay, deal."

"Losing is sometimes like winning." I held his gaze.

"Whatever the lady wants. Promise you'll be gentle."

We proceeded to the first tee box. John hit a spectacular drive and mine rolled into a shallow sand trap mid fairway.

"That's a shame," said John.

"The fairway and I aren't friends," I said as John pulled up next to the bunker. I grabbed my six-iron. "Don't stare. You're making me nervous." I put my head down and swung. The ball came to a stop about seventy-five yards short of the green. "See what I mean?"

He whistled. "If those are nerves, I'd hate to see what you can do when you're relaxed."

John's second shot landed in the deep grass behind the green and then he flubbed his chip. I pitched to the edge of the green then rolled a thirty-five-foot putt to within a few inches of the cup. "That's a five for a four," I said, scooping up my ball.

"I didn't concede that putt. You have just cost yourself a stroke," he said, dropping his putter and walking toward me across the green.

"Concede what? That was a gimme."

"A gimme?" John complained. "We did not negotiate gimmes."

"Did we need to?" I asked.

"If this is a match, yes. There are rules," John said, his argument losing steam.

"This is exactly why there are no doctors on the professional tour. I've never negotiated gimmes. A gimme is like a birthright, it's a given," I countered. John clasped his hands and looked up as if praying for divine intervention.

On the second fairway, I walked alongside the cart looking skyward as John identified the birds he knew and made up names for those he didn't. "Whaddayaknow. That's the Northern Plumb Bob," he said straight-faced, pointing. "Don't see many of those. Over there. Look. An Eastern Duffer. You see those all over the course."

From on high, the next six holes presented like a three-fingered hand resting atop the water. Long swaths of gently rolling kelly-green fairways with tufts of ornamental grasses swayed in the breeze, and a backdrop of lumbering ocean swells met my eye wherever I turned. I whistled at John's legs mid-backswing when I thought he might appreciate a compliment, and he advised putting in a direction not remotely close to the pin when he was all but sunk in the match.

We laughed and laughed and laughed, the world of cops and robbers and killers and con artists far, far away. After nine holes, the sky had clouded; a dank, chilly breeze rolled across the bay. I needed warmer clothing, and we were both hungry. Leo's in Jamestown made the most sense.

* * *

Twenty minutes later, we pulled up in front of the cottage. John rolled down his window.

"You better park and come in," I said. "This'll take a few minutes."

He smiled, turned off the engine, and followed me into the house.

"Help yourself. Beer is in the fridge."

I made my way upstairs, strangely delighted by the sound of the faint clinking of beer bottles and the satisfying pop as John opened them. I pulled on jeans and a thick cotton sweater. Strains of Van Morrison drifted up the stairs. I tamed the wilds of my hair, brushed my teeth, and dabbed on rosy lip gloss. On the landing, I stopped and watched as John danced around the kitchen, a beer in each hand.

As I approached, he set the beers on the island and took me by the hand. "Van the man," he said, dancing me into the living room. He crooned as he swung me back and forth, then spun me around. John felt warm and strong. He was spontaneous and giddy and it was contagious. We danced back into the kitchen singing along with Van about leaving the dark end of the street behind for the bright side of the road. We settled into stools at the kitchen island and I raised my beer.

"To a nice day," I said. "Thank you."

"To a nice day," he repeated. "Thank *you*."

John took the bottle from my hand and placed it on the counter. He caressed my cheeks, his warm fingers tracing the outline of my jaw and lower lip. He searched my eyes for a sign that told him to continue. I counseled myself that this was right, normal. Ever so slowly, he closed the gap between us. His lips met mine, then explored with gentle, prodding kisses that excited and terrified in equal measure. He wrapped his arms around me, and as he pulled me close, we both felt my phone buzz in my front hip pocket. A mounting panic smothered the words "normal" and "right" echoing in my head. And just as John whispered, "Don't answer it," I scooted off the stool and pulled out my phone.

"I've got to take this," I lied. Stepping outside, I declined the call and conducted a pretend conversation. When I returned, I said with feigned disappointment, "Work calls. I need to take a rain check." Before the words were out of my mouth, I regretted them.

"Wow. Okay. Sure," he said.

While the music continued to play, the room felt silent, airless. I wanted him to stay, to kiss me again. But I needed him to go.

"What's the rest of your week look like?" he asked.

"I can make some time."

"I'll call you. Maybe dinner?"

"I'd love that." My words hollow, unconvincing even to myself.

He took my hands in his. Thanked me for a lovely day. Then he was gone.

CHAPTER

28

I WEAVED THROUGH TOWN on foot until I reached Clara's dance studio. She'd been a former soloist with the American Ballet Theater. Twenty years earlier she'd left the bright lights for the quiet of Jamestown, where she opened a school and set about teaching little girls with clumsy slipper-clad feet to prance and plié.

I scrutinized the opaque storefront window, recalling the soft worn barre in my six-year-old hand and Clara setting the needle on a vinyl record that crackled through scratches before launching into a minuet. Then remembered that November, eight years earlier, its expected crisp winds, slate-colored seas, and early morning frost-covered lawns. The discussions with my parents at dinner began to include innocuous sentences that more frequently started or ended with "when you're back at school" or "back in Boston," as if I'd always had a three-month fall break. The reason I was home was never discussed. I soon realized it never would be.

When my apprehension about returning to school made sleep impossible, I'd go out for a late-night run that inevitably ended at Jamestown's deserted main drag. In front of Clara's, my reflection attempted to see beyond the mirrored surface of the plate-glass window. One night the school's wooden sign hung askew. I reattached the chain that had slipped from its s-hook and noticed the almost indecipherable script at the very bottom. It said: *self-defense.* I had all but forgotten about Clara's partner, Vi, a former captain with the NYPD. Her career ended when she'd been disabled by three bullets, still lodged in her body. When I first began ballet lessons, I'd seen glimpses of Vi, but as I stood in front of the dance studio, I realized I hadn't seen her in years.

There was no posted schedule or number to call; all I could remember was that whatever Vi did, it had been late at night. The following evening, I waited across the street under an overhang out of the rain. It was after eleven when the punch and grind of heavy metal music quieted and light streamed through the open door. I expected a handful of students to scatter onto the sidewalk, but none came. I crossed the street and stepped inside. The room was bathed in a peculiar amber glow that emanated from the back room. A figure appeared in the trajectory of light. Strapping a knapsack over her wide shoulders, Vi stiffened then turned as I approached. Her silvery eyes scanned my face; the shorn bristle of her salt-and-pepper hair sharpened the jut of her chin and nose.

"I need to learn how to take care of myself," I said. "I have eight weeks."

The answers to her unasked questions seemed to come to her during the long, uncomfortable silence as she looked me up and down. As if wordlessly, I'd shared a confidence, Vi nodded, then laid out her rules—committing to five nights each week, no Wednesdays, no Sundays, and no excuses. If I agreed, we could start the next night. She explained that my work ethic would be my payment. I balked, but Vi repeated her conditions with a take-it-or-leave-it tone of voice. I understood the subtext: somewhere along the way, someone had offered her a hand, and this was Vi's way to pay it forward. One day, I would do the same. I accepted.

"Eight o'clock," she said, then walked up Narragansett Avenue like she owned it. Her shadowy figure dwindled into a pinprick, then vanished.

The first night she brought me to my hands and knees again and again until finally, too exhausted and angry, I lay prone, unmoving.

"Rule number one, Andie," she said. "You've got to get back up."

She held out a hand, pulled me to my feet, and read the look on my face.

"That's right. Get mad. Take whatever is rolling around in your head and use it, give it purpose."

Vi taught me to defend against an assailant who was not only larger and heavier, but had the advantage of surprise. She explained how to free my mind in order to overcome fear and panic, and how to react instinctively. Within seconds of hesitating, she'd have me pinned.

"No thinking," she said, a crack of her palm into the mat. "Your body knows what to do."

At the end of class, she shared nothing more than a "next time" or "tomorrow," or sometimes just a simple nod, and then she was gone. At the end of eight weeks, she plodded along beside me. In silence, we walked shoulder to shoulder, heads down, bracing against the frigid January wind that kicked up off the water. And I wondered about her law enforcement career and if it had been worth it, given the risk and the injury that, no doubt, nearly took her life.

"Ask," she said, as if reading my thoughts.

"Would you do it again, even though, you know, you risked your life?"

She stopped, examined my face. "Again and again and again," she said. "Even for one life saved, for one family given closure. I made a silent promise to every victim I encountered that I'd find the bad guy, make him pay for his crimes, deliver justice."

By the time we reached the harbor, the wind had eased and wet clumps of snow fluttered around us as if angels flung handfuls of confetti from the heavens. Like tiny figures beneath the protective bubble of a snow globe, we stood in the absolute quiet of the swirling snow that crystalized the sodden branches of the magnificent blue spruce dominating the square and, with an artist's flourish, painted our little world white. As the magic unfolded, renewal seeped into my bones.

"There's one exception to the 'no thinking' rule," she said, her voice like smoked whiskey. "When it's either you or them, you can't forget the most powerful tool in the bag."

"And what's that?" I asked, in a whisper, afraid to break the spell.

"Your personal storm on steroids."

It sounded ominous, otherworldly, something I didn't possess.

"Imagine why," she said, her eyes finding mine. "Why you need to be on this earth until whatever God you believe in comes beckoning, and not one minute sooner. When you call, your resolve will answer—with a tsunami of purpose. Visualize it. Keep it close. Your determination to live is a force to be reckoned with and, if you ever need it, it will carry you through."

I knew I couldn't be "fixed" in eight weeks. Naively, I had hoped.

"You have the physical skills, but the rest of the journey, my friend, is the hardest part." She tapped her head. "Advanced self-defense is self-belief." Vi rested a hand against her heart. "You might struggle, slip. It happens. But remember what I told you that first day." She said it one word at a time: "You've got to get back up."

I met her eye and nodded.

"If that becomes impossible," she said, her voice drifting on the falling snow, "know that I'll be there, my hand outstretched to help you over that last hurdle."

She was a block away before I could utter a word, her shape a mere smudge that became one with darkness.

I hadn't seen Vi in years, but she'd told me the door would be open, her space available whenever I needed it. It was after nine when I walked across the unlit dance studio and into Vi's domain. The light on low, I gazed at the sparse selection of worn equipment, twenty years past its prime, fallen into disuse. I swept the dust from the top of the nineties boombox, then rifled through her music until I found an old classic rock cassette. I slotted it in and turned up the volume until it was as loud as a dogfight, then gloved up and circled the heavy bag.

Jab, jab. Jab, cross. Right roundhouse. Slip left. Cover.

Front hook. Back hook. Back roundhouse. Cover. Cover.

Vi's voice silenced the doubt chattering in my head: *This isn't about defense. Fight, damnit.*

Jab. Jab, cross. Slip left. Slip right. Uppercut. Left roundhouse.

There are only two choices, Andie, what's it going to be?

The shadows loomed, but Vi, circling, prodding and provoking, felt more powerful than anything darkness could deliver.

CHAPTER 29

I WOKE ON THE couch with a start, the familiar tingle of regret easing upward from some seemingly endless well of fear and doubt. As my surroundings came into focus, I saw the ugly remnants of my solo pity party on the cocktail table and felt the beginnings of a world-class hangover.

I trudged into the bathroom and turned on the shower, then washed down four ibuprofen, wiping the water that spilled down my chin with the back of my hand. As the bathroom mirror fogged, I surveyed my body for signs of past damage, looking for remnants of yellowed bruises. None had been visible for years, yet they haunted me like the ache of a phantom limb. In the shower, I let the hot water pelt my neck and shoulders until the tension eased, then scrubbed with hot soapy water until I felt human.

Installed at the kitchen table, I checked my phone. A missed call from DelCarmen and two from my mother. Mother telephoned every morning like clockwork, and it warmed me; inevitably, a pang of regret whispered in my ear and overwhelmed the warmth as I recalled the weekend that changed our relationship.

* * *

I returned to school for the winter term at the end of that January.

A few months later, I learned of Elizabeth's death and relapsed under the guilt and shame for having a part in it. I listened as Kay Matthews, the nurse practitioner, insisted it hadn't been my fault, but believed none of it. And as I sat in the armchair, blankly staring into the image of *Flaming June,* the painting became another stark reminder of my failure. In the weeks that followed, my emotional state spiraled and, finally, ready to tell her everything, I called my mother. I told her I needed to speak with her; it was important. "Dad is away on business," she'd said. "Come home, we'll have a girls' weekend."

I skipped my Friday afternoon classes and arrived at six to an empty house. I'd later learned she'd dined with clients. On Saturday morning, a note on the kitchen counter said she was attending an all-day business retreat, and we'd talk the next morning. But before she woke that Sunday, I was driving back to campus recalling none of the cars that passed, none of the exits taken, as I worked out on my own how to deal with the guilt that consumed me for my role in Elizabeth's tragic death, telling myself that our opportunity had come and gone, and feeling unable to forgive my mother. By the time I reached Boston, I'd decided to simply bury what had happened to me—never discuss or address the what and the why, never think of it again.

Of course, my resolution hadn't been thought through; it became a mistake my childish, stubborn nature hadn't allowed me to make right. Her patience seemed infinite, but my mother wasn't the faithful dog who, despite being repeatedly kicked, would forever greet me with unconditional love. In that moment, I swore to make amends and to do it soon. I dialed her back.

"Good morning, Mother," I said cheerfully.

"Your voice mail is full. Did you misplace your phone?"

"No. I'm on vacation."

"What does that have to do with the price of tea in China?" she asked.

Her oft-asked question made me smile. I answered with a version of my standard response. "I'm not sure I see the connection, either, Mother. Tea? China? Voice mail? Anywho, most wonderful Mother, how are you on this spectacular morning?"

She waited a beat. "Is everything all right?"

"Perfect," I said, sounding unconvincing, even to me. "Did you call about anything in particular?"

"Yes, I did. I called to let you know about the fundraising event. Remember? Marble House? I didn't think you'd have other plans, so I accepted for you and Peter, of course."

"Of course," I managed, less perky. "Who's sponsoring again?"

"Silver Oak Equity. You know, the Philbricks. Tragic about their daughter. I can't believe they haven't bowed out."

"Right. I mean, how awful. When is that again?"

"Three weeks from Sunday. You'll need a gown."

I had a closet full of them.

"I'll figure it out."

"Now, Andrea, this is important to me and to your father. God rest his soul."

Such drama.

"Yes, Mother. I'll be properly dressed and coiffed."

"You and Peter are representing the family," she reminded me. "Now," a dramatic pause, "I will lend you some family heirlooms if you promise that you won't, won't . . . act up."

Good Lord.

"As you wish, Mother."

"You need to promise."

"As God and Dad are my witnesses, I promise."

"Be specific."

For the love of Pete.

"I promise not to physically assault anyone in the presence of your high-society friends, thereby maintaining the dignity of our family name."

"I do love you." She sighed and clicked off before I could tell her that I loved her, too, even if she was completely nuts. And thankfully, she didn't ask about golf.

Work was a reliable distraction. I opened my notebook and atop the first blank page made a note: *Four days since Hope Philbrick's death.* It felt like four weeks had passed. I underlined the notation and dialed DelCarmen. He picked up and said, "For the record, I stopped by and called you last night."

That was the great thing about men; they didn't hold grudges. They said what needed to be said, or punched each other, and bang, done.

"Saw that." After returning from Clara's, I'd found ten years' worth of reports for sexual assault on my kitchen island. The note from DelCarmen told me to enjoy and chided me for my unlocked door. With no appetite for it, I'd watched Hitchcock's *Notorious*, swilled martinis with Ingrid Bergman, declined my calls, and prayed that Cary Grant would bust down my door, carry me off, and save me from myself.

"Where are we on Rodriguez?" I asked.

"Lybrand has her. Postmortem is scheduled for tomorrow afternoon. End of next week before we have preliminary results. Not expecting any surprises."

"Prints?"

"No prints on the flashlight. We have a shoeprint. A sneaker, men's size ten. Brand not yet identified. Rest of the forensics will take a couple weeks, but the shoeprint is a coup."

DC explained that there'd been nothing exceptional about the scene: Rosa had been the intended victim, her assailant knew her schedule and went after her. Squad members were still knocking on doors, but so far, no witnesses.

"Anything else?"

"Shorty confirmed the CCTV shows Jacob and his date entering Swing as he stated at about eight ten."

"That would clear him."

DC gave me a rundown of the rest. He'd sent Shorty back to Jamestown to check alibis and to get a list of household staff and the grounds crew who worked Tuesday, and was now cross-referencing it with anyone who may have worked the party on Saturday night.

"Did the Philbricks offer up their whereabouts?"

"They did. Mrs. P. was home all morning, she had a visit from her priest, and Mr. P. said he was at the office."

"Did anyone verify their statements?"

"Not yet. And we will, but not sure it's a priority."

"Why is that?"

"Besides the fact that neither are a suspect, our bartender, Frankie Moran, is looking better and better. I'll tell you all about it when I see you. We've got the wife at nine and he's coming in at nine thirty. Can you make it?"

"I'd love to, but my invisibility cloak is at the cleaners."

"Not necessary. O'Sullivan is at one of those interagency meetings and then taking a few personal days."

"My presence will not go unnoticed."

"I'll deal with it."

"I'll see you at nine."

CHAPTER

30

When I arrived at the detective division, DelCarmen was escorting a brunette, maybe all of five feet tall, into an interview room. Door closed, DC joined me in the hall and opened his notepad.

"Here's what we know. Moran admits leaving his bar and ducking out, but states he drove home and was there by about eleven or eleven fifteen."

"Did we check with security?" I asked.

"They clocked his arrival at two forty. Didn't monitor anyone leaving after nine. His coworker said he didn't see him after about ten. And his wife swears that on Saturday, he did not come home." DelCarmen handed over a folder containing two files and as we each held one half of the folder, he met my eye. "All yours," he said. I didn't understand. "All yours," he repeated.

Then I got it: I'd take the lead. DelCarmen's gesture seemed small since interviews were conducted in tag-team fashion, but because I'd always been the wingman, I recognized it for what it was: a step up.

I nodded, wondering what had prompted his decision, then ducked into an empty interview room and started with Mary Moran's medical file. She was thirty, more than ten years younger than her husband and, unless he was beating the crap out of her, relatively healthy. Mary Moran had a different explanation for her injuries: she was clumsy. She told the emergency room doctors and her own internist slightly different variations of the same story. She claimed to have fallen down a flight of stairs, off her bike, over toys scattered on the living room floor.

Over the past nine years he'd broken her nose and her jaw, fractured her cheekbone. She'd been hospitalized for a major depressive episode—which sounded like she'd had an epic nervous breakdown. Only twice had she filed charges, both times for spousal rape. Never had she followed through and prosecuted. Coming here today was big.

I did a quick read through of Frank Moran's file, then gathered both and headed into the hallway where I watched through the one-way glass. Mary Moran sat rigid as DC poured coffee; Shorty Long smiled and made small talk. She'd once been pretty. One could imagine an energetic girl untroubled by her diminutive stature, popular, and with an amiable smile. The Mary Moran who sat at the interview table was weary, guarded. Deep frown lines had replaced her smile, her doe-like brown eyes permanently ringed in a smoky bluish haze. Long gave her a reassuring pat on the shoulder, then left the room as I joined DC at the table.

I introduced myself, let her know we'd be taping the interview, asked her to state her name and address. "I'd like to begin with some background information, Mrs. Moran. Can you tell us about your relationship with your husband? It would be helpful if you started at the beginning."

She gave a resigned shrug. "We met at the gym. I was a senior in high school."

"At the gym where he trained?"

"Yeah."

"What about you, Mrs. Moran, what were you doing at the gym?"

"Gymnastics." Her eyes brightened, and I imagined her smile after nailing a vault or complicated tumbling routine. "All-State," she added.

"You need good balance for that."

Our eyes met.

"Ancient history, Detective." The look on her face told me she was sticking to her story of sudden clumsiness. "I got an eleven-year-old little girl who needs her mother." She took a deep breath and continued. "A few years later, I got pregnant, we got married. Things were going well. Frankie was training hard, winning. Then he flipped his motorcycle and tore his rotator cuff, shredded his bicep, and dislocated his shoulder. That was the beginning of the end. Whatever they gave him for pain didn't cut it. The doctor prescribed opioids that, eventually, he couldn't live without. Like many addicts, he did the ugliest things for more."

"Did he get help for his addiction?"

"I can't count the stints in rehab."

"And now?"

"For the sake of our kid, I hope he's kicked the opioids for good. He's a hotshot bartender at Rumpelstiltskin's in Newport and has the catering thing, so I guess that's an improvement, but I don't know."

I asked about their impending divorce. In another month, it would be final. Frankie's mother lived near Delray Beach in Florida, and Frankie planned to move in with her and open a gym in the area. He'd been back and forth scouting for a location, setting up the business.

"In the meantime, where does he live?"

"We still share the house, but it goes in spurts. I told him not to bother if he's high or drunk. On those nights, he stays with his sister or whoever he picks up. I don't want our daughter to see him like that."

"Running interference?"

She scowled. "It's been a necessary evil, Detective." She looked me in the eye. "But not today."

Those words gave me hope.

"And on the night of Saturday, September first, did he come home?"

"He didn't."

"How can you be certain?"

"When he gets home, he's got this nasty habit of slamming the front door. It shakes the whole house, wakes me up. Besides, he usually leaves some sort of crap near the couch, and there was nothing."

"Does he have any sort of regular schedule?"

She shook her head. "He shows up anywhere between ten and two or three in the morning."

"What time do you go to bed, Mrs. Moran?"

"Maybe ten or eleven. It depends."

"Do you take anything to help you sleep?"

"Not lately."

"Can you recall if there was a time when he came home and you didn't hear him?"

"I'm sure there must have been, Detective. But these days I don't know which Frankie is coming through that door and I've learned to be ready."

I asked about the bathroom, its proximity to her bedroom. Mary explained he showered at his sister's, and there was no need for him to go upstairs because of the half bath off the kitchen.

"Let's get back to Saturday. Frankie says he came home."

Mary Moran didn't blink. "Well, he's lying."

I watched for a shift in her body position, any hesitation, a dip or rise in her voice, anything that might indicate doubt or deceit on her part. I saw nothing.

"One last question, Mrs. Moran. Is Frankie capable of murder?"

She looked away, silent, somewhere else, involved with harsh memories. Finally, with a slow turn of her head and a stare that made me think she could see straight through to the inside of the back of my skull, she said, "When he drinks or is high, Frankie is capable of every imaginable evil."

DelCarmen closed his eyes and gave a slow nod, offering his blessing.

"Thank you, Mrs. Moran." I noted the date and time and the conclusion of the interview, then turned off the tape.

The mind-boggling jigsaw was taking shape, a picture emerging from the haze, but the word that nagged at me was "motive." Then I thought, *Where does a guy like Frankie Moran find the money to open a gym?*

CHAPTER

31

LONG STUCK HIS head into the interview room. "Frank Moran just called. He's got a conflict. Can be here at two. We good with that?"

"We are," said DelCarmen.

"Eddie is due in Jamestown from Block Island at eleven," I said. "We have plenty of time to have a look-see and be back for two."

* * *

When Eddie motored into the cove, DelCarmen and I were waiting. He greeted us with a lopsided smile. We'd been expected. Eddie opened an arm and invited us to do whatever we needed. The boat had been tidied. Trash removed, bunks made, the bathroom wiped. The galley's fridge contained nothing but neat rows of bottled water. Eddie invited us to look through his leather duffel. Its matching toiletry kit contained a razor, shaving cream, and cologne; some of his clothing was still wrapped in monogrammed tissue paper and affixed with a custom seal from a men's clothing store in Newport that wasn't known for bargains. An hour later, DC and I had a handful of bagged items, mostly papers and manuals from the cockpit, and one pacifier coated in dried saliva and fuzz.

We sat across from Eddie at the galley table. When DC held up the evidence bag with the pacifier, Eddie's face momentarily clouded, then cleared as if he just realized what he was seeing.

"Oh, geez. Where'd you find that?" he asked, looking from me to DelCarmen.

"In the back berth, behind the bunk."

"My buddy has a baby. He stopped by for a visit, put him down for a nap."

"Nice," DelCarmen said. "What's the kid's name?"

The cabin felt airless. "Patrick," he said, finally.

"Your buddy lives on Block Island full time?" DC asked.

"His parents have a cottage they rent out for the season and he's out there with his wife and kid for a few weeks doing odds and ends, you know, repairs. Sort of a vacation."

"Sounds like a good deal," I said.

Eddie nodded.

"You've no doubt heard about Rosa Rodriguez?" I asked.

He shook his head. "So terrible."

"As a matter of procedure, we'd like to know where you moored the boat," DC said.

"Bob's on The Block," said Eddie. He pulled a slip of paper from his wallet and pushed it across the table. The receipt was for the marina, dated and time stamped, noting the boat's arrival and departure.

"And your friend's name and his phone number?" I asked.

"He stopped over . . . only for a few minutes."

I thought about the nap and resisted a smile.

"That's okay," said DelCarmen.

Eddie scribbled the requested information on a slip of paper and handed it over.

"The last time we spoke, you mentioned a bartender had been dancing with Hope. The bartender who worked the bar next to the dance floor at the party also tends bar at Rumpelstiltskin's. His name is Frankie Moran. Do you know him?"

Eddie cocked his head. "I've been to that bar, of course, but you know, I uh . . . I don't think so."

I tapped my phone's home screen and googled Frankie, then showed Eddie his press photo.

"That's the guy who was dancing with Hope, but like I said, I don't recall seeing him before the party."

"Rumpelstiltskin's hosts private high-stakes card games. Is that where Jacob plays cards?"

Eddie shrugged. "I know nothing about that." Then he added, "But I suppose it's possible."

Beads of sweat formed on Eddie's upper lip, and the tips of his fingers tapped a nervous melody on his thigh.

"Easy enough for us to check," I said.

Eddie offered a tight smile.

"Anything you want to tell us before we head out?" DC asked.

Eddie considered the question, then shook his head. DelCarmen had Eddie sign for the items we'd removed and let him know we'd be in touch with more questions. Eddie watched us leave with a wide-eyed stare.

"Interesting," I said, as we made our way back to the car.

"Which part? The pacifier, Frankie Moran, or the contents of his overnight bag?"

"All of it. I mean, who shops for new clothes or bothers with cologne on an impromptu visit to see a buddy? And I expected an angry reaction when I showed him Frankie's picture—the guy who might have been the linchpin that set off this whole tragic event."

"There's no question," said DC, "that Eddie Field has more he doesn't want to tell us."

Intersections. Connections. Six degrees of separation anywhere else on the planet, but in Rhode Island that percentage was at best, half that. Eddie exhibited distinct tells of deception, and for the first time it occurred to me that I'd been wrong about Eddie Field. I saw the gambler with debt, the bartender with muscle, the brother with money, and the tendrils that stretched between them. I looked forward to meeting Frankie Moran.

CHAPTER

32

LIKE THE PRIESTHOOD is for the priest, fighting for the boxer is a calling. The boxer embodies his sport; the priest, his faith. There is no nine-to-five in boxing or say-you're-sorry-on-Sunday for the faithful. Boxers eat, sleep, and dream of nothing else. They obsess over their last bout and fantasize about the next. Toss in relentless pain, drugs, and alcohol, and the potential to slip into the shadows that exist in the deep recesses of the boxer's mind is frighteningly easy. Lashing out is the intuitive response to almost everything for a quick, efficient hurting machine.

Frankie Moran reclined with his legs stretched beneath the table, his hands clasped behind his neck and his eyes closed. When DC shut the door behind us, he startled, his eyes watery and blinking.

"Not getting much sleep?" DC asked.

"Nothing regular," he said with a small smile.

"Federal Hill" Frankie was five eleven, weighing in at 172 pounds, a former middleweight. His hero was Marvelous Marvin Hagler. Frankie, a troubled ten-year-old, sat wide-eyed with a hoard of inner-city kids at the local Boy's Club as Hagler danced around and threw punches into the air. He recounted the story of having his ass handed to him in a street fight with a local boxer. The next day, Hagler began training. A year later, he fought the same guy, this time in the ring, this time with a resounding win. He told the boys that if a fourteen-year-old school dropout could succeed, they, too, could be anything they wanted to be. Frankie wanted to be just like him.

Frankie Moran's press photo portrayed a rakishly handsome man, his nose a bit off center: the imperfection gave him some style. Today, he looked like a guy who had a black eye and white medical tape stretched across his swollen, broken nose. Still, with his curly black hair graying at the temples, piercing cornflower-blue eyes, and ruddy full lips, I understood the appeal.

That he had readily agreed to come to the station to give his statement, without counsel, gave me pause. Frankie didn't appear to be nervous, didn't fidget, and he looked us in the eye. I opened my notebook and cleared my throat.

"So, Frankie, you may or may not know, but Miss Philbrick died the night of her prenuptial party. We've asked you here because we need some help piecing together the events of Saturday night."

Frankie made no objections when I explained that the interview would be recorded. He sat forward, opened his hands, and said, "Yeah, whatever I can do."

I started with background questions: address, employment, routine, meals, his movements on the day in question up to his arrival at the venue. I was most curious about his involvement with a local bookie.

"You helped Carmine Figueroa collect debt," I said.

He shrugged. "At one point in my life, I had to do what I had to do."

"Because?"

"Because I needed the cash."

I rephrased and asked again. His response was unchanged. I moved on. Frankie took us through his station prep: he'd worked the outside bar, near the band, described cutting fruit, opening wine, inspecting glassware. Guests arrived just as it was getting dark; he recalled the waitstaff lighting the Tiki torches.

"Was there anything at all unusual about the evening?"

"Typical party. The crowd was on the young side. Hitting it hard."

"Hitting it hard?" I asked.

He tipped his head back, his thumb positioned above his mouth.

"So, how much of a good time were you having?"

"Open bars are magnets for big spenders. Like to buy everyone a drink, bar staff included," he joked.

"So, a pretty good time for a work shift." Frankie nodded, and I continued. "Tell me about your interaction with Miss Philbrick."

"The first time I saw her, she and her fiancé were having the first dance, you know, to open the dance floor."

"What time was that?"

"Maybe eight. Then the father came over to the bar and had me open a bottle of Champagne while the couple and her mother were going from table to table."

"She drank just one glass of Champagne?"

He shrugged. "I poured the Champagne, went to restock some ice. When I got back, all four glasses were empty. The mother, the father, and the couple were walking away."

"Then what happened?"

"Not sure what time, maybe an hour later, everyone's dancing, having a good time and uh . . ."

"Miss Philbrick," I supplied.

"Exactly. She's trying to get everyone on the dance floor."

"How'd she seem?"

"Drunk."

"Other than the Champagne, had you served her more alcohol?"

He held up his hands. "She had to have more to drink, but I didn't serve it to her."

"And then what?"

"She comes to the bar, grabs me by the hand, and pulls me onto the dance floor."

"You danced with her?"

"More like she was dancing with me. Kind of all over me. Then her fiancé comes over, and he's trying to be nice and cut in. And I thought, hallelujah. But she's not having any of that and tells him to buzz off."

"And?"

"And that's when it got ugly. She's hauling me off the dance floor, saying she wants me to see her boat. I told her, you know, I gotta get back to the bar. She's laughing, got me by the hand, pulling me toward the platform they got over there. I'm trying to beg off. Next thing I know someone taps me on the shoulder, I turn around, and wham. Fucking guy lands a right hook. Broke my fucking nose."

"I can see that," I said, feigning concern.

Frankie Moran's criminal career had begun with barroom brawls. Simple assault quickly escalated to aggravated assault, assault with a deadly weapon, then on to second-degree robbery, and finally, armed robbery.

"Then he grabs her by the hand, she's yelling at him, and finally he drags her off."

"When you say, 'drags her off,' what do you mean, exactly?"

Frankie shrugged. "He seemed really frustrated—"

"Frustrated? He'd just taken a swipe at you and broken your nose. And according to you he's 'dragging' his fiancé. You'd think he'd be angry."

"Yeah, I mean. I don't know. I guess he was. But I was watching her."

"Why were you watching her?"

"It was amusing, you know. She's like one of those little dogs." Frankie snapped his fingers. "The whaddya call it, a terrier, digging in her heels and I was thinking, you know, good luck with that. Poor bastard needed everything he had to get her to budge. Then she started laughing like she was messing with his head and off they went."

"Where'd they go?"

Frankie lifted both hands. "No idea. That's when I decided it was time for me to leave. Didn't even go back to the bar."

Early in Frankie's criminal spree, judges had been sympathetic, reducing charges, ordering community service, anger management classes, and rehab. Sympathy waned as his crimes increased in regularity and severity, resulting in frequent jail stints.

"Why not?"

"I had blood pouring from my nose, all over my shirt."

"What time did you leave?"

He shrugged. "It had to be around ten or a little after."

"We tried to find someone to verify the time you left the party," I said. "But no one seems to have seen you leave."

"I walked around the side of the house to the place they set up for parking."

"On your way to the car, did you see or hear Miss Philbrick and her fiancé? There was a garden with tall hedges nearby. Do you remember seeing the garden?" I asked.

"No. I got in my car and drove home."

"What time did you get home?"

"I don't know, sometime around eleven."

DC cleared his throat. "Here's the problem, Frankie. Your wife says you didn't come home on Saturday."

"She's wrong," he said, with Mary Moran's same calm conviction. If I hadn't known better, I'd say that both believed what they'd told us was the truth.

"Mary said you sometimes go to your sister's house. Did you go to your sister's house, Frankie?" DC prodded.

"I did not go to my sister's house or anywhere else. I went home." He looked from me to DelCarmen and said, "Mary is mistaken."

"Did you see a neighbor? Stop at a convenience store? Get gas? Anything at all to help establish the approximate time you arrived home, Frankie?" asked DC.

He picked at his bottom lip, then shook his head. "I didn't stop anywhere."

"That confuses me, Frankie," I said, "because you have a pretty good story. I think you could have explained what happened without repercussion. In fact, your boss told us that until that night you were a stellar employee. In your version of the events, it appears you were, for once, the victim. I almost feel sorry for you."

I wanted to see the Frankie Moran described in the police reports, the one who beat up his wife, the one who the sportscasters called vicious, the guy who picked fights with those who had the misfortune of crossing his path.

I looked over at DelCarmen. "What's that they say about 'almost,' DC?" DelCarmen shrugged, pretending he hadn't heard my spiel a hundred times. "Oh yeah," I said, returning my attention to Frankie. "Almost only counts when you're throwing horseshoes or hand grenades. Strike that. I don't feel sorry for you."

He closed his eyes. I drummed my pen on the table. "Why'd you run, Frankie? Why the panic? Based on some well-documented history here," I said, tapping on his file, "I'd say you're not the type to walk away from a guy that slugs you." His eyes found mine. "You know what I think, Frankie?"

"I'm dying to hear," he said.

"You would not back off. You'd bide your time, wait for an opening and take your shot."

He tapped an index finger on his lips. Finally, he said, "Look, Detective, I was a good fighter and a quick study. After he broke my nose, I knew I needed to remove myself from the situation."

It sounded like he was quoting an anger management checklist.

"Reading through your rap sheet, a theme emerged. Do you know what that is, Frankie?"

An angry look formed on his face.

"Not one of these incidents was started by the other guy. You were the aggressor, Frankie. For whatever demented reason, you went after these people. And now you want me to believe that some badass cleans your clock and you're, what, happy to let it go?"

"Yeah, I was pissed," he said, raising his voice. "Pissed at that woman for dragging me onto the dance floor. Pissed I got sucker punched. Pissed that she fucked up my job."

"And what happens when you get pissed?"

"This time," he said through gritted teeth, "I ran."

"Time after time, Frankie, you did not allow one of these guys, not one, to get the better of you. So now, you want us to believe that after boozing it up for hours, you had the good sense to leave?"

"It's been a long, hard lesson, Detective, but I've finally learned how to walk away."

I shook my head. "Not buying it."

Frankie cleared his throat. "You know what? I can't control what you believe." He gestured to the file on the table with his name written across the top. "And, yeah, I did all those fucking ugly things, and I paid for them. But I had nothing to do with that girl's death."

"And no one to verify your inordinate peace of mind and self-restraint?"

He paused, held up a finger, then smiled. "When I was going to the parking area, I went past the fire pit. The fiancé's brother was sitting there."

Frankie had my undivided attention. "He has two. What did he look like?" I asked.

"Tall. Skinny. Shiny suit. Tight at the ankle. By himself. Smoking."

DelCarmen raised an eyebrow. We had Jacob on CCTV at 8:10 PM in Newport. And just like that Frankie held up a hand grenade that recalibrated the balance at the table. It was time to pretend I knew things I didn't.

"Why are you calling him 'the brother'? The man you're describing is Jacob Field. He plays cards at Rumpelstiltskin's—a well-known host for high-stakes poker—where you're the full-time bartender. Surely you know him."

"I was introduced to him on Saturday when he came to the bar at the start of the night with the fiancé, who told me to take good care of his brother."

"Funnily enough, Eddie Field, or the 'fiancé' as you referred to him, said that he, too, isn't a stranger to your bar."

"The first time I saw either was on Saturday."

"Never at your bar?"

He shrugged, shifted in his seat.

"I mean, I could have seen the brother before, but you know, a lot of people come to my bar," he said.

"Fair enough," I said. "And can Jacob Field confirm he saw you?"

"No idea. Saw him sitting there. I walked past."

I asked again about knowing Jacob, giving him an out. "Think, Frankie. Rumpel's is a small place. Certainly, at the very least, you've met Jacob Field before? Easy enough for us to check."

"Like I said, it's busy, and the lighting's bad. Chances are good we've crossed paths, but I can't say for sure."

A definitive maybe. DelCarmen and I shared a look. I smiled at Frankie, waited for anything he might want to add, but he said nothing. DelCarmen crossed his right leg over his left. I moved on.

"What size shoe do you wear?"

"Size ten."

"Are you a runner?"

"More of a jogger."

I resisted a glance at DelCarmen.

"We're asking everyone who worked the event to provide us with a DNA swab. We'd like to clear you from our very long list."

Frankie shook his head. "No, thank you."

"Any reason why not?"

"Are you going to arrest me?"

I inclined my head toward DC.

"Look, Frankie, no," DC said. "We aren't going to arrest you. I understand how you feel, but truly, if you want us off your back, this'd be the way to do it."

Frankie smiled. "Ah, DNA. It's like a knife that cuts both ways. It could be my saving grace or what does me in. I decline to volunteer."

DC glanced at his watch. "How about we take a few minutes, get a cup of coffee?" he asked.

Frankie looked from me to DelCarmen and said, "That's real nice, but no thanks. I've got no idea what happened to that girl, and nothing more to say. If that should change, I'll be saying it with my attorney present."

Frankie Moran pulled a card embossed with the scales of justice from the front pocket of his jeans, and dropped it on the table. And with that, he stood and left the room.

CHAPTER

33

Within minutes, DelCarmen had the manager of Rumpelstiltskin's on the phone. He confirmed Jacob was a well-known client. We'd made some unexpected progress connecting a line between Frankie and Jacob, and it wasn't a leap for Eddie to complete the triangle. The most interesting fact was that Frankie was a runner and wore a size ten shoe, but questions remained unanswered. We opened our notebooks, and DC clicked his retractable pen.

"Who benefits?" I asked.

"Eddie," said DelCarmen. "And Jacob. If Hope isn't around to protest how it's spent, what prevents Eddie from helping his brother? And if Frankie is the hired gun, he gets paid for killing her."

"Theoretically, Eddie came into cash—was set to be financially comfortable—when they married."

"We took it for granted the relationship was solid. But if it was rocky, and he was about to sign an agreement that left him with what he brought to the marriage, there's your motive," said DC.

"The Fields are by no means on par with the Philbricks' wealth, but I doubt they're poor. Frankie Moran, however, is not well heeled. I bet opening a gym takes some capital."

DC had three years' worth of Eddie's financials on his desk. They'd pulled anything tied to his Social Security number. As far as a gym was concerned, Frankie would need cash for the lease—three months to a year in advance, and the buildout—unless he found a space that had already been a gym, then equipment. We'd get Long to look into it.

"Can we make a case to subpoena landline and cell phone records for all three?" I asked.

"I'll file the paperwork."

"Timing is pretty tight with Frankie moving south," I told him.

"We don't want him in the wind. I'll talk to O'Sullivan, see what he's willing to do with some extra support."

"Shorty reviewed the CCTV from Swing, but let's take a look at it again. All of it."

An old monitor with an even older VHS player was shoved into a corner of the detective division. DC slotted in a beat-up videotape. Frame by frame, we scrutinized the back and side views of anyone leaving, and finally, at 9:27 PM, there he was. Unlike the others who had left before him, Jacob turned and faced the camera as if he was going back inside. Instead, he looked up and smiled. I hit stop and rewound. After smiling for the camera, Jacob adjusted the collar of his suit jacket, turned, and walked away.

"Not subtle," said DC.

"Without side trips, that'd get him back to the party at about ten or a few minutes after. Keep it rolling."

When the time stamp read 11:58 PM, an unkempt Jacob, his shirt haphazardly tucked into his pants, his jacket slung over his arm, reentered the club. Time of death provided by the medical examiner was between midnight and two AM. It was damn close.

"If this is premeditated and Frankie is our killer, how do they get him there?" I asked. "His catering gig is part time, his shifts, sporadic."

"Maybe a plan was conceived once the catering company was confirmed, and he was on the schedule."

"Mrs. Philbrick had used the word 'new' when she mentioned the caterer. I assumed it was a caterer they'd never used, but maybe she meant 'replacement.' Let's find out when they were hired."

Last-minute made sense. Planning seemed minimal. And when Hope dragged Frankie onto the dance floor, it turned any plan they had sideways. This could explain why the events that followed were haphazard, sloppy.

"And then there's the punch," I continued. "It makes me think Eddie wasn't involved. But then, what's the motive for Frankie and Jacob? No payday without Eddie."

"What if," said DC, "Eddie had been involved, but at the last minute decided not to see it through? Then Eddie slugs Frankie, and maybe Eddie tells him the deal is off. It sets Frankie into a frenzy. He wants his money, he's banking on it. Frankie watches Eddie walk away, then finds Hope in the herb garden. Now it goes further sideways. He's got a penchant for rough sex. Hope doesn't resist because she's drugged, not thinking straight. This part is not premeditated."

"An opportunity presents itself, and he gets her over the cliff."

"Makes sense. He's more than capable," said DC.

"Then there's an urgency to get away from the house. He's not lying about being unnerved; he simply adjusted his story. But why did Frankie say he doesn't know Jacob?"

"A mistake. Easy enough for him to back pedal," said DC. "He'll say he was confused, thought we were asking if he knew the other brother sort of thing. Now let's talk the tough stuff—evidence."

I groaned. DC and I agreed it made little difference if we found Frankie's DNA, or fibers or what have you on Hope's body or clothing—they'd been in close proximity. However, if we found his blood, we'd establish they had further contact after he claimed to have left. Timing was problematic: it'd be weeks before we got results for blood that didn't belong to Hope from her dress.

"Let's say that Frankie offs Hope Philbrick. Why does he then go after Rosa Rodriguez?" I asked.

"Because she's a witness, or he thinks she's a witness. Is it possible she left the house?"

We had no reason to believe Frankie went back into the house. I'd never considered that she might have ventured out.

"Get Detective Long back out to the house to see if anyone on staff saw her leave," I said.

Rosa Rodriguez lived in the golden triangle—two blocks controlled by one of the toughest gangs in the city—and DelCarmen thought it impossible that she hadn't witnessed criminal activity and, consequently, become a liability. He was on the fence that her death might be connected.

"Do we have a make on that flashlight?" I asked.

DC flipped through his notebook. "It's a fancy one. Sold by some suburban company called Front Door for about a hundred and twenty bucks. Heavy sucker."

He dropped an eight by ten photo on the table.

"Not what we typically find on our local gang members," I said.

DC shrugged. "No doubt stolen."

"Do we have any CCTV?"

We had a camera on the corner of Atwells and Bradford, but it had been shot out three weeks earlier. DC had Long checking on video surveillance from the few surrounding businesses and the gas station on the corner.

"And what about Eddie?" DC asked.

"We'll need to have another discussion with him, but not until we know a little more. Have you looked at the financials?"

He shook his head.

"I'll take them. And Hope's computer?"

"Digital Evidence has it."

"Maid of honor?" I asked.

"She said Hope had been excited about the private ceremony, didn't think there'd been any coercion."

We had Eddie's time-stamped receipt from the dock, but we'd send someone down to the Block Island Ferry to pick up the surveillance video and question employees. It was a longshot, but certainly possible for Eddie to have taken the morning ferry to the mainland, committed the murder, and been back on Block Island by the afternoon.

"I'll give the friend from Block Island a call. If Eddie checks out, we can cross him off the Rodriguez list," I said. "And let's bring Jacob in, discuss his return to the party, find out what he has to say about seeing Frankie and any relationship they might have."

DC had the confident glint in his eye that came when information filled the blank spaces on the page and the path to the solution unfurled with clarity before him. I could see the happenstance of last-minute poor planning, but a crucial, unanswered question whirled: What was so fundamentally broken with Eddie and Hope's relationship that nothing less than her death would fix it?

CHAPTER

34

AT SIX O'CLOCK, I sat at the kitchen table with a pint of chicken fried rice and three years of bank statements for both savings and checking for Eddie Field and the same for his father—Eddie was his dad's power of attorney and listed as a co-owner on his accounts. Between them, they had five credit cards.

The transactions on Eddie's bank accounts were routine—utilities, rent, credit cards, student loans, car loan—but his credit card expenditures were dense, and you learn a lot about someone when they use their credit card for seemingly everything. Eddie was a committed coffee drinker and enjoyed a steady diet of Mexican food.

I'd reviewed two years of Eddie's accounts when I moved on to his father's. The elder Field didn't pay a mortgage or a car loan. He received two substantial pension checks and Social Security, paid estimated taxes, and transferred ten thousand each quarter to what appeared to be an investment account; his savings account was robust. The field card for his five-bedroom home on the East Side of Providence showed an assessed value close to a million, which meant its market value was significantly higher. The snapshot of his assets confirmed my suspicions that the Fields were financially comfortable.

By ten PM I'd reviewed two years of the senior Field's bank statements and found what I had expected, checks written to Jacob that amounted to roughly twenty thousand, supplementing either Jacob's drug or gambling habits or both. Still, the money to Jacob didn't negatively impact the bottom line nor was there anything that clarified motive.

I yawned, stood, and stretched, then moved from the table to an armchair. I eyed the untouched stack of incident reports for sexual assaults. Ten years' worth amounted to 504 of them. Deciding to switch things up, I swapped out the bank statements for the reports.

It was a long shot, but we needed to not only link the three men to each other, but the drug to one of them or at the very least, some tangential connection with any of the three to where the drug might have been procured. Drug-facilitated sexual assaults were typically initiated at bars. Frankie was a bartender. If any of the victims had been at a bar, it'd be identified in the report, and we'd issue a subpoena for employment history. There were two other well-known drinking establishments that catered to private card games and that might lead to Jacob and, of course, Eddie's credit cards revealed three bars he frequented and a slew of restaurants. The minutiae of the work ahead overwhelmed me. My phone chirped. It was a text from John. I smiled.

What r u up to?

I gave him a rundown.

Need some help?

I'm good.

I know how to read.

Sensitive information.

A GIF of a child tentatively petting a cat, looking up at an adult for her approval. Underneath it said: *I'm sensitive.*

Sure, I'd love the help, but I'd have to kill you if I let you read these. Your call.

Hope you have a great night.

I laughed, felt my cheeks redden.

I responded with a picture of a woman with plumes of smoke shooting from her ears, the top of her head ready to explode. Then added:

Sorry I bagged out on dinner the other night.

We all have jobs.

They can be inconvenient.

Or convenient if those troublesome houseguests The Jitters decide to drop in.

Hmm. You got that, huh?

Thought that might have been it.

Smart man.

I'm fluent in pig Latin and can decipher the ever-popular smoke signal.

Impressive!

Can't read minds.

I knew where he was going with this.

Mindreading is a tough skill.

Plenty of ways to tell me what you need.

No good at pig Latin. And if the embers creating the smoke ignite, and my house burns to the ground . . .

John sent another GIF. This one of a fireman hosing down a burning building.

Not on my watch.

Incorrect, stinging assumptions filled the void that silence created. The easier to navigate truth was what John asked for and deserved. But my wounds sparked unbidden flashing red lights that warned of potential danger. Since it was doubtful that all the king's horses and all the king's men could ever put Andie back together again, exposing my vulnerability seemed pointless. And the words I needed to say, the ones that explained my skittish behavior, refused to be spoken.

I filled the sadness with another glass of wine, then did what I did best, and got back to work. I set aside three hundred reports that were beyond the geographical cusp of my target area. By midnight, I had twenty-seven reports from four area townships for sexual assaults committed by someone known to the victim, and ten reports with victims who'd been drugged anonymously.

I was through five when I read a report filed by a woman from the Washington, DC, area. It was November, the Friday after Thanksgiving. She was renting for the week in Newport and the report made at the Newport PD, but the incident had taken place in Jamestown at the Voyager. The woman had joined friends. They waited for a table.

She knew people from the area, had chatted with several groups her friends didn't know; she struck up a conversation with a man. The woman told her friends she was going home, was too tipsy, and no longer felt like food, but was getting a ride and would pick up her car the next day. The woman was discovered passed out in her car in the parking lot of the Voyager after closing by one of the bartenders. The staff and her friends had been interviewed. No one, including the victim, could provide a description of the man she left with. The toxicology report, however, revealed Rohypnol. I set the report aside.

Losing steam, I did jumping jacks while Tom snoozed on the couch, then forced myself to tackle the few that remained. Of the final four reports, one piqued my interest. It was dated three years earlier. Filed in Jamestown, Steve O'Donnell had been the duty officer. Like the first, the victim had been from out of town—New York State—and renting during the last two weeks of August. Both incidents had taken place on a Friday night; she, too, had been at the Voyager, alone. In the summary statement, she explained that her friends hadn't shown, and she'd struck up a conversation with a man. The next thing she remembered was waking up in the driveway of her rental home, in her car. She'd been sexually assaulted. Steve had conducted a standard investigation, interviewing employees, her friends, patrons to the extent possible. The background check for the victim, however, was not favorable. Her ex-husband had filed a restraining order and several domestic abuse reports for stalking and emotional abuse. In the end, the victim was deemed unreliable. The only evidence to corroborate her statement was discovery of Rohypnol in her system. I sent a text to Steve and asked if we could meet to discuss the case.

On my notepad I wrote *Voyager*, *summer vacation*, *Thanksgiving week*, and *invitation-only celebration*, *perpetrator*, *drug dealer*. Summer and Thanksgiving were periods for transients or former residents who still had ties. The only common denominator between the Voyager and the party was either the staff or a guest. The Voyager's service staff made little sense in terms of the perpetrator: they wore uniforms and were easier to identify, but still, an employee could have supplied the drug. What made more sense was someone with ties to the area who returned for the holidays, the summer. I emailed DelCarmen. We had a guest list for the party that we could cross-reference against credit card receipts for the customers at the Voyager for the dates of both incidents. But if our guy was a predator and smart, he'd have paid with cash. All of it would be a tedious trip down the rabbit hole. We'd need to subpoena employment records. DelCarmen responded saying he'd get Long on it, first thing.

I started on the final year of Mr. Field's bank statements and all was routine until June of this year. By the end of August, steady withdrawals in various amounts of cash totaled an even $50,000. There'd been a few checks written to Jacob during the same period, and I wondered if they were now just giving him cash. It was two AM, and I started in on Eddie's January credit card statement. Still, I found no smoking gun among the single cups of coffee, the tacos, and the gas.

No, that wouldn't come until morning.

CHAPTER 35

THE CHECKS WERE written monthly beginning in January and made payable to an Amanda Fellowes. At first I guessed landlord, then roommate. I stopped guessing and typed her name into my search engine. The baby had been born the previous September and was a year old, conceived almost two years prior in December. Going back further, I found that Eddie and Amanda had been a couple, but in October of that year, Amanda posted her status as single. I reviewed my notes: Hope and Eddie had begun dating at roughly the same time.

Eddie's friend on Block Island provided the expected answers: he'd visited with his one-year-old son. Yes, he'd put the baby to sleep on the back bunk. After a friendly conversation about the ramifications of making false statements to a police officer, he told me what I needed to know.

DelCarmen visited Rumpelstiltskin's. According to the manager, Jacob Field was a well-known client and of course Frankie knew him. When DC produced a photo of Eddie, the manager said he wasn't a regular, but back in mid-June, Jacob had hosted a bachelor party for him. A dozen or so guys had gathered in the bar area for appetizers and drinks, and Frankie had been the bartender.

On a dreary, wet Friday morning, as the Philbricks buried their daughter, DelCarmen made the case for warrants and peripheral support to O'Sullivan, my vacation was cut short, and I rejoined the team. That first morning back, O'Sullivan called me into his office. He explained that my vacation had been covered, there were budgetary concerns and, as expected, cited my indiscretion, all of which made him less inclined to put himself out. But DelCarmen had asked.

"You get my drift?" O'Sullivan asked.

And I did. O'Sullivan trusted DelCarmen who trusted me, so he'd go with it. His unspoken parting words were: don't fuck it up. Regardless, I felt an unexpected boost as I left his office.

* * *

As we tugged, the tightly wound stitch loosened in tentative increments; connections and motive filled the empty gaps.

We believed the baby was the seed that sparked the motivation for Hope Philbrick's death. Before Hope became aware of his child, Eddie had convinced her to tie the knot in advance of the planned wedding, perhaps confident that it would be harder to leave him if they were already married when she learned he'd fathered a child. Then something disrupted that confidence. With the realization that there was no signed prenuptial agreement, a better solution had been hatched. Eddie's alibi was fuzzy: after leaving Hope in the herb garden, he'd wandered around for an unspecified amount of time, then met up with three friends at the poolside bar and drank excessively.

Although uninvited, Jacob and his date arrived at the party at six. By eight, they were seen entering a dance club in Newport. Two hours later, Jacob returned to the party alone, and failed to mention it when questioned. Jacob was picked up on CCTV returning to the club at 11:58 PM. The timing was tight, but still not impossible for him to have played some role in facilitating Hope's death. We considered him to be part of the motivation, the guy with massive gambling debt, the initiator.

Frankie was the muscle. The head chef and owner of the catering company the Philbricks initially hired had a heart attack and canceled in June. In a scramble to find a replacement, Eddie had recommended Cornerstone Catering, saying his brother's employer used them exclusively. A call to Cornerstone Catering and Altman Auto confirmed that no, in fact, Cornerstone Catering had never worked an event for Altman. I wondered if the catering company mishap was how it had all begun.

For the next two weeks, it was all hands on deck; every facet of our team worked around the clock. We'd been issued warrants for computers, cell phone records, and text messages. The Digital Evidence Unit recovered and reviewed deleted files, providing us with reams of data. DC and Long read email after tedious email. I read the text messages between Eddie and Amanda, which produced a clear picture of a rekindling of their relationship. Our tech team reviewed a massive data dump from cell towers in and around the areas our suspects worked and lived, to triangulate their phones. The night of Eddie's bachelor party seemed to be the starting point, but it had been the only night the three could be placed in the same location prior to the prenuptial event. In the months since, Frankie and Jacob's cell phones crossed paths three times when Jacob had been admitted to high-stakes poker at Rumpel's. He'd been seated in a private room with seven other players; two waitstaff ferried drinks. The bar had closed and Frankie long gone before the card game had ended in the wee hours of the morning.

The tendrils that I'd expected to stretch between, at the very least, Frankie and Jacob, failed to materialize. A break came when we identified four calls to Eddie's cell phone, all placed after midnight from the same burner phone, each call less than two minutes in duration.

The first call was placed the last week of June, and the last, three days before Hope's death. We traced the burner phone's purchase to a Walmart, three miles from Frankie Moran's home. Walmart held their surveillance video for sixty days and we were well beyond that and, of course, the phone had been purchased with cash. But burner phones needed to be activated by a third party call to a 1-800 number.

It took a subpoena to learn that the third-party phone belonged to Mary Moran. The burner had been activated at three in the morning and used for the first time the next night. The burner was switched off during the day, but after eleven at night we triangulated its location to the cell tower three blocks from Frankie Moran's home. We received a copy of a signed lease from Frankie's landlord in Florida and copies of emails confirming Frankie still owed the $30,000 balance for the up-front security. The landlord made it clear that if Frankie didn't pay soon, he'd lose his initial deposit and the space for his gym. Frankie's response confirmed he'd be sending what he owed within the next two weeks. We put a surveillance team on Frankie Moran.

Over the weekend, DelCarmen and I prepared for interviews. I returned home at midnight on Sunday to find Tom atop a mountain of reports and paperwork, glaring and thumping his tail. He followed me into the kitchen and I fed him some fresh tuna, massaged his ears. My absence and lack of attention forgiven, we retreated upstairs: me into the shower and Tom, and a handful of files, onto the bed.

* * *

Monday morning at nine, sixteen days after Hope Philbrick's death, we interviewed Amanda Fellowes. She was as tall as a man with the shoulders of a linebacker, and a look on her face that said: Come on. I dare you. Amanda explained that her relationship with Eddie had been over; she'd started a new relationship and so had he, but in transition, they shared an apartment. It had been a one-off thing, a weak moment. Lo-and-behold, she'd conceived. She hadn't thought Eddie was the child's father, but as the baby grew, the resemblance was uncanny. Still, it took a paternity test to convince Eddie. She'd asked for child support and money for the child's future education. In the end, she asked for an amount that far exceeded what Eddie had paid to date. If she didn't get a signed written agreement, she'd sue.

I presented her with a sheaf of papers that listed phone calls between her and Eddie over the past six months. Her expression remained unchanged as she scanned them. I started with the question I knew the answer to.

"Doesn't your boyfriend mind?" I asked.

"We don't live together."

"Yet you had lived together?"

"We had," she said, matter of fact.

"On Monday, September third, you spent the night with Eddie on Block Island. Given the current circumstances, does this mean you're reuniting?"

"He's got a right to see his son," she said.

"Are you reuniting as a couple, Miss Fellowes?"

"We aren't."

The transcripts of their text messages started businesslike, but soon softened, describing regrets and memories of better times and promises to be the parents they'd never had for their child. I dropped them in front of her and after she'd sifted through page after page, she bristled.

"What I do know is that the father of my child has decided to be a part of his son's life. The fact that Hope is gone has nothing to do with it."

"Can you explain how not even forty-eight hours after the death of his wife, he's with you?"

"It's just what happened."

"Why the secret and rushed marriage to Hope if you and he were reconciling?"

"I have no idea about any of that, and we're not reconciling. We're trying to figure out how to co-parent our child," she said.

"Hope's death and Eddie's subsequent inheritance simplifies that, wouldn't you say?"

Amanda stood, her amber eyes narrowed into slits and her shaggy golden mane standing on end like a dog's hackles. "I'm done here," she said.

We couldn't hold her, but we had a few parting shots to give her something to think about. Amanda glared as I outlined the definition and consequences for an individual found guilty as an accessory to murder and encouraged her to tell us what she knew. We advised her that the correspondence and phone calls between her and Eddie supported motive in our murder investigation and made other promises that were less than truthful. What we hadn't mentioned, however, was that we'd been granted a court-ordered wiretap on her phone, and on those belonging to Eddie and Jacob Field and Frankie and Mary Moran. Convinced she'd give us an earful, we pushed every button available.

CHAPTER 36

IN THE DAYS that followed, Eddie's three friends showed up, impeccably dressed, well-spoken and accompanied by their highly paid attorneys. After several hours in the hot seat, none budged from their original statements that provided an alibi for Eddie from eleven o'clock forward on the night of the prenuptial, leaving barely an hour unaccounted for. All three had also attended the bachelor night at Rumpelstiltskin's and testified under oath that when they left, well after midnight, Eddie had been engaged in a drunken heart-to-heart with his brother. Data from nearby cell towers told us it wasn't until two thirty in the morning that Eddie, Jacob, and Frankie left Rumpelstiltskin's.

When I arrived on Friday morning at eight, DelCarmen handed me an updated binder with an outline for the interview. Eddie's formerly sketchy alibi had been bolstered by his three friends. Jacob's was tight given the two-hour differential of Hope's time of death provided by the medical examiner. A search of the Morans' house turned up three pairs of size ten high-end running shoes, but none matched our print. Still, Frankie Moran had lied under oath about his whereabouts during the time of Hope Philbrick's death; he had no alibi and no foreseeable way to conjure one. We spent the next two hours reviewing, preparing our evidence in a manner that showed Eddie we had enough to convince a judge to indict, at the very least, Frankie Moran. And Frankie wasn't going to take one for the team. When faced with the prospect of a jail term, we expected that Eddie would accept a plea deal and give us the details DelCarmen and I had yet to uncover.

Eddie sat hunched next to his attorney looking rattled, his face wan. Weeks earlier, his muscular body stretched the seams of his clothing. Today, it looked like someone had let his air out: his shirt collar gaped at the neck, his pant hems dragged at his heels, and his bluster had been swapped with a meek countenance. After the standard background information, I started.

"Do you know why you're here?"

Eddie nodded.

"The interview is being taped, Mr. Field. Please speak up for the benefit of the recording."

"Yes," he said. "Because I didn't tell you about my son."

"We're here to find out what happened to your wife, Mr. Field, but if you want to start with the child, we can. You neglected to tell us about the baby, and when asked, lied about it. Why did you lie?"

"Because I didn't think the information was germane."

"You fathered a child with your former girlfriend. Concealed the child's existence from your fiancée, then convinced her to marry you in secret before the planned ceremony and before a prenuptial agreement was signed. Then your new bride died suspiciously, and we discover an unexplained, dangerous drug in her system that likely contributed to her death. Without the signed prenuptial agreement, you are the heir to her substantial estate. Is that not germane enough?"

"That's not how I see it."

I dropped the thick stack of paper in front of him listing the dates and times of phone calls and the transcripts of text messages from the past six months between he and Amanda. I gave him my *Reader's Digest* version of what he already knew: they'd spoken daily, sometimes several times a day. The tenor of the text messages had begun impersonal, but soon Amanda broke things off with her boyfriend and the tone became caring, tender.

"Less than forty-eight hours after Hope's death, you reunited with the mother of your child. In many respects, that's good, but—"

"I'd never held him."

"Not having held your son." I shook my head. "That must have been difficult, but you do understand how this looks?" Eddie met my eyes and dipped his head, conceding it looked bad, worse than bad. "I'd like to talk about the night of the prenuptial party. We've pieced together much of what took place, but really, Mr. Field, or may I call you Eddie?"

"That's fine," he said.

"Thank you, Eddie, we'd like it if you helped us with the details we don't have."

His mouth fell open in disbelief.

"You think I had something to do with this?"

"We believe that Hope's death was the result of a confluence of poor decisions, other people, their actions."

Eddie's attorney whispered in his ear.

"I had nothing to do with Hope's death," he said softly. "I loved her," he added.

"We know you loved her," I said, matching his tone. "But we also know that you were terrified you'd lose her when she found out about your son."

Eddie studied the table. "I was," he said.

"And all the while, your brother Jacob is badgering you. He reminds you that the people he owes money to are threatening his life. You may have sworn him off, but he's your brother, and you consider him your responsibility."

Tears soaked his face.

"And then there's Amanda." I tapped the stack of paper. "It's obvious what you both wanted for your son."

Eddie explained that from the time he was a child, his father had no time for anything except work, and when Eddie's mother left town—even with three boys between the ages of eleven and fifteen at home—his father became even more absent. All three handled their unsupervised teenage years differently. Jacob found gambling and drugs and flash; Jeffrey tried to be perfect, to not rock the boat, and Eddie, the eldest, was the fixer, the one who stepped up, tried to plug all the holes. Eventually, the only thing that mattered to the lone adult in the household was alcohol. Eddie wanted something better for his son.

"Given your son's inauspicious start, and your childhood, the pressure to do the right thing must have been epic. And under such strain, poor decisions were contemplated and maybe in the end it was an accident."

Eddie dropped his head into his hands, and his shoulders shook.

"Did all this begin at the bachelor party?"

"What? How did you . . ." He looked from me to DelCarmen. "That's right."

"And you met Frankie that night, even though you told us you first met him at the prenuptial party."

"I was so drunk. I'd forgotten."

"On the night of your bachelor party, the other guys had left, and now it's just you and Jacob and Frankie at the bar at Rumpelstiltskin's. What did you talk about?"

Eddie told Jacob about the money Amanda needed for the baby and how scared he was that Hope would find out and what he thought would happen if she did. Jacob described what debt collectors for bookies do when people don't pay what they owe.

"Jacob said we needed to figure out how to come up with the money for all of it."

"What did you figure out?" I asked.

"A few days later, I discussed it with Hope."

"You discussed what with Hope?"

"The money for Jacob, sort of a last ditch effort."

"Not about the baby?"

Eddie shook his head. They'd discussed the money for Jacob's gambling debt. Hope refused, insisting that once they started, it'd never end with Jacob, he'd be back for more.

"But Jacob kept at me. Finally, I agreed to try to help him, but he needed to be patient."

"Is that when you decided to get married secretly?" I asked.

"We'd been talking about that all along. Everything kind of fell into place."

"When you say, 'fell into place,' do you mean when the first caterer canceled and Cornerstone, the company that Frankie worked for, signed on?"

Eddie looked confused. "That had nothing to do with it."

He explained that the family home was unmortgaged. At first, his father had said no to a line of credit. A month ago, he still said no. Eddie could have done it without his blessing because he was on the deed and his father's power of attorney—but he hadn't wanted to.

"So instead you began withdrawing cash from your father's checking account, but you needed more than the fifty thousand you siphoned."

Eddie froze. "I was withdrawing money, but I didn't give it to anyone. A week ago, my father agreed to take a line of credit against the value of his home and it's in the works."

DelCarmen scribbled on my notepad.

"All put in place after the fact, after Hope's death, correct?"

Eddie nodded.

"You stood to inherit from Hope's estate well over what your brother and Amanda needed. So the line of credit is all well and good, but the horse, you know, had already left the barn. It hardly cuts it."

Eddie rambled on about how he'd finally convinced his father to help end Jacob hassling him for money. They'd decided to give Jacob a third of the value of the house now, as his inheritance. The trust would pay out the rest to Eddie and Jeffrey when their dad passed and a third of the remaining cash to Jacob. The trust was ironclad. Whether Jacob liked it or not, there wouldn't be any more.

"Ultimately, it's not going to help Jacob. He'll squander everything he's given, but we hope it'll help the rest of us," Eddie said.

"That's admirable, but again, it feels like a poor attempt to make up for a terrible mistake."

"I swear, I'm telling you the truth," he said.

Eddie's words felt flat. Last ditch. But this was the typical path of these arguments. They circled and circled then lost momentum as they skirted the drain. I dropped the transcript of the burner calls to his phone in front of him.

"You received four phone calls placed after midnight, one month apart beginning in June and the last, three nights before Hope's death. All from the same burner phone."

"That's what the money from my father's bank account was for," Eddie said, exasperated. "That guy threatened me. Said he'd tell Hope about my son if I didn't pay him fifty thousand. I told him I needed time to get it together."

"That guy? Eddie, these calls were between you and Frankie Moran."

"What? The bartender? I didn't know who it was or how he knew." Eddie stared off, remembering. "At Rumpelstiltskin's . . . serving us drinks when I told Jacob about the baby . . ." Eddie looked from me to DelCarmen. "I didn't put it together. But when I realized he had information that was never going away, I decided not to pay him. I still have the money."

"So, was Frankie getting greedy? He didn't think the agreed upon fee to deal with Hope was enough?"

"You mean getting paid to kill Hope? That's outrageous. There was no plan to kill Hope. He was blackmailing me."

Early in the investigation, we'd considered that Eddie had either reneged or never agreed to a plan to kill Hope. This version of events did explain a few things—the "punch" and some of what happened the night of the prenuptial—but not all of it. Of course, Eddie claimed ignorance, denied any knowledge. It was smart; his friends, as they already had, would testify he was intoxicated the night of the bachelor party. A savvy attorney could use this to argue reasonable doubt to beat a murder rap if it ever got that far. Until we had another shot at Frankie and Jacob, both of whom would be formally interviewed after the weekend, the veracity of his statement couldn't be confirmed.

Eddie maintained that the caller was unknown to him. He'd been told to place a gym bag with the cash inside a locker at the downtown YMCA, had been given a three-digit combination lock to the padlock. It wasn't much, but the Y had surveillance cameras and we could review the film. Still, we kept at him.

"When he called that last time, I told him to fuck off. I'd made up my mind to tell Hope about the baby. And I did. I told her the morning of the party."

"You see the problem with that, Eddie?" I said. "We've read her texts, emails, there's nothing in writing and, of course, we can't confirm that with her."

"It's true," Eddie said. "I told her that morning. Hope said she needed time to think things through. We'd get through the night then . . . uh, we'd talk about it. By then I was so frazzled, I'd have accepted whatever she decided to do. But that night when things got crazy, I thought we'd be okay."

"Because?"

"She got really drunk—"

"But she hadn't been drinking, Eddie, had she?"

"No. But that's what I thought. And all the flirting . . . She was trying to make me understand how much I'd hurt her. When we first started dating, we'd been at a party. This girl was hitting on me and I was being polite, too polite. Hope made her point, flirted with some other guy, drank more than she normally would have. I got the message, and we got through it."

"But that's not how this story ended," I said.

He shook his head. His lower lip trembled as he fought back tears.

"What happened to Hope, Eddie?"

He repeated his original story, the one his friends supported. He sat up straighter, leaned forward, provided all the physical tells of innocence. An hour later, his story remained unchanged. We told him we had enough to charge Frankie Moran with Hope's murder, and when that happened, Frankie wasn't going to spare Eddie.

It had been two hours and forty-five minutes since we'd begun. We took a break. Eddie and his attorney sat on a bench at the end of the hallway. Eddie shook his head in a manner that indicated a decision had been made, while his attorney pleaded in hushed tones.

Twenty minutes later, we reconvened at the interview table. DelCarmen and I had seen our fair share of witnesses who had finally made peace with the wisdom of Elvis: that the truth like the sun can be concealed, but neither are going away. We'd seen relief gush like joy; Eddie looked every bit the goddammed geyser.

As we completed our preliminaries for the recording, Detective Long rapped on the door. The look of distress on his face and the get-out-here-right-now flap of his hand said it wouldn't wait. DelCarmen and I followed Long to interview room number four.

We looked through the one-way glass and saw Mary Moran, a weary but set look on her face and a single sheet of folded paper on the table in front of her.

CHAPTER

37

I HELD A COPY of Mary Moran's cable bill.

"I didn't lie," she said, after I'd read it twice. "I didn't know."

The highlighted entry showed *Million Dollar Baby* rented on Saturday the first of September at 11:10 PM.

Incredulity and anger juddered like a train about to jump its track. I scrutinized Mary, who shrank beneath my stare, then met DC's eye.

"A word," I said. The glass pane rattled when I flung open the door. DC followed as I stomped off to the farthest interview room.

"This means nothing. By no means is it an alibi. *She* could have rented that film." I gesticulated wildly in the direction from where we'd come. "That burner was activated from her phone."

DC allowed me to pace and rant without interruption for a full five minutes. I insisted we get back in there, work it until she admitted giving her dirtbag husband a false alibi, threaten to charge her with obstruction of justice, accessory after the fact, and everything else we could throw at her. I wondered out loud what kind of money Frankie had promised or what dirt he had on her.

The cooler head spoke. "We need to rethink next steps and stick to our plan," DC said. "She's not going anywhere. We can bring her in at any time. If we don't do it right, it won't hold."

"You're suggesting we back off?"

"For the time being."

"And Eddie?"

"We've been at him for almost three hours," he said.

Horror echoed in my head; my temples throbbed. Worse, I knew he was right.

* * *

Lunch, a cop's euphemism for alcohol, delivered like a crack ambulance crew. After the first beer, the edges felt softer. The death rattle of defeat, less strident as a second dripped into my veins.

DelCarmen coaxed me out of my tree by focusing on the positive, detailing our progress and devising a concrete plan of next steps. My anger anesthetized and my attitude surgically reattached, we agreed that the next person we needed to speak with was Jacob Field.

My hand was up before anyone else could volunteer.

CHAPTER

38

I DROVE TO ALTMAN Auto and was told that Jacob was having lunch with clients then taking the rest of the afternoon off. My badge and bitchy demeanor encouraged the receptionist to tell me he was dining at The Black Pearl.

When I arrived, Jacob sat alone in the far corner of the upper deck and was flirting with a waitress deftly sidestepping her way around the table as she removed espresso cups and the remnants of lunch for three.

"May I?" I asked.

Jacob shrugged and offered a mischievous smile. "Drink?" he asked. "Sammy's G and T's are delightfully refreshing. It's the dash of muddled pineapple," he added in a stage whisper.

He was more than drunk, his pupils the size and color of a corroded penny. I reconfigured my face into a fake smile and ordered a Perrier.

"By all means," Jacob said, "ask away."

"Did this start as simple blackmail?"

"Oh, my." Jacob laughed. "Detective, I'm so rarely surprised. Blackmail?"

"We know about the demand made to Eddie on a burner we traced to Frankie Moran. Eddie admitted he was being blackmailed to keep the existence of his child from Hope."

Jacob put an index finger to his lips in thought, then his eyes brightened. "Ah, the bachelor party. Eddie had been all boo-hoo about his predicament. And Frankie," he said, shaking his head. "He'd been right there, wiping glasses. How much?"

"Fifty thousand."

"Short money." He sniffed in disappointment. "Could have asked for more."

"About the same time, there was the issue with the caterer and you recommended Cornerstone Catering to Eddie."

Jacob chuckled. "Eddie called me in a panic. I told him I'd see who Altman used. I was distracted, so when he called back, I gave him Cornerstone."

"Why Cornerstone?"

"First name that came to mind."

"Frankie Moran works part time for Cornerstone."

He shrugged, nonplussed.

"Your friend Frankie."

"Bartenders are a friend to one and all. Frankie's the bartender at Rumpel's, somewhat of a local celebrity. Makes a damn good drink."

"Did you meet him when Carmine needed to collect payment on your gambling debt, back in the day?"

He looked offended. "Carmine has never needed to send his minions."

We discussed Eddie's day-saving heroics, yet Jacob insisted that he and Carmine had an arrangement to repay his debt before his brother's magical bailout.

"Then what was the purpose of your return to Eddie and Hope's party on Saturday?" I asked, tenting my fingers.

"You're a smart lady."

Like a bone that had been chewed clean, my last iota of nice had been culled. I leaned forward, felt the menace in my eyes. "Enough with the fucking bullshit."

"Eddie and I had discussed a small, short-term loan."

"Your arrangement with Carmine wasn't solid?"

"Solid, but pricey. Thought I'd give it one last try, brother to brother. I figured later in the evening would be better, when all the hoopla died down."

"How did you get back to the party?"

"My boat, of course."

"What time was that?"

"Close to ten."

The waitress deposited our drinks and scurried away. I sipped my Perrier and looked out at the slice of harbor. The water looked black as crude oil; surly fishing trawlers heaved from the wake of the boats that passed as if mustering a sigh of patience.

"Is there a reason you neglected to mention this when we first spoke?"

"Maybe because nothing happened. Eddie and I didn't connect. Forgot all about it."

"You docked your boat, and then what?"

Jacob had gone to the fire pit, where Eddie usually enjoyed stargazing and a late-night cigar before turning in. He had two Arturo Fuente hundredth-anniversary cigars in his coat pocket for the occasion.

"Did he show?"

"Well, almost. I was sitting there, and I heard a *thwack,* then someone said, 'What the fuck, man. You broke my nose.'" Jacob shook his head. "Then Eddie told whoever it was to fuck off."

"I'm sure you realized that was your friend Frankie?"

"Frankie isn't a friend, he's the *bartender.*"

"But you know him, right?"

"Correct."

"Why would Frankie Moran tell us he didn't know you? That he hadn't laid eyes on you before Saturday night?"

"Who knows?" Jacob said, throwing his hands up. "Rumpelstiltskin's is one of the oldest drinking establishments on the East Coast, in business since the late seventeen hundreds. Management thinks it's still the Gilded Age. They don't approve of clients and staff mingling. When you enter those hallowed halls, it's like you've joined a grand game of dress-up, a one-act play on repeat. Everyone has their role, and they play it flawlessly."

"And, what? You're an heir to the Getty fortune?"

Jacob laughed. "Well, they've run out of those, but when you entertain and tip the way I do, close enough."

"What did you do when you heard the scuffle?"

"You've seen my brother." He lifted both arms and flexed his negligible biceps.

"Then what?"

Jacob made a childish, frowny face. "Then nothing. I sat there hoping Eddie would wander over, but he didn't."

I asked about Frankie, and he denied seeing him walk past.

"But I did see two other people."

Surprises were like minefields.

"Twenty minutes later, a kinder, gentler Hope showed up. I'd never seen her, shall we in sailor parlance say, three sheets to the wind. Such a different kitty cat. Toppled over the Adirondack next to mine. I caught her at the last minute, and she planted herself on my lap."

I cringed, understanding where this was going.

"So uncharacteristically friendly."

He filled the silence.

"What's that old Johnny Lee song?" Jacob crooned in a baritone about a woman looking for love in all the wrong places, then stopped, held my eye. "And she wasn't taking no for an answer. It was like she'd taken an extra helping of some good old Spanish Fly. What else could I do?"

I drummed my fingers on the table.

"Funny, I could only come up with one thing. I gave her what she wanted and then some."

"Have you no sense of decency?"

Jacob held up his thumb and forefinger. I choked back the Perrier.

"It's just sex. She wanted it. And as I like to say, I live to serve."

He continued to bait me while I imagined upending the table, wrapping my hands around his throat.

"And the mouth on her, shocking. But then we heard the old battle-ax calling her name, mommy dearest, on the hunt for her little she-devil."

Mrs. Philbrick's momentary hesitation in response to the question of her whereabouts flashed across my mind's eye.

"What happened when she arrived?"

"She took one look at that daughter of hers and the smoke came shooting out of her ears, like a mama coyote ready to eat her young. Then it started, the two of them hissing at each other, she's trying to grab Hope by the hand and Hope swiping back at her like the Siamese cat I knew she was."

The tiny amount of skin found under Hope's nails. The long scratch on Mrs. Philbrick's arm.

"And then what?"

"Are you kidding? I skedaddled."

We had him on tape at Swing. Nevertheless, I wrote down the harbor master's information. "I'll need a formal statement. First thing tomorrow."

"Your wish is my—"

Some internal switch sparked, then exploded. I pounded both hands on the wrought-iron table, rattling the glasses and sending the salt and pepper shakers skittering to the ground. In one swift lunge, I was in his face, gripping his knobby shoulders, holding him vicelike in his chair. "You're nothing but an opportunistic fucking punk, with no regard for anyone but yourself." I imagined grabbing him by his collar, pulling him to his feet, delivering a swift kick to the balls with the toe of my cowboy boot. But I wasn't defending myself, nor was I that kind of cop. "If you're fucking bullshitting me," I said, tightening my grip, "you'll regret it."

I released my hold, stepped back. Jacob smiled and straightened his shirt collar as if he hadn't a care in the world.

CHAPTER

39

Mrs. Philbrick had been in a physical altercation with her daughter at a time critically close to her death and had lied about it. That we'd missed her stung. Nevertheless, it put Penelope Philbrick at the top of the suspect list.

I'd had the sense that death was following her around—in our business, you meet those unfortunate souls—but now I suspected she was bringing it with her.

"This changes everything," DelCarmen said after I recounted the conversation.

"Despite the shoeprint, we need to revisit her alibi for the Rodriguez murder. We've been fooled before. Her husband's too, all of it. It feels like we're starting from scratch."

"Progress," DC said.

We agreed that DelCarmen would verify Preston Philbrick's alibi for Rosa Rodriguez's murder, and I would take a swing at Penelope. I called Bliss Manor, the home where her sister had lived and died, unexpectedly, four years earlier, and was told the director would be there until five and available to speak with me.

I cruised east along Route 195, rambled through the town of Barrington then Warren, and finally, into Bristol. I didn't know much about Bliss Manor, but I did know about Charles Bliss, the man memorialized in bronze with a hooked nose and plummy cheeks, his eyes blazing angrily on a plaque at our yacht club. His knowing stare had terrified me as a child.

To assuage my fears, my father told me about his wife, her tragic accident and how Mr. Bliss spared no expense to transform their home for her care. The story, told in my father's gentle, lesson-to-be-learned voice, was romantically carved and the significance of Bliss's unwavering dedication not lost to my ten-year-old heart and mind. In my teens, I learned that in the late eighteen hundreds he'd been the captain of a sailing clipper, enormously successful in the wool and tea trade, but it had been his philanthropy in his later years that earned him the scary plaque.

A half mile along Seaview Lane, a massive stone structure amid mature gardens with a sweeping view of the bay sprung into view. Laura Canning, the facility's director, waited on the veranda.

"Detective Andrea Stuart." I extended my hand. "A pleasure to meet you."

"The pleasure is mine," she said, as we shook. "Would you care to see the grounds? We can talk as we go."

We strolled along a wide footpath dotted with benches and shaded by ancient weeping willows, their long feathery tendrils rustling as they swayed in the breeze.

"Thank you for seeing me on such short notice," I said.

Laura nodded. "I've always hoped someone would ask about her death."

"So, you remember Bea Harrington?"

"I've been here for almost ten years. When she died, I'd been the assistant director. Since there are at most twenty residents, we know them all quite well."

We passed the tennis courts and stopped to watch a couple in their seventies volley a ball back and forth across the net.

"I hadn't expected this. I thought the house was for the infirm."

"Most people think that. Charles Bliss renovated the house for his wife after she became paraplegic, but it has been, how shall I say it, improved upon since then. When he died, he left the house and the property in trust for the creation of one of the first independent living facilities for anyone who wanted to age gracefully in place. There is a directive to ensure that the property will evolve along with 'new inventions,' as he put it, and 'with the needs and whims of its residents.'" Laura chuckled.

"By anyone, you mean anyone who can afford to pay for it?"

"Exactly. The trust pays for the upkeep of the property and the house."

There were ten two-bedroom apartments, all with beautiful finishes, patios, and views. The residents paid rent that included amenities such as full-time housekeeping, a fine-dining restaurant, a salon, a library, a gym, and a car service to transport residents wherever they wanted to go. We reached the entrance to a hiking trail. A large multicolored map displayed a series of named routes that crisscrossed through the woods.

"Seventy-five acres of wildlife preserve. All the trails are marked and maintained and wind down to a very pretty sandy beach."

"Impressive."

"Our residents are well cared for and have no objection to the price they pay. For the most part, they are here long-term."

The setting was magnificent. The long swath of Narragansett Bay glimmered in the sunshine. Jamestown appeared to be minutes away by water, but the drive was almost an hour across two bridges and along small roads clotted with traffic. We circled back toward the house. The afternoon sun cast a soft pinkish hue on its stone facade.

"And how long had Bea lived here?"

"About twenty-seven years—since she was eighteen."

"It doesn't seem like she was your typical resident?"

"She wasn't. Most have your normal age-related health concerns but, on the whole, they are independent. Bea had a severe form of cerebral palsy. She had great difficulty communicating and caring for herself."

Bliss Manor had aides and a registered nurse to administer medications, but didn't provide nursing or medical treatment. Accordingly, Bea's family had arranged for an independent nursing staff. Eventually, her care was delegated to trustees of the family estate.

"When her mother finally passed, the trustees were instructed to tell Mrs. Philbrick about her sister."

"That must have been a difficult time for Mrs. Philbrick."

Laura shook her head. "It wasn't an easy transition for either sister. Routine was a critical component for Bea's demeanor and Penelope mucked it up for a while, but eventually," Laura stopped, considering this, "eventually, it was a gift for both."

"What was Bea's routine like prior to her death?"

"Penelope came every day, at eight thirty or nine in the morning, relieving the overnight nurse. At the beginning, the on-duty nurse would stay, but with guidance from the private nursing staff, Penelope began to care for her sister. I don't want to say Bea was improving but, when the two were together, she was more even, softer, less inclined to have a seizure or bouts of frustration."

"Amazing," I said.

"My brothers are twins," Laura said. "Mirror-image twins—a lefty and a righty. One got the mother lode of good genes and the other, just the opposite. They were one person in two bodies, two halves of a whole who could never develop a rhythm for life independent of the other. I expect it was similar for Bea and Penelope, but because of the precarious nature of the pregnancy, Bea had been deprived of the necessary resources to develop normally. No one's fault, really. Penelope Philbrick is a tough bird, but there was something about her that made me think she felt responsible."

We reached the formal garden that flowed along curlicue paths of trimmed boxwood, segregating rose bushes from lavender topiaries. Laura gestured to our right. "That was the patio for her apartment."

The bluestone terrace wrapped the southwest corner of the house. A white pergola festooned with lush, heart-shaped English ivy gave shade to a table and chairs set beneath it. The three-tiered fountain at the patio's center sent crystals of water in endless, cascading circles.

"Quite something," I said.

"It was nice even before Mrs. Philbrick renovated it."

Penelope had added the fountain—which delighted Bea—then extended the patio so it could be accessed from the bedroom and the living room, and installed a ramp to help get Bea to the car more easily. Penelope's stonemasons made it look like it had always been there.

"And what happened the day Bea died?"

"Penelope arrived as she always did, eight or thereabouts. Sometime after eleven, maybe eleven twenty, she stood at the threshold to Bea's apartment, frantic, screaming that her sister was having a seizure. For a crazy few seconds, our receptionist thought we'd need to get help for Penelope as well. She stood at the door, stock-still, unable to form words, as if she, too, was having some sort of episode. Then she snapped out of it—as an aide described it—as if she'd been plugged back in."

"And then?"

"We're not a hospital, so we dialed 911. Within minutes, an emergency medical team stormed in. They hadn't been here five minutes before they took Bea away. She was pronounced dead at Newport Memorial."

"What killed her?"

"Officially, it was a sudden cardiac death," said Laura.

"A heart attack?"

"No. A heart attack is more of a plumbing problem, caused by a blockage. Sudden cardiac death can be caused by many things: overdose, renal failure, drowning, suffocation, and, of course, seizure."

"Seems straightforward."

"Maybe, but she hadn't had a seizure in almost two years."

"I see. Would an overdose of any or all her medications prompt a seizure?"

"Her meds were administered by the nurse at our dispensary and accounted for. So, no."

"Why do you think her death was suspicious?"

"Medically, I couldn't come up with a reason. She was fragile and had been taking high doses of numerous medications for many, many years, so I couldn't disagree that it might have been the culmination of her treatment. But there were two things that made me think otherwise."

That morning, Mr. Philbrick had arrived. He'd dropped off a book Penelope had left at home, something she'd been reading to Bea. He explained to the receptionist that Penelope had asked that he leave the book at the desk because she and her sister would be out for a stroll on the property and the door to the suite would be locked. Mrs. Philbrick would pick it up when she returned.

"Was that unusual?"

"I hadn't seen him in years, but no, I didn't consider it unusual. The units are private, so doors were routinely locked."

The staff had keys, but used them only in emergency situations. An aide saw the book on the desk, a slip of paper with Penelope's name taped to it. She hadn't known the book was to be picked up, so she attempted to deliver it. She knocked on the door, but no one answered. The aide looked for them in the garden, walked the grounds, but they were nowhere to be found.

"Maybe they went for a drive?"

Laura shook her head. "We would have known. Penelope needed help to get Bea from the wheelchair into her car."

We passed the reception desk and followed a wide hallway with dark wood floors and sconce lighting. At the end, we peeked in through the open doorway.

"This unit was already beautifully done," Laura said, "but when Mrs. Philbrick got involved, she hired a team of designers, craftsmen. The resident who took the apartment after Bea didn't change a thing."

Three women in navy blue monogrammed T-shirts and khaki trousers bustled about the apartment dusting furniture, plumping pillows, vacuuming, and swabbing the kitchen. It was magnificent. Floor-to-ceiling windows flanked the west- and south-facing patio; the French doors were open, and the sheer draperies billowed in the crisp breeze.

We retreated along the hallway and onto the front veranda.

"And the second thing?" I asked.

Laura eyed me carefully. "I hadn't known about the book and the aide unable to find Penelope and Bea until a few weeks later, and it bothered me. Then about a month after Bea died, we had a non-life-threating 911 call."

The same team responded. As they were leaving, Laura took one of the medics aside, inquired about the time they had attended to Bea. The medic was not new to the job, had more than twenty years' experience, and she swore that Bea had been dead well before they arrived.

"And when I further questioned her, she said that Mrs. Philbrick told them 'to get her the hell out of here.'"

Motive was the elusive common denominator.

"What do you think happened?"

Laura shook her head. "I can't begin to guess. But here's the kicker: an autopsy is not mandated when the death is deemed natural, which Bea's was. Typically, an extensive external exam is conducted and is usually sufficient. But whoever did the exam flagged it for a full autopsy. Two days later, when the medical examiner opened the locked body bag, they found the body of a man already autopsied and slated for cremation."

"Are you saying Bea had been cremated in his place?"

"Exactly."

"Was there an investigation?"

"They said there'd be one, but there was just finger-pointing and feeble explanations. A few months after her death, I inquired again." She shook her head. "Nothing but crickets."

CHAPTER 40

PENELOPE PHILBRICK'S ALIBI for the morning of Rosa's murder was her priest. I called the rectory at St. Matthew's, and Father Fred said he'd welcome a distraction from the mountain of paperwork on his desk.

I headed along East Main Road, thinking about what John had said at Hope Philbrick's autopsy. It was about the evidence of suffocation, that the dotted skin around the lips and eyes wouldn't develop if the victim didn't struggle. I considered the possibility that Bea Harrington had been given medication that calmed her, made her drowsy enough that she wouldn't have struggled. But that would indicate premeditation, and when I speculated why anyone would have wanted Bea Harrington—a harmless disabled woman—dead, nothing sprung to mind. The Harrington family trust had supported Bea's housing and care, and the ultimate beneficiary was indeed Penelope Philbrick, but her net worth prior to her inheritance was more than she could spend in three lifetimes. So it wasn't for the money. Pulling into St. Matthew's parking lot, I recalled Penelope's sailing debacle. I wondered if it had been an early indicator of her tenuous emotional state.

* * *

The oak door that welcomed congregants to St. Matthew's looked twelve feet high and at least six inches thick. Closing it against the sharp grate of light, its door sweep shivered along the stone floor, the click of its latch volleying from stained glass to stone until it receded by small increments of sound, reverberating like a somber bell, into the darkened nave.

I hadn't been inside a church in eight years and felt inconsequential beneath its towering, gabled ceiling. An urn of holy water sat against the back wall. Without thinking, I dipped two fingers into its center and made the sign of the cross. Stepping into the nearest pew, I lowered myself onto the prie-dieu, set my forehead against my clasped hands, and closed my eyes.

Wrapped in a blanket of darkness, the cool air was soothing, like a cold compress against a feverish forehead. I felt safe inside these stone walls, as if sheltered behind the old mahogany door of my childhood home—my barricade from the real or perceived missteps of my day. I'd slip into Dad's study, find him in his reading chair or at his desk. No doubt, he could read minds; he knew what troubled me with little explanation. He offered even-toned observations and gentle questions that were more like answers, aha moments, solutions that felt like my own. Relief chased away uncertainty when he helped me discover a glimmer of positive in a poor decision or from the disappointment of something tried and failed. I couldn't pray, but it felt necessary to thank Dad for knowing and saying the right words when I needed them most.

I breathed deeply and as the tension eased in my jaw and my shoulders settled, the lights of the cathedral snapped on. A man dressed in black, save for the small square of white cotton peeping from beneath his chin, bustled along the front of the altar. Catching sight of me in his peripheral vision, he turned and smiled.

"Oh, there you are," he called. "When you didn't turn up at the rectory, I thought I might find you here."

"Father Fred," was all I could manage as I jerked up, landing clumsily onto the pew. I gaped at him, blinking beneath the bright lights, as if I'd been caught wearing only a bath towel, doing something shameful. But he hadn't seemed to notice.

"The quiet. Lovely, isn't it?" he said, approaching. His soft brown eyes flecked with amber were crowned with the intuitive brows of a spaniel.

"Peaceful," I said, extending my hand. "Detective Andrea Stuart."

He took my hand in both of his, infusing it with warmth. I imagined dulcet tones, the flutter of an angel's wings. "A pleasure to meet you."

"It's beautiful, my first time here." Sadness swept over me, knowing the feeling would dissipate when I left the sanctuary these walls provided.

"Ah." He tilted his head to the side, considering me in a way that made me think he was channeling my dad and could read the doubts that tumbled endlessly in my mind. "You are always welcome here, my dear. Anytime you need some quiet—or maybe some assembly," he added, brightening.

"Thank you, Father."

His jaunty smile, round wire-rimmed glasses, and scrubbed, polished face gave him the look of a much younger man, one full of optimism, a man whose life had been filled with nothing but joy, kindness. But I knew that wasn't true. His lustrous inner peace was the result of his unquestioning faith, a shield more stalwart than any formidable door. I felt a twinge of jealousy.

"You mentioned questions regarding Penelope Philbrick?"

"Yes. I understand you visited with her the Tuesday morning after her daughter died."

"I did. We made plans to meet at eight. She is an early riser, as am I."

"Can you describe her demeanor?"

"As I like to say, bereavement is my business. She acted as I expected, given the loss of her daughter. Her housekeeper as well, I'm told."

"Yes, that's why I'm here. Her housekeeper's death is suspicious, and I—"

"Oh, heavens, that is a tragedy," Father Fred interrupted. "She'd been with Mrs. Philbrick for some time. Even before Hope was born." He retreated into his thoughts. An awkward moment passed as he seemed to be grappling with a memory.

"She was murdered that same Tuesday morning. We need to account for Mrs. Philbrick's whereabouts."

"I see. So terribly strange," he murmured, still elsewhere.

"Was there anything unusual about the visit? Something that came up in conversation that surprised you?"

"She was . . . well, there's no polite way to say it, she wasn't her regular put-together self."

"How so?"

"Mrs. Philbrick is particular about how she presents herself. Her clothes were mismatched, and her hair, always impeccable, was, well, a bit askew." He fluttered his hands around his head.

"Other than that?"

"We'd intended to discuss the service for Hope's funeral."

But Mrs. Philbrick hadn't been up to it. Father Fred hadn't found it unusual, given the circumstances. He told Penelope he'd prepare the service in a manner she would approve of and promised to call her on Thursday, when they'd review what he'd planned.

"And what time did you say you met Mrs. Philbrick?"

"We'd set the meeting for eight. I think I mentioned that. Poor dear, she was confused, thinking it was nine. All part of it. I waited, of course." He shook his head. "You see, the unexpected death of a child will extinguish the soul of the parent. And she had been so . . . so renewed. Yes, that's the right word. Joyous, even, while planning her daughter's wedding. It had been difficult losing her sister, and this seemed to help her. It brought happiness back into her life."

"So, she showed up at nine?" I asked.

"Yes, well, right about. I was returning emails on my phone." He paused, and with a mischievous look, answered my unasked question. "Yes, even the clergy have arrived in the twenty-first century. I was sending an email to Reverend Mitchell when I heard the car pull into the driveway and the garage door open. A few minutes later, she was tapping on my window. I remember seeing the time on my phone, eight fifty-five. I'm certain of it."

CHAPTER

41

I'D SPENT TWO hours the previous evening looking at the CCTV retrieved from two businesses in Rosa's neighborhood and was at it again. I yawned and decided to brew some coffee, hoping fresh eyes and caffeine would improve the results.

In the kitchen, I thought about DelCarmen, wondering, as I often did, what made him tick. So, I googled him. Not one hit. Then I googled his fallen partner, Sal DiMeglio. His obit mentioned an eight-year-old son, Angelo, and that Sal had been the coach of his son's baseball team, the Warwick Devil Dogs. The Dogs' web page showed a ragtag, scrappy bunch of boys who pulled off unlikely upsets, made wild comebacks—they should have been called the "Underdogs."

I continued scrolling and there was a photo of DelCarmen, his arm protectively around the shoulder of a mini Sal DiMeglio, as they stood at the center of the team. The caption beneath said he'd be stepping in as head coach. So many questions answered in that one sentence.

Every cop in the northeast attended the funeral. DelCarmen had eulogized his partner; someone behind me whispered that he and Sal had been friends since grade school. I hadn't realized it, but as I thought about it now, it had been his closing five words that were most telling: "I should have been there."

DelCarmen and I were opposites in terms of upbringing and education, but as I poured my coffee and settled back at the table, I understood that the regret that motivated us was scarily the same: we were both making amends for our self-perceived tragic decisions. I lived with the certainty that had I told Elizabeth what had happened to me, she'd be alive today, and DelCarmen believed that had he not taken that day off, Sal would be, too. I felt the tug of an ache and the strength of a bond.

* * *

Twenty-five blurry vehicles had driven past in both directions. Seven appeared to be SUVs, six might have been box trucks, and twelve were either midsize sedans or compact cars. Penelope drove a Lexus sedan.

Despite the last-minute alibi provided by Mary Moran, I couldn't exclude Frankie and his SUV from the mix. It was still dark between the estimated critical time of 5:00 to 6:30 AM. There were no working streetlights, and when I enlarged the feed, the clarity became worse. Beyond the general shape of each vehicle, there was little to distinguish them. I instructed the admin to deliver the original feed to Shirley in Digital Evidence to work some magic on the resolution.

DC telephoned at eight thirty. He agreed to get statements from Jacob and Father Fred. The big news was a strand of blond hair retrieved from the Rodriguez crime scene. Despite the inconsistency of Penelope Philbrick's statements and her lack of alibi for Tuesday morning, we decided we needed more evidence before bringing her in for a formal statement or requesting a hair sample. It would be premature and risky—they'd lawyer up and we'd lose access and momentum.

We continued to monitor Frankie's and Jacob's movements and those of Amanda Fellowes and Eddie Field. The reports and transcripts of text messages provided by our surveillance team gave us nothing new to go on. The analysis of bloodstains from Hope's dress was not yet in. I was meeting with Steve O'Donnell, my friend from the Jamestown PD, at eleven thirty at the Gannie to discuss the sexual assault incident reports. Detective Long was knee deep in the tedium of cross-referencing five years' worth of the Voyager's customers who'd paid with a credit card in the months leading up to the dates both victims had filed reports with guests from the Philbrick event. So far, no hits. We were treading water.

I scanned my notes, looking for other threads we could tie off.

"How'd you make out with Mr. Philbrick?" I asked.

"Refused to speak with me. We need to stop in at his Jamestown office. Unofficially. Are you in?"

"I'm in," I said, without hesitation.

"I understand that Mr. Philbrick is redecorating his office space," DC said.

"Didn't he say something about that being on hold?"

"His admin doesn't know that."

"We stop by unofficially to admire the decorating job. And then what? Isn't this is a bit much to verify an alibi?"

"Easier this way."

I didn't need to agree with his approach; I needed to trust.

"Meet me at the park and ride in an hour. Dress for success and find some appropriate wheels."

"Successful wheels?"

"Perfect."

* * *

I pulled into the park and ride in my mother's Mercedes sedan and waited in the passenger seat. DC slipped behind the wheel wearing beige silk trousers, a navy dress shirt and a cream-colored linen blazer.

"Nice," he said, admiring my fawn-colored suit and patent leather heels.

"Yeah, well, I clean up good. So, who are we today?"

"We are consultants, stagers," he said straight-faced. "Well, I am, and you are my assistant. Perkins and Reed have hired us to stage the new furnishings for his offices."

"Who the hell are Perkins and Reed?"

"Philbrick's interior designers."

"Right," I said.

Five minutes later, we pulled up to seventy-five Bay View Avenue. The four-story Victorian structure was a former single-family home, restored from the studs out and repurposed as an office. A tasteful sign indicated reserved parking for guests of Silver Oak Equity was in the rear; DC parked out front. We strode up the stairs onto a lovely mahogany porch. Its ceiling, painted robin's-egg blue, mimicked the unseen sky. A large packing box sat off to the right with a paper taped to its top that fluttered in the breeze. DelCarmen held the door. The waiting area had soft leather chairs and an antique cherry table with detailed turned legs and held various trade magazines for the investment world. Warren Buffett smiled out from the cover of *Investors Weekly.*

A tall woman wearing a boxy ensemble in plaid stood behind the reception desk. She wore her lacquered auburn hair in a tight bun at the nape, and a generous coat of crimson colored her lips. She peered at us over thick-framed reading glasses. The bronze nameplate read *Ms. Sylvia Proctor.*

"May I help you?" Ms. Proctor asked.

"I am Philip Delman, and this is my assistant, Susan. We're here to see Mr. Philbrick." DelCarmen smiled and glanced at his watch.

"I'm afraid Mr. Philbrick isn't here today." Ms. Proctor pursed her lips.

"We had an appointment to tour the space," he said with a subtle undertone of Connecticut prep school.

"Are you certain?" Sylvia furrowed her brow as she sat and opened a leather-bound appointment book.

"Yes. So we can provide suggestions for the upcoming modifications."

She pushed the reading glasses firmly on the bridge of her nose and flipped the pages, then shook her head. Sylvia turned to the computer screen and with a few clicks of the mouse asked, "Are you with Perkins and Reed?"

"No. Well, yes. We work with them. They furnish and we stage," he said impatiently.

"I see. Perhaps you were supposed to tour the Back Bay office today. With whom did you make this appointment?" She eyed us more carefully.

DelCarmen ignored her question. "Susan, is that possible? We discussed the Boston office space, but it was my understanding that we wanted to start with the smaller facility."

I opened my satchel, retrieved my personal datebook. "No, it's very clear."

I held up the appointment book for DC and pointed. The entry read: *Call Vet. Schedule appointment for Tom's rabies and distemper shots.*

"Quite so," DC said.

"This is so unlike Mr. Philbrick but given the circumstances, it's not unexpected. I'm terribly sorry."

"The circumstances?" DC asked.

"Mr. Philbrick's daughter died accidentally a few weeks ago. It's been a bit of a mess."

"How tragic. I'm surprised to hear he's working at all," I said.

Sylvia shook her head, her eyes bright with tears. "He said that keeping busy was therapeutic."

"Perhaps we should reschedule, Miss, Miss . . ." DelCarmen's voice trailed off.

"Please call me Sylvia."

"Yes, Sylvia," DC cooed, "a wonderfully melodious name. Perhaps you should see if he's on his way?"

Sylvia's cheeks colored. She looked at her watch and shook her head. "He's in an executive board meeting."

How did DelCarmen know these things?

"Is it best if we make an appointment with you?"

"Yes, that's best." Sylvia flipped through the datebook.

"How about tomorrow at three? Mr. Philbrick works from this office Tuesdays and Fridays. Of course, I'll need to check if he plans to come in tomorrow."

DelCarmen looked over my shoulder as I thumbed through my datebook. "No. Impossible. You don't have an opening on either a Tuesday or a Friday until five weeks from tomorrow. You're in Dubai for ten days and then off to LA." I flipped the pages. "How does November tenth sound? That's a Tuesday. Does three o'clock work?"

"This is going to delay things." DC sighed. "Well, it can't be helped. Set aside a half hour for the tour. We can discuss our vision for the space at some later date."

"I'd be happy to give you a tour of the office if that helps. What exactly is it that you do?" Sylvia asked, coming around to the front of the desk.

DC didn't miss a beat. "Our mission is to create positive energy in work environments. Energy that can be focused, directed. With simple adjustments to the placement of furniture, we can achieve different goals—creating advantages in power meetings or boosting employee productivity."

"How fascinating." Sylvia batted her eyelashes.

DC arched an eyebrow and inched closer. "May I?" he asked, moving in for the kill.

Before Sylvia could utter a word, he loosened a strand from her tightly pinned chignon and smoothed it, covering her ear, softening her jaw line. He stepped back and admired his handiwork, then wagged a finger, holding Sylvia's gaze. "This is what I do," he said. "I find the one detail that tips the scales."

Sylvia's features relaxed, newly infused with confidence. I stood back and observed in amazement. DC had missed his calling.

"Shall we?" he asked.

"What would you like to see first?" Sylvia asked.

"Let's start at the top and make our way down," DC suggested, motioning toward the elevator.

When the doors opened, I looked at DC and Sylvia, doing my best to appear distressed, and said, "I'll join you in a few minutes. I need to use the ladies' room."

"Oh, sure. Second on the right." Sylvia gestured down the hall.

DC peppered her with questions as they stepped into the elevator; she hung on his every word. The doors snapped shut, and I went straight to the desk. A slight wiggle of the mouse brought the screen to life. Her email was minimized and with one click, it opened. I scrolled backward to the Tuesday in question. An email from Preston had been sent to her at 9:15 AM. Short and sweet, it read:

Sylvia, I'll be working from home. Please reschedule my lunch appointment to same time next week and offer my apologies. Preston.

I forwarded the message to DC's private email address and deleted it in the sent mail file. I retrieved the datebook and headed to the copier. Piece of cake.

I skimmed through the datebook to get a sense of appointments, his basic schedule. When I reached the third Friday in September, it read: *Prescriptions.* And beneath: *Confirm menus and beverages with P.P. Update changes with dispatch.* There were notations about "real" fresh- squeezed orange juice, the name of a bourbon. The first Monday in October read: *Helicopter transport 7:00 PM. Depart OQU 8:00 PM. arrive CDG 8:00 AM.* Philbrick was being picked up by helicopter at his home, flying out of Quonset on his jet, and landing the next morning at Charles de Gaulle in Paris. The dates that followed for months on end were blank. Another personal assistant handled his overseas schedule. Returning to the Friday before the prenuptial event, I copied the pages from that day forward. The copy machine went quiet when I reached Monday. The display read:

Insert paper. Press reset.

Reams of paper lined the top shelves. Four minutes had passed. I tore open a package and filled the tray. The copier cycled and spat out a single piece of paper. Returning the datebook to the copier's flatbed, I pressed resume. Crunching and buzzing announced a more serious problem. The display flashed the two most dreaded words in copier language: "paper jam."

I drummed the help button.

Paper is jammed. Open scanner unit and remove paper. Press reset.

Nothing was labeled, nothing was obvious. I fiddled with parts of the machine that might have been the scanner, but weren't. Despite having the email, I needed to clear the error message on the copier's display. Seven minutes. I started to sweat.

I turned off the copier, peered down the feeder tray. Spying the offending jammed paper, I grabbed hold and pulled, easing the roller forward. Confidence and the clock ticking in my head encouraged me to give it more muscle; half the sheet tore free. A bead of sweat trickled down my nose. I started the copier, hoping it'd spit out the rest of the paper. The words "paper jam" blinked furiously. Nine minutes. I was running out of time.

Paper is jammed. Open scanner unit and remove paper. Press reset.

I reexamined my electronic nemesis. Copier on top. Paper feeder. The middle portion should be the scanner. Patting down the perimeter as if it were a suspect, my hand slid over a ribbed button. It didn't push in, but when I jammed my thumb against it, it moved forward and the scanner unit unlatched. I lifted the top and removed the remaining paper.

I rolled my eyes and stuffed the paper in my satchel as the elevator hummed and the display showed it was descending. I flung myself onto a nearby chair, pinched my cheeks, and pressed a hand to my forehead. The doors opened and out stepped Sylvia, who scanned the room and eyed me suspiciously. DelCarmen followed behind her, still in character.

"Susan, where have you been?" DelCarmen asked, like a parent whose child had missed curfew.

Fanning myself, I pointed toward the ladies' room. "I don't know what came over me. All of a sudden, I didn't feel well."

"Can I bring you some water?" Sylvia asked.

"Thank you, but it'd be best if I got some fresh air," I said.

DelCarmen said his thanks and whisked me through the door, down the stairs, and shoveled me into the passenger seat of the car.

"Nice job, Mr. Delman," I said, as he slid in next to me.

"So, what did you find?"

"An email from Preston to Sylvia saying he wasn't coming in. I forwarded it to you." I handed over the paper. "The datebook indicates she canceled his lunch appointment for Tuesday. Anything interesting upstairs?"

DelCarmen described an elaborate setup, but didn't think anyone except Philbrick conducted business there. There was an office he clearly worked from, then the mysterious third and fourth floors. Sylvia didn't have the elevator code or keys and had never been up there and said the construction had taken at least a year, eight or ten years back.

"A private townhouse-style apartment?"

DC nodded. "That's my guess."

"You know, I don't think the Philbricks are an actual couple. The night Hope died, he said something about Rosa going to 'my wife's bedroom.' It made me think they don't sleep together."

"And so?" asked DC. "Countless married couples don't sleep together. He's got a home in Boston, spends half the year in Paris. Not many nights under the same roof. Probably has someone on the side. Marriages of convenience, the scenarios are endless."

The discovery of Preston Philbrick's apartment and a potential extramarital relationship clarified Preston's silence. We agreed to have a quiet word with Preston regarding his whereabouts on Tuesday morning, then contact his partner to verify his alibi.

"Exactly. Another logistic headache," DelCarmen said. "Besides, what's his motive? Because he and his wife aren't a 'real' couple? Even if he hated her, why would he kill their daughter and their housekeeper? It would make more sense if he'd simply killed his wife, right?"

"Right," I agreed.

"He considers his daughter's death an accident and doesn't feel compelled to answer our questions, doesn't want us involved in their personal drama that has nothing to do with her death," said DelCarmen.

"Understood. For the time being, we tread softly."

My phone buzzed. When I opened the email from Shirley, our tech wizard at Digital Evidence, she explained that the image was captured across five feet of sidewalk and another ten feet of roadway from a camera meant to photograph patrons entering a convenience store. It showed the left profile of a driver from a slight downward angle, a swoop of bright blond hair across the cheek.

I held the phone out for DelCarmen to see. He nodded and said, "When and if we need to, we'll have that quiet talk. In the meantime, we need to understand what possible motive Penelope Philbrick had to murder her sister and her daughter."

I'd first believed Eddie had been the source of the Rohypnol, then Frankie. My confidence that it was either waffled. Even though the evidence against Penelope Philbrick was mounting, she wasn't the source, either. I drove off imagining the elusive, yet integral missing pieces we still chased. Penelope's motive might well be a byproduct of her tenuous mental health, and therefore, not logical or compelling. It was the drug, I knew. And when I found its source, I'd know everything.

CHAPTER 42

I SAT IN THE back of the Narragansett Café. A wedge of sunlight and the intermittent thump of the beat-up wooden door signaled the to-and-fro of patrons. At eleven thirty, Steve O'Donnell strode through the half-empty bar with less hair and more gut than I remembered, looking older than the forty years I guessed he was approaching. The phrase *fat and happy* sprang to mind. I stood and waved him over.

I tried to air-hug, but he was having none of that. He wrapped me in his bulky arms, pulled me to his chest, and planted a big wet kiss on my cheek. He stepped back and said, "Andie, you look terrific! You working out or what?"

"Running," I said, smiling.

We ordered beer and something to pick on, and while we waited, Steve and I reminisced.

"You were a real pain in the foot for a big brother, and you aren't even my big brother," I said.

"Someone had to keep an eye on you two."

"Calling my parents was a bit much, don't you think?"

"Hey, I told my dad about Kate. It would have been hypocritical of me to rat out her and not you. Besides, neither of you dared to do any of that stuff anymore, right?"

"You got that right."

"I think you should thank me for keeping you on the straight and narrow."

"Thank you for scaring me out of underage drinking. As a result, I've taken to adult binge drinking," I teased.

The waitress dropped two beers and a plate of nachos on the table. When she moved away, he raised his eyes to meet mine. I handed him the first report.

"Five years ago, a woman from the DC area was renting for the week in Newport. She was found in her car in the Voyager's parking lot at two in the morning. It was filed in Newport. I've spoken to them, but wondered if you had any further insight."

He gave it a quick read. "As you may or may not know, we don't share. So, yeah, Newport contacted us. They were looking for local knowledge, other incidents. If I recall correctly, it had been the bartender—the one that's been there for years—who found her."

"She'd been there to have dinner with friends, they'd been waiting for a table. And she just leaves?"

"Wasn't that the Friday after Thanksgiving?"

I checked the date and nodded.

The Voyager was typically jammed that weekend. The wait could be hours. Steve interviewed her friends—three of them—who described her as a free spirit; her leaving hadn't been out of character. When she told them she was getting a ride home, they didn't think it was odd. She'd been making the rounds, saying hello to old acquaintances. Her friends assumed she left with someone she knew.

"Did they see the guy?"

"They noticed she'd been talking with a man. But across a crowded bar, with his back to them, all they could say was that he was tall. And the victim couldn't remember who she left with—couldn't even provide a description."

"What about the staff?"

"The victim wasn't remarkable—average height and build, medium brown hair—only one waitress said she looked vaguely familiar. And the Voyager has no cameras."

The report stated she'd had nonconsensual sex. Newport Memorial Hospital performed a rape kit, but she'd showered and they'd found nothing.

"Toxicology detected Rohypnol in her system," I said. "Any idea where it came from?"

He shook his head. Many of the customers were known locals, but Thanksgiving brought out-of-towners, people they didn't know. No one could give them anything to follow up on. I slid the second incident report across the table.

"Three years ago, a woman from New York was in town for two weeks, midsummer, renting. She, too, had been at the Voyager. What do you remember about her?"

Steve scanned the report. "Oh, yeah. She'd taken a ride service to the Voyager. Woke up in her car in the driveway of her rental."

"Exactly. The same sort of scenario as the woman from DC. A Friday night at the Voyager. Left with a man she didn't know and doesn't recall. Nonconsensual sex."

She told Steve she'd planned to meet friends, but they hadn't showed. The friends had been interviewed and the big takeaway had been the victim's nasty divorce. Although she'd rented on and off over the years, the landlord provided very little—she'd paid on time, had been quiet, and left the place in good condition.

"Your notes suggest she was an unreliable witness."

"When we conducted the background check, it wasn't stellar. Her husband had filed a restraining order for stalking and something else."

"Emotional abuse."

"Right. At the time of the incident, they'd been separated." Steve shook his head. "She repeatedly violated the restraining order. And with us, she was understandably difficult."

"What did she tell you about that night?"

"All she could tell us was that she struck up a conversation with a man. The description she provided was vague."

They'd looked at the employees again, but it was the same crew of surly women at the bar and servers who'd been there for years. A few bussers, but those had been fifteen-year-old kids. They didn't take reservations, so there'd been no way to get a sense of the patrons, and of course, besides the regulars, the summer brought transients.

"Did you look at the credit card slips?"

"We did. And we checked credit card receipts on the night when the other woman was drugged and compared them."

A handful of the same couples dined early in the evening. The staff described them as steady Friday night dinner patrons. In at five, out at six thirty. The Voyager had been a cash only establishment, only in the last five or six years had they accepted credit cards. Accordingly, there had been a lot of cash tickets, especially at the bar.

"What else can you tell me about that night?"

"Not a lot. She reported the incident on Saturday, agreed to the rape kit, but the entire time, she was either sobbing or screaming. You know, the 'why are you asking me these stupid questions, you need to get out there and find this guy' sort of thing. We did everything we were supposed to do. Professional. By the book."

"I'm sure you did," I said.

"She came back to the station on Sunday to tell us she thought she might have been in a car accident. We checked. Nothing reported that Friday night. She went batshit. We offered to call our mental health liaison, but she refused. Ultimately, we thought she was unhinged."

After we said our goodbyes, I sat in the darkness of the Gannie amid a cacophony of glassware, the clatter of voices. Our person with the Rohypnol hadn't been staff; it had been someone with a connection to Jamestown, someone who visited family in the summer, over the holidays. Had they been a guest at the Philbrick event? I thought about what John had said about clues, information that encouraged you to look in the wrong direction.

Had I simply been looking in the wrong direction?

CHAPTER 43

I SAT WITH THE case notes and a copy of the guest list. The party had been primarily for friends of the couple. Logically, most guests were similarly aged, mid- to late twenties. Five years ago, they'd have been closer to twenty. I thought about one of the parking lot attendants at central station. He was either side of twenty, but if I'd been asked to describe him, I would have said he was a kid, not a man. And these women were older—late thirties, early forties. Both had described their attacker as a man. That it had been a guest seemed less likely.

Starting from the beginning, I reviewed the notes, searching for what I'd missed. When I reached the interview with Dr. Maxwell, I read it twice. There had been something he'd been either trying to say or trying to hide. I needed to scrape away the chaff, understand the origin of its seed. Uncertainty scrambled my thoughts. Repetitive movement provided clarity. I needed a run.

At mile five, a thought came to me. I skipped the last part of my route and headed for the cottage. Cross-legged on the couch, I dialed the medical examiner's office.

"How can I help, Miss Stuart?" John asked.

"You knew I had a question."

"I'm psychic."

"Perhaps you can conjure Hope Philbrick's blood type?"

Fingers tapped on a keyboard.

"Do psychics typically summon information with their computer?"

"What else would they use? It's AB," he said.

"You're a funny man."

"Pretty soon you'll be calling me just to get your smile on for the day."

I was smiling, wasn't I?

"So, a week from Monday, I'm biking in a benefit race," he said. "It starts and ends at Fort Wetherill. It's an end of season ride. We're having a weenie roast."

"A weenie roast?" I laughed.

"Probably vegan weenies."

"I haven't been to Fort Wetherill in ages," I said.

"Well, let me know. Spouses and partners are coming. It's a fun group. I'd love to introduce you to my friends." He gave me the date and time. My insides twisted as the words "spouses and partners" echoed in my head.

I brushed the thought aside and googled Preston Philbrick's corporate blood drives. I scrolled through page after page of press articles. An official phone call might raise some unnecessary attention. Dialing the beneficiary of his efforts, Newport Memorial, I did my best impression of Mrs. Philbrick, who I assumed was listed on his medical privacy form.

"My husband has been asked to promote a blood drive for a high-profile cancer patient but wants to be sure he can donate before he commits. He can't remember if he's O positive or O negative. Can you check?"

Preston Philbrick's blood type was O. When I researched blood types and the various possibilities for parentage, I found what I had suspected. There was, however, a minute chance, and I needed to be certain.

* * *

Dr. Maxwell was in the kitchen making what he called his world-famous chili. If he was surprised to see me, he didn't show it. He rummaged through drawers in the refrigerator, retrieving a bunch of parsley, humming as he chopped, then swept it into the large stockpot on the stove. He wore, without embarrassment, a woman's apron adorned with tiny pink flowers and a ruffle bordering the bib and hem; its strings strained the flimsy tie at the small of his back. Max added cumin, then coriander, stirring, tasting; the thick lenses of his glasses fogged in the rising steam. He adjusted the gas valve until the chili settled into a low simmer.

"Did you find your bracelet?" he asked.

"I did. I hope you didn't mind that I let myself in?"

Max flapped a hand at me. "Everyone knows my door is open. Once Gladys from next door was hunting for a stick of butter in the fridge when Roger from across the street popped by—he was entertaining and out of half-and-half. Gladys just about hit the ceiling. When Lady and I came back from our walk, Roger had a cold compress on Gladys's forehead and was making her a cup of sweet tea." Max smiled. "Glad you found it."

Our eyes met.

"I expected you'd have more questions." Max filled a battered teakettle, ignited a burner, and set the kettle on the stove. "Milk with your tea?" he asked. I nodded, and he placed a creamer beside the pot of sugar on the table. "She had quite the collection, but this was Gracie's favorite." Max set a bone china teacup with an ornate French loop handle in front of me and retrieved a mug for himself.

"I'm honored," I said, examining the lovely hand-painted peonies on his wife's teacup.

"She was English. Tea every afternoon, even at the end. And a baker, too—sponge cakes, scones, her own jam. I don't have the patience for measuring and all that hooey, but I still like my cookies," he said, loading a plate with boxed shortbread.

When the tea was served, Max sat and gestured for me to begin.

"You mentioned giving blood for Hope when she was first born. I'm wondering why Mr. Philbrick didn't donate?"

"His blood type isn't compatible."

"Because he isn't her biological parent?"

Max heaped two teaspoons of sugar into his mug, rattling the spoon as he stirred. "He isn't."

"Is there a reason you hadn't mentioned that?"

"Why would it matter?"

"It probably doesn't, but sometimes background information helps, provides clarity, allows me to separate the chatter from the significant."

"What do you need to know?"

"What can you tell me about Hope's biological father?"

"It's not the right question," he said.

I eyed him with a quizzical look. "And what is the right question?"

He slurped his tea. "All I meant to say was that he . . . he was never in the picture."

Max fidgeted. I smiled, and as I'd hoped, he continued.

"This began the summer the America's Cup was in San Diego. Penny's family had one of their boats in the running as the defender, and she'd been on the West Coast for the trials. The Cup brought yachtsmen from all over the world. Though I can't say for certain, I suspected he was a foreigner who eventually went back to where he came from."

I recalled the photo of the sailing team with Penelope at the center.

"She's still a beautiful woman, but back then . . . tall and fit with that glossy blond hair, those eyes—they all chased her—but she'd been so caught up with riding, sailing, and her education, she scarcely noticed them. This young man, however, he'd been different. It's an old story, but it shaped her life. The young man asked for Penny's hand in marriage. Her parents disapproved, said they'd disown her if she accepted."

"How did Penelope react?"

Max shook his head. "Penelope was hell-bent on having her way. She played her trump card—getting pregnant—on purpose, no doubt. The young man was persistent. Met with her parents, asked for their blessing. Instead, the Harringtons offered him an obscene amount of money to go away."

"And?"

"He took the money. Signed an ironclad agreement, giving up everything—contact, rights, every eventuality their lawyer could think of to keep the child from him."

"Did Hope know Preston Philbrick wasn't her biological father?"

Max nodded. "But until four years ago, Hope hadn't known her real father's identity. It was the first and last time I saw Penny go back on her word."

I wondered what had prompted the change of heart then thought of my own naive, emotionally charged declaration. My plan had been simple: dig a hole, deposit the burning coal, and be done with it. Yet when maturity and hindsight scrape the scar from the lens, the difficult things we've flimsily buried continue to haunt, like a restless ghost with unfinished business.

"Has he ever contacted Penelope?"

"After it ended so badly, I doubt it."

"Would Penelope have reached out to him?"

Max considered the question. "Her father once said that if you crossed Penny, you'd cease to exist in her universe. She'd throw up her three-foot thick steel wall, banishing you forever."

If that were so, the idea of them reconnecting seemed improbable.

"So she married Preston?"

"Penny's parents, God rest their misdirected souls, had been quietly courting the Philbricks for years. Preston was much older, twelve years, but very much in love with her."

Given the circumstances, Max believed it was of little consequence to Penelope that Preston loved her, had been willing to marry her and accept the child as his own. She'd been smart enough to know, however, that she'd been outmaneuvered.

"And as these folks do, Penny did what she was told. Before she could blink, Penelope Jane Harrington became Mrs. Preston Philbrick. At any rate, happy ending. Preston stepped up and raised Hope as his own."

The arranged marriage to Preston might have made some sense, yet I was doubtful it erased the pain created by a union not of her own choosing. Penelope's naivety had been the means to her parents' end. I had a new appreciation for what Penelope Philbrick had endured.

"Were they close, Preston and Hope?"

"Preston traveled to France from the fall and into the spring for business. In the summer, Hope sailed, and when she wasn't sailing, her mother kept her busy with this and that camp."

Max had skirted the question, but the subtext was clear: they didn't have the opportunity to become close.

"The last time we spoke, you said that Penelope had trouble adjusting to Hope's schedule after her birth. Did you prescribe anything to help Mrs. Philbrick sleep?"

"I'd need to check, but my go-to is melatonin."

"Had Mrs. Philbrick asked you about medication for jetlag? Maybe taking that to help her sleep?"

It was a guess, of course, since the questioning phrase *medication for jetlag?* had been in Penelope's medical file with no explanation or further notation.

Max glanced at his wristwatch and stood as if he had some place to be, then dusted nonexistent crumbs from his shirt. "Penny wasn't breastfeeding, she could have taken anything, but had she asked, I would have recommended melatonin," he said, removing our half-full cups from the table. "I don't mean to be a poor host, but I need to pack for a little weekend trip."

"Dr. Maxwell, if there's something you think I should know, please tell me."

But he was already filling the sink, clattering the dishes as he washed, inspecting as he rinsed. "I've told you what you need to know. I hope you understand," he said, placing the teacup, then the mug on the drainboard.

I left the house dissecting our conversation. Max had given me a significant piece of information, but he'd been cryptic and evasive. My mind reeled, suddenly weary with the effort to unmask the opaque Dr. Maxwell. And now I had more questions that only Penelope Philbrick could answer.

CHAPTER

44

PRESTON PHILBRICK WAS still at his Boston office; Penelope would be home and likely alone. My questions would tip my hand, but I saw no other way to get what I needed.

A delivery man hurried down the front steps as I pulled into the driveway at the Crow's Nest. I rang the bell; inside, heels clicked along the wood floor and the door swung open. Penelope Philbrick glowered at me.

"I've said all I'm going to say to you," she said, then slammed the door shut.

I leaned closer and shouted, "I need to speak with you about Hope's biological father."

Options were being weighed.

"And about Rosa Rodriguez."

When the door reopened, Penelope's cheeks were wet, an expression of disbelief on her face. "I have nothing to say about him, and we've already answered questions about Rosa," she said.

"I have different questions."

Penelope steeled herself as she considered me. Without a word, she turned and clicked away. I followed her into the kitchen and watched as she feverishly searched, opening and closing the same cupboard doors; she found the coffee beans in the freezer.

"Well, what is it, then?" she asked, contemplating the coffeemaker as if she'd never seen one before. Her hands shook, her tenacity like a piece of fine lead crystal.

"Please," I said. Something in me softened as I extended a hand. "I have the same model."

Penelope's resolve teetered. She relinquished the packet of coffee beans, then deflated onto a stool at the kitchen's island. "I never learned how to use that thing," she admitted.

"It takes some figuring it out, but once you get the hang of it, it's not so bad." I ground the beans, added water, and started the machine. "Milk? Cream?" I asked, retrieving a mug from the cupboard.

"Black, thank you." She eyed me as if considering one last attempt to rally. But weariness was the victor. With a heavy sigh, her determination slipped then shattered; the shift in energy felt exhilarating.

"When did Hope's father first contact you?" I was convinced that Penelope's about-face when she told Hope about her biological father meant there'd been some extenuating circumstance that couldn't be explained otherwise.

"On my birthday, the year Hope turned five."

The milestone struck a chord. Hadn't Hope been five when Penelope's boat malfunctioned, then sank?

"He wrote to me. In his letter, he begged for my forgiveness. Leaving me and the baby had been the worst decision of his life. He hoped I'd found happiness." She met my eye. "We'd been so young, so foolish, and we'd both made the fatal mistake of trading each other for money."

Max hadn't known the entire story.

"Before he left for good, he told me about the money my parents had offered, assured me that we could make our way without their financial support or approval, making it clear that crewing for the New Zealand team was just a summer stint. He'd completed his degree in boat architecture and planned to design and build boats, and, of course, over the years, he'd done just that. But my parents painted a different scenario, made his ambitions seem farfetched. And I'd been with him for mere months and with them for twenty-two years. I chose the devil I knew. I told him I couldn't be poor. In a fit of anger, he took what my parents had offered and returned to New Zealand."

"When did you respond?"

"A few months after I received his letter, I emailed."

"Have you been in touch since?"

"Every year on my birthday. Sometimes I'd reply, sometimes not. Four years ago, when Hope turned twenty-one, my parents long dead by then, I gave Hope her biological father's contact information, let her know she was free to take the relationship where she wanted. Hope reached out to her father when she decided to wed."

"Was he at the party, Mrs. Philbrick?"

"He'd been invited, but declined the invitation. We had a hundred and fifty guests, Ms. Stuart, many arrived by boat, many I did not personally greet. It's possible that he changed his mind unbeknownst to me. But I can tell you that Hope had invited him to her wedding, and he was planning to attend."

"Did Mr. Philbrick know?"

"I don't know," she said, distress clouding her face as she jotted his contact information on a slip of paper then handed it to me. The coffee hiccuped and spat its last drops into the carafe. I filled a mug and set it in front of her. What I'd learned from Max had altered my line of questioning, I was at a crossroads between continuing or shifting to the original purpose of my visit. Time was at a premium; I moved on.

"You've spoken to my colleague, but I need you to tell me where you were between the hours of five and eight forty-five on the Tuesday morning Rosa was found dead."

Penelope wrapped her arms around her waist, not meeting my eye. "Sleep hasn't been easy. By six, I'd gone for a walk to Beavertail. I returned home a little after eight."

"Can anyone confirm this?"

She shook her head.

"Father Fred said you'd agreed to meet him here that same Tuesday at eight. He knocked, but no one was home, so he waited in his car."

"I'd written 'nine' in my datebook. One of us got it wrong."

"He saw your car pull into the driveway at eight fifty-five. You went for a drive that morning. Where did you go?"

Penelope examined the countertop, then shivered as if suffused by a cool breeze. "I didn't drive anywhere," she said. "After returning from Beavertail, I went to the chapel at the cemetery, the one on our property."

"Did you see or meet anyone? A member of your grounds crew?"

Another shake of her head.

"Father Fred was very explicit—"

"Father Fred is wrong. I came into the house through the back patio doors. At some point, I was in the kitchen and noticed him sitting in his car." She lifted her chin toward the bank of windows in front of the table; the driveway was a few yards beyond. "I went out and tapped on his window."

Unease gnawed at my confidence.

"When was the last time you drove your car?"

"The afternoon of the party."

"It's been weeks," I said.

She shrugged. "I'm not ready."

"Do you keep a flashlight in your car?"

"I expect there'd be one."

I placed a photo in front of her. "Is this your flashlight, Mrs. Philbrick?"

She scanned it without reaction.

"It doesn't look familiar."

"Please, take another look," I said, moving it closer.

Her eyes darted back to the photo. "Is that what killed Rosa?" she asked, clutching the gold pendant that hung from a thin serpentine chain around her neck.

"It's shape and heft is consistent with the weapon used."

A thought seemed to form then crystallize. "This is why you're here? Because you think I had something to do with Rosa's death?" She regarded me as if I was some pitiful lost dog. "You have no idea who and what you're dealing with, Ms. Stuart."

Penelope was warning me, telling me my actions would have consequences. I wanted to laugh. I'd been thinking the same about her. "You lied about being in bed on Saturday at eleven. And Rosa lied for you."

She scrutinized my face as if trying to discern what else I knew. "I didn't ask her to lie."

Rosa had been special to her, part of the Harrington household long before Penelope had married; the lie had been Rosa's initiative.

"We have a witness who can place you at the fire pit with your daughter close to the time she died. What happened when you last saw Hope?"

"I went to find her. To tell her she was making a fool of herself." Disgust spread across her face. "She was at the fire pit with Jacob, that . . . that degenerate brother of his. It was despicable. I told him to leave."

We'd clocked Jacob on CCTV at the marina where he docked his boat on the cusp of the two-hour differential of Hope's time of death.

"What happened next?"

"I tried to bring Hope back to the house. She screamed at me, not much of it made sense. The things that did make sense were terrible, but true—how I'd commandeered her life, how she'd had no say, had been kept away. I'd never told Hope why, knew an explanation was long overdue. I just wanted to get through the night." Penelope drew a deep, shaky breath. "I decided right then to tell her everything the next morning."

That Penelope would never get the chance was a gut punch. It made me think of my mother, what I needed to tell her and hadn't.

"And then?"

"I grabbed Hope's arm, but she lashed out, pushed me away." Penelope wrung her hands as if squeezing the last drops from a wet towel. "I left her there and found Rosa. Asked her to bring Hope back to the house."

"What did Rosa say when she returned without her?"

Penelope swiveled her stool, turning away, her face only visible in profile. In a practiced voice, she said, "Rosa said she couldn't find Hope."

Penelope's inflection, lack of hesitation, and facial expression conveyed that until the last sentence, she'd been telling the truth. Rosa had been at the fire pit, and what Rosa saw signed her death sentence. Without a doubt, Penelope Philbrick knew what Rosa had witnessed.

CHAPTER 45

THE WOMAN FROM New York was named Emily Rollins. She'd divorced, retaken her maiden name, and moved to the outskirts of a small village called Knotty Pine, near where she'd grown up in New Hampshire. A telephone interview might have sufficed, but I wanted to see her. For some, body language was silent; for me, it was dependably verbose.

I turned off the main road and drove upward on a narrow, rutted dirt track. At the three-mile mark, I followed left at the fork through the open metal gate. The nose of the wagon pointed skyward. Five miles farther, I turned into a semicircular driveway that fronted a midcentury deck house. Solar panels blanketed its roof and that of the barn off to its left; surveillance cameras hung from every corner.

A petite woman in jeans cuffed midcalf and an oversized navy sweatshirt, her hair a tight-clipped pixie, sat on the front steps tossing a tennis ball for two German shepherds. Both jerked to a halt, ears pricked, tails high; their gaze followed the path of the car, then flicked to their mistress. She lay her hand diagonally across her chest and they retreated beside her.

As Emily led the way into the house, efficient and well-trained, her dogs trotted between us. I reminded myself to move slowly, speak softly.

Emily poured iced tea into tall glasses. "Sugar? Lemon?" she asked.

"Both," I said, marveling at a series of landscape oil paintings that covered the living and dining room walls. An antique rolled top desk dwarfed the sitting room. Cubbies held notecards, stamps, a collection of erasers. A handsome Montblanc pen box made of black calfskin with a gray suede lining sat at its center. The pen's guarantee papers and ink cartridges were tucked into the spaces provided, yet the slot for the pen was empty. Emily appeared next to me, then frowned as she followed my gaze.

"It was a gift from my father for my college graduation. I was going to be a poet," she said. "Somehow words became color, form." Emily gestured to her paintings and handed me a glass of tea. I followed her onto the back deck; we settled into rockers, and the dogs flanked her like statues.

"How long have you been here?" I asked.

"Almost three years. After my divorce, I needed to find a place to live. Closer to family made sense."

Emily's words were the happily-ever-afters we desperately want to believe in. But when someone so easily plucks you from your ordinary day and does what they will with you, when you finally claw your way out of the abyss they've dropped you into, the world you once breezed along in, like a child drifting through and endless summer day, has disappeared. Danger no longer uniquely existed in Hollywood's dark alleys, it waited in the empty hardware store; it drove past and circled as you entered the bank; it watched while you pumped gas.

Emily had built her fortress.

"It doesn't feel close to anything," I said.

She pointed. "See those ants down there? Those are my cousins."

I laughed, appreciating the levity.

"The house was a bonus. I walked the land first and knew I'd buy it even before I came up here."

She opened a hand to the gently sloping valley, a crooked stream wending through it and the massive, elegant white pines standing guard. It was the sole subject of her landscapes, each unique in its light, time of year, perspective.

"An old-growth forest is rare. The most intriguing part is the understory—what lies beneath the canopy."

We sipped the cold, sweet tea. When I set my glass on the side table, her dogs, Winnie and Roo, swung their heads in my direction and watched. Their whimsical, storybook names were a nod to A. A. Milne's Winnie-the-Pooh and Emily's own Hundred Acre Wood below. But the dogs weren't part of a children's story. Both came in for a closer look. Emily eyed me like a wary cat. I held out a hand. They sniffed. Tails and ears dropped. Winnie let me pet his head, massage his ears; Roo nudged his snout into the palm of my hand. The canine contingency had offered their blessing. But I knew the drill. I would let Emily lead the way.

"So, Jamestown," she said.

I nodded. "Two years before your incident, another woman filed a similar report—same venue, same drug. I have a case where a woman has died. She, too, had Rohypnol in her system. It did not, however, take place at the Voyager. I'm looking for something that might connect any or all three cases. The notes in your report were thin. Perhaps you can tell me what, if anything, you remember."

Emily looked out over the valley. "It was a low time for me. I was in the middle of a bad divorce. Things got worse after what happened. Let's just say, I've come a long way since then."

I knew all the scenarios of *worse*.

"Can you give me a little background?"

She'd spent summers in Jamestown as a kid. Eventually her parents divorced, sold the house. Her mother went south, her father, west. She'd kept up with a few girlfriends and they got together in Jamestown for a few weeks every summer for years. But that summer, with the divorce, she'd told her friends she wasn't coming. They'd insisted, said the change of scenery would be good.

"So I went. My friends had been right. The island lull was soothing, the colors of the sea and sky, inspiring. I spent days alone, walked, swam, in bed by nine. I dreamed of putting brush to canvas again, began to believe I could move forward with my life. That first Friday, we'd planned to meet for drinks at the Voyager. The odd thing was that I'd tried to beg off; I was tired. The sun and the sea can do that. They told me they were trying to cheer me up, it'd be fun, like old times."

"So you showed."

"I'm polite to a fault."

"And then what happened?"

"It was warm, so I went out to the deck, sat in one of those Adirondacks. The stars were brilliant, the bay, a mirror, the full moon reflected like a delicate necklace of gold beads across its surface, the water lapped at the hulls of sailboats. Like so many things Jamestown, it was hypnotizing."

A man had been standing at the railing. He'd turned and as he passed, said something about it being a good night for stargazing. Emily joked she had a hard time finding the Big Dipper. "He stopped and pointed it out."

I laid out the eight by tens of Eddie, Jacob, and Frankie Moran. The police report had stated she couldn't provide a description, so I knew it was a long shot. She examined each photo. After a few minutes, she shook her head and continued.

"He chatted about the stars. Oddly enough, I felt sorry for him. Seemed lonely, thankful for the opportunity to discuss what was so obviously a passion. It was a relief to talk about anything other than my woes or myself to a stranger."

"I can see how that would be welcome."

"He said it was unfortunate that we couldn't see one of his favorites, Orion."

"Ah, yes. The mighty hunter. The wrong time of the year," I said.

"He'd explained that in Greek mythology, Orion had chased one of the seven sisters of the Pleiades on earth, so Zeus put them in the sky to protect them. I said that would make old Orion a skirt chaser, and he laughed. I told him that I was a Taurus. That I'd been told Orion was squaring off with Taurus, the bull."

An anxious feeling rattled through me.

"The only identifying feature you gave the police was that the man was tall. Can you remember anything else?"

"He stood slightly in front of me, looking out. The moon was rising, casting him in shadow. He wore a suit. I assumed, businessman."

Emily had told him about her friends that hadn't shown. Like magic, her phone chirped. It was a response to a text she'd sent earlier.

They'd gotten their signals crossed, thought she'd backed out. She got up to go. No, stay, he'd said, and asked if she'd she join him for a drink. She couldn't think of a reason why not. He returned ten minutes later with two drinks.

"Not long after, it was like watching myself in a movie—from above, my voice far away, then bits and pieces, then nothing. My next memories are fractured—waking in the driver's seat of my car, being propped up in bed, my friend talking to me, the plastic bucket held beneath my chin."

Emily's eyes shone. She was all of five two, maybe 110 pounds; the dose she'd been given had been devastating. I thought of Elizabeth Samms, the college student who'd choked on her own vomit. She'd been alone and had died. Emily's friend had saved her life.

"The next day was a blur. My friend drove me to the police station, but I couldn't tell you what happened. They took me to the hospital. I remember thinking I was having a nervous breakdown, thinking I wanted to die."

"I'm so sorry," I said.

Three useless words were all I could manage. She read the pain on my face, put her hand on mine.

"I'm doing well now," she reassured me. "I've come to realize that healing is going to be a lifelong practice. And I'm not sure I'd have made it this far or at all if I'd done it alone."

Her words resonated.

"For a long time," Emily said, "alcohol became the only way to get through the day. It anesthetized me."

I understood too well. During the first few years after my assault, by ten AM I was drinking just enough gin and tonic so my hands no longer shook, the doubt no longer clawed, and I could put a checkmark on the calendar indicating I'd survived another day.

"Meds helped me sleep. And if things didn't improve . . ." Emily let the reference to taking her life hang in the air. "But that same friend from Jamestown kept calling, checking in."

And hadn't Mom kept calling? That Sunday morning when I'd slunk out of the house before she woke, and drove back to school, my dorm room phone had rung before I had the key in the lock. Then she'd made the two-hour drive to campus the next weekend and every week thereafter and taken me to dinner. She'd asked, and I lied, time and again, insisting there was nothing to talk about, that I was fine. Given no alternative, she'd backed off.

"One sober morning, it occurred to me that my friend was offering help, but she knew it was impossible to help someone who didn't have skin in their own game. I had to want it, to ask for it. She showed up a few hours after I called and didn't leave for three months."

My mother had offered and cruelly, I'd refused her help, refused to forgive her, continuing to punish her for that one weekend.

"Your friend," I said. "No truer sense of the word."

Emily nodded, held my gaze, quietly considering me. "What she told me the day she left is worth hearing."

"Please," I said, gesturing for her to continue.

"I told her I didn't know how to thank her. She said there was no need. I had already thanked her. I'd allowed her to help me. The alternative, watching someone she loved, helpless from the sidelines, slowly killing themself, would have been pain beyond measure."

I drifted downward, a current dragging me in a soundless, hazy green sea, praying it wasn't too late to make amends for the pain I'd no doubt caused my mother.

I followed Emily and her dogs into the kitchen, set my glass in the sink.

"You know," she said, "I told the cops this, but I think the car I'd been riding in slammed into something, maybe another car."

Steve had mentioned it but had dismissed its veracity. I was all ears. "What can you tell me?"

"I heard the screech of brakes, the sound of metal against metal, being thrown to the floor."

"Anything else?"

She shook her head. "The cops said nothing had been reported in Jamestown or nearby. But it had been one of those rare lucid moments that stay with you."

I knew what she meant.

"That's when I last saw my Montblanc. I kept it with me always, along with a tiny notebook, in case I had a thought and wanted to jot it down. It had been in my purse when I left the rental. When I woke in the car that morning, the purse was on the passenger seat. Days later I realized the notebook was there, but the pen was gone."

"Wait, when did you tell the cops about the car accident?"

"On Sunday."

CHAPTER

46

"YOU SAID THAT Preston Philbrick was involved in a fender bender, a hit and run," I said, when DelCarmen finally answered. "Can you tell me the date of the incident and the date it was reported?"

"Give me an hour," he said, and hung up.

Along narrow, twisty roads, town after town drifted past in an anonymous blur. I pushed aside what I knew—the lies, half-truths, the unrelated and misleading—and attempted to let what I'd missed bubble to the top. I couldn't make sense of a motive—yet. But it was coming. That telltale prickly sensation on the back of my neck subtly indicating that the subconscious had cobbled together some vital information, a few seemingly innocuous phrases; something seen but not recognized that had yet to surface to my active mind.

DelCarmen called with the information I'd expected: the hit and run had taken place three years prior, on a Saturday in August at 2:30 AM, yet not reported until the following Thursday. I'd check the dates against my notes but was fairly certain they'd line up. Emily Rollins's statement about the car accident had not been verified, because it had yet to be reported. The complainant testified that Philbrick rear-ended him as he was stopped at the four-way intersection of Walcott and Narragansett Avenue. When he stepped from the car, he expected Philbrick to do the same. Instead, Philbrick had backed up, made a

U-turn; the victim noted the license plate before he sped away. Philbrick's statement said that he hadn't been aware that he'd hit the man's bumper. He paid for the repairs and apologized. The conventional wisdom was that Philbrick had been drinking and by driving away, avoided a DUI. This sort of behavior was not uncommon, but the assumption had been incorrect.

I told DelCarmen I'd call him later.

It was dark when I pulled into Jamestown and parked at the pier. I strolled along the deserted wharf. A somber moon illuminated the edges of thick cumulous clouds, the light from the lampposts cast long shadows, my footsteps echoed on the pavers. All the while DelCarmen's question from two days earlier pestered me like a bothersome fly. And then there it was again, a nuisance buzzing around my head. "It would make more sense if he'd killed his wife, right?"

I dropped onto a bench, pulled out my phone, and searched backward through my emails until I found Dr. Maxwell's medical notes, much of them still unread. I scrolled to the beginning, to Hope's birth, and reread the notes in the margin regarding Penelope's difficulty sleeping: *Medication for jetlag. Fluni?* I then read Max's notes regarding the second pregnancy: *She doesn't understand—diaphragm, spermicidal jelly.*

What didn't she understand about the second pregnancy? How she became pregnant?

I skimmed along until I read that a year after terminating the pregnancy, a tubal ligation had been performed while Preston was in Europe on business. Hadn't Dr. Maxwell said that Preston Philbrick had hoped for a houseful of children?

This was where Max had been pointing me. This was Penelope Philbrick's three-foot thick steel wall. Penelope's rejection of her husband, his child, her marriage. Then I recalled what Father Fred had said about the death of a child: it extinguished the soul of the parent.

Was it that simple? Was the score even now?

And all of Penelope's bad luck or mental illness had been neither. When Hope turned five, her biological father had reached out to Penelope and they'd corresponded. At about the same time,

Penelope's boat had sunk, nearly killing both her and Hope. Four years ago when Hope turned twenty-one, Penelope disclosed to Hope the identity of Hope's biological father. And about the same time, Penelope's twin, Bea, had died without explanation. And I expected that the fire that killed Cricket had been triggered by something similar that Penelope Philbrick had no idea her husband knew about.

And finally, I typed "fluni" into the search engine. Within less than a tenth of a second, I had hundreds of thousands of results that provided the same answer: Flunitrazepam was the medical name for Rohypnol. "Fluni" was one of many street names. I had the drug and what I considered the motive, yet I was miles away from connecting my suspect to the drug or to the crime.

On my front step was a glass vase overflowing with white tulips, their petals open, bright orange stamens bursting. A tiny cream-colored envelope dangled from a slender pink silk ribbon tied in a simple bow around the neck of the vase. I stooped and gently brushed my face against the silky petals, breathing in their delicate aroma. I eased the card from its envelope and held it beneath the light of the porch lamp. It read:

Roses are red,
Golf balls are white.
Don't break my heart,
Say we'll have dinner tomorrow night.
John

I picked up the vase of flowers and pushed through the front door. A smile spread across my face and a feeling I vaguely recalled from a lifetime ago fluttered in my heart.

CHAPTER 47

AT FIVE AM Saturday morning, I drafted an email to DelCarmen asking him to file the paperwork for a search warrant for the Philbricks' medical records and for Penelope Philbrick's car.

I needed to be certain, however, before pulling the trigger and making it official. I drank the last few sips of my coffee and headed upstairs. Slipping on black running pants and a T-shirt, I strapped on my runner's belt packed with a tape measure, phone, gloves, lock-pick set, night vision binoculars, flashlight, and pepper spray.

At the kitchen island, I opened my laptop and with satellite imagery, reviewed the Philbrick property.

A helipad lay at the property's southern tip; beyond a stand of thick evergreens was a tiny chapel and a family cemetery. The herb garden, observatory, and well-defined footpaths lay between the chapel and the house, and the garage was located on the property's northern end. Aerial photography showed a good stretch of dense woods—at least a half mile—with no apparent paths or thinning on the neighboring property to the north. The Manchester property, just south, looked more promising. Better still, the Manchesters were summer residents. Their driveway hugged the left corner of their own lot before veering off in a southerly direction. Not far to the north of their driveway was a perimeter path that skirted the Philbricks'.

Mrs. Philbrick and I were roughly the same height; the distance from the seatback to the steering wheel in the Parisienne was sixteen inches. I cuffed my black ski mask until it resembled a cap and slipped it on, stuffed my sunglasses in my pocket, inserted ear buds for show, and set off toward Beavertail.

Twenty minutes later, I trotted past the entrance to the Crow's Nest and turned into the Manchesters's driveway. The perimeter path was twenty or thirty yards beyond a low stone wall. I walked along the paved drive until it turned south, then climbed the wall and headed along the wooded edge of the dirt path. Crouched in a stand of trees in front of the car park, I surveyed the garage and house. All was quiet. I retreated west through the scrub pines, crossed the driveway, and made my way to the north side of the garage.

Four lights with motion sensor detectors were positioned above the three vehicle doors that I assumed operated primarily by remote control. Sweeping my binoculars along the pedestrian door at the far right, a few steps from the kitchen entrance, I noted a manual keypad to its left with a push-button locking mechanism that activated what was likely a deadbolt securing the door. I slipped on gloves and crept along the side of the garage then circled around back. There was no rear door, but there were two twelve-over-twelve wood-framed windows that would, without a better option, work. Neither had visible alarm contacts, but both were latched shut. While I'd seen an older security system keypad in the house, it didn't appear that the garage was wired. At the window situated farthest north, I removed the flashlight from my running pouch and tapped on a small pane of glass until it cracked. Piece by piece I removed the glass, then retreated into the wooded area and waited to see if I had tripped a glass-break sensor. Fifteen minutes later, certain no alarm was in place, I unlatched the window, lifted the sash, and climbed into the garage.

A tall metal two-door storage unit stood off to my left against the back wall in the center of two parking bays. An old workbench topped with tools and assorted bric-a-brac sat in the corner to my right. Oddly enough, the Lexus was alone and, fortunately, unlocked. Where was Philbrick at this hour? It was ten minutes to six and sunrise was thirty-three minutes away. There was no time to worry about it. I stretched the tape measure from the driver's side seatback to the steering wheel. While the Parisienne had measured sixteen inches, the Lexus measured twenty-four. Several strands of thick blond hair lay on the headrest. I put one of them in an evidence bag.

As I repacked my running pouch, my flashlight fell to the ground and rolled beneath the car. I dropped on all fours and, as I scanned beneath the chassis, heard the unmistakable sound of tires crunching along gravel. Pulling the ski mask over my face, I crawled into the corner next to the workbench and crouched behind a trash barrel. Within seconds, the garage door rose, the interior lights flashed on, and a black BMW pulled in and rolled to a stop. The idling engine muffled the words of a heated conversation. Minutes passed until, finally, Preston Philbrick cut the engine and popped the trunk. When the car door opened, the overhead lights timed out, and the garage went dark. He grumbled as he rummaged through the trunk, groaning as he retrieved what sounded like a suitcase; he set it down and closed the trunk. I expected the patter of footsteps, but none came.

Nonsensical scenarios inundated my mind: wondering if I'd silenced my phone's ringer, if he could see me from where he stood, or if he'd noticed the nonexistent pane of glass, the flashlight beneath the passenger side door. I clutched my pepper spray, slowed my breathing, and concentrated on remaining perfectly still. After what felt like an eternity, he lifted the valise and walked toward the side door.

The suitcase thumped as it dropped to the ground, then Preston pivoted and charged in my direction. My heart hammered as I unlatched the safety on the pepper spray and prepared to take aim. The door to the metal cabinet, a mere two feet to my left, screeched open, my hands clenched in fists to steady their shaking. He sighed with relief and laughed as he closed the door, then retreated across the garage, retrieved his valise, and this time hauled it along the concrete floor. As he neared the door, he stopped. Seconds passed in interminable silence, until I heard the crack of his knees, then a faint scraping sound. Preston whistled as he unlocked the deadbolt and pulled the door tight behind him. A minute later, I heard a faint *thwack* as the kitchen's screen door slammed shut.

The air seeped between my gritted teeth, and although I knew it was no longer there, I crawled to the side door of Penelope's car and searched in vain beneath for my flashlight. The window complained as I hoisted it open; I tumbled over the sill and headed into the neighboring property to the north.

Following the phone's compass west through the dense woods, I made my way to Beavertail Road, then sprinted for home. Thirty minutes later, I lugged the stepstool from the back hall up the stairs and into the closet. Retrieving my mother's blond wig, I clipped a strand from it. When I compared the hair from Penelope's car to the strand from the wig, another piece of the puzzle fell into place.

CHAPTER

48

LIKE THE SEA, my purse never gives up its dead. My phone vibrated madly somewhere in its depths.

As soon as it stopped, it started up again. I pawed through the rubble without success, then tipped its contents on the kitchen island. Plucking my gun from the chaos, I slid it into my shoulder holster, then retrieved my phone; four missed calls from DelCarmen.

"I was starting to think you were avoiding me," DC said.

"Wash your mouth out with soap," I said. Then, hoping something else would magically shake out I asked, "What do you have?"

"The postmortem report for Rosa Rodriguez confirmed the obvious. Cause of death was blunt force trauma to the head. The diameter of the flashlight matched the head wounds. Time of death between six to eight AM. The rest of the evidence from the apartment will take more time to process, but they're working on it. We identified the sneaker, though. It's a Saucony running shoe."

"How many gangbangers do we know that wear Sauconys?"

"Frankie Moran wears a size ten."

"Hmm," I said. "What about Eddie and Jacob?"

"Both wear size eleven. How about you?" DC asked.

I took DelCarmen through Max's notes; the street name, "fluni," for flunitrazepam, its common name, Rohypnol, which was conceivably the referred to jetlag medication. Given that Philbrick spent six months of the year in France for business, in all likelihood, it had been prescribed there to ease his jetlag with the frequent back and forth. We discussed my interview with Emily Rollins, and I cited the covered telescope mount on Philbrick's office patio and at the observatory platform.

"He's on the board of the Rhode Island Astronomical Society," said DelCarmen. He was silent for a while, then said, "Serious, yes. But there's no connection to Hope Philbrick other than having the same drug in her system. It simply means they have the drug at the house, easily accessible by almost anyone. Hope could have taken it herself. We could be back to her mother, or Eddie."

"I read something else in Max's files. At first I didn't think it had anything to do with anything. But now I think it was the linchpin."

"And what was that?"

"Penelope had an abortion."

"Many women terminate pregnancies, Andie. Often, for medical reasons."

"She didn't want the child."

"I'm not following. She aborted their baby, so twenty-five years later he drugs and kills their daughter?"

"Her daughter," I corrected, and recounted my conversation with Max about the biological father and the Philbricks' arranged marriage. "Penelope became pregnant almost two years after giving birth to Hope. It's clear from Max's notes that Penelope wasn't sure how she became pregnant. She'd been using a diaphragm and spermicidal jelly."

"Are you saying he drugged her, too?"

"Hard to know, but I'd say it's possible. And then Penelope aborted his child."

DelCarmen was silent. "Revenge?" he asked finally.

"I'm not sure 'revenge' is the correct term, but, yes, it might be that simple."

DelCarmen listened without interruption while I gave him the history of Penelope's boating debacle, and about the fire that caused the death of her horse and what I believed to be the real circumstances of her sister's death.

"My guess is that he'd been trying to get her attention for years. Maybe she didn't get it or give him the satisfaction he needed, and it escalated. Isn't that what Dr. Maxwell described when Preston Philbrick courted her? Penelope had ignored him, and it spurred him on."

"It's a stretch to think that he gave Hope the Rohypnol and expected to find the perfect opportunity to chuck her over. Besides, even though he isn't her biological parent, he raised her."

I thought about Max's cryptic answer to my question about Hope and Preston's relationship. I recalled Penelope flinching when he reached for her hand the afternoon I told them about the Rohypnol detected in Hope's system, and Penelope's regret that she hadn't had the chance to tell Hope the reasons she'd sequestered her—the away camps, the boarding school—throughout her childhood. At the very least, Penelope suspected he was dangerous.

"I don't think they were as close as Preston made us believe. In fact, I think all of it was a charade. And you're right, the premeditation angle is unlikely. But if he's trying to lash out at Penelope, her daughter's public drunken behavior would humiliate her. After Frankie poured the Champagne and left to restock ice, maybe he gets the idea to spike her drink with just enough of the Rohypnol to make her seem drunk. Perhaps that's how it started."

"Then what?"

I shook my head. "The final piece, that's what I don't know."

"That's fair. You think this was a great big 'fuck you'?"

"Well, now they're even. You asked a question yesterday, one I couldn't shake. You wanted to know why he didn't just kill his wife. The answer is, he did. And in the cruelest way, something he knows firsthand."

"Why wait so long?"

"He hadn't been waiting. It started soon after she terminated the pregnancy of his child. Maybe with the realization that there would be no big, happy family. Who knows, there could be more."

"And Rosa Rodriguez?"

"Penelope asked Rosa to bring Hope back to the house. Rosa saw something, or at least Philbrick thought she saw something."

Against my better judgment, I told DC about my visit to the garage. That the seat position was where you'd expect given a taller driver, and the strand of hair I removed from her car appeared to be a hair from a wig, and my suspicion that Penelope wore a wig, not for fashion, but because of hair loss due to stress.

"He drove her car, wore one of her wigs, used her flashlight. A sick game of cat and mouse, incriminating her, toying with her, and then intervening if need be to save her."

DC cleared his throat. "Look, Andie, maybe you're right. Philbrick spikes the Champagne. As a lark. But I don't think he's got the stones for murder. Even drugging women with Rohypnol, what does that tell you?"

"Perpetrators who use this drug are typically someone without confidence, and Philbrick's got plenty. But the drug offers one thing that absolutely fits—anonymity. Rarely are drugged victims able to identify their attacker."

"Well," DC said, "we can't place him at the scene."

"Nor could we place her at the fire pit, but Mrs. Philbrick had been there."

DelCarmen sighed.

"One last question, DC, what's his shoe size?"

"Size ten."

After a long moment, DC said, "The reality is that what you've got on Philbrick is all circumstantial. Without physical evidence, it's next to impossible to prove."

"Worst-case scenario, we start at the Rodriguez scene and work backward. I'm willing to give next to impossible my best shot."

My participation with ridiculously long-shot situations typically required much prodding. I had jumped from the high diving board.

"What are the chances we'll speak with someone at the Voyager who's worked there long-term?" DC asked.

"They die on the job over there."

"Let's meet at eleven."

"Badges?"

"Absolutely."

CHAPTER

49

THE BUILDING THAT housed the Voyager handled all the needs of the seamen who made a living on Narragansett Bay. Over the years, its brown boxy structure had been shored up and cobbled together, adding a kitchen, another room for dining, and, finally, a deck. Nestled amid the Jamestown boatyard like a place that didn't want to be found, there were no obvious signs to direct you through the maze of shrink-wrapped boats and the assortment of water-soaked nameless structures. Newcomers usually mistook it for a bait shop or the harbor master's office.

The Voyager was a paradox: you never seemed to run into anyone you knew, but everyone you knew went there. The bar always drew a crowd, but even at full tilt, the atmosphere was eerily quiet; conversations and sound seeped into the dark recesses of the walls. To stave off the perpetual damp, a fire crackled in the massive stone fireplace year-round. The three-item menu had been served without exception since the early sixties: no steamed if it's fried, no put this or that on the side, no salad instead of fries, no exceptions, no kidding.

A tall, wide-hipped brunette dressed in khaki pants and a white polo shirt pushed backside first through the swinging kitchen doors. Both hands held five-gallon pails filled with ice. She emptied them into the bins beneath the bar and said, "We don't open for another half hour."

DelCarmen flashed his badge, and she rolled her eyes. "I have an ironclad alibi for whatever it is you're investigating. And I'm busy."

"We appreciate that you're working," DC said. "Tell us what we need to know, and we'll get out of your hair."

She looked from me to DelCarmen and shrugged. "Shoot."

"How long have you been working here?" I asked.

"For what seems like an eternity . . . give or take fifteen years."

"Always as a bartender?"

"Always."

"Do you work nights?"

"I've worked doubles Thursday through Sunday for the past ten years. Can I ask what this is about?"

"We're following up on two reports from a few years back," DC said. "Five years ago, a woman came here, had a few drinks, left with someone she met, then woke up in her car in the early hours of the morning in the parking lot. She can't remember leaving or anything other than this is where she started the evening."

"Five years is about, oh, I don't know, a thousand drunken women ago. People meet other people and leave with them all the time. Someone passed out in their car is not unheard of, either. You got a photo?"

I pushed an eight by ten across the bar.

The bartender nodded. "Yeah," she said. "I found her in the lot, slumped over the steering wheel. Tapped on the window, she didn't budge. I opened the door, shook her, she was hard to rouse."

"Did she say anything when you finally woke her?" I asked.

She shook her head. "Gibberish. I went through her purse and found her phone. I dialed the last number called and reached a friend who came down and took her home."

"You didn't think she needed medical attention?"

The bartender narrowed her eyes. "I didn't."

"Had you recognized her from earlier in the evening? See her with anyone? A man?" I asked.

She thought about it, then shook her head. I slid the photo of Emily Rollins across the bar.

"This woman was here three years ago. She had a drink with a man and her next recollection is waking up in the front seat of her car in the driveway of her rental. Do you recall seeing her?"

"Nope," she said.

DelCarmen placed photos of Eddie, Jacob, and Frankie in front of her. "Can you tell us if any of these men are regulars or ever worked here?"

She studied each, then tapped Frankie's headshot and said, "He sort of looks familiar, but I couldn't tell you if I know him from here. And that one," she pointed to Eddie's. "He's been here. With a bunch of big guys. Beers and shots. But not lately."

DC dropped a photo of Preston Philbrick on the bar.

"Mr. Philbrick is a regular. But, you know, super nice guy."

DelCarmen and I shared a look.

"Tell us about him," I said.

"Like I said, nice man, quiet, comes in for a few pops after work."

"Any particular day, time?"

"Midweek, Fridays. After six or so."

"And?" DelCarmen prompted.

A flush swept across her throat and along her cheeks.

"And nothing. Keeps to himself."

"How does he pay?" I asked.

"Cash," she said, without hesitation.

"We hear he likes the ladies," I said.

She put her hands on her hips. "Discretion is a big part of my job. I get paid very well to pour with a heavy hand and to keep my mouth shut."

"We can do this the easy way or the hard way," DelCarmen said slowly.

She scowled. "Yeah, he likes the ladies. Like a million other guys."

"What are these women like?" DC asked.

More silence. "He goes for the cheap date."

"Meaning?" I asked.

"One or two drinks and they're open to suggestions, if you know what I mean."

"Does he leave with them?"

"Sometimes." She looked from me to DelCarmen. "Look, we have an understanding. He doesn't let them get behind the wheel of a car. If they were unescorted, I'd take their keys and call a ride service."

"More job security?" I asked.

"Knowing those women aren't getting behind the wheel . . . that's all I can do from here. Once they leave, whatever else happens between them, is between them."

"Anything at all you can add about any of the women he's left here with, anything that struck you as odd or out of place?"

She shook her head.

I looked at DC. He nodded, dropped a twenty on the bar, and said, "We appreciate your time."

We had almost reached the door when she called out to us. "You know, there was something about that woman, the one from the car in the parking lot."

She shifted from foot to foot.

"It'd been late November, and we'd had an unusually frigid few days, the nights dipped close to zero. She hadn't been wearing a coat. I was concerned, you know, about hypothermia. But when I shook her, she wasn't the least bit cold."

CHAPTER

50

DC HELD OPEN the door of the Voyager and met my eye. "Well done, Stuart," he said.

We agreed to meet at the office to outline next steps, file the paperwork for warrants. I stopped at the cottage to feed Tom. As I pushed through the kitchen door, my cell phone vibrated. I felt my cheeks color when I saw the caller was John.

"Hi," I said, slinging my bag over one shoulder.

"Hi back. Did you get my note?"

"I did. Thank you. I can't remember the last time anyone sent me a poem. Certainly not one with golf balls in it."

"I don't know that many words." He chuckled.

"It was very sweet. And I got the beautiful flowers that were attached to the note. Tulips are my favorite." I glanced at the flowers on the kitchen's center island, the gesture felt enormous. "But seriously, unnecessary."

"Are you kidding? Beautiful women deserve to be spoiled, and believe me, trying to pick out the right flowers for you was nerve-wracking. I had a committee helping me at the flower shop."

"Oh, wow." I suddenly felt anxious.

"So, are we on for dinner?"

I put the phone on speaker, set it on the countertop, then rinsed and dried Tom's bowl.

"Uh, yeah I'd love to but, unfortunately, tonight's tough. Work calls."

I looked around but didn't see Tom as I retrieved a can of his food from the pantry, opened it and spooned it into the bowl.

"Oh." John hesitated. "What happened to your vacation?"

"Cut short. It's getting complicated."

An uncomfortable silence volleyed between us.

"Have you given the bike race get-together some thought?"

"When is that again?" I asked, cringing when I remembered it was a cookout with spouses and partners.

"A week from Monday."

"Right. Well, with work ramping up, you know, I'd hate to commit then have to back out last minute." Then I heard myself utter the classic brush off. "How about I call you when work settles down?"

Silence echoed down the line as I made my way upstairs toward the bathroom. "Sure, Andie. Although we could . . ."

But I didn't hear whatever John was about to say. "Oh, Christ, I've got to go."

"Is everything okay?"

"Uh . . . yeah . . . fine. DelCarmen is ringing me on the other line," I lied. "I've got to take the call." I closed the phone, slipped it into my jacket pocket, then read the message scrawled in red lipstick across the bathroom mirror. By the time I registered the faint smell of cologne, it was too late. The door slammed into me, propelling me forward on hands and knees, and the toe of a boot struck my side. I curled to protect my vital organs as a man wearing a black ski mask repeatedly kicked my gut, my ribs, my legs. When I heard the hammer of his gun cock, an ungodly caterwauling echoed up from below. His coat rustled as he looked over one shoulder toward the stairs. The high-pitched screaming intensified as the barrel of a gun connected with the back of my head, then quieted to the footfalls of my assailant's retreat, then nothing as darkness gathered me, stroked my forehead, and soothed, *"There, there. There, there."*

* * *

I woke hours later, paralyzed with fear. Those confused moments stretched like hours. My thoughts dizzy with the uncertainty of what had happened and where I was, the events of eight years earlier reared up and played before my eyes.

* * *

When I came to, I was naked and standing in a hallway, shivering uncontrollably. I recognized none of my surroundings, unsure how I came to be there, where my clothes were, nothing. I could have been standing there for a minute or an hour. I was terrified.

The back of my head throbbed with indescribable pain, and I desperately needed to urinate. I staggered down a dark hallway, opened the closed doors in search of a bathroom, horrified at my nudity and my inability to cover myself. Behind the doors, stark outlines of bed posts, tall cabinets and the pale fringe along the length of oriental wool rugs shone in the sliver of moonlight through large windows. I retreated into the hall and cowered, trying to figure out what to do; hot urine dripped down my legs and pooled at my bare feet. Taking in great gulps of air, I struggled to quiet the sounds that erupted from deep inside as I wept.

My eyes adjusted to the dark. A landing and a set of stairs materialized. Clothing lay in a heap below. The floor swung beneath my feet. I reached for the banister and clung to it, nauseated, black spots danced before my eyes. When the swaying stopped, I sat on the top step like an unsteady toddler, then eased myself to the bottom. I crawled to the clothes, fingering them, slowly recognizing they were mine. From somewhere in the house, three sonorous chimes tolled. The floorboards overhead groaned.

I struggled into pants and a shirt and scrambled to the wooden exterior door. The deadbolt refused to budge; the doorknob slipped in my trembling hands. The sound of footsteps escalated my panic. Tears mixed with mascara made it almost impossible to see. I wiped my hands along my thighs, twisted the deadbolt, wrenched open the door and ran forward. Cold air overwhelmed me, bile filled my throat; the stairs turned over and over. The sound of my head and body connecting with the wooden treads seemed to be coming from far, far away. I willed myself to my feet. The word "run" echoed through my head. The front door swung open as I collapsed into the darkness of the thick shrubs along the driveway.

I walked aimlessly down tree-lined streets that felt more residential than urban hoping to recognize something, anything. Turning right then left, unable to remember where I'd just come from, I passed endless thick hedgerows, gated stone courtyards with glimpses of grand homes beyond. I crouched and vomited until my insides ached, then lay on my side exhausted. My head spun. And the cold. I was so incredibly cold. The soft pillow of wet grass offered no comfort.

When I opened my eyes, a faint strip of light breached the tree line. A man knelt before me. Relief registered in his weathered face as I showed signs of life. In broken English, he tried to tell me I needed medical attention. I shook my head and repeated the word "college." Finally, he nodded. I wasn't going to the emergency room. I was a student and was going back where I belonged.

He took my hand in the warmth of his own, wrapped an arm around my shoulder, lifted me on wobbly legs, and led me to a nearby red pickup laden with gardening tools and parked in the adjacent driveway. At the passenger door, the dawn sky swirled chaotically. When the spinning stopped, I was unable to move. I sobbed, gasped for breath. His wizened, kind face now radiated pain, pity. In a soft voice, he told me I was safe. We both knew he was taking chances: a beat-up female college student was trouble for a Hispanic gardener. I let him help me into the truck.

My next memory was the sound of the pickup pulling away from the curb. The stone gates at the entrance to the college towered before me. Poignant gaps in my memory made it seem like I was dropped from the sky to where I now stood and to the places I'd so recently found myself, as if the moments in between did not exist.

Dorothy Gale from Kansas had nothing on me.

I passed no one as I made my way to my dorm room. Standing with the lights off under the shower, I scrubbed until I was raw and the water ran cold. I piled all the blankets I had on the bed and burrowed beneath, searching my mind for answers and finding none. There had never been a time when I wasn't exactly sure of where I was, where I'd been, or where I was going. The small comfort I found from the gaping holes in my memory was the nonexistence of the horror I knew I'd experienced.

I fell to sleep that morning praying I would never remember. And still, I hadn't. The before and after, however, never failed to return in detailed clarity at my lowest moments. I sobbed without restraint when, finally, I realized I was in my home and on the bathroom floor.

"Rule number one, Andie. You've got to get back up."

I staggered to my knees, winced in pain, my tongue swollen from biting it; dried blood caked my lips. I stood shakily, listening. Across the bathroom mirror read: *The sins of the daughters shall be visited upon the mothers.*

"Find your anger. Give it purpose," Vi had said.

A swath of red crimson snaked along the white marble floor; my lipstick tube lay crushed at its end. Thoughts shrieked like a boiling teakettle. The need to cower wasn't among them.

I was certain that I was alone. Regardless, I pulled my gun from its holster and cleared each room, and wondered about the noise, expecting to find a juvenile fox or opossum under a chair or the couch, but found nothing. There was no sign of forced entry and nothing else appeared to have been disturbed. In Providence, this would have never happened, but this was Jamestown. I engaged the deadbolt before going to bed, but had never locked it when I left; I couldn't recall even having a key.

I choked down four ibuprofen, grabbed a pack of frozen peas and tucked them under my arm, then checked my phone. There were six missed calls from my mother and two from DelCarmen.

I called the house. It rang and rang. Calling my mother's cell phone defied logic, but out of desperation I tried it anyway. The call went straight to voice mail. I redialed the house phone. The mournful wailing droned on. I hung up and redialed, the threat on the mirror filling my mind with frightening images. As I was about to hang up and call for an ambulance and backup, I heard a click and then Mother's beautiful voice commenced with its blessed reprimand.

"Good Lord, Andrea, what's all the fuss about?"

So choked with gratitude, I almost wept.

"Hey, Mom, what's up?" I said, stifling my emotions, trying not to alarm her. "I saw you called—"

"What did you say?" she asked.

"I saw you called," I repeated, but my swollen tongue garbled the words.

"What? For the love of Pete, Andrea, stop mumbling."

"Dentist . . . Novocain," I managed.

"I see," she said, then continued. "Why in heaven's name do I bother leaving messages if you don't listen to them?"

"Everything okay at the house?"

"Course it is. Well, now it is. Never mind that, tell me all about what's-his-name and golf."

"What do you mean 'now it is'?"

She let out a dramatic sigh. "I thought," she said, pausing for more drama, "there was something wrong with the landline. The phone would ring and I would answer. Someone was on the other end, but for the life of me I couldn't hear them. Maybe they couldn't hear me. Since I couldn't reach you or your brother, I called Barbara next door and asked her to dial the house. It rang as it always has. My guess is that it was the other person's phone because it's happened a few more times. As Barbara pointed out, it could have been one of those pesky telemarketers."

"Did you check caller ID?"

"Honest to God, Andrea, who cares? Whoever it was will call back if it's important. Now, enough about my silly telephone trials. Tell me about your golf date."

I hesitated, unable to focus on the question. "Hard to talk," I mumbled. "I'm going to stop by." Then I asked, "When did you say your phone was on the fritz?"

"Andrea, you're like a broken record. It was this morning, dear. Are you having trouble hearing me?" She continued without waiting for a response. "I'll see you later," she said, then hung up.

God bless her. Mother was being stalked, and she was oblivious. I checked the cottage for Tom and found him asleep in a shoebox in the closet. I gargled with icy water to help the swelling and waited for the ibuprofen to kick in before dialing DelCarmen.

"Where the hell are you?" he asked.

I told him about the attack, the message on my mirror, and my mother's unknown caller. "I'm all right," I said, "but threatening my family is unacceptable."

DelCarmen said nothing.

"He wore a ski mask, but I'm pretty sure it was Preston Philbrick."

"Hmm," he said, finally. "Not sure how he'd know we were asking questions."

Philbrick was in possession of a flashlight with my initials carved into the handle. The realization that my sloppiness had not only jeopardized my mother's safety, but likely tipped our hand, was difficult enough to accept. Telling DelCarmen would change nothing.

"I'm heading to my mother's now and plan to stay until I'm certain she's safe."

"Good. I'll be at your place in an hour. Don't touch anything. I'm going to dust it."

"No need. He wore gloves. I'm going to need surveillance and muscle."

DelCarmen had a friend whose private security firm we'd used before.

"Short notice will be pricey, but doable."

"They'll need to change the locks on my doors and provide me with keys. Whatever the cost."

We agreed to talk when I'd assessed the situation at the main house. I took three calming breaths, then redialed my mother.

"What have I done to get all this attention?" she asked.

"I forgot to ask if you wouldn't mind some overnight company? Tom and I need a place to stay."

"Of course you can. Why do you need to a place to stay?"

"Tom is having a little flea problem. I thought it'd be prudent to fumigate the cottage. The pest company said it would be best if we moved out, for at least a day."

"Well, if Tom has fleas—"

"Tom is fine," I interrupted. "He's already been dipped. Clean as a whistle. I'll be up shortly."

"Lord knows I've got plenty of room. It'll be fun. I'll whip up something for dinner. See you soon."

I stuffed a few cans of cat food, some jeans, and a T-shirt into a backpack and set off in search of more important things. In my sock drawer, I found my ammo pouch and crammed it with more ammunition than I hoped would be necessary. My Glock was safely tucked into my shoulder holster, but since I adhere to the Girl Scout motto "Be prepared," I retrieved my Smith and Wesson from the gun safe and more ammo, then tossed both into the backpack and drove up to the house.

The main house presented security challenges, but making it safe was not impossible and despite my pounding head and what I thought might be a cracked rib, I was more than up to it. I started on the front porch. As I dragged a large packing box into the front hall that obscured the sightline from the formal living room, I heard it. My mother was at the piano playing Claude Debussy's magnificent *Clair de Lune.* The momentary frisson of joy that tickled the base of my spine was swept away, no longer by fear, but by sadness knowing the music that once evoked images of family and the happy times we shared would forever be sullied by the memory of my sexual assault. I was desperate to take my beloved Moon Song back, to once again make it my own.

Minutes later, she was silhouetted in the doorway. I fought back tears of relief, then felt furious at the audacity of the threat leveled against her. I wanted to run to her, hug her in a way I hadn't in years, but knew it'd create questions I didn't have time to answer.

I cleared my throat and asked, "Are you moving?"

"Family Services is collecting gently used men's clothing. Those are suits and shoes Peter no longer wears. Donation pickups were scheduled for last Friday, but they never showed. I called Ralph, you remember him?"

"Ralphie Tomatoes? How could I forget the only man brave enough to join your garden club? Thick as thieves, the two of you, back in the day."

She swatted a hand at me. "If he could hear you," she said. "He's a Webster, dear, not a mobster."

"Excellent. He'll give you a run for your money at Scrabble."

"You're referring to Noah Webster; Ralph hails from the Daniel Webster line. Anyway, he said something or other had happened and they'll be by this Friday."

"It's supposed to rain," I fibbed. "I'll put the box back on the porch at the end of the week."

She met my gaze. "I'm so glad you're here."

"I'm glad, too, Mom," I said, and turned before she could see my tears.

I started in the basement and worked my way to the attic. Mother didn't ask, and I didn't explain as I methodically checked and secured each window and door. As promised, Mother exhibited her still remarkable telephone prowess and whipped up a wonderful French dinner—delivered from Chez Pascal. We noshed and sipped wine until almost eight, when she retired to the upstairs sitting room to watch her show.

As I turned off lights and meandered through the first floor, my phone chirped with a text from DelCarmen confirming that surveillance and a security detail was in place. I sat by the windows in the living room listening to the wind swish through the leaves on the old maple and remembered the wooden swing its boughs once held, my euphoric whoops as Peter pushed me ever higher.

An hour later, I wandered into my father's study, turned on the desk lamp, and sat in his chair and swiveled. Everything was exactly as he had left it: his cardigan draped across the back of his chair, a draft of a note on his blotter to someone named Carl, a list of books he'd been planning to order. I scanned the framed photos on the wall, ran my fingers along worn bindings: the wisdom that served him well, the words that had delighted him. His study told the story of time well spent, of family, of laughter; regret was nowhere to be found. I heard his words, those offered for poor choices, in defeat: *"There's always the tiniest pearl of wisdom in the error. Find it, learn from it."*

Dropping into his recliner, I opened the leg rest, closed my eyes, and savored the comfort of its supple, worn leather. My mother, too, felt present. It occurred to me that she'd left the room unchanged because this was where she came when she needed him, needed his strength.

I climbed the three stories to my bedroom. It'd been eight years since I'd slept here. The faint scent of lemon oil, the crisp percale sheets of summer, swapped with the soft warmth of autumn's flannel. A fresh sprig of lavender hung from the bedpost. Down comforters piled high at the foot of the bed. That my stay could not have been expected, that the room was prepared and waiting, brought fresh tears. I propped open the balcony door, turned off the lights, and slipped between the sheets, pulling the heavy down comforters over me. Serenaded by the familiar trill of crickets and the softness of sea air, sleep came quickly.

CHAPTER 51

MY CELL PHONE rang, coaxing me from my paralysis. The phone chirped, indicating a text. I read DelCarmen's message.

Action at Dr. Maxwell's house.

It was seven AM, Sunday. I pulled on jeans and a T-shirt, tiptoed to my mother's bedroom door, heard her rhythmic breathing, watched the rise and fall of her chest, and smiled. I gave the house a once-over and headed out, locking the front door behind me.

When I arrived at Dr. Maxwell's, a Jamestown police cruiser was parked out front. Steve O'Donnell yammered into his cell phone and paced the length of the front porch, a distressed look on his face. I waited impatiently until he hung up.

"Steve, what's going on?"

He shook his head. "Suicide."

I pictured Max in the apron, heard him humming as he stirred the pot of chili, and stumbled over my words. "Are you sure?"

"I'm sure," he said.

"Who found him?"

"I did. Dr. Maxwell's son, Greg, called me and asked me to swing by. Greg and I are friends," he explained. "He'd been trying to reach his dad since yesterday. Max was supposed to drive up late Saturday, spend the night, but he didn't show."

"Note?"

Steve shook his head.

"Where's his dog?"

"We found her in the kitchen. My wife has her."

"I'm going in," I said, giving his shoulder a squeeze.

I pulled on gloves as I walked through the office. Nothing appeared to be out of place or disturbed. In the sitting room, everything looked as it had when DelCarmen and I had first interviewed him except, this morning, Max lay dead in his recliner. His head was cocked to the left, a bullet hole in his right temple. Pieces of his skull coated the headrest. Large amounts of dried blood speckled his face and plaid shirt and spattered the wall behind the chair; the gun lay in his right hand. The red light from the telephone answering machine blinked in the half-darkness: a flashing *8* indicated the number of unanswered calls. I pushed the button.

Beep.

"Dad, it's Greg. Call when you get a chance."

Beep.

"Dad . . . Dad . . . You home?"

Beep.

"Hello, Dad, please check in. I'm getting concerned."

Beep.

The machine clicked five times indicating a series of hang-ups.

The persistent hum of the hearing aid that lay on the table next to Max's reading glasses receded as I retraced my footsteps to the front door. I hustled up to Steve, who was again on the phone. "I'm so sorry," I heard him say. After a few more muffled words, he ended the call.

"That was Greg," he said. "Tough call to make, but I guess it was a matter of time."

"What are you talking about?"

"Greg had this nagging feeling about his father. Always thought his dad was depressed after the Mrs. passed. Beyond that, Max is—well was—sick. Cancer—he wasn't going to beat it. Greg thought he might, you know, do something." Steve looked away. Sweat glistened on his brow and stained the underarms of his shirt.

I moved out of earshot and dialed DelCarmen. "We've got another body. Dr. Maxwell is dead. A poor attempt to make it look like a suicide."

"On my way," he said.

* * *

Twenty minutes later DelCarmen hurried up the driveway, pulling on gloves. "You take the office, and I'll take the residence."

We went our separate ways and a half hour later, met on the porch.

"Well," said DC, "he had enough food in his fridge for a week plus four big containers of chili. The pot he cooked it in is unwashed in the sink. There's a duffle bag packed with a few wrapped gifts, and clean clothes laid out on the bed. Looks like he was going away for the weekend."

"According to Steve O'Donnell, Max had terminal cancer. His son, Greg, was concerned he'd take his own life."

"Yeah," said DC, "maybe in the final stages and suffering. You saw him?"

"I did. Engaged and very much the happy clam."

"Regardless," DC shook his head, "no one makes a batch of chili, packs a suitcase, wraps gifts then kills himself."

"When we analyze a writing sample, we'll find he's left-handed. The gun is in the wrong hand."

"What did you find in the office?" DC asked.

"It's what I didn't find that concerns me. Some of Max's medical files are missing—the Philbrick files." I recalled the sound of Philbrick dragging the heavy valise from his car. "One thing, DC—"

As if he could read my mind, he said, "Anthony's team is ex-military. The best money can buy. Your mother is safe."

I nodded. "Let's get to work. The next round won't be easy."

* * *

Crime scene analysts and a pathologist from the medical examiner's office descended on Max's house. DelCarmen established a log, roped off the scene, and gave instructions to the uniformed officer. I briefed the criminalists on what we expected to find and where to focus beyond what they'd normally do, and handed them a sample of Max's handwriting.

Then, DC and I headed to central station to present our case to the captain.

CHAPTER

52

CAPTAIN O'SULLIVAN LOOKED unhappily from me to DelCarmen. "Are either of you aware that the Sox and the Yankees are, at this very minute, about to throw the first pitch at Fenway?" he asked with a calm that was frightening.

I looked at DelCarmen, who shrugged. "No, sir, we weren't," I said.

"Well, this better be good," he said, narrowing his eyes and pointing at me.

DelCarmen laid it all out for him, from the heartbreak to the deep-seated anger and finally, an opportunity to even the playing field. The level of devastation Penelope would suffer at the loss of her child at this pivotal moment, the same moment Penelope had been denied so many years ago, would be equal to, if not greater than Preston's own. DC methodically walked O'Sullivan through the evidence.

"So why now? Why'd he wait so long?" asked O'Sullivan.

Attempting to be thoughtful, I took him through the history of Preston's campaign of terror against Penelope. "He wasn't waiting. I see a man who tried to make a marriage work that was doomed from the start. She wanted no part of it or him. It did a number on him emotionally. Maybe he thought this was the solution to his woes."

"One lunch short of a picnic?" O'Sullivan asked, looking at DC.

I rolled my eyes.

"He blew a gasket," DC said. "It'd be a waste of time trying to figure out what made him snap. Besides, we understand the motivation. Who gives a rat's ass about the timing or the trigger?"

"I certainly don't," O'Sullivan agreed.

The lighthearted humor tailed off and O'Sullivan fixed his eyes on me. He nodded as if formulating thoughts, or maybe, counting my transgressions. Then, the corners of his mouth lifted into what appeared to be a grumpy smile. I almost stumbled backward.

"Fine job, Stuart," O'Sullivan said.

The uninitiated would consider his words run-of-the-mill, something people say, but DelCarmen and I knew better, and we silently appreciated the enormity of the moment. Then the three of us put our heads down and went to work.

* * *

We reviewed our evidence. From the Rodriguez scene, we had a size ten print of a man's Saucony running shoe with no match, but it was the same size shoe worn by Preston Philbrick and Frankie Moran, a strand of blond hair found in the back stairwell, and the flashlight. The flashlight was identical to the one that had been bought two years earlier when Penelope Philbrick purchased her car and was paid for by her credit card. We had CCTV of a black sedan with a blond driver. It was too grainy for a match and had no view of the license plate, but it was logged coming and going at about the right time.

The Maxwell scene was too new, but the Philbrick medical files had been removed and the gun was in the wrong hand, indicating not a suicide, but murder. We had probable cause for a warrant for both the Jamestown and Boston homes, and Penelope Philbrick's car, but not for the Bay View Avenue office/residence or Preston Philbrick's car. Pulling the handle prematurely had its risks. We'd be at the window with our noses pressed against the glass. We needed a month and an army of investigators.

"A week from tomorrow Philbrick is flying to Paris," I said. "Typically, he's there through March and returns for a few days each month.

But he doesn't need to. He can conduct business as usual from France."

"Can we extradite?" asked DelCarmen.

"Philbrick has dual citizenship and France won't extradite its nationals."

"We need a Hail Mary," said O'Sullivan.

"And a Bigfoot sighting," I added.

Even DC smiled.

CHAPTER

53

In the end, it was all we had. A pass spanning the length of a football field to a receiver who sprinted, arms wide, toward the end zone. But when the ball finally appeared, spiraling downward, woefully shy of its mark, the fans shuffled into coats, defeat a foregone conclusion.

The following day we applied for the moon—warrants for both cars, both houses, the garage, and the Bay View Avenue property. As expected, we were granted a warrant for Mrs. Philbrick's car, both houses, and the garage. The second part of all we had was fast tracking the crime scene evidence analysis. Two days later, we had a match on the strand of hair collected at the Rodriguez scene to one of Mrs. Philbrick's wigs. O'Sullivan was a hero, approving overtime pay and extra manpower.

A team of three detectives led by Shorty Long searched the Boston property. Long's report stated that the home was infrequently used—no food in the fridge, no unopened tubes of toothpaste or used toothbrushes, toiletries or medications of any kind, rows of professionally laundered men's clothing hung in garment bags in the closets, dress shoes in dust bags—and meticulously maintained—no hair in the drain traps, no lint in the dryer filter, a clean bag in the vacuum. And not a sneaker on the premises. Privately, Long said it was the sort of creepy house where you'd expect to find Lurch in the foyer and leg irons in the basement. Sadly, the only instruments of torture were dull kitchen knives and nothing heavier in the utility closet than a flimsy wooden rake used to straighten the fringe on the oriental rugs. In other words, it'd been a bust.

Our search at the Jamestown property did not yield Saucony sneakers, but a pair of men's Brooks running shoes that showed little to no sign of wear. Since Brooks were my running shoe of choice, I knew there were only a few stores that carried them locally. Tracing the purchase wouldn't be difficult. The big prize was a pharmaceutical vial found wedged behind a slide-out shelf in the kitchen cabinet. The medication had been prescribed to Preston Philbrick for high blood pressure by a French physician, and filled by a French pharmacy. It was not our smoking gun, but when we contacted our French frères we were given a list of three prescriptions, including a copy of the contraindications and labeling for each. They were filled upon Philbrick's arrival in France each October and refilled during his time abroad as prescribed.

And there it was, a prescription for flunitrazepam, the benzodiazepine more commonly known as Rohypnol. The discovery was a triumph and a curse—neither the label nor the contraindications contained the word "Rohypnol" which provided plausible deniability to Philbrick's assertion that he'd never heard of the term we'd used for the drug he'd been prescribed. Nonetheless, we were gathering circumstantial crumbs that collectively we could draw logical conclusions from and, upon which, a case could be built. But crumbs were tiny and scattered; assembling them took time.

In our pre-interview conference, we made decisions on who'd take the lead, our questions, the inevitabilities, our approach, and so forth based on the profile we developed for Philbrick. I argued that we'd get more from him with testosterone at the table, advising that DelCarmen take the lead in the interview with O'Sullivan as his wingman. I'd watch and listen in from the one-way mirrored window with the ability to communicate to DelCarmen via earpiece. In the event we got a second shot at him and needed a friendly face, my absence might come in handy.

Looking every bit the upstanding philanthropist, Preston Philbrick arrived at central station with his lawyer in tow. He played a flawless round of the game cops had perfected called "I'm here to help."

Philbrick readily admitted to an ongoing battle with chronic insomnia triggered by jetlag. His parents divorced when he was fifteen and when his mother returned home to Paris, his frequent commute between households was arduous. Flunitrazepam, prescribed more than thirty years previously, was the only medication that helped. When asked why he denied knowledge of Rohypnol, as expected, he said he hadn't recognized the term since the medication had been called flunitrazepam: it had never been referred to as Rohypnol.

For some unknown reason, the flight east did not acutely affect his sleep. He carried a dozen pills each time he returned from Paris and kept them in the bathroom vanity. His assertion that the medication had been consistently stored in a location accessible to anyone in the household including his wife, Hope, Rosa, and even Eddie, had been expected. He neither counted nor kept track of the pills.

"Mr. Philbrick," said DC. "You have a three-day-old pair of Brooks running shoes in your closet, but no others. What did you do with the old ones?"

"I must have donated them when I purchased the new pair."

"We contacted the store where the Brooks were bought. They have a box for shoe donations, but they said you hadn't worn running shoes that day or brought any with you. We checked the box to be sure. Where else might they be?"

Philbrick shrugged. "If not in the donation box, they were likely thrown out."

"When we searched both of your homes, we went through a week's worth of trash. No sneakers were found."

"As you well know, our lives have been in turmoil for almost a month. We have staff that handle domestic and quotidian tasks. They shop for groceries, prepare our meals, and sometimes dispose of our used clothing. I have no idea where they might be," Philbrick said.

DelCarmen continued to press. "What brand had you worn previous to the Brooks sneakers?"

Philbrick considered the question. "I don't know."

"Have you ever purchased Saucony running shoes?"

"I'm sure I have," said Philbrick.

"Can you recall when you last purchased a pair of Saucony running shoes?"

Philbrick shook his head.

"How often do you buy running shoes?"

"Whenever I need them," said Philbrick.

"Every six months?" DC asked.

"I don't run as much as I used to."

"Every eight or ten months, a year?"

"I can't be definitive."

"We reviewed your personal credit card statements for the past two years, and other than the most recent purchase of the Brooks, there are no purchases for running shoes. Is there some other means of payment you'd use?"

"It's rare, but I might have paid in cash," said Philbrick.

"The manager at Newport Athletic Gear says the Brooks sneakers are the first pair of running shoes they've sold to you. Where else do you shop for your sneakers?"

"I think the last pair was bought in Paris, but I can't say for certain."

"There are personal checks written fairly regularly to your assistant in Boston. Are they reimbursements for personal items bought by her on your behalf?"

"That is correct."

"Would she have purchased running shoes for you?"

"Most recently, she purchased a shirt and tie for me when I spilled coffee during my commute."

"And running shoes?"

"Not that I can recall."

The interview stretched on for another hour, Philbrick answering the same questions rephrased and restated with Eagle Scout forthrightness, the patience of a clergyman, and a fierce fence-straddling lack of recall.

Philbrick left the station as unconcerned as when he'd arrived.

We had five days before Philbrick's departure to Paris. While we were making progress, we didn't have enough.

Philbrick's personal assistant from his Boston office had boarded an airplane the previous day and was still en route to her honeymoon in Fiji. It was a twenty-eight-hour flight and with the time difference and layovers, we didn't expect to hear from her until at the earliest, late in the day on Sunday. The three of us sat in stunned silence at the improbability of it.

We'd contacted every athletic gear store in southern Rhode Island and within a twenty- mile radius of Philbrick's Boston office. There were fourteen in all. Neither management nor employees recognized Philbrick or, for the Boston locations, his personal assistant by photo; neither appeared on any customer list.

Four squad members and a secretary from traffic sat hunchbacked over reams of computerized printouts in the incident room at a conference table that was scattered with remnants of the lunch we'd had delivered, coffee cups, half-eaten baked goods, and boxes laden with records from ten of the fourteen stores. Most vendors had inventory and sales software and the squad segregated all Saucony sales, regardless of gender or payment type. So far there were no Saucony sales paid for with cash and until we could speak with Philbrick's personal assistant or get the warrant issued for her financial records, we had no credit card number or numbers we could cross-reference.

At last check, our engine was wheezing and threatening to stall.

DC and I sat in O'Sullivan's office. None of us had given up, but I was certain the same thought crossed our minds: we were screwed.

"We'll find the purchase," O'Sullivan said. "It just won't be in time."

DC stared into nowhere, deep in his typical otherworldly rumination. He snapped out of his trance and asked, "When's the party?"

It took me a minute to figure out what the hell he was asking, then said, "Oh, you mean the thing at Marble House, the one Philbrick is hosting for the Preservation Society?"

"Exactly," said DC.

"Sunday," I said.

"You're going, right?"

I sighed. "I promised I would. But honestly . . ."

O'Sullivan asked, "Will Philbrick show?"

"Anyone's guess," I said.

"Will he know you're going?" O'Sullivan asked.

"My name is on the guest list and he'd have access to it, but it's doubtful he'd look at it."

"Long, long, long shot," DC said. "What if we concede defeat—the whole nine—an apology from the department and officially rule Hope Philbrick's death an accident. Can you get up close at this event?"

"Why?" I asked.

"Because triumph breeds arrogance, and arrogance and alcohol and a kingly stage breeds sloppiness. And if it's done right, maybe even bragging."

"That'd make for a hell of a Hail Mary," said O'Sullivan. "But, what the heck. For a wiretap to be admissible as evidence in a court of law in Rhode Island, only one party has to agree to it."

"Are you suggesting that I sidle up, ply him with a few conciliatory drinks, then ask, just between us, to tell me how he pulled it off? And, what? Get a recorded confession?"

DC smiled. "I thought you believed in Bigfoot."

I rolled my eyes. "He's too sharp to fall for that."

"Got anything better?" he asked.

O'Sullivan reconsidered and said, "Maybe we appeal to another judge for his car and the apartment?"

"The Bay View Avenue property was rezoned commercial, and the construction for the living space was never permitted by the town. With the evidence we have, no judge will warrant a search for a place of business. Besides, he's been two steps ahead at every turn. He's likely dumped his clothes and shoes," I said.

A thought popped into my head. "Wait a minute," I said. Opening my laptop, I searched the registry of deeds and within minutes, found what I was looking for. "The property is deeded to both Philbricks. We need only one of them to approve a search."

DelCarmen said, "Penelope Philbrick is one shovel of dirt away from being buried alive. She's our best bet."

"Do you think she knows?" O'Sullivan asked.

"She does," I said, thinking it over. "For whatever reason, she appears to be standing by her man. She'll lawyer up. We don't have enough time."

In the end, team underdog put all options in play. Despite the late hour, O'Sullivan crossed his fingers behind his back and informed the Philbricks that the medical examiner had ruled Hope's death an accident and the case was closed. Preston Philbrick had three days to bask in our absence. Since there were things Philbrick knew about that had not been made public, it was likely he had a friend on the force feeding him information. We prepared for the recorded admission with a device no longer used by the department—which was key, since it didn't need to be requisitioned and there'd be no record of it. O'Sullivan would petition a judge in the morning for warrants for the office and Philbrick's car.

If we didn't get what we asked for, we'd appeal to Mrs. Philbrick. And finally, we'd continue to scour sales for the running shoes and attempt contact with his PA, calling her cell phone and the hotel where she was due to arrive.

It was two AM when I drove through the stone columns of my mother's property and made my way up the winding drive. I stopped in front of the cottage as was my habit. Before I could put the Beast in park, my cell phone rang. DelCarmen didn't bother to say hello.

"Pull all the way up the drive and park in front of the main house. Lock the car and the front door. And in case you were wondering, there has been no activity, not even an errant squirrel on the property."

I climbed the steps to the front porch, stunned, thinking about how Julian DelCarmen didn't take side jobs, and why he was at the helm of the team monitoring my mother's safety. DelCarmen hadn't wanted a partner; he'd done that once before and his loss couldn't be put into words. So he picked me. But we are who we are from that first breath and no amount of willpower is going to change it. That I'd crossed the threshold, no longer a compliant warm body, and been accepted as his partner felt monumental. I crawled between the sheets, a sleepless night no longer a foregone conclusion.

C H A P T E R

54

"CHOP, CHOP, CINDY!" DC called from the bedroom.

DelCarmen had waited patiently for me to shower, style my hair, and apply makeup to my satisfaction. It was five. Primping time had come to an end.

I poked my head out of the bathroom door. "For the last time, I'm not Cinderella."

DC sat in the rose-colored chair with a book open on his lap, his feet resting on the matching ottoman. He inclined his chin and looked at me above his reading glasses, saying nothing. I took in his hazel eyes, the soft crow's feet that edged them and the thick eyelashes any woman would kill for. Goosebumps covered my bare skin.

"Pass me the tape. I'll do it myself." I held out a hand.

"Andie, we're trained professionals. This is strictly business. I'll keep my eyes closed the whole time."

"Honestly?"

"No, it needs to be attached properly. But I thought it was the right thing to say."

A few minutes later, I came out of the bathroom wearing a white terry-cloth bathrobe. DelCarmen and I stood face-to-face.

"You ready?" he asked.

He placed the device on top of the robe at the small of my back. I shook my head. "Lower, especially if I'm dancing."

"Right. What are you wearing underneath?"

"Nothing," I said.

"Nothing?"

"Well, panties." I retreated into the closet and returned with a navy Versace in chiffon. "They built a bodice into the dress," I explained, handing it to DC.

He examined the dress, then said, "Perfect, plenty of fabric."

I slipped the robe from my shoulders, draped an arm across my breasts and closed my eyes.

"Holy shit," DC said, surveying the bruising on my abdomen. "Did you get this checked out?"

Our eyes met. DC read my thoughts—an exam would have risked a medical determination of unfit for duty—then nodded. He taped the cold wire under one breast then to my stomach. His fingers pressed gently at my waist, indicating that I should turn as he attached it along the side of my hip. Finally, he placed the transmitter well below the small of my back and secured it. DC rifled through his knapsack, then handed me a thigh holster that was heavy duty but sleek, like a second skin. I strapped it on, inserted my loaded Glock and a spare magazine, and both lay tight against my inner thigh. DelCarmen held out wireless earbuds that he'd paired with my cell phone.

"They're long range, which means fifty feet, but they won't transmit through thick walls, between floors. Where's your flashlight?"

"MIA," I said, avoiding his eyes.

DC passed me his new tactical flashlight.

"That's hardly necessary." I waved it away dismissively.

"Humor me, will you?" He held up the sleek black cylinder. It was five inches in length and weighed maybe five or six ounces at most. "You twist the top for a steady beam and tap the tail-cap button once for momentary illumination and twice for the emergency beacon. It doesn't look like much, but this little sucker will temporarily blind someone if you flash it in the eyes."

"Are you sure? It didn't work out so well last time."

"This one is waterproof, bulletproof, and Andie-proof."

"Touché," I said, slipping it into the empty slot alongside the Glock. "I won't run this one over."

We both smiled.

"Now the dress," he said, turning back around.

I removed the robe, slipped on my heels, then stepped into the gown.

"Can you zip me?"

The back of the dress formed a deep V. DelCarmen's hands felt warm and strong as he eased the zipper to just above my waist, then skillfully attached the hook-and-eye clasp. I turned and held my arms open in a dancing stance.

"Dancing is obligatory at these things. Let's try it out."

DelCarmen took my right hand in his left and held my eyes as we waltzed in silence, turning me this way and that with the ease of a professional dancer. Brushing a hand over my lower back, DelCarmen shook his head, indicating he couldn't detect the transmitter's presence.

"In all likelihood, none of this will be necessary," I said. "We'll convince Mrs. Philbrick to consent to the search. You'll find what we need at the Bay View Avenue property."

"Exactly," said DC. "We'll have the mobile crime lab from Newport on hand to blood type anything we find on the shoes. If it's Rosa Rodriguez's blood type, we make the arrest and hope for a DNA match."

Not only did we routinely fib to our suspects, but we spun fairytales, like gold from straw, for ourselves, and delivered them with the same conviction a Baptist minister preached the word of the Lord. The good guys always came out on top; it kept us in the game. Yet, we both knew the prospect of finding evidence at the apartment was negligible. Philbrick had had weeks to cover his tracks. And the recorded admission was a pipe dream. By the time we could connect him to the shoeprint or other irrefutable evidence from the Rodriguez and Maxwell scenes and could indict, he'd be in Paris and couldn't be extradited to face charges. Still, we had no choice but to continue with the far-flung rhetoric and the unshakable belief in the long shot.

"He's smart, prepared, and not going to go down easily. Do not underestimate the situation, no unnecessary chances. If he feels threatened and is given the opportunity, he won't hesitate to kill you."

His words stiffened my resolve. "I haven't come this far to fail."

DC nodded. "You good?"

I took a mental inventory and held up my index finger. In the closet, I loaded my silver beaded bag with my phone, lipstick, and compact with mirror, then wrapped a matching chiffon scarf around my shoulders. I stepped back into the bedroom and, in the vein of the charade, announced with a twirl, "Cinderella is ready for the ball."

DelCarmen held my gaze for a long minute, gave an approving nod. Then we shared a sobering smile that said: Game on.

CHAPTER

55

We received word from Shorty Long that Philbrick had exited his driveway at five thirty sharp. I called Mrs. Philbrick. There was nothing warm about our conversation. She said the front door would be unlocked.

One dim lamp shone from the study in the otherwise dark house. I found her wearing the same bathrobe, sitting in the same wingback as I had that first night. She stared into the unlit fireplace, unflinching even as a gust of wind rattled its damper and shook the windows. A brass-handled bar cart sat to her left, a half-full bottle of vodka and glassware atop. Shards of a crystal decanter menaced like a den of snakes, their eyes blazing from the darkness of the area rug and the wood floor. The room reeked of bourbon and damp ash. Mrs. Philbrick hadn't bothered with her wig. Pale wisps of hair dotted her bony scalp. She took a long draw on a highball glass three-quarters full of clear, iceless liquid, then met my gaze.

My planned speech of planted physical evidence implicating her at Rosa Rodriguez's apartment fell by the wayside. Instead, I listed the dead, then made a foolish promise, a promise I desperately wanted to keep.

"I will find out what happened to your daughter, but I can't do it without your help."

She drank the last of her vodka then hurled the empty glass at the slate hearthstone, watching with detached interest as it disintegrated into a million little pieces and scattered across the floor. Penelope Philbrick shed no tears, wasted no words. "What do you need?"

"Your permission to search the Bay View Avenue property. We need full access, exterior and elevator keys, alarm codes."

She nodded. I recorded her invitation to search, then followed as she weaved into the kitchen, opened a cabinet door lined with keys on hooks, and gave me what I needed. Then she delivered information I hadn't expected: "He left the house with his carry-on. The helicopter is picking him up tonight. Eleven thirty. It's about thirty minutes to get him to the airfield and situated on the jet."

Minutes later, I pulled alongside DelCarmen, handed him the keys, and gave him the bad news. "We have twenty hours less than we were banking on. He's leaving for France at midnight."

DelCarmen didn't flinch. "I'll call when we find what we need," he said, then closed his window, made a U-turn, and headed toward the team waiting at Bay View Avenue.

I drove on to Newport.

CHAPTER

56

THE HISTORIC PRESERVATION Society annual fundraiser was the finale of the summer social season for Newport elite. The sense of arrival at Marble House, its stately elegance, transported many to a time when the details of their family's glamorous lifestyles dominated the front pages of popular newspapers. A short ride home in hired limousines reminded them that the opulence was a thing of the past dragged out for weddings and twice-a-year black-tie society events, and cruelly, of dwindling trusts and crushing tax burdens. Most unpleasant, however, was the long-suffering charade of the exceedingly wealthy bon vivant they obediently portrayed to others.

Marble House was the thirty-ninth birthday present for "the indomitable Alva" aka Alva Vanderbilt, from her husband, William K. Vanderbilt, or "Willie K." The Vanderbilts commissioned Richard Morris Hunt to design for Alva the finest "summer cottage" money could buy. Of course, summer cottages on Bellevue Avenue were nothing at all like cottages. Three hundred artisans and three years later, at a cost of $11 million in 1892, Marble House was everything Alva had hoped for: Mrs. Willie K. had pummeled her competitors in the social arena.

It's funny how things work out. With all the money in the world at their disposal, the Vanderbilts still made a mess of their lives. Personal happiness eluded them. Distracted by the enormity of their wealth and the illusion of their importance, they failed to take care of and for each other. Alva and Willie K.'s marriage was more like the first little pig's house built from straw than the indestructible marble fortification they had so painstakingly designed, constructed, and furnished.

Willie K. was suspected to have been carrying on with a variety of women. Alva, never one to be outdone, took a lover of her own. The Vanderbilts only daughter, Consuelo, fell in love and became secretly engaged to Winthrop Rutherfurd. By all accounts a fine man, but Alva wouldn't hear of it—it wasn't enough that he was a direct descendant of both Peter Stuyvesant, the onetime governor of New York, and John Winthrop, the first governor of Massachusetts, after whom he was named—Alva had her sights on English aristocracy for Consuelo and had been quietly arranging a match with the ninth Duke of Marlborough.

Everyone except Consuelo had something to gain from the marriage.

The Duke was in love with another woman, but his considerable familial debt and the dowry that accompanied Consuelo Vanderbilt made the union irrefusable. For Alva, too, the stakes were high. With her own marriage on the brink of divorce, Consuelo's wedding to the Duke would solve the problem of Alva's postdivorce social standing. In true form, Alva stopped at nothing, including threatening to shoot Winthrop Rutherford should he dare interfere, as well as feigning a life-threatening illness, insisting that any further upset would be her end.

Not wanting to be the cause of her mother's demise, Consuelo relented, and allowed herself to be married off like chattel to the Duke.

The Vanderbilts had a coat of arms. It had some lofty inscription and displayed symbols of valor, strength, honor, and other ridiculous affirmations that bore no resemblance to the way they conducted themselves. As I thought about the Vanderbilts, I came up with something more suitable, more honest as their coat of arms: Appearances above all else.

Mother made me promise I wouldn't valet the wagon. At six o'clock, I stood next to the incredibly chic yet corroded 1979 Pontiac Parisienne on Coggeshall Avenue, one block parallel to Bellevue, waiting for Peter. Soon enough, his two-seater convertible pulled alongside.

"Dapper," I said, as I slid in.

"Lovely," Peter countered, shifting into drive.

A minute and a half later, we pulled into the stunning tree-lined drive of Marble House. Illuminated from below in a manner that accentuated the creamy white marble exterior, the house floated, glittering like a fairytale castle. We rolled behind long black limousines and highbrow shiny sedans, watching the procession of tuxedoed men and women clad in haute couture gowns as they drifted up the sweeping marble steps then disappeared behind the elaborate bronze grille doors that welcomed guests to Marble House.

The valet helped me from the car and delivered me like a prize to Peter, who took my arm in his. We entered the grand foyer and approached an enormous marble table flanked with attendants who supplied us with our table seating and a brochure for the silent auction. Peter and I made our way to the main bar. When our drinks arrived, we clinked glasses.

"I'm glad we're doing this, Peter. But next year, get a date, will you?"

"I will if you will," he said, as if it was a childhood dare.

"Pinkie promise," we said in unison and laughed.

The orchestra played Sinatra. The waitstaff passed Champagne and hors d'oeuvres on silver trays. Peter excused himself to make the rounds. Women dripping with gold and silver encrusted with fat jewels strolled from table to table like peacocks showing off their finery. My mind drifted to my mother. I had called en route to Newport to remind her the dinner I ordered would be there shortly and that the poached salmon was for Tom. She teased, telling me "Thomas" was enjoying the wine and that neither of them—as if she and the cat had discussed the subject at length—could figure out what on earth the pint of cream was for. I imagined Tom atop the kitchen island wearing one of my father's bow ties, a haughty look on his face. The delivery man was at the door and the call, cut short. But what she had whispered before signing off made my heart soften; a smile formed on my lips each time I replayed her stilted words:

"I've been critical about your work . . . I haven't made it easy. I realize it's meaningful to you . . . I'm proud of you, my love, for doing what's in your heart."

As much as I needed to hear her words of admiration, of love, she, too, needed to hear mine; she needed to hear that I'd forgiven her. *Tomorrow*, I thought. *I will make everything right between us tomorrow.*

I was halfway through my cosmopolitan when I spotted Preston Philbrick working his way through the room, missing no one with either business or social clout. I'd been waffling about how to handle Philbrick. DelCarmen and O'Sullivan recommended I flirt—honey trap protocol as old as dirt. Yet hadn't Dr. Maxwell said that Penelope's lack of attention made Preston chase her even more? And hadn't Peter said that women who ignored suitors and rebuffed advances drove the poor buggers to the point of madness? Maybe none of that would work, but that was how I'd play it, if we needed it at all. A team of three investigators led by DelCarmen was at this moment scouring the Bay View Avenue property for physical evidence.

I left the bar and followed at a distance until Philbrick took a seat at table twenty-two with the governor and his wife and two other couples I failed to recognize. When I passed Philbrick's table, my eyes focused on my destination, the heat of his gaze made the hair on my neck rise.

Let the games begin.

* * *

Peter waited at our table, which was otherwise unoccupied. I surveyed the place cards and rearranged them to make sure that I had a side view of table twenty-two. Preston sat facing toward our table. Perfect.

"You are sitting next to James and Charlotte Jarvis, and I have a Dr. Joseph and Mrs. Judith Barber to my left. Harold and Susan Stamford are over there," I told Peter.

"Great. Do we know any of these people?" he asked.

"I don't think so. But if they know us, we can always pretend to know them."

"Right," he said, deflated.

"This might surprise you, but I'm going to make the best of this."

Peter stared, dumbstruck. "Fifty bucks says you won't make it to ten o'clock."

"Deal," I said, then turned and smiled at a newly arrived group of four who introduced themselves as the Jarvises and their daughter Susan and son-in-law Harold. Even though no one asked, James informed us that he was CEO of Pegasus Systems, a newfangled biotech company whose operations were so complicated us normal folk couldn't possibly understand it, so he wouldn't bore us with the specifics. But he was important, which was his point. We masked our skepticism with feigned fascination except for Harold, who seemed incapable of speech. James Jarvis eyed his daughter's choice for a spouse like he had leprosy, then sent the waiter off for a round of martinis.

Dr. Joe and Mrs. Judith Barber arrived fashionably late. Joe was exceedingly drunk and Judith, teetering on strappy gold stilettos and sporting a towering mane of red hair, didn't seem to notice. She introduced herself and played the speaking parts for Joe without offering any sort of résumé. Joe was dressed seventies retro in a white tuxedo jacket with wide lapels, a white ruffled shirt, with an oversized black bowtie and a glint of mischief in his eyes. Judith, who looked to be twenty years her husband's junior, wore a gorgeous red satin Valentino accessorized with matching red claws. Judith propped Joe in the chair next to mine, wagged her finger at him, and said, "Now you behave, or we won't be able to stay and you'll ruin everyone's evening. Especially mine."

Judith struck up a conversation with Peter. Joe promptly slumped forward and examined my cleavage. "I'm a doctor," he said to my left breast. Without lifting his head, he raised his eyes to meet mine and smiled.

"How intriguing," I said, batting my eyelashes. "I'm a stripper."

"How delightful," he said. "Would you care to dance?"

To my surprise, Drunken Joe was transformed on the dance floor. He staggered right to its edge and then snap, out popped Fred Astaire. Joe led me through the fox trot then the rumba. The other dancers cleared to admire Joe's footwork. As we retreated to the table, Joe stumbled out of dance mode and plodded military style all the way to his chair. We were right on time for the first course.

I sent a text to DelCarmen.

Status?

Still working the apartment. Mr. and Mrs. Clean have been busy. You?

My stomach knotted.

He's seen me. No contact.

The waitstaff ladled creamy pink lobster bisque tableside from steaming tureens and as they placed the bowls before us, floated a buttery puff pastry crouton on top. Judith passed on the bisque and drank her first course. Susan and Charlotte critiqued gowns and hairstyles while Peter and James discussed golf, and Joe napped sitting straight up in his chair. Harold sulked and spoke to no one. As the waiters removed the soup bowls, I nudged Peter. "Ask Judith to dance."

He looked in her direction and frowned. "She's not my type," he complained, eyeing her heavy makeup, spray-on tan, and chunky gold jewelry.

"Suck it up. I want to dance with Joe again."

"He's sleeping."

I elbowed Joe. He opened his eyes, looked around, and muttered, "Ah, right. Here we are." He rested a hand on his double old-fashioned glass like a small child clutching his blankie and was a new man once he'd taken a big slug from it.

"As you wish," said Peter.

I patted his arm. "You are a prince among princes."

Peter set his napkin on the table, stood, and flashed his million-dollar smile at Judith Barber. Peter, like my father, was elegant: tall and handsome with his leading-man chin and smoky brown eyes. Women rarely said no. She took his hand, and he escorted her to the dance floor.

"Well, Joe, shall we?" I asked.

"Let me get a bit more comfortable, little lady," he said, removing his jacket, loosening his bowtie, and polishing off the rest of his drink. I led the way past the Philbrick camp to the dance floor.

Joe outdid himself leading me through a smooth waltz, cuing me like a seasoned dance instructor. Out of the corner of my eye, I saw Preston Philbrick approach the dance floor with the governor's wife, Sondra, in tow. A few dancers moved back to give the evening's host and the state's first lady some room. Peter and Judith, Joe and I, and Preston and Sondra Cunningham strutted and twirled on the crowded dance floor.

After three consecutive dances, we made our way back to the table. Joe chucked his tie under his chair, then removed his cufflinks and rolled up the sleeves of his tux shirt. "Ah, that's better," he said.

My earpiece chirped. I checked my phone.

Apartment clean. Heading into basement.

It was 7:40. As I sipped my drink, I had that unmistakable feeling that someone was staring. I turned and glared at Philbrick, who smiled and, to my horror, winked. I angled my chair so all he could see was the back of my head.

Our waiter announced the fish course: a roast monkfish with a horseradish beurre blanc.

"The wine is a 2002 Château LeFebvre Chablis," he said as he opened the bottle.

"Is that red or white?" asked Charlotte.

The waiter cast a disapproving glance at Charlotte. In one deft move, Joe commandeered the bottle from his white-gloved hand, loudly tut-tutting as the waiter protested. "Not to worry, I'm a doctor," Joe assured him, resting a hand on his shoulder. "It appears, however, that we have a serious problem, and you, my good man, are the only person who can fix it. We have eight thirsty guests and one itty-bitty bottle of wine. Do us proud, son. We're counting on you." Joe slapped the waiter on the back and, like a platoon leader sending a soldier into battle, sent him on his way.

The waiter returned and placed two uncorked bottles on the table. "This is white wine," he said before he huffed off. Joe gleefully played waiter, pouring wine all around.

The fish course dragged on. The previously amusing conversation felt tiresome. We listened politely as James, who suggested we call him Jimmy, explained that Pegasus was one of New England's most prolific excavation and septic system installation companies. After three martinis and many more glasses of wine, Jimmy repeated his hackneyed slogan. "Our goal is your hole," he said, slapping Dr. Joe on the back. "All the boys have T-shirts with the slogan on it," he said, gesturing. "Sort of wrote that myself. Clever, huh? The trucks got 'em, too. Have you seen the trucks?"

Peter would have handily won his fifty dollars if I hadn't been on a job.

I texted DelCarmen for an update.

Still in basement.

Anything?

We think we found Jimmy Hoffa.

I signed off with a bomb emoji.

Domed dinner plates were set before us while waiters, with ninja-like stealth, appeared behind our chairs then simultaneously whisked away their tops. Oohs and aahs echoed throughout the ballroom as the showmanship was repeated like a succession of toppling dominoes.

"Dinner is served," announced our waiter. "Beef Wellington prepared medium rare, steamed asparagus, and potatoes Lyonnais. The wine is Pinot Noir. Which is a *red* wine."

My companions applauded.

"Red wine goes well with red meat," chirped Charlotte.

"And it matches my hair," said Judith.

Dr. Joe stood, raised his glass, and stoically informed the table, "The rugs and the curtains and the wine all match."

Jimmy stood, tapped his wineglass with his spoon, and toasted, "To Judith, to her matching curtains and rug."

"I must get the name of your decorator," said Charlotte.

Everyone laughed and glasses clinked all around. The waiter cast a heavenward glance, then handed Dr. Joe the bottle of red wine. A few minutes later, he placed two more uncorked bottles on the table.

CHAPTER

57

According to my dining companions, the Beef Wellington was delicious. I rearranged the food on my plate, then hid the vegetables under the beef like a seven-year-old until, thankfully, it was removed.

It was nine when I received the next update from DelCarmen. They'd searched the basement and found little more than half boxes of flooring and tile, and broken-down empty packing boxes. An officer was sifting through the dumpster we'd already searched earlier in the week. They were moving on to the office and wouldn't find a thing. We were running out of time.

My phone chirped. It was a notification for John's bike race. I'd put it in my calendar when he first mentioned it. It was tomorrow at two. I looked around. Couples laughed, danced, held hands. It didn't look difficult; it looked normal. Without thinking, I typed.

I was just reminded that your bike race is tomorrow. My work obligation is going to end tonight. I regret not accepting your invitation. If you don't have other plans, I'd love to join you.

I hit send. Seconds later, three blue dots pulsed across my screen.

Hmm.

John had asked for honesty, truth. Truth he deserved.

For what it's worth, I've been through something I'm uncomfortable discussing. It's why I'm not girlfriend material.

Says who? I'm an adult. Adults make their own decisions about who is or isn't right for them. I'm sorry for whatever you went through. When and if, I have big ears.

I appreciate the offer.

It's a standing offer.

He sent a picture of a Howdy Doody marionette. I laughed at the dumb smile and large ears then typed a response.

Here's what I know. You make me laugh—in a good way. And I enjoy your company.

Laughing is good. Right?

It is.

Too much too soon?

Yes.

How about friendship and

He'd hit send before finishing his thought. I responded similarly.

Friendship and

Dots pulsed on the screen.

No expectations where or how the story

I can handle that. See you tomorrow at two?

Tomorrow at two.

An outburst of laughter snapped me out of my reverie, and I swung around to see Philbrick and the two women who flanked him dissolving in fits of hilarity after what appeared to have been the punchline of a joke. Anger seethed. It felt good. I thought about the second part of our plan—the impossible recorded admission—and considered different scenarios, but none seemed viable. Checking the time, my watch read "now or never." Dinner was done. Philbrick would be leaving the venue in little more than an hour, maybe sooner. I scanned the room. The governor was at the bar holding court. Although he and my father had been acquaintances, I'd never been introduced. None of his companions looked familiar. Nothing looked promising.

Something niggled. I reread DelCarmen's text: *Nothing but empty packing boxes.* Then it came to me: the box of clothing donations on my mother's front porch. A similar box on the front porch at Philbrick's Bay View Avenue property. A piece of paper taped to both. I sent a text to DelCarmen.

There was a box on the front porch. Is it still there?

DC sent a speedy response.

Not here.

I googled my mother's old colleague Ralph Webster, found his home address and a phone number, and dialed. It rang eight times before a voice hollered into the handset, television sirens wailing in the background. Ralph had a soft spot for my mother and, therefore, was grumpily polite. He explained that they'd picked up roughly thirty or forty boxes two days earlier. Seventy-five Bay View Avenue had been on the list. The boxes were at the collection center still unopened. Yes, he had the keys. I told him I'd send someone to pick him up. I dialed DelCarmen.

"I think the sneakers are at Family Services, in their collection center."

"Why do you think that?"

"Because his initial response to your question of where the sneakers might be was that he'd donated them. He was laughing at us, playing a little game he never imagined we'd figure out. Do you remember when we visited his office, there'd been a box on the front porch? My mother had the same box on hers. Family Services reached out to those who regularly donate asking for gently used men's clothing and *shoes*. They drop the box, you fill it, and then they pick it up."

"I'll take two guys with me," said DelCarmen. "Let's hope that old saying holds true."

"What old saying is that?"

"No good deed goes unpunished."

Adrenaline simmered in my veins. I needed to hedge my bets. If I was going down, I was going down swinging. Me and my newfound self-confidence swept arm-in-arm past Philbrick's table. Three heads, six eyes, and whispers followed as I made my way to the bar, sidling up to the governor. I ordered a cosmopolitan, then introduced myself. The governor fondly recalled my father; they'd played golf on several occasions.

"Fine man, Peter was. Far too young."

The scent of his cologne struck like an icepick into the nape of my neck. Fear prickled in the cavity it created. I considered my drink, knew a generous sip would calm my nerves, knew it wasn't the solution. Closing my eyes, I breathed deeply then counted backwards from ten as I exhaled.

"A Beefeater martini," Philbrick said to the bartender.

When I opened my eyes, I saw crimson everywhere. The ever-burgeoning shadowy figures of women in my head gathered around, patted my arm. Fear dissipated. Calm, then focus filled its place. I picked up my drink and turned; it spilled over the edge of the glass and splashed onto my dress. "Oh, dears" and a flurry of napkins were offered.

Philbrick signaled to the bartender as I rummaged through my bag, retrieved a useless tissue, and switched on the recorder before feigning an exit.

"Please," he said. "The bartender is making you another."

I muttered something about the wet dress and waved him off. Unanimous dismay erupted from the governor and his two companions.

"Please, stay. I have a story I must tell you about your father," said the governor.

The bartender delivered the fresh drink and Philbrick made a production of picking it up and setting it closer to me. An arctic chill slithered up my spine as I watched the liquid swirl then settle in the glass. Finally, I returned my attention to the governor as he launched into the details of the final hole of a charity fourball golf match; he and my dad had been partners.

"Your father and I were playing out of our shoes; it was a miracle we were still in contention. We were all square going into eighteen. My approach shot flew the green. Your father pulled out his eight-iron and said, 'Well, Albert, this is the best club in the bag, let's see what it can do.' Our hopes sank as we watched his ball sail a good twenty feet to the right of the green. Then, it was as if that large oak, you know the one, reached out and swatted his ball. The bloody thing ricocheted left and landed forty feet from the pin at the very top edge of the green."

The group crooned sympathetically.

"An impossible two-putt. We'd all but lost. Then, all of a sudden," the governor stopped for effect, "your father's ball began to roll. Our opponents watched in horror as it trickled down the hill, finally coming to rest within inches of the cup. Your dad tapped it in for the win."

Everyone cheered. Preston Philbrick raised his martini glass and proposed a toast. Glasses clinked all around. The governor and his little group turned their attention to a constituent who had approached. I held Philbrick's gaze, lifted my glass to my lips, then shook my head and placed the drink back on the bar. He raised an eyebrow, and for a long moment, intently scanned my face. I reached for my bag.

He stepped left, blocking my exit. "You're here with your brother?" Philbrick asked.

"I am."

"My family has supported this organization's efforts for more than thirty years."

"How admirable," I said, stepping right.

"Please," Philbrick said, gesturing to my cocktail. "If that's not to your liking, I'd be happy to order something else for you. Maybe you'd prefer a beer, perhaps one of those citrusy ones."

It's not the type of drink I object to.

"That's kind, but I'm no longer . . . in the mood."

"A familiar theme. Women are never in the mood until suddenly they are." He watched for a reaction.

Was that supposed to be funny? I felt my cheeks redden.

"Thank you. The cosmopolitan is fine."

"Then, perhaps you will do me the honor of a dance?"

I almost laughed. "A dance?"

"An ending to all of this . . . unpleasantness."

Unpleasantness? If looks could kill, I thought. But he remained upright.

"A truce," he continued. "As you know, we have our answer and can begin to heal. All of us can put this to bed," he said, drawing out the word "bed," cracking a wry smile. "Move on. No hard feelings."

The sophomoric references to sex seemed to be an inside joke I didn't get. As distasteful as it would be, a dance might work. I took a deep breath and, in keeping with my plan to snub him, rearranged my face into what I hoped resembled a polite "no thank you."

"Really, I'm all danced out," I said, then turned, signaled to the bartender, and asked for a side of ice I didn't need.

As I'd expected, the trio swiveled its attention back to the evening's host with a rousing chorus, insisting we dance. And just like that, Preston Philbrick was leading me through the crowd, then guiding me expertly around the dance floor.

"Well, Ms. Stuart, you look lovely tonight," he said.

I forced an icy smile.

"I must say it was a shock to our little community to hear that you had pursued a career in public service. The kind that pays," he added. "It's beneath you."

"Yes, well . . ." I was at a loss for words.

"I can't even begin to guess what possessed you to enter the police academy in the first place," he said, then he leaned in and hummed a few bars of what sounded like "Blue Moon." As if he was wooing me. I shivered.

"It was an odd turn of events," I said. "It couldn't possibly be of interest to you."

"Nonsense, regale me! I'm sure it's a most interesting tale." He laughed, then incomprehensibly, crooned, "I saw you sitting alone, da da dum de dee da . . ." His hot breath on my ear made me recoil; the pressure of his hand on my lower back wouldn't allow it. No doubt it was the melody of "Blue Moon." The lyrics, however, were his own. "You hadn't known what I was there for . . . what I was saying a prayer for . . . da da dum de dee da . . ."

I recalled the cryptic yet purposeful message on my bathroom mirror and wondered what the fuck he was trying to tell me. I avoided his gaze until I could get the anger in check. My thoughts spun; the canned response to the question skittered away. The voice in my head howled: *I enrolled in the police academy because of a sick bastard like you.*

When I didn't respond, he asked again, "What *was* the allure, Andrea?"

I breathed deeply; an acute twinge in my ribs shot through me. The pain calmed me, yet the easy lie failed to come. I heard myself say, "I'm fascinated by the brilliant criminal mind. I'm fascinated by people like you."

"Tsk, tsk," he chided. "Andrea, dear, you don't think of me as a criminal, now do you?"

I met his eye with a smile, and shook my head. "No, no. Of course not. I meant that I thought you were brilliant," I said, in a feeble attempt to right the ship.

"That's where you're mistaken," he continued, nonplussed. "I am justice in the purest sense of the word."

"I see. Justice." *Judge, jury, and executioner. I should have guessed.* "Clever."

"Not clever, it is 'just.' You see, the scales of justice represent a balance, yin and yang, tit for tat, an eye for an eye."

"A child for a child?" I asked, as if these might have been his next words.

Preston beamed like a teacher who had finally helped his dimwitted student understand an intricate concept.

"Lest we forget the old adage," he said. "Never judge a man until you've walked a mile in his shoes."

"Guilty as charged," I said, as if in apology. I attempted a commiserating tone while trying to keep the conversation on point. "Now I understand the need for Penelope's boating mishap."

"Adversity had been her strength. Managing to summon some otherworldly power. Could never figure out where it came from." He shook his head as if remembering. "Of course, she'd been an extraordinary athlete. Somehow I'd forgotten she'd been a swimmer."

"And tenacity has been your strength."

He grinned.

I thought about the fire at the barn that had killed her horse, and how the evidence pointed to Penelope. Her unhappiness had been his mission. "And Bea?" I asked.

"My, my, you have been a busy beaver. Penelope called to see if I would drop some book at the home and I said no, but then reconsidered. Poor Penelope drove all the way to Jamestown and when she returned, her dear sister wasn't breathing. A stretch of bad luck," he said, shaking his head.

"You had a visit with her, no doubt?"

I smiled and held his eye. *Come on. Say it. Tell me what you did, you bastard,* I thought.

"Oh, yes," he said gaily. "The patio door was wide open, and Bea was sleeping. It looked like her pillows needed a bit of fluffing. I was already in a helpful sort of mood, fluffing the pillows seemed the right thing. She didn't make a peep."

"And, what? She had the misfortune of putting her head beneath one of them?"

We both laughed. "You naughty girl. How could you think such a thing?" he said, winking.

"Well, I suppose to make things right, you had no other choice but to take her daughter from her, too." I held my breath, praying for his admission of guilt.

But all he said was, "Had she only shown some remorse."

He shook his head as if all of this could have been avoided had Penelope only said she was sorry. It felt as if someone had just kicked the stool from beneath me and I was desperately trying to stave off the inevitable.

The song was coming to an end and Preston attempted a flamboyant finish. He twirled me, reeled me in and dipped me, and then, to my surprise and his, he stumbled. His right hand landed on the base of my lower back and the transmitter. Our eyes locked, and his haughty smile wilted into a grimace.

Preston held me in the dip until my legs ached and my back cramped while he reached into my dress, ripped the transmitter from my lower back, disconnected the wires, and shoved it into his jacket pocket.

A confident smile returned to Preston's face. He leaned close, brushed his lips against my ear, and whispered, "Were you expecting some grand admission? Recorded, no less?" A lively waltz began to play; he lifted me to my feet and continued dancing. "When I arrived at the observatory, she was sitting at one of the high-top tables." He pulled me into a tight embrace, his lips inches from mine. "I asked what she was doing. She mumbled something, then stood on the chair and stepped onto the tabletop. I said she should get down. She laughed. Told me to mind my own business. I climbed on the chair next to her and offered her my hand. She said it was too late to start acting like a father. Then she . . . she said that, in fact, her real father would be attending the wedding and maybe he and I could both walk her down the aisle." I felt his fury as his grip tightened on my waist, the pain in my ribs excruciating. I wanted to scream that it had been the drug doing the talking. That Hope had been the one innocent party in all this. "And then," his eyes drilled into mine, "she asked if that would be fine with me."

"And what did you tell her?"

He leaned in and whispered, "It would be, I assured her. But she wasn't convinced, needed me to set her mind at rest."

In concert with my intake of breath, the boisterous sound in the grand ballroom screeched to a halt like a stylus skidding angrily across a vinyl record into the repeated murmur of a scratch. My question was barely audible.

"And?"

His eyes became endless empty black holes as he appeared to watch the memory unfold. "And she raised her arms overhead as if in triumph. And I thought, a firm pat on the back would do the trick."

The background noise surged. My earpiece crackled. DelCarmen's voice said the words I'd waited for all night: "We've got his sneakers. Blood type is a match. In fifteen minutes, make the arrest. By the time you walk him to the door, I'll be waiting."

As if he'd heard DelCarmen's directive, Preston Philbrick pulled away, and I grabbed his arm. I didn't have fifteen minutes. "Preston Philbrick, you are under arrest for the murder of Rosa Rodriguez," I said, sotto voce. His body bristled with anger. I continued with the Miranda warning.

"You are a fanciful and imaginative young lady who is grasping at straws." He refastened his grip, attempting to dance.

"This is not fantasy," I assured him through gritted teeth, trying to retain purchase, my heels scraping along the parquet in protest. Laughter echoed, dinnerware clattered on metal trays, and marble columns swirled dizzily as he danced me toward the side of the room. "We can do this quietly or I can make a scene, your call. We have a team covering all exits," I lied.

"Quite a disappointment. I had expected so much more from you, Ms. Stuart. A more formidable—"

"Adversary?" I finished his sentence. "Don't underestimate me," I hissed.

Then he spun me wildly into the crowd.

I landed full force into Earl Butterworth, attached to his wife, Agnes, both in mid-dip. We fell like dominoes: me on top of Earl, both of us on top of Agnes, and finally, the three of us barreling into a waiter carrying a full tray of cocktails. We crashed in a heap, spewing glass and ice and alcohol. The guests at the edge of the parquet scattered like mice. As I disentangled myself from the center of the ruckus on the dance floor, Preston Philbrick strode, unhurriedly, up the marble steps, out through the vast bronze doors, and into the night.

CHAPTER

58

SCRAMBLING TO MY feet, I hurried to the bar and grabbed my purse. As expected, the recording device was gone. It didn't matter; Philbrick hadn't admitted to anything before disconnecting the wires. I fired off a quick text to DelCarmen directing the team to proceed to Quonset, where Philbrick's plane was set to depart at midnight, that I was in pursuit.

I weaved through the crowd then ducked out the side service entrance that backed up to Coggeshall Avenue and where I'd parked my car hours earlier. Heaving open the driver's side door, I slipped off my heels and chucked them along with my purse across the bench seat. The bag hit the passenger door, spilling its contents, including my phone, into the footwell. The engine spewed a throaty growl as it revved; I slammed the gearshift into drive, completed a 360 and sped toward Jamestown.

The wagon swerved as I circled the entrance ramp onto the Newport bridge; I gripped the wheel tight and stepped on the accelerator. The deafening sound of the Pontiac's V-8 pushed to its limit parted the cars on the bridge as I crested its span and caught sight of a black sedan heading through the toll station. Preston Philbrick passed the main drag and took a sharp right onto Hamilton; he was going home to meet the helicopter transport. I hung back as he turned onto Beavertail Road, cut my lights, and followed, then watched in amazement as his car whizzed past the entrance to the Crow's Nest and continued south toward Beavertail.

I needed to call DelCarmen, but when I reached for the earbuds, they were gone; I'd have to pull over to find the phone. Instead, I kept my foot on the gas. A detour didn't matter; we knew his final destination and would be there in time to make the arrest. A quarter mile down the road, doubt whispered in my ear. Preston Philbrick should have been making his escape, fleeing the country. This excursion was an unreasonable risk. He was too smart for such an error in judgment.

Then doubt asked the inevitable question: What had I missed?

I deflated with the realization. The carry-on. I'd missed the significance of the carry-on. Philbrick hadn't underestimated us; he'd planned for all eventualities. Penelope Philbrick said he'd adjusted his itinerary; I'd thought time, but never considered location. His flight and transport crews could be mobilized with little notice; one phone call could change where he'd meet the helicopter—it could land almost anywhere. The same for where his plane waited; there were a dozen private airfields within a ten-to-twenty minute flight time from Jamestown. I'd shown my cards on the dance floor. Philbrick was smart enough to guess we'd counted on the helicopter at the Crow's Nest then the jet at Quonset and had called en route to adjust the location of both.

This detour had been, no doubt, unplanned, but his escape route was solid: he was going to be picked up at Beavertail, deposited at some remote airfield, then gone. Nevertheless, we were still dancing; he led and wanted me to follow. Which meant that Philbrick had something else he needed to take care of. What had DelCarmen warned? Preston Philbrick didn't take prisoners. The one thing I did know for certain, however, was that it had to end here.

I veered left—in the wrong direction—onto the one-way road that exited the park. The element of surprise was somewhat problematic in a seventies station wagon that sounded like thunder ripping through a canyon at dawn. But I'd had plenty of practice with the Parisienne as a teen, and I shifted into neutral, killed the engine, and coasted downhill and into the parking area farthest from the lighthouse.

When I cranked open my window, I heard nothing but the croak of bullfrogs and the crash of the surf. After a short internal debate, I decided to keep it simple. I had a gun and cuffs. I'd go to the lighthouse on foot and wait him out. He'd park his car in the open hoping to bait me, while he hid nearby. When I didn't show, and the helicopter began its approach, he'd have no choice but to go back to his car to retrieve his carry-on, at which point I'd bring him in. We'd ride back in his Beemer, this time with my gun to his head.

Stepping from the car, an unsettling gust of air made me realize I was woefully underdressed in chiffon and equally unprepared with strappy heels. There was nothing in the back seat. In the way back were Dad's golf clubs. Rifling through the zippered compartments of the golf bag, I struck gold—rain gear. Men's size large, crumpled black plastic jacket and pants, vintage 1980. Despite the coup, I found no shoes. I swept the thought aside and stripped, suited up, and re-strapped the holster to my left thigh, clipped the cuffs to it, then slipped the Glock, tactical light, and spare magazine securely in place. Two steps was all it took to realize the rain pants weren't conducive to stealth: my stride mimicked a horde of children unwrapping candy in a quiet movie theater. Time to call DelCarmen.

There was no phone in the passenger side footwell. As promised, the tactical light produced an impressive, blinding light. On hands and knees, I scanned beneath the bench seat and plucked the phone from the debris. Its signal was negligible. Still, I punched DelCarmen's number on the keypad and hit send. The numbers glowed an eerie yellow, then the screen went dark. A second try produced the same result. With time for nothing else, I opened the car's ashtray and stuck the phone inside, retrieved the keys from the ignition, and zipped them into the right thigh pants pocket. Admittedly, on most days, I considered myself smart. And the smart thing to do was to get back in the wagon, drive until I found cell service and call DelCarmen. But I'd risk losing Philbrick, and that wasn't a chance I was willing to take.

While Philbrick hunkered in some hidey-hole waiting for me to blunder in so he could finish me off, I walked off into the night thinking how perfect his plan had been, how this foolish detour might risk it all, and why he considered me a loose end that needed to be dealt with.

I headed south to where Preston Philbrick awaited my arrival.

CHAPTER

59

THE BEAVERTAIL LIGHTHOUSE and museum were perched at the tip of the peninsula surrounded by enormous, elegant boulders that in the daytime were well-suited for climbing, picnicking, or sunbathing. At night, slick and unnavigable, they were more likely to contribute to a first-class crippling. For more than a century, the lighthouse had served two purposes: standing as a beacon of safety while ushering sailors into the lee of the harbor and simultaneously warning of the danger of the rugged shoreline. The fourth-order Fresnel lens sat like a diamond in the lantern room rotating and sending out beams of light like giant spokes of a wheel that could be seen for miles, all from a single tiny bulb. The lighthouse flashed its conflicted message. *Safety! Danger! Safety! Danger!* I wondered which was on offer tonight.

Reaching the lighthouse unseen was the tricky part. The southernmost tip of Beavertail was a flat, grassy expanse bordered by the narrow one-way road that followed up and around the lighthouse at the island's edge. Both the road and the field were exposed. Neither was an option. I'd follow the perimeter path and see how close it took me to the point. The sea was a minimum of twenty to thirty feet below the road. To see me, he'd have to be standing at the edge looking down. It was a safe bet in the dark.

I chose a well-traveled trail through scruffy shrubs. A tremendous full moon shone and sparkled on the ocean; the wind whipped through my hair, making it difficult to see. I tucked it into the nape of my jacket and, for the third time in a few minutes, felt for my Glock, then proceeded like a cat clad in plastic wrap through the bushes. Small animals scattered as I passed. *Swish, swish, swish.* I might as well have used a bullhorn to announce my arrival.

The path thinned and dipped toward the water. Fifty feet farther, it ended abruptly. I had two, less than ideal, choices: scaling the cliff and risk being seen, or attempting a few hundred yards with limited vision on slick boulders. I clambered onto the rocks, dropped to my knees, and crawled. My bare feet became scraped and numb as I moved steadily forward, securing my hands and feet from one crevice to the next, my mind clear and focused.

Ten minutes passed; I was almost there. I climbed the precipice and, as expected, Philbrick's black sedan was parked in front of the lighthouse, glimmering in the moonlight. Retreating onto the rocks, I continued toward the point, trying to think of the places he'd choose to hide and how I'd get Preston to show himself.

The sound of gunshot shattered my thoughts, and a bullet whizzed past my shoulder. Our eyes met. He smiled smugly as he raised the gun and aimed. I dropped behind a rock; his second shot pulverized its top. Shale and dust fell like rain. A round shredded the tip of a boulder to my left, knocking me off balance and sending me careening and landing waist deep in a pool of icy water. The jagged edge of a stone tore into my right thigh as I scrambled out; my car keys clattered along the rock then sank into the sea. I aimed and fired as he ducked out of sight.

Adrenaline kicked in. I scaled the cliff, catching sight of Preston rounding the north side of the lighthouse. Blood oozed from the gash in my thigh as I shifted into overdrive, ran full tilt to the southernmost point of the peninsula, then ducked behind one of those informational signs warning of the dangers of the precipice below. It wasn't the best cover, but not an obvious choice, either; it gave me distance and a solid vantage point.

Water and blood pooled at my feet. The wind howled; sound and shadow bounced chaotically. It was unnerving knowing the two senses I needed most were compromised. The moonlight cast an eerie glow on the lighthouse; the eastern side was in darkness. I waited for an interminable few minutes before deciding that if I was disoriented, so was he.

"Preston," I sang like a mother calling her children in to dinner. "We found the sneakers. They were at the Family Services collection center. Come on out now, before anyone else gets hurt."

Like you.

"Preston, it's over. I've got help on the way."

Leaves rustled. I leaned right, searching the shadows of the lighthouse. No sign of him. I leaned left and, remarkably, there was Preston Philbrick heading straight for me, his gun in one outstretched hand, scanning from side to side. Two things were obvious: he had no fucking idea how to handle a gun and no idea where I was. A few seconds later, he did an abrupt about-face, still holding the gun with one hand.

Manna from heaven.

I rounded the sign with my gun drawn. "Drop your weapon!" I commanded.

He turned. Twenty yards and approaching. My heart hammered. No option. He had to be stopped. My first shot was wide, and the second grazed his shoulder, sending him stumbling backward, the gun in his right hand raised skyward as he hit the ground. I charged and kicked the gun out of his hand, and it skittered out of reach.

Philbrick rolled sideways, righted himself into a crouch, then dove headlong, knocking me on my back and the gun from my hands. Before he could pin me beneath him, I jammed my right foot into his hip, then watched in disbelief as his hand extended from his shirtsleeve, and inched incrementally forward, near enough to see the pale circle on his pinkie finger where a ring had been long worn, and the intricate engraving in the rose gold of his exquisite timepiece. His face, crimson, contorted and beaded with sweat, mutated into a victorious grin as my knee compressed into my chest allowing him to wrap a thumb and forefinger around my throat. I bucked and thrashed, dislodging his grip; he slammed me into the ground like a ragdoll. My foot, still wedged into his hip, now bent impossibly backward, felt as if it might snap at the ankle as he delivered the full weight of his body into mine and pushed the heel of his palm against my windpipe. Then we both heard it, a faint metallic click; a tiny lever in his watch had slid into place and the unmistakable opening chords of Debussy's *Clair de Lune* filled the space between us.

Philbrick watched as the door to the long-sealed vault in my mind flew open, its trapped memories hurtling forward through time: Mother's hand squeezing mine, whispering that the music was a reprieve, the server pointing, Kari laughing, the two of us drinking the citrus beer. Pinpricks of light, then clearer images, like those from an old film, unfolded before my eyes. I looked from the hand on my forearm into Preston Philbrick's tanned face and said I needed to find my friend.

Commandeering me through the crowd and onto the wet sidewalk, his echoing baritone assured me that Kari was on her way back to campus and he was taking me home. Next, I was naked, and he was on top of me, hurting me. When I struggled, he hit me, becoming louder, angrier, and more violent. He raped me repeatedly.

The movie stopped. My eyes fluttered open; my wordless horror met his grimace. I twisted and Preston's sweaty hand slipped. A burst of anger propelled him forward, seizing my throat, this time with both hands. My leg cramped and shuddered, began to give way. Dark spots danced before my eyes; consciousness dwindling. Letting go seemed the thing to do, peaceful even. I had no more fight in me. They say you have eight to ten seconds before it's all over.

God, let it be over.

"You've got two choices, Andie. What's it going to be?" I was at self-defense and pinned on the mat. Vi urgently whispered in my ear. *"He's taken what no man had the right to. It's time to take it back."*

"It's over."

"It's not over. Your leg is longer than his arm. Hold him back, wait for your opportunity. It will come."

"I know all of that, goddammit. I just can't do it."

My foot slipped. His hands tightened around my neck. Vi's voice faded.

I gazed down upon *Flaming June*, laying on the rocks—Hope Philbrick's rocks—the sun showering me with piercing gold rays that blind, yet radiate a sublime warmth. When I looked up, I luxuriated in its benevolence. Surely June was asleep.

I dropped to my knees and reached for her. Yet when I lifted her into my arms, I pressed the broken body of Hope Philbrick to mine. *"Live, damn it. Live,"* I begged, as her blood, bright crimson and viscous, coated my arms, my body, the warmth hemorrhaging from me. In the next moment, all I held was a skeleton, its brittle bones snapping, dropping away. As I scrambled to hold on to the disintegrating bones, the face atop of what I carry was my own.

"Dig deep, Andie," whispered Vi. *"Find your anger. Find the one thing you need to live for."*

I pictured my mother and thought of the second chance for both of us that I had so desperately wanted, the promises I'd made to myself and to all those women. Thoughts and images flickered like black and white pixels on an old television screen, diminishing as life swirled, ever smaller before my eyes; all my dreams nothing more than the worst kind of lie. How had I let this happen?

The high-pitched cacophony accelerating inside my head sounded like a detonating grenade.

The promised opportunity arrived. Philbrick let up. The sound of air filling my lungs caught him off guard; I exploded into his shoulder, trapped his hands, and drove the crown of my head into his chin. Pummeling him with a left hook then my right elbow, his nose snapped, releasing a torrent of blood. As he attempted to shield his face, I thrust my knee deep into his groin. Preston recoiled just far enough for me to put both feet under his abdomen. I grabbed him by the collar of his tuxedo and, with an unworldly bellow akin to a battle cry, rolled backward, the force of our collective weight sufficient to hurl him over my head. His body landed on the rocks below with a sickening thud.

Scrambling to my feet, gasping for air, I found my gun and holstered it, then loped off toward the car hoping he'd been knocked unconscious, but knowing the drop hadn't been steep enough to kill him. I needed to find cell service and call for backup. Then I remembered I had no goddamned keys.

Warm tears bathed my face as I began to pray. I prayed to God for my life to be as it once was, for the comfort and security of my family. But who was I to ask for God's help? A God who I wasn't certain existed. And if He did exist, He had abandoned me when I'd needed Him most.

A new movie played in my head. Peter was twelve, and I was ten. We sat side by side in the back seat of the wagon. Without seatbelts, we climbed like monkeys over the second and third seats playing a game of some sort while my father drove and my mother sat unconcerned in the front passenger seat, smiling and chatting. Life had been simpler. While I ached for what once was, a flicker of warmth flowed through me as my father's words echoed in my head. I began to run.

Wrenching open the driver's side door, I shimmied across the Naugahyde bench seat and reached beneath the mat. The spare key was Dad's idea. *"You never know when you'll lose those keys. Besides,"* he chided, *"I won't be coming out at all hours of the night for either of you."* Years of beach sand and debris stuck to my bloody fingers. And then there it was, cold and heavy in my hand.

"Thank you, Dad," I whispered.

My breathing slowed. I inserted the key in the ignition and fired up the engine, its deafening roar, a symphony. Shifting into reverse, I placed my arm over the seat and checked behind the car. When I turned back, Preston Philbrick stood aiming a shotgun at my head.

I hit the gas. The car bucked and stalled, knocking Philbrick off balance. The windshield shattered; a windstorm of glass shards pummeled my arms, face, skull. The force of the shot knocked Preston to the ground, but within seconds he was pulling open the passenger door. Mine wouldn't budge. I scrambled into the back seat and then into the next, pushing the tailgate open and tumbling onto the ground, Dad's golf clubs, assorted golf paraphernalia, and an umbrella clattered around me. I rolled left into a crouch and reached for my gun. The holster was empty.

As Philbrick took aim at my head, his glance skyward at the sound of the approaching helicopter was enough time to grab the flashlight and hit the tail-cap. A blast of light exploded from the small cylinder, and Philbrick's hands went to his eyes. I thrashed at the heap of gear around me and came up with the eight-iron. My first shot knocked the gun from his hand. I swung again, crushing his right hand on the fender as he tried to climb out.

"You're not going to make the flight," I said, bashing his left hand. "You want formidable? I'll give you formidable," I ranted as I swung. Unprecedented strength surged, took control. He leaned back, but I connected with his chin with an ugly crack. "You took my sense of self-worth. What was that you told me? How's this for justice?" Philbrick looked up in shock and reached for his chin with his bloody, swollen hand. "I prayed for death, Preston. Thought it'd be kinder than the living hell you put me in."

My next shot hit him above his left ear. He crumpled to the ground. I was beyond myself, an out-of-body experience. "Start praying, you evil bastard." The thud of the club against flesh and bone was nauseating; blood sprayed everywhere.

Preston Philbrick lay in his bloodied tuxedo, his hands cradling his head, moaning. I stood over him gripping the club tight, numb, my ears ringing, the wind howling, the sound of the helicopter touching down in the clearing, too far away to see us.

I cuffed him to the back of the wagon, and for the second time that night, read him his Miranda warning. Pulling Preston up by the back of his tuxedo jacket, I leaned in close. "You had everything, every goddamned blessing the world had to give. Why the fuck did you do this?"

The gurgling terrified me. Then it came, those moments people tell you about before death, the moments of clarity before the dying slip away.

"Our baby . . . all I'd ever dreamed of. They called me . . . too late. The baby was dead. Could never forgive her." Preston Philbrick closed his eyes and slumped forward.

How it had all started was no excuse. I sat at arm's length and listened to his labored breathing, hoping each would be his last. When finally, I glanced over, his left arm was raised between us, his wrist bowed, as if presenting the rose gold watch like an offering. I released its clasp, slipped it from his wrist, and leaned in. "You took my life, Preston. And now, I'm taking it back."

I stood and with everything I had, hurled the watch. It's gold casing glinted in the moonlight then flamed out like a spent shooting star as it sailed over the scrub pines and into the sea.

* * *

Still clutching the eight-iron, I lowered myself to the ground and leaned the back of my head against the bumper of the wagon. Slivers of glass dug into my face, penetrated my scalp; it was nothing short of a miracle that my eyes had been spared. It seemed like an hour, but it was minutes when I heard it. I shielded my eyes against the headlights as a car door opened then slammed shut and deliberate footsteps approached.

DelCarmen knelt beside me and checked my wounds. He felt for Preston's pulse, then radioed for an ambulance. Our eyes scanned skyward as we listened to the rotors of the helicopter as it lifted, then watched as it flew off.

"No jet at Quonset?" I asked.

DelCarmen shook his head.

"Is he going to make it?"

He nodded.

DelCarmen loosened my grip on the eight-iron. "I thought you were bluffing when you said you were a lousy golfer." When he took the club from my hand, every inch of my body shook. "Fabulous outfit," he said, as he untied his shoes, removed his thick woolen socks, and gently pulled them over my cut and swollen feet. Gesturing to my face, DelCarmen attempted some uncharacteristic humor. "The glitter transforms the entire ensemble seamlessly from daywear to eveningwear." He removed his heavy overcoat and wrapped it carefully around me, then pulled me onto his lap and held me close, warming me as we waited for the medical team. "You are okay, aren't you?" he asked.

I was beat up and bruised, looking like hell, worse. But I knew better than to believe that appearances told the whole story. Nothing about the way I looked could have been further from the truth. A sense of peace and incredible calm filled the depths of my battered soul. I closed my eyes and felt something akin to a smile as the first traces of warmth returned to the tips of my fingers, my toes. Shrugging the heaviness from my shoulders, as if an oppressive winter coat, felt like taking one decisive step forward out of the darkness.

And there at the edge of a clearing, I caught sight of a path I was certain would become more distinct with each deliberate stride and would soon enough lead to a road, and from there, onward toward home and the way back to me.

EPILOGUE

When I opened my eyes, sunlight streamed in through the window and Mother was dozing in the chair beside the bed.

"Good morning," I said.

Her hand found mine. "My love," was all she could manage through choked tears.

"How did you know?" I asked.

She wiped her eyes. "Julian," she said.

"Ah," I said, finally. I rarely used DelCarmen's first name.

"He spent the night on the couch and called me at six. He had things to do. Asked me to look after you."

"I'm grateful you're here."

She nodded, more tears threatening.

"I tried, you know," she said.

Warm tears bathed my cheeks. "I know you did."

"And when Julian called me, for a terrifying moment, I thought we wouldn't have the chance."

"I'm so sorry, Mom. For far too long, I couldn't figure out how to let you in. Can you forgive me?"

Mother squeezed my hand and said, "There's never been a need."

It was a new day. Perfect for second chances. I closed my eyes feeling grateful and began to drift off.

"Wait, what time is it?" I asked, sitting up.

"Just eleven, dear."

"Plenty of time," I said.

"For?" she asked, concerned.

"I have a date," I said, "at two."

She regarded me as if I'd said the most absurd thing in the world. But the look of teenage angst that I imagined described my facial expression stopped her reproach.

"Can you help?" I asked, pointing to my face. The ER doctor had painstakingly removed each sliver, but pockmarks of glass cuts remained.

"The doctor?"

I nodded.

"I'd love to," she said.

* * *

A week later, I drove north to Knotty Pine, New Hampshire. Emily Rollins met me with a quizzical look as she scanned the hideous scabs that covered my face.

"Sheesh," was all she could manage.

"Bike accident," I said.

She narrowed her eyes. "It looks like you drove your Harley through a plate-glass window."

I smiled. "Something like that."

"More questions?" she asked.

I wanted to say I was delivering answers. Instead I said, "An ending, but I hope what I have is the prologue to a new story. Your new story."

I retrieved the reason for my visit from my coat pocket and presented it like an offering. She looked from me to what I held in uncertain silence.

"We found it beneath the passenger seat, jammed against the floormat," I said. "We contacted Montblanc, and the serial number indicates it belongs to you."

When recognition of what I held dawned, so did her tears.

* * *

True to my golfing skills, Preston Philbrick survived. He was eventually indicted for the murders of Dr. William Maxwell and Rosa Rodriguez, and finally, years later, found guilty by a jury of his peers. He was sentenced to two consecutive terms of life in prison.

No one was held responsible for the murder of Hope Philbrick.

ACKNOWLEDGMENTS

I AM INDEBTED TO the talented Tash Barsby and to Sorcha Rose and Emily Kitchin and the wonderful community at The Novelry. I am equally indebted to Maya Shanbhag Lang for her close reading and invaluable comments. With special thanks to Jeffery Kurz, who read the book in its infancy and offered kind, professional direction. Enormous thanks to martial artist Vicki Dorfman, who not only read an early draft, but provided guidance with the fight scenes and weaponry. I am grateful and fortunate to have had the expertise of Detective Billy Mattera, former member of the Major Crimes Unit for the Providence Police Department, who provided seemingly endless technical and procedural information. While this is a work of fiction, I strove for some level of authenticity, and any inaccuracies or adjustments to police procedure for the sake of the story are my own.

In no particular order of importance, the following have either read and reread, then read again, offered in-depth notes, cheered me on, or are guilty of all the aforementioned crimes. A mention here seems trivial in comparison to the time, encouragement, and kindnesses shown to me. My thanks to Janette Talento Ley and her partner in reading and, no doubt, in crime, Ellen F. Kasle. Huge thanks to Theresa (LaFleur) Sculley, Andra Geana Armstrong, Ralph Hardy, Steve Caldas, Julia Techentin, Sara Beauchamp Hiebner, Mike

Warmington, Margaret Kinnecom, Lisa Seely, Diane Quattrini, Sarah Eron, Barbara Hesketh Bender, Deb Beauchamp, Dave Loewenstein, Debra Whalley, and Cindy Warner.

And finally, warm thanks to my agent, Mark Gottlieb, for his kindness and for believing.